BLACK MIRRORS

EVERYTHING = NOTHING
‖ ‖
NOTHING = EVERYTHING

by the same author

Prisoners of their own prayers – parts 1 and 2
Museum
Frozen movements

BLACK MIRRORS

FAROOQ KHALID

Translated from the Urdu by
ERIC CYPRIAN

JONATHAN CAPE
THIRTY-TWO BEDFORD SQUARE LONDON

First published in Great Britain 1987

Jonathan Cape Ltd, 32 Bedford Square, London WC1B 3EL

First published in Pakistan 1977 by Maktaba Meri Library, Lahore-2,
under the title *Siah Ainey*.
This book was awarded the highest literary prize, the Aadamji Award, in Pakistan, 1978

British Library Cataloguing in Publication Data

Khalid, Farooq
Black Mirrors
1. Title 2. Siah Ainey. *English*
891'43937 PK2200.K421/

ISBN 0 224 02382 9

Photoset by Rowland Phototypesetting Ltd
Bury St Edmunds, Suffolk
Printed in Great Britain by Hazell, Watson & Viney Ltd
Member of the BPCC Group
Aylesbury, Bucks

GLOSSARY

Ammi	mother
Asalam Alaikum	God bless you
Baboo	Mr
Baratani	a game similar to draughts
Bearer	waiter, butler
Burqa	a veil completely enveloping the woman
Charpoy	wooden bed with a jute rope base
Dopatta	muslin scarf to wrap around the head or shoulders
Godown	warehouse
Hakim	a doctor practising traditional Indian medicine
Jinab	sir
Khan	form of address for a Pathan
Maund	approximately 80 lbs
Munny	an affectionate way of addressing a young girl
Newar	broad, coarse tape for weaving the base of a plang
Pao	approximately half a pound
Pathan	someone from the north-west frontier
Phiaji	dear brother
Plang	superior charpoy with webbed base of Newar
Qalima Taieba	the important Muslim article of faith: 'There is no god but God, Mohammed is the Apostle of God
Sahib	Mr
Seer	approximately 2 lbs
Serai	inn for travellers
Seth	a prosperous businessman
Shalwar	loose trousers
Tonga	horse-drawn taxi

ONE

The moment dusk fell all the bathrooms were occupied and everyone had to wait a long time for a turn. People gathered here in the mornings, but in the evenings there was always a large crowd waiting – labourers from the nearby lock factory finished for the day, and also a number of hotel residents back from their work wanting to refresh themselves. There were three bathrooms in a row on the second floor of this ship-like hotel. Their doors were made of old wooden planks roughly nailed together by some unskilled person. The attempt to join them had not been entirely successful and in many places there were gaping cracks. When a person was bathing, parts of his body could be seen as easily as his voice could be heard. The first bathroom on the right was the worst in this respect.

The interior of the bathrooms was even more deplorable. When you opened one of the doors you had immediately to negotiate two steps, each about three feet wide and six inches high, leading to a somewhat wider square area. It was not easy to bathe here due to the combination of the inevitably slippery floor and the particularly low ceiling. Therefore most of the bathers would stand on one of the steps supporting themselves against the closed door, in order to pour water over their heads, and while bathing would loudly curse the men who had built the bathrooms. The salts from the water, the acid chemicals in the cheap soap, and the dust and sweat from the bathers' bodies ingrained the bathroom floors and steps with layers of foul-smelling dirt and slimy moss. From time to time before turning on the tap, a bather would scrape the steps with an old fish slice which lay around there, and he would glare angrily at the low ceiling. The reason the bathrooms' ceilings were so low was that a small rectangular attic had been built above them, to the height of the other rooms along the corridor. This attic was the abode of a decrepit old man who for most of the time lay there silently like a chronically ill patient, so that for days on end nobody noticed his existence. He did, however, occasionally open his mouth and when he did he created such a noise that everybody's attention was drawn to him and it was difficult to scold him into silence.

In addition to the defective doors, slippery floors, disgusting stench, troublesome low ceilings and the ridiculous steps in the bathrooms, their finish was equally distressing. The walls dividing them were innocent of plaster except for the wall facing you as you entered. This wall was part of the adjoining building and had been already plastered. The side walls were uneven and the bricks, roughly laid and close to each other, seemed to look like sex-starved girls, who, dodging their over-vigilant fathers and evading the assiduous control of a strict society, peep slyly from doors and windows to catch a glimpse of what is going on outside and become the very picture of pitiful deprivation as their despair and longing are laid before your eyes. In their effort to stand out as individuals, these badly laid, pink bricks shared the same brazenness, the same crude exhibitionism and the same shameful existence of such girls.

Apart from the awful bathrooms, the second storey was chiefly characterized by the small coop-like rooms, the narrow corridor, the dirty, dim staircase and the irritating discomforts everywhere in the unhealthy semi-darkness. Before it became a hotel, the building had been single-storeyed, the property of a Hindu Seth. This man had been middle-aged and unmarried. He had built the house with loving care under his own supervision and this was why the ground floor contained a spacious hall. This now held some twenty-five tables and a large number of chairs. It was magnificent and visitors would admire its decorated ceiling. Although with the passage of time the colours had faded and the embossed designs worn out, in some places the original workmanship remained resplendent.

The Seth was a great lover of music. On summer nights when the moon was bright and the air was calm and peaceful he had spread a carpet on the steps and the adjacent raised area on the roof to make a small stage and enjoyed singing and playing musical instruments with his friends. He had not the slightest idea that after he had left his house in the 1947 Partition of the country, someone would come here who would transform it into a third-rate hotel and who would erect walls on the steps to make bathrooms.

The owner, who was also the manager of this hotel, was stingy and was constantly scheming to make money. If there was the slightest hope of gain in any project he would immediately pursue it without counting the cost in terms of labour or time, which might far exceed the profits obtained. There was a well fitted bathroom in excellent condition on the ground floor, but he had prohibited entry to it, reserving it for his exclusive use, and he had built these wretched bathrooms on the steps and platform where the hotel residents used to sit in the sun in winter and to get a breath of fresh air on summer evenings. When some people protested against the construction he gave this answer: that if they did not like to live in the hotel they were free to go elsewhere; he had done it for their own good. It was the least appropriate place for bathrooms but this rogue had made them without even taking the trouble to dismantle the steps, and had then made matters worse by allowing non-residents – shop boys, loafers, pilferers and other hangers-on – to use them for a small payment. How this mean and malevolent person met his death will be related later in the story. I shall first describe the extraordinary incident which occurred that day outside the bathrooms.

One evening people were standing as usual awaiting their turn to bathe. Two lads from the lock factory were laughing and chatting. Along with Rafiq, the dyer, I was standing in one corner with my towel over one arm, thinking that I should bathe quickly so as to reach Aziz's place. He had told me that his mother was ill and to come to his house at six o'clock. I looked at my watch and found that it was half past five and I was worrying how I would be able to get there in time. Just then a boy working at the shoe shop came panting up and stood beside the two lads, glum and silent; his lips were trembling and he looked frightened. He said something to his friends and then the two lads from the lock factory also looked scared and the three of them moved slowly over to the rest of us. The eldest of the three said hesitantly, 'This boy has just found a newborn baby lying on the floor.' Rafiq looked at them suspiciously and his face moved under the stress of some unknown emotion. The boy led us all to a small, semi-dark room behind the stairs where broken furniture and other odds and ends were stored. We soon fixed our anxious and curious gaze upon the body of the infant. It was hardly a day old; its eyes were closed and all but the face was bundled up in a white denim coat like those worn by railway guards. We held our breath as we looked at it. Then Rafiq stepped forward and picked up the infant and said, 'What a lovely baby it is. Look how peacefully it is sleeping.'

'Not "is" a lovely baby, but "was".' We heard these words from behind us, and turning round saw Fiazi, a hotel resident, standing close to us. It was then that we realized that the child was lying quite still, that Rafiq was holding a dead body. Fiazi looked at us with wide open eyes and said to Rafiq, 'What a lovely baby! I wish your words were true, but you must have realized how far they were from reality.'

While he was speaking I noticed the old artist, who usually kept to his room, standing near us, busy trying to reach some conclusion. His presence was indeed the embodiment of distracted thought in that gradually darkening room at the close of the day.

'How did this child die? I mean who left it here?' Rafiq asked us innocently.

'A wrong has been done,' Fiazi said in his own peculiar way. 'Mistakes are made and the signs of these mistakes are spread about.' He took the infant's corpse from Rafiq and left the room with composure. He went out with complete assurance, not once looking back to see if we were following him or if we were reduced to inactivity, confused by his cryptic words. Rafiq put his hand on my shoulder and drew me along with him, saying, 'Come, let's see where he has gone.'

We all left the boxroom and rushed towards the stairs. We realized that the artist was not among us; perhaps he had gone into his room before Fiazi left. Half way down the stairs another hotel resident, Qadir Ali, also joined us. He seemed trapped by his own eagerness to know everything. On such occasions when he was ignored or imagined that he had been ignored, he became a real headache, and it was always difficult to reassure him. I had no direct relations with him, nor had I had any opportunity for prolonged conversation with him. Before I explain what happened when we got downstairs, it seems appropriate to say something here about myself, and more about the hotel and its residents.

I used to live in my family house with my elderly father. My mother died when I was a child. Three months ago when my father caught a lung infection and died I was compelled to bring about some changes in my life. The three-roomed house was now too big for me, and my father's pension, which had been coming regularly each month, had stopped. I had found no means of livelihood as yet. I therefore thought that the only way I could manage was to rent out my house and live in a small cheap room. Rafiq the dyer was employed in a shop in our neighbourhood. One day I was standing near the shop asking people if they knew of an inexpensive room, when he told me about this serai-type hotel where he himself lived on monthly payment. I immediately went to the hotel. The crafty manager treated me in a friendly manner and told me the rent for the room was ten rupees more than the sum Rafiq had told me it was. When I said that I knew what other tenants were paying, he answered ruefully, 'Well, Jinab, you can also pay the same amount, but remember that it must reach me by the third of each month.'

Along the corridor on the second floor of this hotel there were eleven poky, badly built rooms and, additional to them, the machan-like attic, from which sometimes the strange screams of an old man were heard. The first thing you saw as you climbed the stairs were the loathsome bathrooms. Some space opposite them had been taken up by the stairs, and from the few square feet that were left, excluding the very narrow passage which led to the boxroom, a longish 'room' was constructed with an iron-barred door. This room was hardly three-and-a-half feet wide, but was the length of a proper room. An old beggar used to live here. At night, before sleeping, he played the tambourine on a tin box. Two months ago, when he died, the hotel manager installed here a few enormously big earthen pots and his 'lovely' hens. These flea-bitten birds were always clucking from hunger and if anyone stopped in front of their door they raised a terrible racket. On that side, where the hens were kept, there were five rooms. They were exactly the same size as those opposite, but they had windows which opened outwards, while the other rooms, on the bathrooms' side, had no such facility, except the last in this row, because they backed on to the wall of the adjoining building. The men who built these rooms had had the consideration to provide an open space above each door through which some air, at least, could enter. At first the rent of the rooms on both sides was the same. The people demanded that the rent for those rooms which had no windows and no satisfactory arrangement for light and fresh air should be less than for the rooms opposite. The despicable manager made a strange decision; he didn't lower the rent of those rooms, but asked more for the rooms with windows and convinced the people that the increase was essential and must be paid by all means.

Apart from the manager's detestable character and his beggarly thoughts, the place's squalid and sordid condition suggested that it deserved some suitable epithet. This fat and ugly person, however, had given his two-storeyed building a romantic Moghul name, 'The Bara Dari Hotel', and had had a small sign fixed to the front of the building. Once he asked the artist to do a larger, brightly-coloured sign to enhance the glory of the hotel, but the artist quietly paid for his tea and went upstairs to his room.

The artist lived in the last room in the left-hand row of rooms with windows. He had been living here for a long time. He never came down for his meals on time and quite often when he appeared for breakfast the servants had moved all the chairs and tables to one side and were washing the floor. He stood at the big marble table near the steps and when he had finished he retired to his room. He did the same at dinner. Although he did not come in time for meals, he disliked the idea of their being brought to his room at fixed times either. Despite his long residence in the hotel he had not developed a single friendship. He did not believe in having even a nodding acquaintance with his fellow residents. His indifference and negligence towards others did not cause uneasiness in them but they wanted to know what thoughts he was lost in and what kind of sadness had taken possession of him. He, however, never allowed anybody to find that out.

The artist was a solitary person who led a barren, secluded kind of life here. His face was stony; it looked as if sorrows and afflictions alighting again and again in the same place had left permanent marks which could no longer be removed by any means. His grizzled beard grew up to the jutting cheekbones. He had a wrinkled forehead and deep-set eyes. When he walked, with his back bent, his eyes downcast, oblivious of his surroundings, he gave the appearance of a man suffering. Anyone seeing him for the first time would have felt pity. He was a great artist though nature had painted his figure with inferior colours.

Occasionally he had a woman visitor. Sometimes she came with a man who looked like a labourer and when they left he would be carrying paintings wrapped in newspapers. We shall learn later what kind of paintings the artist did and how good they were. However, a wooden frame above his door to the left is worth mentioning. A beautiful vase was painted lying on its side and light seemed to flow out from it. Below it in red letters was written, 'LOVE CAN WAIT, BUT LUST CANNOT'.

Next to the artist lived Qadir, who worked in a soap-making factory. He was obstinate and conceited and sometimes, in his angry moments and with his rapid way of speaking, he would say things that were altogether wrong or self-condemnatory, but he was never prepared to correct himself. He was one of those persons who in a rage would abuse his own brothers or sons, and when it was pointed out to him that such language reflected on him as a relative of the person abused, he would retort in anger, 'No, Jinab, he is exactly like this. I know the bastard well.' The room next to Qadir's was occupied by a clerk who used to go off in the mornings and return late in the evenings. In fact he had nothing to do with the other people living in the hotel, and even when he returned from the office he seemed preoccupied with its affairs. I was given the room next to his. Next to me was a room that I had never seen open. Whenever I chanced to look at it I found a handcuff-shaped padlock on the door. Gaman lived in this room. I learnt from the hotel servants that Gaman came here very occasionally and that when he arrived everybody was frightened and the manager was scared out of his wits as long as he stayed and so took great pains to provide all conveniences for him.

Gaman was a cut-throat and a professional murderer and when he had no other place to hide he was compelled to spend a few nights here. The oldest cook in the hotel told me that the police were always after Gaman just as Gaman was on the lookout for the police, and he killed the constables detailed to search for him, one by one. God knows what his real name was. Ghulam Ali or something like that. Nobody knew, but they called him Gaman, referring to him in fear and trembling. I had been living in the hotel for about two months but had never set eyes on him.

The first two rooms in the row next to the bathrooms were taken by some trader who used them as stores. He came here every few days and these rooms were usually locked. The third room was occupied by Rafiq the dyer and an oculist lived next to him. This oculist looked like a beggar, but in fact his profession was to make collyrium and he sold this and other medicinal herbs on the pavement. The last room, the only one in this row with a window, was taken by a man whose speech and conversation were beyond me. This man also seldom came out of his room and had little to do with the other hotel residents. He was about fifty-five years of age. His eyes were extraordinarily bright and his face had a strange kind of magnetism which gave the impression of seriousness and forbearance. Perhaps his appearance alone did not give this impression and he may have been considered an ordinary man, but his words and manner of speaking compelled you to notice him. He spoke impressively, quite differently from other people; and you did not know where he got his ideas from. He was the only one in the hotel who did not eat there. His name was Sharafuddin, but the people of the hotel knew him by the name of Fiazi.

As we hurried downstairs we were all thinking seriously. We quickly reached the hall where we caught sight of Fiazi, walking with dignity. He stopped at the counter and addressed the loathsome manager, 'Jinab, this has been found in your hotel.'

The hotel manager stood up and bent forward to look at the thing wrapped in white cloth. The sight shocked and upset him, and he asked haltingly, 'Wh . . . who . . . who left this here?' Both his hands were resting on the counter and in utter amazement he looked first at the baby's face and then at us.

'Who left this here?' he asked again.

'I regret to say that it is not alive, it is dead,' Fiazi replied. 'It is better you inform the police so that proper arrangements can be made for the disposal of the corpse.'

'Corpse . . . ?' the manager exclaimed, 'But how did this child's corpse come here?'

People were sitting in the hall drinking tea, absorbed in their own conversation. A foreigner who was eating something was the first to come to the counter and smiled when he saw the baby in Fiazi's arms. He touched its nose and started to whistle, but was surprised by the seriousness of everyone's expressions. He was about to say something when he glanced back at the child and at once understood the situation; he closed his eyes in fear and made the sign of the cross on his chest in confusion. Muttering, 'My God, my God', he went back to his table. Picking up his travelling bag and some pamphlets he went to the counter, placed some money on it and left the hotel.

'Fiazi Sahib, where did you get this dead baby?' the manager asked, implying that Fiazi had brought it to the hotel from outside. He came out from behind the counter and started looking at the small corpse and at the people around him, in bewilderment. He approached Fiazi and whispered a few inches from his ear, 'Please take it out and throw it somewhere.'

Fiazi gave him a stern look and said through clenched teeth, 'What's this nonsense? Send a servant to call the police. It's necessary to have the police on such occasions. For one thing it provides them with raw material for their formal procedures to show their efficiency, and secondly the child's corpse would not be wasted. The post-mortem might reveal something to the doctors, although one cannot expect our doctors to get anything from a dead body, because they only know how to profit from half-dead bodies.'

Taking my eyes off Fiazi, I again examined the face of the dead child. I was all agog to learn more about the case. Fiazi placed the corpse on the counter and started to undo the knotted sleeves of the white coat. We all watched him. Carefully he unfolded the coat. When this was done, another cloth was revealed, a man's vest wrapped around the child's body. He pulled this to one side. The flesh lay lifeless in front of us. It was the dead body of a girl whose neck was the thickness of a wrist. Fiazi wrapped the corpse back in the vest and coat as before, but without knotting the sleeves. Different emotions crossed his face. A terrible conflict seemed to be raging behind his bright, angry eyes as if it would continue its destruction into infinity.

Qadir, who had been restraining himself with difficulty, said to Fiazi,

'You're wasting time. How long must this innocent corpse continue to be exhibited here?'

'Innocent? Can the innocent come to such a sad end? An end which is without any beginning and which is reduced to a deep, dark, hateful, black full-stop?'

The manager passed his tongue over his dry lips and blinked rapidly three or four times. He looked as though he wanted to say something but his power of speech forsook him. Fiazi turned away from him and gave us all a look and then started to say something extraordinary and significant, but a man who was unknown to us, who had never been seen in the hotel before, came forward swiftly, making space for himself, and it was his haste that prevented Fiazi from completing his sentence. The man quickly picked up the child's corpse and passing through the crowd in the twinkling of an eye went out of the main door. Fiazi had started to say: 'I know this child and her father . . .'

There was a hand-pump under the spreading tin roof, beside its supporting pillar. Some six feet beyond the pillar was a brick wall about nine feet high, topped with broken glass, the glitter of which dimmed as the sun sank in the evening. At about ten in the morning when the sun rose up behind the hotel these glass pieces shone brightly in the slanting rays of the sun, and it hurt the eyes to look at them; but now the sun was sprinkling its yellowish light on the branches of a cluster of sheesham trees, and sinking behind an ashen-coloured building. A crow cawing hoarsely alighted on the pump handle and jumped from there on to the pipe and, putting his beak to it, sucked out some water. Soon he flapped his wings and flew away. I got bored and came away from the window and sat on my bed. A little earlier I had gone to Fiazi's room and had knocked at the door. Fiazi had come out, but his face was wooden and devoid of any sign of emotion, and he had shown no reaction to my coming to visit him. His unexpected attitude had made it impossible for me to say anything, so I had left with an excuse.

I started thinking about the recent incident. Who had the man been? The way he had come forward and picked up the corpse, and the rapid and decisive manner in which he had left, had stopped anyone from challenging him. But who was he and where had he come from? Then I brushed aside my speculations and poured myself a drink of water from the jug. I had hardly taken a sip or two when I remembered I had to go to Aziz. In my recent preoccupation and all the excitement I had forgotten about meeting him. I hastily closed the door and rushed downstairs. Near the main door Rafiq asked me for a match, but with a wave of the hand I indicated to him that I had none, and ran across the road and down a side street. Darkness was fast approaching. I asked a passer-by the time and he told me it was twenty minutes past seven. I realized then that there was no point in my rushing to Aziz's house, and because he lived only three streets away from the hotel I slowed my pace.

Aziz was a youth of nineteen or twenty who easily attracted attention because of his strange appearance and odd conversation. He would ask questions to which it was difficult to find answers. He would go about expressing his petty desires in short clipped sentences so that you could not help pitying his inadequacy. He was a miserable type and, for some reason, his pitiable condition reminded you of weeping trees. Sometimes he would become extremely emotional and then would start whining and complaining; he would seem not so much to be speaking, but to be plunging his twisted and deformed hands into his own being and bringing from it heavy and unhealthy bits and pieces of the situation in which he was involved. Sometimes he would be in such a mood that it would place anyone walking with him in a labyrinth of confusion. He was a young man who dreaded his own being, who was running away from a terrifying loneliness from which he could not find any haven and who appeared to be doubtful and disgusted with everything. He would listen to and understand what others had to say and was also capable of acting accordingly, but despite this his whole personality seemed to be in the grip of permanent and unchanging compulsions before which he was helpless and which filled him with fear and dread. With everyone, even to common shopkeepers, he behaved with a great show of respect which he sometimes carried to extremes. As a result he became the butt of laughter for them or else they seriously worried about him and wanted quite sincerely to do something for him.

His father was old and worked at a service station on a busy road. He was about sixty and took great pains to remain silent. Each time I had been to Aziz's house I found a deep sad silence on his father's old face. Every time I met him he was either very busy at some ordinary and unimportant task, or was sitting on a stool wrapped in his usual awful silence. So lost and so motionless was he that after some time you began to wonder whether he was there or not. It looked as if the moment before some tyrannical photographer had ordered him to sit still and silent for a long period. Either his eyes would be fixed on a particular part of the nearby table, or his large head would be raised on its weak neck and he would be staring patiently, wonderingly, at a small patch of sky just visible through the window. He seldom spoke to me and if ever he asked me anything he seemed utterly unconcerned about the reply, as if he had had his say and did not need an answer. It is necessary to explain that his silence and indifference did not mean that he was denying the existence of the person he had addressed, nor was he trying to assert his own importance. In reality, shadows of guilt were wandering about in the wilderness of this silence in search of a place to hide, as when a man commits a great sin he cannot tell anyone about and his face mirrors the guilt which is torturing him and compelling him to forswear the sin and its consequences. For some time now he had stopped calling me 'son' and called me 'brother' instead. Though his long spells of silence and absence from home gave him little opportunity to address me at all, whenever he wanted to say anything he would tack the word 'brother' to the beginning of the sentence and this stressed his utter miserableness. His whole personality gave the impression of a ruined wall about to collapse and one felt sorry that he had no one to give him a helping hand. Some features of his face resembled those of the artist, but the shape and cut of his beard was quite different. The beards of both men showed carelessness and neglect, but Aziz's father had more white in his beard, and furthermore his dirty, tangled hair made it look as if his beard and face had been lying around somewhere and had become rusty with time.

Aziz's mother was slim and frail, and her face was the colour of milk into which a large quantity of water has been mixed. Just as the whiteness of milk is lost when too much water is added to it, so the signs of vitality on her face appeared to be fading. Her hard and bitter experiences had left permanent traces on her face. She was small of stature and she lived in the two-roomed house as the mind lives in the body. She was familiar with every nook and cranny, and she knew everything lying about the house, even insignificant things, just as someone knows the moles and marks on his own body.

I was going to Aziz's house after two months or more. Since moving to the hotel I had not been to these poverty-stricken rooms. I had run into him in the morning when he was holding a weak old woman by the arm and was crossing the street. It was simply not proper for him to help anyone so entirely dependent upon him. Although I was in a hurry I took them both over and before he could start a conversation I waved and turned back. As I was half way across I heard him say, 'Please come to my house at six in the evening, my mother is ill.'

I was sorry to learn about his mother's illness and there and then I made up my mind that I would go to visit him. He had told me to come at six o'clock and now it was half past seven when I got there.

Aziz's house was at the end of a narrow cul-de-sac, on the second storey of a three-storeyed building. The building had long outlived its life and was now in a state of dilapidation. The plaster was falling off the walls and dust was coming out of the cracks between the exposed bricks. Other houses in the street were in a similar state; a few steps away one had collapsed and the debris was still lying there, no one having thought it necessary to remove it. The atmosphere here felt heavy and suffocating and it became even more mournful after sunset. Dirty water flowed through the open drains in the street. Although these could not be seen at night because there were no street lights, the stench made one aware of their presence. As I was about to enter Aziz's house I saw two small children squatting over the drain easing themselves. They were laughing and exchanging obscenities. Male and female private parts figured frequently in their talk and they referred to the sexual act in the first person singular. I paused to listen. Just then two men came out of a nearby house, one of them blaspheming and uttering obscenities involving the other's sister and the other person taking him along saying, 'Brother, there is nothing like this. Everything will be all right.' After a while the small children stood up and ran barefoot into the same house.

At the entrance to the building where Aziz lived was an arched door. It was dark here. When my eyes got used to the darkness I saw two goats tied up by strong chains, eating their fodder. The staircase was even blacker and felt very threatening. The first time I had come there had been a bulb burning dimly in the doorway and no goats but now there were a lot of obstacles in my way and the place seemed terrifying. I groped cautiously upstairs. At last the stairs took a right turn and brought me to the first floor landing. From there I could see a bit of sky through a small shutterless window. Opposite to that there was an empty bag hanging from a nail, almost flat to the wall. A few steps further was the door of the tenement where Aziz lived. I knocked softly. At first there was no answer, but after a short while Aziz's father opened the door. I greeted him respectfully, but perhaps he did not hear me because he returned and, crossing the room, sat down on the stool by the table. Aziz's mother was lying on a charpoy behind the stool. Her eyes were closed and she was sleeping soundly. Standing at the door, about eight feet from the charpoy, I could see that she was not ill but that something else was the matter. I rushed to her and found her eyes closed in deep sleep. A fine muslin cloth was wrapped round her forehead and under the bandage just above the left eye was a piece of cotton wool stained yellow with a medicament, indicating that there was a serious wound underneath. How had she come by it? Who had taken her to hospital down those difficult stairs? How long had she stayed there? What had it cost and who had paid? All these questions passed simultaneously through my mind.

The old man was sitting wrapped in his usual enigmatic silence, his back to the charpoy. There was a smaller charpoy in another corner of the room where the old woman whom I had seen crossing the street with Aziz that morning was sitting very still, as if holding her breath. The way she was sitting, the faded features of her face and the expression in her eyes showed that she was unable to see things further than a few feet away. A dusty bulb suspended from the ceiling by a thin gut-like wire illuminated the room with its weak yellow light and made her look like a ghost. I felt melancholy and depressed in the room. As yet there was no sign of Aziz. The old man continued to sit still and silent, paying no attention to anybody: it seemed as if his weak, frail body had been stretched out on a last. I was standing in front of him near the far end of the large table which was about four feet long. This table was unusually high, made of strong wood, and an aluminium tumbler and a dirty rag were lying on it. I wanted to ask something and had almost formulated my thoughts when the old man jumped up and, placing one hand on the table, spoke loudly and in gasps: 'Why have you come? What do you want? Aziz is not here. Go away, go away!' He said this with all the passion that he was still capable of. The effort made him out of breath and he paused briefly, looking at me with wrathful eyes. There was hatred in his cross, insulting tone. I began to have doubts about the wisdom of coming and wanted to say something partly to justify myself and partly out of sympathy for these people, but he screamed again, 'Aziz is not here. Go away. Otherwise I will curse you.' The old man's unkempt beard trembled with rage and he was being shaken by convulsions. I was taken aback by his extraordinary behaviour. My idea of him as someone who sat still and silent was shattered at a blow and I felt helpless. I did not know what was going on, or what had happened in the past few days. I wanted to know why Aziz's mother had a bandage round her head. It was evident that the wound was fresh and that the bandage had been tied some time that morning, but how had she been hurt? What was the meaning of the old man's present behaviour? I had no answer to these questions but all sorts of speculations passed through my mind. I decided to slip away and wait for Aziz on the stairs or downstairs at the main door. I shot a parting look at the old man. His face was the picture of misery and becoming more and more agonized. All of a sudden he got up from his stool and taking short steps dragged his weary body across to the open door of the other room. It was pitch-black inside. At the door he looked round again, then dropping his eyes vacantly to the floor, turned back to go into the room. Just then an inhuman-sounding scream emanated from the old woman as she struggled to get down from her charpoy.

'Go to hell! Go to hell! All are sick here and no one cures anyone,' the old man said as he entered the dark room, his voice trailing away as his body was lost in the darkness. He soon came out again and walked back to the stool but instead of sitting on it he kicked it over, which sent it under the charpoy of Aziz's mother. Looking at me he shouted passionately, 'Tell me, when everyone falls ill who will do the work?'

'When who fall ill?' I asked timidly.

'People, people. I say people,' he repeated.

'What people? I don't understand who you are talking about.'

'I do not have to make you understand,' he said, resting both hands on the table, 'I want to explain things, but I cannot. I have a lot to say, but it is better to remain silent,' and he subsided into silence. However, this was only temporary and he again burst out: 'No, no . . . I will not keep quiet today. I will not remain silent. You come here; tell me, tell me quite frankly why I am not respected. Why don't I get respect?'

'Well . . .'

'No, no. First listen to me and tell me, why am I not respected? Why is my honour not considered my honour?' He tried to speak furiously and impressively. This put him in a worse state and he almost choked, but he continued nevertheless.

'I want to live properly, and . . . and to be respected here. I respect others but I want them to show some consideration for me too. I desire good things in life. I want peace and comfort. I want a place where I can sit and be happy. I want to live, so why am I not permitted to live? How can one live when one is not being taken care of?' he screamed. 'I need money myself, and here everyone swallows my share of the food.'

On hot summer afternoons, amidst shiny cars at the service station, and during the quiet lonely nights here, these dark, melancholy rooms gave birth to a tumult of agonizing ideas in a mind fatigued by labour, and all that he had suffered now boiled up and he bitterly gave vent to them. He was demanding the rights that he could not even clearly evaluate.

He soon became tired trying to speak rapidly and in his helplessness looked for a place to sit down and rest. Apart from the two charpoys and the big table there was no other place to sit. Seeing his need I stepped forward and took out the stool from under the charpoy and placed it to one side. He picked it up and replaced it in its usual place and stood beside it. He did not sit on it but kept staring at its top. It was an ordinary stool, the type usually seen outside the government offices for peons to sit on. He went on staring at the worn-out red paint on the stool. After a while he slowly walked out of the room, towards the stairs, muttering as he went.

Meanwhile the old woman had lain down on her charpoy and was silent again. I turned my attention away from her and thought with dread of the condition of Aziz's mother. I felt doubtful that she was sleeping deeply and suspected she was in a coma. The vehemence of Aziz's father's words and the way he had kicked the stool under her charpoy had made enough disturbance to wake her if she had been merely sleeping. My fears proved correct, Aziz's mother was unconscious and breathing with difficulty. I ran to the old woman, and, shaking her, said agitatedly, 'Aziz's mother is unconscious. I know no more than that.'

The old woman did not answer me, and started weeping and sobbing fit to choke herself. She was crying as if her soul had become disgusted with her. I made no effort to stop her, but looked here and there for water. My eyes fell on the aluminium tumbler on the table. There was water in it. I dipped Aziz's mother's dopatta in the water, but then realized that this effort was useless since the whole of her forehead was bandaged and there was no place to which I could apply the wet material. She was still unconscious. Her pale face had grown paler and in the yellow light of the electric bulb it seemed to be doubtful of its own existence. Her hand was cold when I touched it. Although I was unsure of its effect, I soaked the dopatta in the water once again and squeezed it out and placed it over her face and began fanning her gently with a fan. She seemed so weak that I was afraid fanning her might cause her to get pneumonia.

The old woman got up too and a peculiar sound drew my attention to her. I turned and saw that she was standing, her right hand stretched forward, not quite towards me but trying to find some support to hold on to, and all this time she was slowly shaking her head as if she was denying the existence of some dreadful reality before her. Her heavy khaki sheet was left behind on the bed, and her small body seemed to be held together by a small shirt and green shalwar. I took in these details in one glance and they, together with the old woman's poverty-stricken body, became for me both a question and a challenge.

I rose and took her by the arm. She said something as she walked, perhaps asking where Aziz's father had gone, but I could not understand her properly. Supported by me, the old woman walked to Aziz's mother's charpoy and sat down on the side. She held her hand and again cried the inhuman-sounding scream which shook me once more. The inhuman shriek from that wretched voice was horrible. A moment later, Aziz's mother seemed to screw up her eyes even more tightly. I suppose the scream ended her long painful unconsciousness. The old woman was sobbing and crying and Aziz's mother was gazing at us in amazement. The old woman's sobs ceased and she stared into the face of the woman whose hand she was holding. After a while Aziz's mother seemed fully to recover her senses. She looked first at me and then upwards. Her eyes were strange and lifeless; they seemed to bore a hole in the ceiling. After a while she closed them as if she was going back to her previous condition. Keeping her eyes closed, she spoke with all the anguish of her life, 'Where is Aziz?'

I was about to answer and tell her how I had met him that morning when she asked the old woman, her eyes remaining closed: 'Mother, where has Aziz gone? When did he come?'

I glanced first at the old woman, and then at the face of Aziz's mother, which appeared to be as utterly lonely and sad as the sunset in unknown forests. Then her eyelids opened and, passing her tongue over her parched lips, she asked for water.

I got up and turned round, but stopped because I had used all the water in the aluminium tumbler to soak the dopatta and now it was empty. I picked it up from the floor and asked Aziz's mother where the water was kept. She said that it was in a bucket in the other room. I went towards the dark room and turned on the light and saw . . . But wait, let me first take the water to the ailing woman, because the room was full of details and to study these would have delayed my taking water to her. I filled the tumbler from the bucket and came out of the room.

Aziz's mother had sat up by now. I gave the water to her and went back to the room at the side. This room was smaller than the other and was in complete disorder, unclean utensils on the floor on the right with cockroaches running about. The bucket of water was close by. It was from this bucket that I had just filled the tumbler. The bucket handle was missing. I realized that either this bucket was always lying here or else the person bringing water in it must experience great difficulty. Two paces from the bucket on the floor were some dirty clothes, some of which were so worn out that it would have been better to have thrown them away than wash them. A pair of black trousers hung on a wire stretched across the middle of the room. These also needed washing but they were so dirty that the dirt and stains had nearly changed the original black. About seven feet away from the trousers a vest had been thrown carelessly over the same wire and under this vest on a low charpoy, without any bedding on it, Aziz lay senseless. He was wearing only dark trousers and was on his side with his knees drawn up to his stomach. His mouth was open but it was difficult to tell whether he was breathing through his mouth or nose. He was fast asleep and his stomach rose and fell slowly as he breathed. There was a window next to his charpoy which opened outwards like the window in the other room, except that it had no shutters. The lighted bulb was observing all this with wonder and disapproval and was using up its energy quietly. I looked at Aziz for some time. Then I switched off the light and came out of the room.

Aziz's mother was sitting up in the charpoy and the old woman, who had turned out to be her mother, was sitting near her. Aziz's mother was tired and could not speak coherently and the old woman was answering affirmatively with 'Hoon' and 'Han', nodding her head as she did so. I asked Aziz's mother whether she wanted anything else. She looked at me in gratitude and went on talking to her mother. I sat down close to her to tell her about Aziz: 'Auntie . . .'

'Wait!' screamed the old man from the door. I do not know how long he had been there watching us. His voice had the same horrifying tone and the word 'Wait!' rang out like a hammer blow. For some moments he stood in the door but his eyes were not directed at us but at something near his feet. Aziz's mother turned pale. Her face, already colourless, now appeared more lifeless, and the same extraordinary scream was choked in the old woman's throat. I was distressed. By now it was half-past eight or nine and at this hour of the night in a room on the second floor of a dismal house an aged man was standing demanding proof of his individual worth and dignity.

I racked my brains to think of something to say or do but came up with nothing. The old man raised his ferocious eyes and fixing his fiery gaze on me came nearer. He caught hold of my arm and in a clear, calm voice, expressive of all his deprivations, said falteringly, 'Brother . . . my brother, I will tell you everything. This woman will not let me live. I have done nothing. What can I do? I am an old man and subjected to all kinds of indignities in this house. I was searching for my shoes near the table and she says that I pushed her down the stairs. This is incorrect. It is a lie. How could I have pushed her? She has never done anything for me and has always considered me a redundant thing. I bring money home, while everyone here eats my share of the food. Everybody's ruining me, everybody's tormenting me.'

'Did Aziz's mother hurt herself falling downstairs?' I asked.

'Yes, yes, falling downstairs . . . I have often warned her to be careful when going up or downstairs. Where is my fault in that?' he asked vehemently and, catching me by the hand, brought me near the stool.

'Brother, tell me where my fault lies? What have I done wrong?' His face was one big question mark. Weighed down by years of painful labour, he did not want to accept his degradation, and was offering his peculiar reasoning about everything. Aziz's mother lay down once more, and stared indifferently at the ceiling. I wanted to go to her, but the old man held me firmly and his grip tightened as he talked. His old, feeble hand had the same hardness that is found in the bones of the sick and weak too. The old woman was looking attentively at her daughter, gently pressing her arm.

'I can live alone,' the old man said in his crazed voice, using it to lash the two women on the bed. He went on in a fury: 'Don't imagine that I cannot live alone. I can live by myself, or I will beg for food. The world is large, there is plenty of room out there.'

God knows what more he would have said, but just at that moment came the sound of many people rushing downstairs together. The noise reached the door and it was flung open. There were not many people, but just one person at the door. His hair was neatly combed and he seemed just to have had a bath. He stood trying to express his rage through his blazing eyes. All he was wearing were white trousers and thick leather sandals on his feet, their buckles undone. His fingers and lips were smeared with curry grease. It was evident that he had been drinking and that the old man's loud talk and screams had disturbed him. The old man was scared out of his wits and lost all power of speech. The drunkard gave him no opportunity and said in a decisive tone, 'Now keep quiet and go to sleep.' Saying this he left the room, slamming the door with even greater violence than when he had opened it. It would certainly have been smashed if it had been made of inferior wood. His heavy steps were clearly audible as he ascended the stairs.

When he had left Aziz came silently into the room, probably awoken by the drunkard slamming the door. He was looking confused and had some difficulty in standing. His coming into the room was like a wandering dream entering a strange body. The old man's face twisted in pain and he came close to me and whispered, 'You will see that this son of a pig will now trouble you.' Saying this he lost no time in getting up and again leaving the room silently, and this time briskly.

I went over to Aziz and took him to the charpoy. I was thinking of taking my leave when he made an effort to chase sleep from his eyes and said, 'When . . . when did you go away?'

'Go away? What do you mean? Where am I supposed to have been?' I really was at a loss to understand his question.

'I mean . . . when did you go away from here?' he asked in a mournful tone. 'I am very sorry that I was asleep when you came. I was supposed to meet you, but could not help falling asleep.'

It was obvious that he wanted to sleep some more, because he was not articulating properly and seemed to be groping for each word. He sounded tired. Suddenly he opened his eyes wide and said, 'Munir, tell me one thing . . . Why haven't you been to see me?' He was placing the words in the proper syntactical order with great care and this had the effect of slowing down his speech. 'Brother Munir, tell me one thing . . . just tell me . . . you didn't come to see me. Why didn't you come to see me? You think I am bad, but I tell you I am not.'

As he stopped talking I heard the strangled sound of sobbing from Aziz's mother. I felt suffocated. There was such a dreadful feeling of disaster and desolation here that even the walls seemed horrified. I wanted to say nothing but continue to listen to Aziz's mother weeping; I wanted to see her melt into tears moment by moment and listen to her in silence. I had no desire to be an aloof spectator but I was so deeply moved that I wanted to see the absolute end of it all. I wanted everything to weep so much that the whole room would be filled with scalding tears. I consoled Aziz and assured him that I would try to meet him again the following evening. I gave him the address of the hotel as I was leaving; he nodded in assent and got up with me. I stood a while near his mother's charpoy without any purpose, then went out feeling extremely sad.

TWO

Fiazi entered his room, bolted the door and lay down on his charpoy. He closed his eyes, seeking peace and quiet. He was comfortable lying straight like this, his mind composed to induce a particular mood. After five or ten minutes he would be wonderfully refreshed and cheerful and ready to get up.

It was now a quarter to seven and the only window in the room was open, letting through the dim blue evening glow. He got up and turned on the electric light. Near the window was the large charpoy. To the left of it was an armchair and to the right side was a longish table with three books piled up on it. A library card peeped from the pages of one of them. There was an ink pot with very little ink left in it, and next to the books and the ink pot a closed cellophane bag containing about twenty dry rusks. Near the long table was a round table, a little higher than the other. Its diameter was not less than two-and-a-half feet. There were more books on this round table, a jug of water with a saucer on it, an upturned glass and a small tin.

Fiazi picked up an umbrella lying in one corner. A nail stuck out just above the handle. Earlier that day he had intended to fix it properly but had then opened the pages of a book and had postponed the task until the evening. He had just taken a heavy iron tool, shaped like a pestle, from the cupboard to repair the umbrella when a knock came at the door. He got up and opened it. A fellow hotel resident was standing there. Fiazi looked at him with an expressionless face and the visitor, seeing the lack of a welcome, left with an excuse.

There came a second knock at the door some half an hour after the man had left. This had never happened before. People rarely came to him. He did not eat in the hotel and so the bearers had no dealings with him either. The room he occupied was his sanctuary where he could cut himself off from everybody. Therefore it was natural that he should be uneasy. Nevertheless he got up again and opened the door. This time the man who had taken away the infant's corpse was standing in front of him. He had a small flower in his hand. Fiazi stepped aside to let him into the room. The stranger sat down on the chair and said, 'I have come to say a few important things.' The man's voice had the power to attract attention and he seemed not only to be in command of his own feelings and thoughts but also to be able to dominate his surroundings. 'Someone near the stairs told me the number of your room,' he said, placing his elbows on the arms of the chair. 'Tell me, how did you know that I was the father of that child?'

'Oh,' Fiazi said, coming over to him. 'In fact I have to go out shortly, so it would be better if you could come some time tomorrow.' They agreed on four o'clock the next afternoon. When the man had left, Fiazi noticed the flower on the table and picked it up before locking his room and going out. He went to the place where he usually ate his dinner. After dinner he left for the store where he was a night watchman. He was still holding the flower. He looked at it and started thinking:

When we pluck a flower we rarely, if ever, consider the length of its stem as we pick it; we may pick it casually as a means of passing the time, and then throw it away down a drain or on a patch of grass. The flower and our plucking it has consequences in our lives, as does the length of its stem at the time we plucked it, the time of day, whether we were alone or in company, whether we wanted to show the flower to someone else or picked it for our own pleasure; all these and similar factors come into play, either to disturb or please us in the days to come. The question is, why did we pick the flower in the first place? What were we reacting to? Some external condition. But what took us to the place where the flower was? Circumstances. Do circumstances influence a man and shape his habits and qualities or do we create circumstances? One man cannot be responsible for circumstances, just as he alone cannot be responsible for the birth of an individual. Here 'alone' does not merely mean the individual, but his own union with his surroundings with which a man, from birth to natural death, protects himself.

For the past three years Fiazi had been employed as a watchman at a godown. The godown contained machines and tools. He was satisfied with the job. He had been under no compulsion to take it but it fitted in with a plan he had which would give him time for study. His employers had no objection that he spent his time with books while on duty; their main requirement was that he would remain awake all night. In this way Fiazi used the night like the day, with the minimum of interference from anyone. He slept in his room at the hotel for five to six hours in the morning and this was sufficient for him.

Fiazi had been a primary school teacher before becoming a night watchman, and before that a professor of philosophy at a college. He had taught at the college for thirteen years before deciding to go and teach small children and live among them. He spent nine years at the primary school. Then he gave up teaching and simply drifted for three or four years. He studied life with an open mind and heart and gathered much experience as he went along. He battled with the conditions and incidents around him and discovered new directions for his thoughts. He achieved this by passing through the burning desert of ideas which had been firmly established within his being. In the process he destroyed much that was inside him, and was known, for an existence which opened many doors to his latent perceptions. He had known his parents and other relatives but he believed that over-attachment of parents to their children was one of the worst things for a man, something which lodges in him like a disease. It tries to hold him back a whole generation. He believed that escaping from them and casting off the subtle net of theism was an important personal revolution: that the future was now cut off from the fossilized past. He was not against parental love, but was against the immediate or distant personal motivations lying behind this feeling. He believed that things should be looked upon as they really are. Rivers should be left as rivers, wood should be used as wood, stones should be used to construct buildings, the doors of which should not be open to the floating heavens beyond man's reach. The dike of false hopes should be broken. There is no flood behind it, no fire and frenzy on the other side, and the dust raised by the breaking of the dike will be readily dispersed. Some people go beyond reasonable limits in the way they behave and in the ideas they pursue, while he believed that they should behave with moderation. Whenever anyone exceeds reasonable limits he either entangles himself in difficulties or else becomes the target for the hatred of others, and if the person hated happens not to recognize his place then he becomes no more than a joke. It is very important to know our limits. We acquire this knowledge in the extensive river of experience where we all must learn to swim, and those who do not swim drown, even if they remain out of the water. This particular insight enables us to understand the link between thought and action. To gain knowledge of the essence of things is a real task; once this has been attained, other knowledge will follow. In this way everything should be understood and things should only be called by the name they deserve. We are troubled when we give something a name which does not correspond to its identity. Once we give a wrong name to a thing or we misunderstand its identity, that thing will express its anger and will curse us. Reality presents itself in its simplest and most comprehensible form, but we, through foolishness and delusion, are lost in a maze of errors. We run away from reality and are for ever chasing mirages and illusions. The same can be said about falsehood. When a person deliberately tells a lie it eats into him and destroys him; it is like an acid eating into his heart and brain. A lie is sure to take its revenge, it lives on imperceptibly and wherever it gets an opportunity and conditions are favourable, it continues to harm those who perpetrate it. They cannot understand the cause of this harm, and start searching for reasons, but the old lie which they thought was insignificant and harmless mocks them.

It was now ten past four and Fiazi was waiting in his room for the stranger, who was late. Sitting in the chair he could see the clear blue sky. It was the month of August and the weather was pleasant. In his mind's eye he had flown far away into the vast space of the sky; with one movement of his eye he could create an arch and support it in the air and stretch it from left to right. He continued doing this for some time but could not make the floating arch stay in any one position. He got up, took the padlock from the round table and went out of his room. He locked the door and, keeping the key in his hand, crossed the corridor and went downstairs. Outside the hotel, some fifty paces away, he saw the stranger walking rapidly towards him. He looked apologetically at Fiazi as he drew close, but then his eyes began to shine, looking eagerly for change and stimulation.

'Come with me. I'm going this way,' said Fiazi, turning down a side street.

'I'm sorry I was a bit late, but where are you going now?' the stranger asked, walking beside Fiazi.

'I was sitting in my room waiting for you and when you didn't appear I thought you might be coming another day instead. So I left the hotel intending to visit someone. But it doesn't matter, you can come too.'

'Can we discuss such things there?' the stranger said doubtfully.

'Why not? Anyway, what's so special that you want to discuss?' Fiazi asked. The other did not reply but continued to walk beside him. After about twenty-five minutes they reached a junction where a narrower road turned left down a slope. A casual glance at this sloping road gave the impression that everything was running away to some unknown destination. Fiazi always felt this at this point. It would occur to him that just as the rotation of the earth is not felt, so the area round that road was in imperceptible but certain motion.

'Look. All those houses seem to be flowing downwards,' Fiazi said, stopping a moment. 'I do not know how far they will all go before they stop.'

The other person, lost in thought, had not been paying attention and said, 'Excuse me, I didn't catch what you said.'

'I was saying that looking at the houses in this locality, I always get the feeling that they are floating downhill. What do you think?'

'What can I say?' replied the other, and laughed unexpectedly. His laughter was strange. After his mood over the past twenty-odd minutes no one would have expected him to laugh, but it disappeared as suddenly as it had come and, with his former gravity, he said, 'How much farther do we have to go? And please tell me where we are going.'

'I don't understand why these houses are floating. It looks quite something from this height.'

'Forget the houses. Just tell me, why did you say that you knew that child's father?'

Fiazi did not answer, but went on walking, turning down a lane which was so desolate and quiet that one felt all the inhabitants had gone away leaving their houses lonely. The doors and roofs were wrapped in a mournful silence as if awaiting some final decision about themselves. At the far end of the street was a date-palm and there was a turning into a broad road lined with bungalows. After some fifty paces Fiazi stopped before a house with an impressive facade. He knocked at the door and just at that moment they heard the sound of breaking glass inside the house, followed by complete silence. Fiazi knocked again and an old ayah opened the door. Recognizing him, she stood aside and Fiazi and the other man entered the sitting room.

The walls were light green which, in combination with the fine turquoise-blue curtains, looked attractive. There was a beautiful, clean glass ashtray on the table, without any cigarettes or matchbox near it. Placed thus, it looked more like a decorative piece than an ashtray. Near the sofa was a long table under which was a pair of woman's sandals. These sandals were so elegant and delicate that it seemed that the feet had been taken out of them in order to give them rest. One door of the room opened on to the street. The remaining rooms lay through the door which had no curtain. There was a plang beside it spread with a white sheet, its pillow propped against the wall. The pillow and sheet indicated that someone had been sitting here, leaning against the wall only a moment ago. To the left of the bed was a wall cupboard with glass doors. There were two shelves in it. On the lower shelf was a cloth doll and a small carved wooden box, and then two empty brass vases.

On the upper shelf was a framed picture of a woman and next to it a picture of a child of about seven.

Fiazi had not been here for some four months and the room was exactly as it had been when he last saw it, except for the picture of the boy which had been added. He picked up the ashtray and just then the door opened and a woman of forty-six or so entered the room with dignity. She was neither too fat nor too thin; in fact one did not have time to look at her figure, because the expression on her face caught one's attention. Her grave and sober face showed that she was a little annoyed though she could not give vent to her annoyance in the presence of a stranger. Fiazi smiled at her and made a gesture of getting up and then sat down again. Shadows of unknown thoughts crossed the woman's face, and they made her otherwise good-looking face desolate.

'What am I supposed to be doing here?' The first person to speak was the stranger. He got up and looked at Fiazi as if asking for an explanation, and said, 'I do not understand why you brought me to this house. I came to see you, but you had to drag me here.'

The woman looked straight into the stranger's eyes and asked Fiazi loudly, 'What is he saying?'

'Kausar, to begin with, I apologize for staying away so long,' said Fiazi, ignoring both their questions. 'I was unable to come for quite a while, but a few days ago I made up my mind to visit you.' He paused and then continued, 'See how helpless this man is. He says he is the father of a child, one whose dead body he took away immediately after its birth.'

'Utter nonsense,' said the other man softly under his breath.

'No . . . no, this is not possible.' Kausar spoke excitedly on hearing what Fiazi had said.

'What is not possible? Anything that the human mind can conceive is possible.' Fiazi turned to the stranger and said, 'You abandoned the infant's corpse in the hotel and went away, thinking that no one would find out that you were the father of an illegitimate child. Remember, nothing is illegitimate except for our thinking, which labels certain things as legitimate and others as illegitimate. What is at fault is the kind of thinking that tries to understand things in their superficial relationships. We are trying to repay the debt we owe for our borrowed thoughts, a debt that our parents did not pay, nor their parents before them. We undertook to repay it and in return we surrendered our thoughts. We gave our thoughts to our creditors and expected justice to be done to us. This was our mistake. How helpless we were, and how cruel it was. Man wanted to redeem his thoughts, then found that they were not his but those of others and polluted by others. He found they had been grossly adulterated by concepts of legal and illegal, good and evil, sin and reward for good deeds. All the time we remain unaware of the existence of a great universal force and suffer agonies, troubles, doubts and inequalities and become the battleground of confused ideas.'

As Fiazi spoke a strange light in his eyes brightened. He said to the stranger, 'You are responsible for the murder of that child. Your ideas and thoughts will remain with you and torture you. You will try to escape from them, but you will not be able to. You will have to endure them. It is you yourself who has sown this sorrow and it is you who will reap the consequences. When I saw the child's dead body I said that a wrong had been done. Arguments about legitimate and illegitimate, holy and profane, about rewards and punishment are futile. Things cannot be categorized in such terms; they are either wrong or right. Wrong things harm our health and disturb our peace of mind and right things facilitate life. By right things I mean those which arise from man's awareness of the realities of nature and his capacity to learn how to use them. Things should be tested from the point of view of nature and science, and the most likely consequences should be kept in mind. If this had been done that child would not have come to this sorry end.'

'Fiazi!' Kausar almost screamed.

Fiazi was talking to the stranger, ignoring Kausar, but that scream drew his attention to her and he turned and looked at her with surprise. The stranger's hands were planted on the back of the sofa and the expression on his face showed that he was engaged in deep thought and that the moment he freed himself he would immediately leave the room without exchanging any words with anyone. Fiazi looked attentively at him and said, 'You may live in any country, but don't fall foul of the law of that country. Do not create conditions in which you have to kill children. You should always bear in mind the consequences of your actions. The law does not know how to forgive. Don't be scared of it; look it straight in the eye and continue on your way. Be careful not to sail too close to it lest you capsize. The law is like a dog on a leash; if you go too near it, you will get bitten or, at the very least, be frightened by its bark. Remember that the law does not die but causes others to die. It does not bestow life, but snatches it away. Society should give man the opportunity to develop as a human being. Why is man not trusted? If he were, social evils would gradually decrease, and those evils which remained would not in fact be evils, but realities which we have not been able to comprehend and so, in haste or anger, have categorized as evils. We have fitted them with such powerful magnets of our hatred and contempt that these obscure realities are not free to appear in their true form and always dance before us in the shape of evils. Evil, which is in fact not evil, but which we have chosen to call evil, does, in revenge, become evil. I wish more trust were placed in human nature, and if a man is bad, then he should commit suicide. There is nothing inherently evil within man; all he needs is the opportunity to be good. The real problem is the environment and this should be changed.'

The stranger suspected that Fiazi would never tire. His manner showed that words would continue to flow from him, and in this flowing locality, God knows where they would float to. It was the first time he had been in this part of town; it was tucked away in a remote corner and no road passed through it leading to some other important part. He had heard enough and without a word left the room. He did not even turn round as he went out, and he left a palpable vacuum.

The moment the stranger went out Kausar started crying. It seemed that her tears had been waiting for him to leave. Fiazi did not ask her to stop, but brooded on the man who had just left. He liked the way the stranger had left without saying anything, but despite this he was unable to form any definite opinion about him. He would have followed him if Kausar had not suddenly stopped crying and come close to him. She wiped some of her tears away with the palm of her hand and held the others in check inside her eyes and kept looking at him silently. Fiazi found her behaviour strange and couldn't decide what to do. She caught him by the arm and shook his shoulder and shouted, 'You are mean and contemptible. You have placed me in great difficulty. Tell me, what am I to do?' She went over to the plang and, sitting down on it, started weeping again. Fiazi sat down beside her and tried to console her. 'What is the matter, Kausar? My dear, why are you weeping?'

'Fiazi . . . Fiazi,' Kausar said, still sobbing, but then found that no more words would come. Her face was twisted by an undefined pain.

'Why do you behave like this?' asked Fiazi. 'You know I don't believe in things like marriage. I used to sleep with you and I paid you for it. I come now because you insist, even though I feel that everything between us is slowly fading away. There's one thing, Kausar: when I turn at the crossroads to come here I feel that this whole area is flowing downwards.'

It was obvious that Kausar was not listening to him, more absorbed in the ebb and flow of her own thoughts. Moved by some emotion she got up and stood beside him and said through clenched teeth, 'Fiazi, you are despicable.'

Fiazi was troubled and pointing to the plang said, 'You are ill, you are going down with a fever and it's better you should rest.'

'Where are you going?' she asked and then, helplessly, 'Please don't go. Tell me, can you be a father?'

'Father? What do you mean?' He turned back.

'Fiazi, you are a father. Believe me, you are a father.'

'I don't know what's the matter with you, but at the moment you really need rest. I will come again some other day,' Fiazi said moving again towards the door.

'Wait just two minutes,' Kausar said with a choking voice. 'Tell me, where do you live? The people in the house where you used to live know nothing about you. I won't come to see you, but for God's sake give me your address.'

'If you are not to come to see me then what is the use of giving you my address?' Fiazi asked calmly. 'I will come back another day. Now you must rest.'

'No, this cannot be.' She drew close again and said, 'You came today after three months. Why do you avoid seeing me? You have never permitted me to speak frankly. You used to come to me before and then you disappeared for about seven or eight years and said you were working in a school in some other town. I know all your tricks. Don't you trust me enough to give me your address? All right, you can't marry me, because I was a prostitute. But there's another reality, that you are the father of a young man whom you caused to be born twenty-four years ago. I might never have told you if I hadn't received a letter three days ago from your real son in which he expressed certain opinions for the first time. He had addressed the letter to another woman whom he thought was his mother. Look at this.'

She showed Fiazi a yellowish paper which she had been hiding in her fist for God knows how long. She hastily straightened the folds and held it out to him: 'Take this and read it. No, first tell me who the man was that you brought here.' She pulled back the letter. 'Tell me, who was he? Why did he murder his own child? Do you want to kill your son too, Fiazi? Why do you want to? Was that man your brother? He looked just like you. Who was he? Who was he and you . . . you . . . ?'

'Oh, sick woman.' Fiazi jerked away from the small wall of air imprisoning him and hurried out into the deserted street. The woman had troubled him. It was true that he had had relations with her for a long time and she had often asked him to marry her, but never before had she gone so crazy as to risk everything in one desperate obsession. God knows who the young man was whom she was determined to call his son. And then that letter . . . the thought of it made him laugh. The stranger who had come with him had indeed impressed Fiazi, and he thought of him as he walked.

I was startled out of sleep by the sound of my name being called loudly. It was still dark outside. I got up and opened the door to find Aziz standing there. He was wearing the same dark trousers and his shirt was not tucked in. He looked lost. Before I could say anything he entered the room.

If it had been anyone else I would have excused myself and asked him to come some other time later in the day, but it was difficult to convince Aziz with argument. I had given him my hotel address, but I had not expected him to come to see me at four in the morning; on the contrary, we had agreed that I would be going to see him that evening. As he came in his restless quivering eyes looked all around, he came near the charpoy and stopped. A piece of waste paper was lying on the floor. He picked it up and threw it out of the window. Dragging an empty chair to the charpoy he sat down. He was about to speak when Qadir Ali, his eyes heavy with sleep, appeared at the door. He said angrily, 'Munir Sahib, people who come to visit you may, if they wish, knock at the door, and those who visit you should trouble only you.' Saying this he went away, but I felt the force of his words and was quite ashamed. After Qadir left I turned to Aziz and was about to ask him why he had come so early in the morning, but before I could say anything he said, 'In fact, I wanted you to hear my voice.'

'Hear your voice' I said, perplexed, 'Aziz, I don't understand what you really want to say.'

'Yes, just this, that only you should be able to hear my voice.'

'What do you mean?' I asked rather harshly. 'I do not understand you and why the need to come so early in the morning?'

'I meant, if I had knocked at the door you would have thought that the knocking was at someone else's door, that is the reason why I called you.' There was controlled emotion in his tone and I had great difficulty in understanding him. He came over to me and said, 'Munir Sahib, tell me, what can you do now?'

'What can I do? I don't know what you're trying to say, Aziz. I think you're still half asleep.' I tried to make him realize. 'Look, Aziz, the proper thing for you to do is to go back to your house and sleep.'

'I have come to discuss certain very important matters with you. I think they are quite urgent.'

'Aziz, go now, I promise to come to see you this evening. Anyway, you should be with your mother. She is hurt. You should be there.'

'Don't talk about Mother. Whatever she does is all right, and I am sure that whatever she is doing now is all right.'

'Perhaps she's asleep?'

'Not perhaps, she is. When I left home to meet you, she was sound asleep.'

'If she is asleep then what is there to be done? You just said, whatever she is doing is all right,' I replied in frustration.

'Sleep is itself a complete action. No other action is more correct and proper. Don't worry about her for the time being. I have come to you on business. I have two gallons of Kerosene oil* and if they are of any use to you then well and good. The price is not high, and I can assure you that the oil is not adulterated.'

He got up and left the room. I was confused by his talk and actions and even more by his reference to Kerosene. I went to the door, intending to find out where he had gone, but before I reached it Aziz re-entered carrying two small red cans. He put them down near the charpoy and sat on the chair again, just staring at the wall in front. He was as static as a picture. I waited quite a while, thinking that he would say something to which I could give a proper answer, but he remained sitting there silently. The stony silence worried me and irritated me too because I felt quite ignored. Eventually, slapping the words with his tongue, he burst out, 'Brother Munir.' Glancing now at the window, he continued earnestly, 'I really do not want to trouble anyone. I will leave if you wish, but please do not curse me.'

'Where did you get these cans of oil? Why do you want to sell them?' I asked him sympathetically.

'I bought them at Chowk Yadgar market and now I want to sell them at the price that I paid.'

'You went to Chowk Yadgar to buy these? That's a long way away. And why do you want to sell them at the price you paid for them?' I asked him uneasily. What else was there to say to someone who had just arrived at four o'clock in the morning to sell two gallons of Kerosene?

'I only want to sell them, that's all.'

* In Pakistan Kerosene oil is sold in small shops by the bottle or can for domestic consumption, for lamps, oil stoves and the like.

'But why so early in the morning? You could have come later.'

'Munir Sahib, you are my friend, and I trust you and I think you cannot be angry with me and that is why I came straight to you,' he said, trying to convince me. 'It is necessary to sell these cans and I wish to do that today.'

'Why today? And if you bought a can for five rupees . . .'

'No, no. It is not like that. I paid nine rupees four annas for each can,' he said hurriedly, 'and you cannot say five rupees instead of nine and a quarter. Four rupees four annas for the oil and five rupees for the can. I paid in all eighteen rupees eight annas. Go and ask if you like.'

'Very well,' I agreed, 'but I still don't know why you did it.'

'Please, buy these cans.' His desolate face looked pathetic.

'I will buy them, but, Aziz, you do not understand that what you're doing is not right.'

'Dear brother, you also say I am wrong, but I tell you that I am not. Everybody says I do not work. I want to show them I can work.'

'What kind of work is this?' I asked, understanding nothing.

'I will show them that they are wrong about me. The day will come, when everyone will be convinced that I am a hard worker. Brother Munir, please listen to me carefully. I am not doing anything wrong; I am engaged in trade. I borrowed twenty rupees from a Doctor and all I could buy with them was two gallons of Kerosene oil and one meal. You buy them. I want to do some work, some business.'

'But why are you selling these cans at the price you paid for them?' I asked him once again. 'You have a right to demand a little more than you paid.'

'No, no. Not yet,' he replied. 'Training is necessary for everything and this is training for business.'

Luckily I had some money so I took out eighteen rupees eight annas and handed it to him and sat down on the charpoy. Aziz's face brightened with joy as he received the money and now he sat more peacefully and comfortably. After a while he took the money out from his pocket and giving it to me said, 'Munir Sahib, I want to sit here for some time. I will go to sleep on this chair. My money will be safe with you. Please keep it and when I wake up I will take it from you.'

I took back the money and asked him to lie down on the charpoy. He looked at me with gratitude. I do not know whether these grateful looks were for my buying the Kerosene, or for allowing him to sleep on the charpoy; either way deep emotion flowed from his eyes and seemed to push aside the thick untidy eyebrows. Before going to sleep he took off his shirt, did up all the buttons with the exception of the top one and placed it over the back of a chair and, lying down on the charpoy, was soon fast asleep. The shirt on the chair and his body on the charpoy appeared to have separate existences. I stared vacantly out of the window. Dawn was breaking; the morning looked ragged and melancholy.

I was in the habit of going out for a short walk, a mile or a mile and a half. I left Aziz sleeping and went out. It was a depressing day and all the time I was away from the hotel I kept thinking about him. I soon returned and found him still asleep, his brown shirt on the chair as before. I let him sleep, and went to the loathsome bathrooms. When I came back after bathing he was still asleep. I had my breakfast in my room and sat a long while waiting for him to get up. I had to go out, but thought of the money he had given to me, which I wanted to return to him. Aziz slept for three and a half hours. God knows where he had been the night before to make him need his sleep now. Then he got up and undid the buttons of his shirt with as much care as he had buttoned it up before placing it over the chair. After putting it on, he took his money from me and went to the door to go out. I asked him to have tea or breakfast but he gave no reply and went out silently. I do not think he can have heard me or he would have answered.

In the corridor Aziz counted his money again and then went downstairs. A few paces along the street he saw a man walking jauntily towards him. As he drew near, Aziz greeted him respectfully and, taking a ten-rupee note from his pocket, asked for change. The man said that he did not have ten rupees, but Aziz kept walking with him and asked him to search his pockets in case he had them hidden away. The man repeated that he did not and then passed the hotel. Aziz stopped. Watching him go, he muttered, 'You should have money, without it you are nothing.' Aziz spoke sorrowfully, as if he wanted to inform the other of some great reality. He re-entered the hotel and asked for ten rupees change at the counter. Taking ten one-rupee notes he went upstairs and stopped near the stinking bathrooms. He looked to the left and to the right and then took out the notes from his pocket and counted them. He did it again, wanting to reassure himself. He spread them in a fan, like playing cards and tried to count them in one glance. Now he was quite tired. The mental effort was as great for him as four hours' continuous work would have been to another. At last he put the money in his pocket and, heaving a sigh, looked down into the street from a nearby window. The morning was there with all its deprivations. Aziz turned and as he passed down the corridor he found a piece of paper about the size of a bus ticket and one tooth from a comb.

He touched them with his foot and went on to Munir's room and knocked.

I had been about to go out and was not expecting any visitors. I got up and opened the door and found Aziz again standing there. He came straight in and went to the armchair and sat down. His sunken eyes were glittering and restless. He glanced at me and then lowering his gaze said, 'Munir Sahib, all I want to do is sit here for some time. I find this place very restful.' All at once he got up and approached me. 'Brother Munir, I know that this is your room, you pay rent for it. But . . . wait. First tell me how did you pay me this money? Where did you get it from?'

Aziz was standing so close to me that I could feel the breath from his mouth. I felt as if his words were delving deep into my being. He was confident of what he was saying as if all his sorrows would end and he would be satisfied if only he could find out where my money came from. The manner of his speaking was so agonized that he sounded positively mournful. He turned away from me and moved towards the charpoy but did not sit down. He stood with his back to me and said, 'Don't tell me anything. I will ask no questions. Let it be. What's the use of such talk? Brother Munir . . .' Moved by some inner emotion he turned to me and, looking straight into my eyes, suddenly fell silent. The silence deepened and it was torture for me to watch him. At last he broke it with a snap: 'Brother Munir, please tell me, how am I to stay alive?'

'Listen, Aziz . . .'

'No, Please listen to me and tell me whether I can live,' he interrupted excitedly. 'I want to live and obtain money. But how? How do I keep body and soul together? I can work. You can send me wherever you want and I will walk there, but will I be permitted to live or will I not be permitted to live?' His voice grew hoarse as he spoke and I felt that he was about to burst into tears. His whole being seemed shaken by a storm and his lips trembled. Probably he had not slept a wink the previous night and it was obvious that he needed more sleep. I was about to tell him so when he sat down on the charpoy and lapsed into silence once more. His speech, his movements and his rapidly deteriorating state filled me with anxiety. He was sitting lost in thought on the charpoy, his legs hanging down. I had an appointment, but seeing his condition, I postponed my visit. He stared fixedly at the floor and spoke softly but decisively.

'I shall think. I have all day and all night to think. I am sure I shall come to some conclusion.'

He got up and paced the room, sometimes close to me, sometimes further away. His walk betrayed his ill temper. With each step he seemed displeased that he had taken the trouble to walk; as if it would have been better to have remained where he was.

'Munir Sahib, I want to tell you one thing.' He spoke very forcefully and his whole being seemed to have become foggy. I caught his arm and made him sit down on the charpoy. I was worried about what would happen next.

'Munir Sahib, I want to tell you . . . Believe me, what I am saying is the truth, and I shall always keep to what I say.'

'What is it, Aziz? I'm listening.' I looked at him sympathetically.

'Munir Sahib, you have always been good to me, but I am afraid, afraid in my heart and I get very worried. I assure you that I will never come to you for a loan and if you wish I will not sell you anything in future either, or bring anything to you in pawn. I will never let these things happen, never. That is all. This is what I wanted to tell you . . . What am I to do, Brother Munir, what am I to do?' He burst into tears. Tears overflowed from behind his eyelids where they had been imprisoned for a long time. He was trying to extinguish the raging fire within himself with them. Drowned in his tears, in the storm of convulsive sobs, bedraggled in his own vague and incomprehensible thoughts, he continued to weep. I went across to console him and just at that moment the door opened and there was the artist in all his presence. His face was mute and his lips were partly visible amidst the tangled beard.

'I have come here without permission. Please forgive me. But a moment ago I heard the sound of someone weeping. May I ask why he was crying?'

'Please sit down,' I said, offering him a chair. I had not heard the artist speak before and I now wanted to do something to honour him but my plans dissolved when I looked at Aziz. The artist sat down on the chair, looking at me. He may have repeated his question, but just then Aziz wiped his face with his shirt cuff and stood up. 'Munir Sahib, I am leaving.' I told him to sit down and I went and ordered food and drink from the restaurant below. When I came back Aziz glanced at me and went straight to the window. He took a piece of paper from his pocket and after writing something on it he put it and the pencil back into his pocket and returned to his seat. After a while the hotel bearer brought food and drink. The artist had had his breakfast; even so we both kept Aziz company and had a biscuit or two and a cup of tea while he ate. Aziz had some biscuits, a couple of samosas and a cup of tea and then very respectfully shook hands with the artist and with the same courtesy and deference he asked my permission to go. I went to the stairs with him; he turned to me and gave me a blank look and then hurried down.

I found the artist still sitting when I returned. He got up but I asked him to remain seated and we sat facing each other without saying anything. The artist appeared to be trying to count the hairs on his wrist. I was very tired and closed my eyes, seeking peace and oblivion. I was anxious about Aziz and felt unable to help him. Suddenly I remembered the artist and looked up. He had finished counting the hairs on his wrist and was gazing at me. He looked away when he caught my eye and did not say anything. He was wearing a dirt-proof coloured shirt and a pair of blue trousers stained with paint. My attention was drawn to his hands on the arms of the chair. They were dark wheaten in complexion with large pores on the back. His fingers were long and the nails were broken and ugly, the cuticles stained with dried paint. The artist scratched his beard and said, 'I may have caused you some inconvenience. The point is I heard someone crying from my room. The sound was so unusual that I felt compelled to come and find out why the person was crying.'

'I am worried about the boy. I don't know what I can do for him.' I told the artist briefly about Aziz, about his family and home and also that I was going to see him that evening. The artist did not make any comment, and just looked at the table-top. Suddenly he picked up a folded piece of paper from under an empty glass on the table and, giving it to me, said, 'I think your friend left this here by mistake.' He got up and, shaking my hand, went to the door. Half way there he halted. 'If you are going to meet Aziz this evening and if there is no harm in it, I should like to accompany you.' Then he went and I was alone. I opened the folded paper impatiently. Within its folds were two one-rupee notes, along with six hastily written lines.

'Brother Munir,

I am leaving this money. When you went to call the bearer to bring something to eat, I thought of asking you not to send for anything, then I changed my mind, deciding to eat only what could be bought for two rupees.'

THREE

Fiazi reached the hotel at half past nine in the morning; actually he had got there at nine o'clock but had gone on farther to have his breakfast. The previous evening's incident was still fresh in his mind and he was thinking about it. He did not know why Kausar was trying to make him responsible for a son. She had previously asked him to marry her and each visit she would find some excuse to mention the topic, but he had never thought that things would go this far. For the past few years he had noticed a marked change in her behaviour and conversation, but had not imagined that behind this lay a desire to give him a son. He opened the door to his room and found two letters on the floor waiting for him. One he recognized at once by its yellowish paper. Kausar had been holding it in her clenched fist. The other was in a white envelope and looked recent. He opened it and read:

'My lord and master,

You left me in a miserable state. I would have followed you, but the thought that we would become the centre of attention for the people in the street stopped me. You are my own, and the father of my son. How unfortunate it is that he should be in this world and that we should not be prepared to accept him as a son. My desire is that you should give him a father's sincere love and not let him feel that he has been living so far without his real father. Our son is well and healthy, but he does not know anything about his real parents. Give him a father's love and I will show him what a mother is. He is of your blood, so why do you shun him? How can you bear to be separated from your own flesh and blood? For twenty-four years I have hidden this fire within my breast. I would not have told you if Farzana had not brought me Bashir's letter.

I want to hide nothing from you today. How can a wife hide anything from her husband? You are mine and only mine and I am certain you have been mine and mine only. No one else can be your wife or anyone else your son. I had another husband and was married to him, but though living with him I found that I was closer to you because you alone are my husband and father of my son. That other husband is now dead. I barely remember his entering my life or leaving it, but you I have always had in my thoughts. I was not at first interested in you. You used to come to me and go away as other men came and went. I may have treated you with indifference, even asked you not to come. It would have made no difference to me. I would have forgotten you if you had not been the father of my son. I am certain that you are his father. In this I am not mistaken. I was surprised myself that such a thing happened, but it did happen and exactly nine months later the child was born. I left the child at the hospital and Farzana took him from there. She brought up Bashir and he thought Farzana was his mother, though in fact she was not. I am his mother and you are his father. Bashir does not know this, but he has found out that Farzana is not his mother. Bashir is working on a farm in the village where he lives. He wrote this letter to Farzana from there. In it for the first time he has raised certain questions which directly concern us. I want you to consider these matters dispassionately. I know that you do not believe in marriage because I have often heard your opinions on this, but the question is not one of marriage now, it is of one's child and our responsibility as parents. Who are his real parents? This is what he wants to know and it is now our duty to tell him.

You visited me today and with tears I asked you to acknowledge and accept your son. You ignored me and left me weeping. It is true that I was a prostitute, but I abandoned that life long ago; those days are no more than a bad dream. Who does not make mistakes? I did wrong or I was made to do wrong, but I have been punished more than enough. You are my last hope. You are my husband and the father of my child, and if you do not forgive me now, no one will. Even God will not forgive me. I beg you with tears, don't give me such a punishment. I am suffering deeply and am extremely lonely and if I am with you and with my son I will suddenly be happy, all of a sudden I will have everything. I want us to be together so that we can spend our lives as a small family.

Your companion came back to see me immediately after you left. He gave me the address of your hotel. I have been to see you here two or three times but you were out so now I am leaving this letter and Bashir's letter. Read them and come to see me at six o'clock tomorrow evening, without fail. Why are you living in this poor hotel? Leave it and come to me. This house needs you and Bashir very badly.

Yours and only yours,

Kausar.

The other letter was brief:

Dear Mother,

I feel rather strange writing this letter. I cannot tell you all my feelings and doubts, anyway I want to say that you are not my real mother; you took me from someone else and adopted me and brought me up. My friend Gaman told me this, and other things too.

Perhaps this is wrong and there has been some misunderstanding. I am perplexed and do not know what to think. I shall come and see you on the ninth, and I hope that you can give me a clear answer then.

Bashir.

Fiazi read the letters twice. He understood the thoughts and feelings struggling to express themselves between the lines and was able to get a fair impression of this Bashir who was thought to be his son. He put both letters in his pocket and stood at the window, thinking deeply. He considered matters from various angles. He sat down on the chair and closed his eyes, his hands folded in his lap. He groped for the glass of water beside him on the table and, when he had drunk, placed it on the floor. He combed his hair with his fingers, opened his eyes briefly and then closed them again. He rested his head on his left hand, then he rested both his elbows on the arms of the chair and pressed all eight fingers to his temples, the thumbs to his eyes. As his thumbs pressed into his eyeballs he saw golden coloured circles and rainbows forming and disappearing on a vast black curtain. At the top of the curtain circles formed and spread downwards and from them emerged millions of multicoloured suns. Fiazi saw them simultaneously. The rays from the wombs of these suns struck against the white light, giving it new forms and shapes. White light could be seen behind the rays, but the rays were moving so speedily and beautifully that the light was being left behind. The white light was continuously being born and dying. A series of yellow circles formed on the black curtain and flowed downwards. Fiazi suddenly realized that what he had taken to be a black curtain was in fact a black ocean. With circles spreading out across it and multi-coloured waves disappearing into it. Where the waves disappeared was a deep flaming ravine and in the midst of this was a whirlpool of foam which flowed downwards until it became a thin stream. In the foam Fiazi saw countless words with broken arms, deformed legs, weak, writhing bodies, cheeks that had suffered slaps, whipped backs and necks that bore the signs of the yoke of slavery and other parts bearing indelible marks of hatred, curses and misfortune. How wrong these words were, and yet they were nothing more than the counterpart of those intellects which were not witnessing their deaths. It was a terrifying sight because it showed the history of many nations going the way of the foam. Words, words, and words were dying and falling into the flaming foam. Fiazi opened his eyes and leaned back.

'Can words actually die?' Fiazi wondered. No, not words, he thought. No one can kill words. What we see dying are our hateful thoughts and ideas. Words are always protected, but when they feel their last hopes melting away after the death of ideas and thoughts, they go elsewhere to find a place more congenial, and there they settle. They migrate and we see only the remnants and these are not words even though we think they are. They are heaps of filth and whatever we make of them they do not continue along the strong moments of the present representing faith, hope and trust. Rather we vomit obscenities that culture adopts, giving birth to hatred which religion picks up lovingly into its arms, and suspicion which civilization establishes as its monopoly.

Fiazi had entered his room at half past nine and it was now eleven o'clock. He was still seated, his mind in the grip of the recent spectacle. Then, making a plan, he got up, feeling it important to act as soon as possible. As he was closing the door, he heard a sound from the back of the hotel of something like a pot falling. Fiazi crossed to the open window and looked down on the back of a dilapidated bungalow. He saw a fourteen- or fifteen-year-old girl, whose hair was matted with dirt, wearing a wet and faded threadbare shalwar. She was picking up a large brass tray which had fallen to the ground. It might have been used to carry the washing as clothes hung on the line at the back. After picking up the tray she put it back on the ground and squatted beside it to rest. Fiazi looked at her carefully. The girl's shirt was wet in places and too tight for her even with the shirt buttons in front open. It must have been handed down by a girl whose breasts were too large for it. This girl too needed a looser shirt, but she had to manage in this one even though it hardly hid her growing figure. The girl's heels and haunches were on the ground and her knees were about six inches away from those tightly enclosed breasts; she had clasped her knees and was sitting silently, looking blankly in one direction. Then she bent her head and began looking at her breasts. She put her hand inside her shirt to make them more prominent, looking dispassionately at her body as if it was someone else's. She soon tired of this and resumed her former posture, though now her knees were stuck to her breasts and she was nearly bent double as she sat. She was lost in thought. Then a woman appeared from around the corner. She was not old but looked weak and had difficulty in walking. Seeing her the girl jumped up and said, 'I've hung out the clothes, Auntie.' The woman said nothing, just glanced at the clothes and looked the other way. It seemed strange to Fiazi and made him smile for no reason at all. Just as he smiled the woman looked up at him, and Fiazi drew back. The padlock was still in his hand and he left his room, locking the door behind him, and went downstairs.

The road outside was broad and clear. He went first to the godown where he applied for one night's leave. Fiazi seldom asked for leave and whenever he did his employer would grant it. Fiazi thanked him and came out of the godown. He walked along several streets and at last came to the railway quarters. These were all identical and built in a long straight line. He passed seven or eight doors before stopping in front of a single wooden door which was painted khaki. He knocked and waited. The door opened to reveal a middle-aged Pathan in a shalwar and vest, obviously just awake. Fiazi greeted him. The Pathan caught his right hand in both of his and welcomed him warmly, 'So, Phiaji, it's you. Come in, come in.'

They crossed a courtyard whose walls were shared with those of the next quarters and entered a small room. It had a little window with iron bars and wire netting. A charpoy was in the corner against the right hand wall with an old dirty cotton mat too small to cover it. The pillow was even more filthy than the mat. It was unusually long and without a cover. A grimy red comb stuck out from under the pillow and a bottle of mustard oil was next to it. There was a cupboard without a door and with one plank across it, built into the wall like a niche. On the lower shelf were an earthenware cup, a large aluminium bucket, and an old battered enamel mug whose stains and spots on what was left of the enamel looked like smallpox and leprosy scars. The top shelf held only an old rag. Near the cupboard, a nail driven into the wall served as a clothes peg and shirts hung from it. There was nothing else worth mentioning in the room. Fiazi sat down on the charpoy beside Khan who said, 'Will you have a drink or some food?'

'No, Khan, thank you. You know I do not eat lunch. How's work going?'

'The days pass. I've had problems since joining the Railway. Shifts keep changing. Sometimes I'm on morning duty and sometimes night.

How are you getting on in the godown? What's your employer like? Does he pay well?'

'Yes, Khan, everything's all right, but I need a room to live in. Any small room will do. Perhaps you know of one?'

'What's the matter with the place where you are?'

'It's no good.'

'Why? Is it too far from your work?' Khan asked anxiously.

'I can't stay there any longer. I want to move to some other room.'

'Well, come and stay here,' Khan said, laughing affably. 'Consider this your room for the time being.'

'Right, Khan, I'll fetch my things,' said Fiazi, getting up from the charpoy, 'I've got tonight off. We'll search for a place tomorrow morning.'

'Sure, sure. Get your stuff first. I'll come with you, if you like.'

'No, Khan, there's no need, thank you. I'll be back shortly.'

Fiazi left the hotel at five o'clock. He loaded all his belongings on to a horse-drawn cart and returned. Khan was waiting. They went out for tea and as they drank, talked about their past. Khan had worked as watchman at a shop near the godown for about a year before joining the Railway, in the carriage shop. It had taken Fiazi some months to come and see him. After a sip he said, 'I may be back late.'

'What time?' asked Khan. 'I leave at ten. Where should I put the key?'

'Take it with you. I'll come to the carriage shop for it,' Fiazi replied.

'All right,' said Khan, slapping the table with pleasure, making the cups rattle. After tea, they shook hands warmly and Khan left for his quarters.

Fiazi stood there for some time. The sky was clear except for some patches of interestingly-shaped stray clouds. As he walked, Fiazi looked at one of them. It was like smoke from a railway engine which had risen to the sky and hung suspended, its shape intact. On the outer edges he saw boys' heads, looking up into the sky in amazement. Above this cloud was another one like an Edwardian motor car; a schoolgirl was sitting in it with silk ribbons in her hair, touching the collar of her frock. It was all so clear and well shaped that Fiazi soon mastered the details. Then he noticed some smoke rising in the air from a house. Fiazi wondered whether he would become a cloud one day too. Why not? Smoke goes up into the clouds. Then what does 'smoke comes out of a house' mean? Fiazi shut off the regulator of his thoughts and turned his attention from the clouds to the road which was the colour of smoke. He reached the crossroads where everything appeared to be floating. He arrived at Kausar's house and knocked. Kausar opened the door and let him in. The room was in the same condition as the time before. Kausar sat down on a chair in front of him and said after a pause, 'I went to your hotel but you weren't there. I pushed Bashir's letter and another one under the door into your room. Did you read them?'

'If I had not read them why else would I have come here at six o'clock?' Fiazi retorted, looking into her eyes. 'Kausar, I don't think you need me. I thought of something and came to see you for the last time.'

'Why? What are you saying, Fiazi? Last night you left me very worried. Do not treat me like this. I cannot bear it. Why are you acting this way?' She came over to the sofa beside him. Fiazi remained silent, gazing at the ashtray.

'Are you listening, Fiazi? I swear that Bashir is our son and I am your wife.' She spoke with passionate intensity.

'Kausar, stop this drama.' Fiazi got up angrily. 'I don't think that you're altogether mad. Even women like you shouldn't treat me the way you have these past few days. I tell you once and for all, you are not my wife, nor my daughter, nor sister, and cannot be any of these to me. I have no relationship with you and I am putting an end now to anything I may once have had with you. Keep all your sons with you and buy a father for them in the same way that you've been selling yourself.'

'No!' screamed Kausar. She collapsed on the sofa in her frustration. Sprawling there she looked stonily at Fiazi. She seemed to be in a half-faint. Fiazi helped her to the plang and said, 'Look, Kausar, try to understand me. I told you the other day, you are sick, and unfortunately I'm not a doctor.'

'You are a doctor; for me you are a doctor and a father to my son.' Helpless and weak she turned her look from Fiazi to the ceiling and said softly, 'What shall I do, Fiazi? My heart is desolate. I am utterly lonely.'

'You need rest,' said Fiazi, holding her hand. 'Believe me, I can do nothing.'

Deep silence fell. Kausar continued to stare at the ceiling. She made an effort to sit up and started looking at Fiazi. Her throat moved up and down as she swallowed.

'Fiazi, Bashir is my son. I gave birth to him,' she said sadly. 'He is right in saying that Farzana is not his mother. He is coming in a few days. Come, let us tell him that we are his real parents. You tell him this in such a way that he is not alienated from his unfortunate mother.'

'You are indeed an unfortunate woman, I am sorry that I can do nothing for you,' Fiazi said getting up from his seat.

'What? Are you going away?' said Kausar fearfully.

'You can tell your son that his father died before his birth. He will believe it. Many children are orphaned before they are born. There is nothing complicated or incredible in that.'

'But you are alive. I did not stay with my son. I want to be with him. I swear you are the father of my child.'

'Swear?' said Fiazi looking at her, 'I do not believe in oaths.'

'What, do you not believe in God? I swear by God that you are Bashir's father.'

'Which God are you swearing by?' Fiazi looked at her sharply.

'Which God?' Kausar was puzzled. 'By my God, the true God.'

'I do not know this God,' Fiazi said and smiled. The smile stayed on his face.

'You do not believe in God!' said Kausar in amazement, her mouth open. 'That is a sin, a great sin. Oh, my God, forgive me, what torture . . .'

She closed her eyes in agony and stood up holding the wall. Suddenly she turned and hugged him, screaming. Fiazi was sick of trying to understand her and wanted to be rid of her, but she moved away herself and stared at him in fear and dread. She kept staring at him for some time, then she started to speak slowly. 'Why did you come to see me? You should not have come. You could have gone to some other woman; there are others.' She was on the verge of tears and her voice was hoarse. 'Fiazi, believe me, he is your very own son, your own flesh and blood.' She caught hold of his arm and said, 'Look, we'll go to another town and you can live with me there and I will serve you well. I'll sew on your buttons and I'll wash your clothes. I'll cook for you, I will do everything for you. We'll talk about our son and we'll be happy. He is our child. We have given birth to him. Fiazi, let us stay together in one place. Come here, this is a big house. You should be here. I cannot get used to living without you. For days on end I have been silent. But now this must stop.'

Moving past her Fiazi said, 'I'm going,' and he turned to the door. Just at that moment came a knock and then another. Fiazi looked at Kausar who stood where she was. Fiazi stepped forward and opened the door. It was the stranger of the day before. He came in gravely and walked to the chair near the front wall and sat down. He took out a packet of cigarettes, picked up the ashtray, placed it on the floor beside his chair and started to smoke. It was difficult to guess the state of his feelings from his expression. One moment he seemed not to place any importance on anyone there, the next he seemed to be sitting respectfully, not wishing to disturb the people in the room by even the slightest movement or gesture, and then another glance at him would dispel both impressions and one felt that he was convinced there was no one in the room but himself. Fiazi felt as if his body had been pushed away from the door. He kept his eyes fixed on the stranger. Kausar's hands were folded on her breast and she passed her tongue over her lips once or twice. The stranger took a puff from his cigarette and blew it out softly before saying calmly, 'I went to your hotel a little while ago and . . .'

'Let's talk outside,' Fiazi interrupted him. 'I wanted to see you too. It is good that we have met.' Fiazi was standing close to him, willing him to understand the spirit in which he spoke. The stranger glanced up at Fiazi and went on smoking.

'I wanted to talk to you about something important.' Fiazi addressed him again.

'Finish your talk with her first,' the stranger said confidently, blowing out the smoke in one breath. His voice was full of vitality.

'Come on, let's go,' Fiazi said decisively.

Kausar watched them without daring to say a word. Finding herself utterly helpless, she screamed Fiazi's name so loud that it could be heard from afar. She stood where she was, frightened, her hands still folded on her breast. Before the stranger could get up and leave the room with Fiazi, or Fiazi could do anything, the door leading inside slowly opened and a boy of about five entered. It was obvious that he had just woken up, perhaps disturbed by Kausar's scream. The boy was barefoot and was wearing a yellow flowered bush shirt and white knickers. He looked around the room in childish distress and calling 'Ammi, Ammi' rushed over to Kausar and clasped her legs, staring at the stranger.

Kausar looked angrily at the boy but her mood suddenly changed and she placed her hand on his shoulder. Fiazi laughed meaningfully and said to Kausar. 'I think that Bashir has come to meet us himself. In fact, he wants to start his life's journey with us from this age.'

Kausar freed herself and went close to Fiazi as if to convince him, 'This is not my son. By God, this is not my son.'

'When did I say he was yours?' asked Fiazi.

'He is not my son, I assure you. I adopted him. He is my son, but not my real son.'

'Sick woman, sick woman,' whispered Fiazi, turning his back on Kausar and looking blankly at the curtains.

'Fiazi, I took this boy from someone else,' said Kausar helplessly. 'When my own son was separated from me, my own flesh and blood taken from me, I was very upset for a long time. Eventually I could not endure it and I adopted this boy and have been bringing him up, but Fiazi, he is not my own son. Bashir is our son. We will keep this child too, but I swear that he is not my son.' She caught the boy by the arm and brought him close to Fiazi and spoke emphatically, 'How can he be my son? See, he is not.'

The boy was nervous and frightened by all this. He began to cry, looking at Kausar for sympathy. Fiazi went forward and spoke caressingly to him and picked him up in his arms. The boy broke out again in tears. He wanted to cry and, finding security in Fiazi's arms, wept. Fiazi felt the child's sobs echo from the walls and roof. He consoled him affectionately. Kausar pointed to the boy and spoke, looking at Fiazi. 'Why don't you believe me? He was asleep and came in when he was awakened. Let him go, he is not my son.'

'I do not know whose son he is. But you must return him to his parents, whoever they may be. Kausar, you do not know what you are doing. This can be dangerous for you and for others too.'

The stranger stood up, the glass ashtray in his hand. Deep in thought he stubbed out the end of his cigarette. Lifting his eyes, he looked attentively at Kausar, and went to the table, a faint, inappropriate, smile on his lips. He placed the ashtray on the table and, taking a packet of cigarettes from his pocket, lit another cigarette. As he placed it in his mouth, a woman entered the room, the same woman who had ushered in Fiazi the previous day. She looked worried and, snatching the boy from Fiazi's arms, immediately ran inside the house. Her action was so swift and so unexpected that no one understood for a moment what had happened. Fiazi was aghast and looked at Kausar, his eyes blazing. From afar came the sound of the child crying.

'Call the child,' Fiazi said softly. 'Kausar, I want to see that child. Go and fetch him.'

'He is not my son.' Kausar could not think of anything else to say.

'I want to see him. Why don't you bring him? Listen! He is crying.'

'You know . . .'

'Kausar, what else should I say? If you can bring the child here, then bring him. It does not seem proper to me that he should have been taken away like that and made to cry.'

'Let's go.' The stranger suddenly spoke to Fiazi.

Kausar was about to say something. It was obvious from her manner that she resented the presence of the stranger. Fiazi said to Kausar, 'You are a woman, but I do not consider you a woman, nor can I expect a correct answer from you. You have no control over yourself. You do not know what you should really do. You have become disorganized by being entangled within yourself, and you have lost all sense of purpose. You are afraid of the name people give you. You don't want to be identified by this and that makes you helpless. You are so helpless that you have to swear oaths, make yourself cry, scream, indulge in lamentations, and create difficulties for yourself. Why don't you change the names of things, and remember that until you do that and recognize their separate identities, you will go on wasting away in your restlessness. What after all is there to gain by wishing and desiring? Why do you want to love? Why do you want to receive love? Why are you wandering about making yourself wretched in the deserts of constrained and futile love? You are terrified by your present, and the future is a meaningless dream to you. The future is indeed a meaningless dream for you but you should not remain engrossed in the happy revelation of it. I don't suppose you will be able to understand my meaning properly, and that is also part of your self-created helplessness.'

Kausar was sitting on the plang, sobbing jerkily. Fiazi was close to her, and said, 'The most important thing is for you to call things by their true names.'

'Fiazi, all I know is that you are the father of my son,' she said, her eyes brimming with tears, 'and you . . .'

'Stop making yourself difficult,' Fiazi said, looking away from her. Just then he realized the woman who had snatched the boy from his arms had returned to the room. There was no sign of the boy. Fiazi turned to the stranger and, as he did so, Kausar placed a hand on his shoulder from behind.

'Kausar, go and rest. You do not understand that in this place . . .' Fiazi's sentence was lost because before he could complete it he had to struggle to stay on his feet. He had turned to face Kausar when, suddenly, the woman standing silently in the room sprang forward, and pushed him with all her might, shouting and screaming. She had an extraordinarily loud voice. She yelled at Fiazi and the other man to leave.

'You get out. Why did you come in?' asked Kausar, dragging the woman to the door, 'Get out, go away. Stay inside.'

'Kausar, you don't know them,' the woman said angrily. 'They are both scoundrels and they have only come here for wickedness.'

'Go inside and stay there,' screamed Kausar and shoved the woman through the door. They could hear her beating it from the other side and shouting, 'You cannot hit me now, the door is closed. These people are rogues and vagabonds and you are a slut. You . . .'

'Go away, go away,' shouted Kausar, putting her mouth to the door. 'For God's sake, leave me alone.'

'Throw them out of the house. They are wicked rascals. I'm telling you the truth, they are criminals.'

Kausar did not answer this time, but stood there panting helplessly. There was silence the other side of the door. The stranger went on smoking his cigarette with great composure, quite unconcerned with what was going on around him. Fiazi looked again at Kausar, then he approached the stranger and led him to the door. Opening it quickly, they went out. They soon passed beyond the date-palm. There was a deep silence all around which seemed to dog their steps. After some distance, Fiazi said through his teeth, 'Sick woman, sick woman' and went on walking down dark and nameless streets with the stranger.

They reached the crossing where they could see the lights of the city. The stranger had said not a word as they walked. He had just puffed complacently at his cigarette. After a while they turned left down a narrow lane. There were rows of shops on the ground floor, now closed. The stairs leading to the upper storeys must have been at the backs of the houses. If they had opened on the street, one would have seen steps here and there, or people going up and coming down, and then the street would have appeared to have some life, but now it was desolate and the electric poles fixed to the walls looked more like drainpipes.

They walked at a moderate pace. The narrow street opened out into a wide road. Here the houses were just as high, but this road was about three times as broad.

'I went to your hotel first,' the stranger said to Fiazi.

Fiazi did not say anything. Perhaps he wanted to listen to him more and by keeping silent was giving him an opportunity to speak.

'Have you left the hotel?' The man looked straight ahead as he walked, one hand in his trouser-pocket and the other hand with the cigarette swinging.

'It became necessary,' Fiazi replied, taking a deep breath. 'If I had stayed this torment would have come to see me again. You cannot imagine what horrifying thoughts have got the better of her.'

'Why did you waste so much time there?'

'That I do not know either.'

'What was all that about a son she wanted to hand over to you?'

'It's all rather unbelievable. I wonder who the real father of that young man is, whom he's being separated from so dramatically.'

The stranger walked on silently, as if he was not concerned with anything in this world beyond walking. They came to a middle-class residential area with bungalows built economically on small plots. All was silent. The moon was a hazy blur and the darkness was getting deeper. Some way along they saw a tobacconist's stall at the roadside near a bridge over a dirty drain and the stranger stopped to buy a packet of cigarettes. As he paid for it Fiazi had a good look at him by the light of the gas lamp in the stall. He had sharply chiselled features, his lips were thin but well formed, and his nose was well proportioned and seemed to have been carved out of some soft wood. He had an attractive, magnetic face. His hair was distinctive too: smooth as copper wire, it was brushed back and framed his forehead in a semi-circle. Fiazi noticed, as he was asking for the cigarettes, that his lips appeared to move only when he was speaking and that the moment he stopped they closed as if they had never moved. The man lit a cigarette and took a puff before moving on.

'I have to go this way, to the carriage shop,' said Fiazi, slowing down. 'I should like to have a good talk with you. When can we meet?'

'Come along with me now and we can talk.'

'It would be inconvenient for you at this hour.'

'Not at all. Don't worry about me, just come.' The stranger smiled and said, 'In fact I want to discuss some important matters with you urgently.'

'All right. In that case we can talk tomorrow,' Fiazi replied.

The stranger made no comment and laughed softly. To Fiazi it was like fragments of glass scattering in the air. Fiazi continued to walk beside him, looking at him from time to time.

'Why did you murder your child?' Fiazi asked as they turned down another street.

'She was not my child and I did not murder her,' came the answer as the man pulled deeply at his cigarette and blew out a thin line of smoke through his parted lips. It made it look as if he was still smiling.

'If you did not kill her, then whose child was she?' asked Fiazi, scrutinizing his face. The stranger laughed out loud, making large cracks in the darkness. He turned to Fiazi, 'You know whose child it was and where it came from.'

A little farther along the stranger stopped at a metal gate and unlocked it. He asked Fiazi to come in, the key still in his hand. There was a small garden on the left with large plants. The leaves were motionless in the dark as if the air had paralysed them for some offence. The house, too, was still and silent. The stranger crossed a small verandah and rang a bell, keeping his finger on it for some time. Fiazi was surprised. If he had a key to the main gate, why did he need to ring the bell now? The door opened and an old man appeared. He was short and was dressed in a long shirt without any buttons which did not look as if it belonged to him. He had very little hair left on his head, but his beard was thick and completely covered the front part of his neck. The old man looked at them dully and stood aside deferentially. Fiazi and the stranger entered a rectangular room, unadorned by any picture or calendar. There was a curtain facing them, obviously over a door leading to other parts of the house. There were closed windows on the right with square, dark green panes. Above the windows were curtain-rails but no curtains. There were four broad upholstered chairs with sloping backs and in the middle an oval table on which lay an empty glass and a white stone ashtray. A dim electric bulb hung from the wall; in its yellow light the old man looked scared. The stranger switched on the tube light and the room brightened. The lights showed up the cigarette stains in the ashtray. Looking at it, Fiazi wondered who the child had been at Kausar's, and whose son, and his thoughts wandered back to that floating area. The stranger lit his cigarette and disappeared behind the curtain, followed slowly by the old man. About three minutes later the stranger returned, his lips tightly closed. He took a last deep puff from the end of his cigarette and crushed it out in the ashtray. Fiazi looked at the clock on the wall. It was twenty to ten.

'May I have some food?' Fiazi asked, 'I should like to eat if there is anything in the house.'

'Food is coming,' the man answered, looking at Fiazi.

'Good. You are very kind.' Fiazi nodded slightly. 'Afterwards I shall leave.'

'Why?' asked the stranger in a calm voice, without a trace of astonishment or curiosity.

'Because that's how I feel.'

The stranger leaned back on his chair and stared at the ceiling.

Suddenly the old man burst in. He was upset. His words came out in toothless shreds. 'Your . . . your . . . she's coming, your . . .'

'What's the matter?' the stranger shouted, getting up. 'Tell her to go to sleep. I do not want to see anyone just yet.'

The old man had hardly turned when someone came to the other side of the curtain. It was a woman, as was evident from the bangles on the wrist that showed on the left side of the door behind the curtain. After a while she withdrew her hand and only her bare feet and ankles were visible below the curtain, which stopped about six inches from the floor. It was a strange sight, the bare feet which appeared to have grown out of the floor and to have been cut off some six inches above the soles. She went as silently as she had come, leaving the door open behind her. Fiazi got up. The old man had already left the room. The stranger wanted to go after the woman but seeing Fiazi rise he stopped and, putting on a false smile, said, 'Please sit down. I'll be back in a moment.'

'No, I should leave now,' Fiazi said and went out calmly, making no attempt to note the other's reaction. He set off down the lonely road. It was so misty that the stars and moon could not be seen. The houses and bungalows at the side stood like dark stupefied shadows as if waiting for some calamity.

'How black the air has become,' Fiazi muttered, and stopped to look around. Then he continued, for the moment in the direction of the carriage shop, but intending to turn off back towards the floating area where Kausar was. He had decided to make her understand certain things and persuade her to be taken in for her own safety. He had already framed the arguments in his mind. Before him lay the crossroads. He turned left and had hardly gone a few paces when someone softly called his name and placed his hand on his shoulder.

'Come, let's go back.' It was the same stranger, walking beside him. 'Why did you get up and walk away? Come with me.'

'No . . . I must go now,' said Fiazi, halting, 'I have to go right now.'

'What will you find to do at the carriage shop at this hour? I knew that was where you were heading. That's why I was able to take a short cut and catch up with you. Come with me for a little while. You should not have left so suddenly without waiting for the food.'

'I no longer want to eat,' Fiazi said, looking him in the eyes. He continued on his way, but had hardly taken a few steps when the man caught him by the arms and in a mixture of anger and hatred said, 'Come with me.' He spoke confidently, an element of threat in his tone. Fiazi was quick to realize that whoever this person was, he would pursue him whatever happened.

'Please come with me.' This time the stranger spoke with some courtesy and there was a smile on his face; it seemed to Fiazi to be artificial as before.

'And if I refuse?'

'You won't, will you?' He was still smiling.

'Where do you want to take me? What is there to discuss at this hour?' asked Fiazi uneasily, but walking with him.

'I want to discuss some very important matters with you. You know how important they are.'

'I do?' Fiazi asked with surprise.

'Yes,' the stranger said, and smiled again. Although Fiazi hated the smile, he found beauty in the movement of the man's thin lips.

'Is your smile deliberate or spontaneous?' Fiazi asked as they turned into a narrow way.

He smiled again, and this time there was laughter in his voice. 'Never mind my smile . . . just . . .'

Fiazi waited, but the stranger said no more and walked quickly down the narrow dirt road that ran along the back of the bungalows. They soon came to a wider road and then to another, and after a short distance they came again to the metal gate of the stranger's house. They entered and this time the stranger did not feel the need to press the bell, but pushed the door open. When he entered the room Fiazi saw the same woman with the glass bangles round her wrists, sleeping on her side on the carpet. The man left Fiazi standing there and went straight through without a word. He quickly returned, bringing the old man. He signalled to Fiazi and they left the room. For some time they stood on the verandah. Fiazi was blessed with a sensitive nature and was quick to understand the reality of a situation and form an opinion, but this time he was unable to find any signs which might enable him to reach any conclusion. The stranger gestured him back inside. The sleeping woman and the old man had disappeared. The stranger still did not speak. Soon the old man returned, bringing food. While Fiazi ate he wondered what it was that the stranger wanted to discuss with him at this late hour. The old man placed a jug of water on the table and stood waiting for some final order, indicating by his posture that if there was no other work for him he would like to retire for the night.

'Where is she?' the stranger asked the old man.

'She has gone to sleep in her room, Jinab, and I have closed the door.'

'All right, you go now,' the stranger ordered.

They continued to eat in silence after the old man had left. Once Fiazi asked him his name, but got no reply. Fiazi noted that the man sat calmly, eating and drinking with grave contentment. When he had eaten he wiped his lips with a handkerchief and then examined it. One could not say for certain whether he was actually seeing it or was more concerned with his thoughts.

'What is your name?' Fiazi tried again.

'You know why I have brought you here.' The man leaned back in his chair. 'I will tell you everything. First, please answer frankly and without fear. Tell me, since when did you know about our relationship, and why did you look at her and smile?'

'Who are you talking about?' Fiazi asked in surprise. 'Who smiled? I don't understand what you are saying.'

'The woman who was the mother of the dead child that I took away from the counter. You saw her from the window of your hotel room and you smiled and then she went inside. Why did you look at her and smile?'

'The woman . . . ?'

'Yes, she was the mother,' he interrupted, 'but I did not kill the baby. I want to know what the woman told you. You know a great deal, and you have to tell me it all.'

Fiazi had hardly opened his mouth to speak when the old man entered again. The stranger ground his teeth and got up. He seemed on the point of throwing the old man violently out of the room, when Fiazi came between them. Fiazi asked the old man, 'What's the matter?'

He did not answer, and crouched motionless in fear.

'What is it? Speak up!' shouted the stranger angrily.

The old man remained silent, his eyes shifting from one thing to another. Then he gave the stranger a hurried look and said anxiously, 'Jinab . . . she is crying.'

'Let her cry, and you go to bed,' the stranger said loudly and threateningly and then he went out of the room, followed by the old man. Fiazi was embarrassed. He looked round the room and noticed a paperback lying on the floor next to the table. He picked it up. It was an adventure novel. He turned the pages and found a slip of white paper dated two days previously with two lines on it and signed in a corner 'Riffat'. Fiazi was amazed. He had never seen so much human emotion depicted in such a short message. He replaced the book and leaned back. When the stranger returned, his anger was clearly visible in his face. Fiazi felt no need to look at him further, he glanced at the clock, got up and went out of the room. The stranger followed him, having real difficulty in controlling himself. Before he could say anything Fiazi went down the few steps of the verandah and, walking towards the gate, said again, 'How black the air has become.'

'What? Are you leaving?' the stranger asked anxiously. 'I wanted to find out the facts.'

'I do not know anything.'

'How can I believe that? Why did you say that you knew that child and also its father?'

'I did not know you, but I might have done. That is what I meant.'

'How . . . But how?'

'I will come back tomorrow morning, and we can discuss this in detail,' Fiazi said, turning the gate handle.

'Why did she laugh and why did you smile?'

'She did not laugh, you were mistaken. I will come tomorrow. Now I want to leave.'

'Please stop,' the man called after him. Just one minute. I want to ask you one thing.'

'I want to ask you one thing too,' Fiazi said, trying to prise open the thought that he was taking with him. 'Tell me that woman's name.'

'Azra. That is the name she told me, and my name is Arif Nawaz.'

'Azra?' Fiazi was perplexed. 'Which Azra? What is her full name?'

'I don't know.' Arif looked searchingly at him, impatient to know what he wanted to say.

'Then what was the name of the woman we found sleeping here a few moments ago?'

'I must know what it is that you wish to say,' Arif replied immediately.

'Who is Riffat?' Fiazi shot the question at him. This shook Arif. He caught Fiazi by the shoulders and, looking straight into his eyes, said, 'Now you will have to come back inside with me.'

'I have to go,' Fiazi said. 'I shall try to come to you tomorrow between twelve and half past.'

'How do you know Riffat?' Arif asked so peremptorily that it seemed he would raise hell if he did not get the answer he desired.

'I know Riffat better than I know Azra,' said Fiazi in an impressive manner. 'This girl for whom you are prepared to do anything, unfortunately loves you, and is burning in her own passion. You appear to be what she has been seeking for ages, but she does not know your character.'

'What do you mean?' Under the shadow of the dark night Arif boiled over with anger. 'How do you know Riffat?'

'Arif, I must go now, I have been delayed too long.'

'What are you going to do at the carriage shop now? Stay here and answer my questions.'

'There is no need. In any case I must go now.'

'Then you will come tomorrow,' Arif said impatiently.

'I will come. I have already said so.'

'Very well, I will wait for you.'

Fiazi turned down the path behind the bungalow. The piece of paper he had seen in Arif's book was still in his mind and the lines written on it followed him as he walked. The note was dated 'August 17' and below was written, 'Why are you compelling me? I will die, Arif. I did not know that it is very difficult to love.'

These lines were embedded in his mind and burrowed deeper and deeper into his consciousness. It had been a quarter to twelve when he had glanced at the clock and he had been with Arif for an hour and a half or more. The time seemed to have passed very speedily.

Time passes through rain, it passes through storm, and through extreme cold and heat; it passes unconcerned through sad mornings and it passes forward touching the silvery laughter of beautiful evenings, and sometimes it gives you respite only to write two lines.

Night was passing steadily, unaware that it would be smashed to bits and lose its identity when it collided with morning. Night would have to experience this grief. What was this grief? The grief of ceasing to exist? Why should night have to go through this pain of death, why? Was not the disintegration of night called light? Did not those pieces of the night which broke off, of their own free will, cause the birth of day?

Nothing dies, only the conditions and forms of things change and they go on developing and progressing. Doors open and the search for new doors continues; things go forward. Things do not themselves seek new doors, nor do doors seek them, but time takes them along in its wanderings, introducing things to doors and doors to things. It is time which brings about changes within a man. Some conditions change so much that they no longer have a cognitive relationship with each other and when this happens, we are subjectively finished, and that means that we are dead. Actually we are not dead, but others are no longer able to see us or to perceive us through their senses. We change our forms and others cannot understand these new forms. When people understand these conditions time will be recognized as a deity. Time still has a great deal to change and to create, which is itself a form of change.

Fiazi entered the sad and mournful atmosphere of the floating locality and stopped at Kausar's house. He looked like a traveller who had been journeying all night and suddenly came into this street. He knocked softly. The place was so still and so quiet that even the sound of a footstep would have been suspected of being a storm. Fiazi did not need to knock a second time. The door opened and Kausar stood before him. He entered and sat down on the plang and looked at Kausar, inviting her to sit next to him.

'I have come to tell you that I may have caused you distress but I shall not go back on what I said to you.'

'Why have you come? Go, go away!' she shouted.

'All right, I am going, but you must have realized that he is not my son. He is someone else's offspring and I don't know who his father is.'

'He is your flesh and blood, Fiazi, and . . .'

'The same old story.' Fiazi moved to console her. 'Kausar, I want to see you happy. Why do you insist on making me responsible for this boy? Why do you make him my son when he is not?'

'Can you believe a mother?' She flung this burning question at him. 'If you believe a mother, then believe me that he is our son.'

'Kausar, I advise you to sleep and take a rest and don't pain yourself with these meaningless thoughts. You do not know what you are doing, or what you are about to do; you have no idea of the kind of thoughts that have taken possession of you.'

'What am I to do? Oh, what should I do?'

Fiazi heaved a deep sigh. 'You have asked what you should do. The answer is quite simple. Tell me though, who was that boy the woman took inside, wasn't he your son?'

'No, he is not. I took him from someone. I told you that before.'

'Kausar, listen,' Fiazi said, looking straight at her. 'I want you to remain happy. I accept that he is not your son and that you are not the wife of his father, but there is a solution, and that is, consider him and only him as your son, and give up all thoughts of other sons.'

'Fiazi, I like and dislike you. I am afraid of you and yet want to live with you. No one understands my helplessness. Now when everything has happened and I should be becoming detached and unconcerned about everything, even now I desire one thing, that you come to me and we get back our son. I am alone and am waiting only for you.' Kausar fell silent and stared at the floor. Then she started again, in a different tone. She spoke calmly and steadily, as if someone else inside her was speaking. She was clinging to the past, which was all she had.

'It was the most cruel day, Fiazi,' Kausar began. 'Life has never deceived me so grievously. It was terrible, I wish I had known that morning what the day had in store for me. If I had known I would have died rather than go through with it. That day, Fiazi, I had gone to see someone whom I had met a few days previously in the bazaar and who had invited me to her house. It would have been better if I had not agreed. But she had asked me so affectionately that I went. She took me to a room and offered me a chair and then she disappeared, I don't know where. After a while a man entered and, staring at me intently, said, "Now you have to stay here. Forget about going back." I went pale. I wanted to say something, but he went out quickly and locked the door from the outside. I was stunned. Then he came back with another man who had a huge moustache and was very fat. The man with the moustache looked at his companion and said, "She's very good. She'll do." I was shocked. The man who had come in first went out, leaving me with the man with the moustache. I wanted to cry, but was not crying; I wanted to think, but was unable to think. He examined me from top to toe and said persuasively, "Look, if you live peacefully and comfortably, then you will get comfort and peace, but if you cry, then you will spend your life weeping. Consider your body as an office, a factory, a mill where you have to work. It is not yours, or anyone else's. Other people will come here, and you will co-operate with them. You will be provided with everything, but you will have to open the doors of this factory to everyone who knocks." He continued using words like this. Words? They were like molten lead being poured into my brain through my ears.

'I stayed in that house for two days and then at midnight they put me in a taxi and took me somewhere. I was made to wear such a burqa that I could see nothing and therefore did not know where we ended up. I started my new life as I had been instructed and you were the very first person who came to me. It was natural to hate you, and I did, intensely. When you left I told the man with the moustache that I should like to rest for a week or two. He agreed and said, "Have a good rest for ten days or so, eat and drink, and then we will see." They placed a pile of beautiful clothes before me, and every day, morning and evening, I was given the best food. The memory of my parents troubled me. The man with the moustache told me that he had managed to contact them and that they were no longer prepared even to look upon my face. I wept much that day, Fiazi. I have shed many tears in my life, and tried with them to wash away the stains of sin. I heard that you had come again, you or someone else, but they turned you away saying that I had gone out. I rested for about a month and afterwards felt I was pregnant. I was taken to many doctors and lady doctors and took many medicines, but it made no difference, and my son was born in due course. We left the child in the hospital and a woman who wanted a child took him away from there. After a few days I managed to find out where the woman who had taken the child lived. Her name was Farzana. Then I heard that she had left town and I did not know where she had gone. I was separated from my son for six years, Fiazi, and then I chanced to find out Farzana's new address and found my child in her house. By now the people I was living with began to trust me and they gave me freedom to move about so I was able to make friends with Farzana and I used to visit her off and on and see my son. I did not tell Farzana where I lived, nor did I tell her who the child's parents were. You used to come to me, but I never told you that you had a son. In my heart I hated you. You stopped coming to me and then after a long time you came again. Meanwhile many other men had been to see me, and one of them gave me many valuable presents because he was fond of me. You had left an ache in my heart, and though I hated you I could not forget you, because I knew that you were the father of my son. I do not know why you always hated the thought of marriage. I wanted to talk to you about marriage, but each time you checked me and became angry. I decided that one day I would tell you that you had a son. Then Farzana moved again and I did not know whether she had stayed in the same town or gone away to another. I became restless and deeply disturbed. I did not know what was happening or what I should do. I again met Farzana nineteen years later. Only I know how I got through those years. Fiazi, I am in great distress, you do not know how much I have suffered.

'Much changed in that gap of nineteen years. The man with the moustache died and I learnt that the other people had little power to control me, and so I married the man who was fond of me and who used to give me expensive presents. He loved me very much despite knowing about my situation and way of life. After we were married he bought me this house and had it registered in my name. I started living with him and he took good care of me. One day I told him that I wanted to see my parents. I thought they would forgive me now that I was married and that I might be able to give them some sort of explanation which they could accept. I told my husband that I wanted to go to my home-town to see my parents and sisters and brother, because I had been away from them for a long time. My husband agreed readily and said he wished I had told him about this before getting married so that he could have informed them. I felt I had entered another world. Although my heart was trembling with fear, I had great hopes. But my people knew every detail of my life and my brother told me that they were not prepared to acknowledge me ever again. He took me aside and told me that I should leave at once or else he would kill me. I left heart-broken. My husband said consolingly, "Maybe they will change their minds after a while and be prepared to meet you." My younger and elder sisters were married by now and living with their own families. I asked my husband to get a message to my elder sister because I was certain that she would come to see me. She told me that she had heard that I had been to see my parents and met my brother and that she herself would have come to see me earlier, but had not known my "whereabouts". My sister used the word whereabouts, Fiazi. Why did she use that word rather than "house"? However, I tolerated it because by then I had grown strong enough to bear such things. We sat down and talked, mostly about our married life and each other's husbands. As my sister was leaving I asked her whether my mother ever mentioned me and whether she had forgiven me.

'"Mother died four years ago," my sister answered looking at me sadly. Four years had made my sister's eyes very sorrowful, but this was fresh news to me, and I started to weep copiously. I could not control my tears. I embraced my sister and asked her to come again. Then my husband died in an accident. Everyone has to die, I know, but his death caused me great pain and I went to bed for several days. I had one old servant woman who stayed with me and my sister came to see me occasionally. My husband had arranged for his employers to send me an adequate sum of money each month. If he had not, God knows what I would have done. After my husband's death I asked my sister whether I should go to my father now. What was I to do here alone? I said that if she agreed, I would go back with her and live humbly in one corner of the house. She told me that she would ask her husband and other members of the family and if they had no objection, she would come and take me home. The next day she came but she was sad and depressed and she told me that she had first asked Father who had agreed to let me come home. Her own husband had also consented, but our brother had said that if any member of the family even so much as spoke to me, he would not have anything to do with them for the rest of his life. Some days later my father died, and my sister came to bring me the sad news. That day I cried so much that my eyes became red and dry. Fiazi, I have wept much in my life, I have endured many afflictions and have borne many hardships and now I have become too weak to endure more. A few weeks ago I met Farzana in the market and we both went to her house. I inquired about her son, that is, my own son. She told me he was in a village working on a farm. I wanted to know more about him, what he looked like now, how tall was he? How did he speak? How did he walk? Farzana didn't answer me satisfactorily and after some time fell silent. When I asked her why she looked so worried, she told me about the letter and showed it to me. It's the one you have. You must be convinced by now that he is our son. Fiazi, I want to see Bashir, and I want to see him soon.'

After this Kausar fell silent. Speaking so much had exhausted her. She sat down quietly on the plang and tried to get her tired and depressed breathing under control. She had been speaking for quite a while, and had been unable to pause, as her memories gushed out. At times she had broken the thread of narrative and jumped on to unimportant details as if she was in a hurry to tell everything all at once. She repeated certain things which she had already written in her letter to Fiazi. She went on and on, seeming not to care. Listening to her one felt that she had lost control over her thoughts and that she was speaking under some strange influence, or else that she was suffering from garrulity. In fact, she had just wanted Fiazi to know all she had suffered and, in the light of her statement, to believe her. Fiazi sat there like a statue. If his eyes had not been open he would have appeared to be fast asleep. Eventually he took a deep breath and said calmly, 'So?'

'Fiazi, I want to see my son,' Kausar said, pleading with him. 'Bashir is our son and has been separated from us. We will see him and tell him that he is our son.'

'He is not my son, nor am I looking for any such ready-made son,' Fiazi said and stood up. He had spoken these words with the utmost calmness and looking at Kausar said, 'Look, Kausar, I came at midnight and caused you inconvenience only to tell you that you should forget this whole affair. That is the only way you will be able to get rest and peace of mind. It may be that the thought of a son has been in your mind for a long time and then the moment your friend informed you that this boy was searching for his parents, you immediately persuaded yourself to announce that you were his mother. You may be able to become his mother, but I am not his father, in fact I do not feel any need to own a son. I am going now. I do not think that I can be of any use to you in the future.'

'No, this cannot be. It cannot be.' Kausar caught Fiazi by the arm, and spoke with deep passion. 'You are the father of my child. I have told you everything. Don't go, don't leave me.'

'How can I do this, Kausar? You do not understand that I cannot.'

'I will die, believe me, I will kill myself,' she said holding him firmly by his arms.

'You need rest. Go and sleep.' Saying this he tried to free himself from her grip. They struggled slightly and when Kausar realized what he was doing she herself let go, and walked to the plang, and suddenly took out a knife from under her pillow. She would undoubtedly have injured herself seriously if Fiazi had not sprung towards her, caught hold of her wrist and snatched away the knife.

'Let go, leave me. Give me back my knife. That is my knife. Return it. You killed your son, your friend killed his daughter. Give me back my knife . . .' Kausar grappled with him, spitting out words in confusion.

Fiazi pushed her away with great difficulty and, opening the door, quickly went out and walked away without looking back. Dawn was breaking, and the close and oppressive atmosphere had been dispelled. The knife was in Fiazi's hand. It was not an ordinary household knife, but had a long blade with a point bent upwards, and it was nearly new. He put the knife into his pocket and quickened his pace.

FOUR

When I went to meet Aziz the day was drawing to its close and the shadows of the trees and buildings were lengthening. There was more traffic in the bazaars and people were standing around gossiping. The bus I caught was packed and everyone was pushing and shoving. Somehow I managed to get a place for myself and complete the journey. I got out and began to walk quickly. By the time I turned a corner to reach Aziz's house it was a quarter to eight. The street had the same uneasy darkness which I had encountered before. Diffused light shone from the high upper-storey windows and down below in the dark dirty street, people moved about like mysterious shadows. Sometimes there was the sound of someone hurriedly coming downstairs, at other times the noise of a row. I reached the front of Aziz's house. The stairs were as murky as before, I groped my way upwards. It was silent. In graveyards at least one sometimes heard the wind and the soft rustling of leaves; on these stairs the silence was complete and terrifying. I went on until I came to the door. It was ajar; and a beam of light shining through the crack seemed to have been fixed there. I knocked softly and stood waiting for someone to answer. The silence remained undisturbed. I knocked a second time but no one took the trouble to come to the door. I felt worried and, pushing the door, entered the room. A dim electric bulb revealed the real worth of everything in the room. There was no one there, and the stool beside the large table stared intently at me. I was surprised and sat down waiting for someone to arrive. The bathroom and latrine were near the stairs. I had not heard any sound of water and no one had spoken in answer to my knocking at the door. I sat thinking when I realized that I should also look into the adjoining small room where I had found Aziz sleeping on the previous occasion. There was a heap of dirty clothes as before, and some clothes hanging on the wire. Lying on the charpoy, her face to the wall, was the old woman. I called her softly and went up closer. Her eyes were open, silently looking at the wall. I called her again and then placed my hand on her arm to draw her attention. The old woman turned and looked at me with her dim eyes. The flesh on her face had gone flabby, and her mouth remained partially open, her ears were long and soft and she was wearing large ear rings. She sat up. I bent down and asked her about

Aziz, his mother and father, but she kept staring at me blankly. I then put my mouth close to her ear and shouted loudly, 'Mother, where is Aziz?'

'I don't know, I don't know,' she replied in a weak voice, looking at me helplessly. Then she sucked in her lips and started to cry. She wiped her tears with a piece of old rough cloth lying near her on the bed. I felt a deep and shameful sense of inadequacy because I could not think of any means to console the old woman. All I could do was sit like a statue and look at her. Her weeping was strange; it reminded me of old trees being destroyed. The dirty old cloth fell to the floor. Now she wiped her tears with her hands while she continued to sob. She grew quiet after a while and looked at me with her dim old eyes, then she bent down and tried to pick up the cloth, but I jumped forward first and picked it up and placed it beside her on the bed. She carefully put it to one side and carrying, as it were, the heavy stone of silence, sat without making a sound. After some time she looked at me again and placed the fingers of her left hand on my shoulder; they were like thin dry branches of bamboo. I was about to make signs to her to go to sleep when I heard the sound of someone coming into the next room and a groan of pain. It was clearly the voice of Aziz's mother. Leaving the old woman, I went to the other room and found that Aziz's mother had already sat down on the bed and was holding a medicine bottle in her hand, along with something wrapped in a small brown paper bag. She just looked in a daze and said, 'Aziz hasn't come.'

I could not decide whether this was a question or a statement and was not sure what to say.

'Aziz has not come.' Aziz's mother said it again and shook her head in a miserable way. She was in trouble and it was clear that she should be lying down. I helped her and then sat on the side of the charpoy. I was amazed that she had gone to the doctor herself to fetch her medicine. I placed my hand on her feet, remembering my own mother as I did so, and asked, 'Shall I massage your feet?'

'No, no . . . no, no.' It was as if four tear drops had fallen from her pale sickly lips.

'How are you feeling now?' I asked humbly.

'I am all right,' she said. Her last word seemed to bring on drowsiness. She opened her eyes for a moment and then closed them again.

'You don't feel much pain, do you?' I asked softly. 'Please, tell me what I can do for you.'

'Nothing,' she replied through trembling lips. We sat there quietly.

I felt a little awkward asking her any more questions; God knows how much she was suffering. Her lips moved again and she asked me to bring her water. The old woman was now really asleep. I fetched water in a bowl from the bucket for Aziz's mother who was taking out two small pills from the paper bag. She swallowed these with water. Her face was distorted, partially due to her thoughts and partially due to the bitterness of the medicine. She passed her tongue over her dry lips, belched and sat up.

'Son, you are Aziz's friend. Make him understand,' she said to me. 'Yesterday morning he spent an hour and a half in the bathroom and when I tried to call him he shouted at me to stop.'

'Auntie, he . . .'

'Oh my son, my son,' she said in a choking voice. 'Please advise him. Tell him to do some work.'

'Auntie, when I say such things to him he becomes angry and starts talking loudly, and says, "Who am I to ask him to work?" He tells me to mind my own business. "I have not made you my friend to listen to such talk," he says. Pausing, I asked, 'What is he doing these days?'

'Nothing at all,' the sad mother said in a voice pathetic enough to make one weep. 'He goes to many places looking for work, but does not succeed.'

The grief and misery in her voice shook her whole being. She looked as if she had lost hope in everything and yet wanted to see the fulfilment of her few last desires.

'I wish . . .' She did not complete her sentence but stopped and looked at me in bewilderment. I do not know what she wanted to say, or why she broke off. I have no idea what she was thinking about as she looked at me so absently; her eyes were motionless in search for tears or her tongue was helpless to utter the thoughts in her mind. It seemed as if she wanted compensation in one moment for all her past life, that past which had caused grief, which had brought her pain and sorrow, which had given her nothing but blows and scars. Inside she was all wounds, and the painful reality was that her external appearance was also wounded.

'Auntie, where has Aziz gone?' I asked, breaking the uncomfortable silence. I was getting really worried about him.

'Aziz . . . Aziz has not come. He has not yet returned.'

I did not want to increase Aziz's mother's anxiety by telling her of that morning's incident and the story about the oil. I was thinking what to ask next when she got up and went into the small room where I had left the old woman. In a short while she returned and sat down on the charpoy again.

'Will you have some food?' she asked me. 'I can bring you something to eat.'

'No thank you, Auntie, I have already eaten. Why did you go to the doctor's alone?'

'What else could I do? There was no one in the house. I had to go to the doctor to get bandaged. Aziz left the house in the morning. I did not even see him leave. He had not eaten anything. Aziz, my child, Aziz . . . oh.' She groaned and lay down on the charpoy.

'Please go to sleep,' I said sadly. 'Aziz was with me, he will come soon.'

'He was with you? When, until when?' she asked anxiously. 'Did he have his meal?'

'Yes,' I said softly and nodded my head. I was too distressed to be able to say anything more. Aziz's brief note was in my pocket and it had made me weep inside.

'When did he eat? What did he eat? Where is he?'

'We were together for a long while and then he went away without telling me where he was going.'

'Oh, go and look for him. He might be somewhere nearby.'

I got up and went towards the door, thinking that I would go and try to find him in the neighbourhood.

Outside on the landing it was dark as before and the same darkness was crawling in the staircase. Everything was suffocated in black, ill-omened air and, being helpless and uncertain, seemed to commit suicide by the irresistible force of anonymity. I stepped forward to go downstairs when I heard the sound of someone coming up, silently and cautiously. It was a small child carrying a bucket, on his way to the top floor. Then I heard the bleat of the goat below at the door and someone said gently, 'Be quiet, be quiet.' It was undoubtedly Aziz. He must have stopped because there was no sound of his steps coming up.

'Aziz,' I called out in a loud voice.

'Brother Munir, I am coming; please wait for me.'

I reproached him as he came into sight. 'Aziz, your mother is ill and you are gadding about. You should have stayed at home. You are needed here.'

He stood silent. 'Come, let's go in,' I said. 'Where were you?'

'Munir Sahib, I was only outside, just here, and I would have come home.'

'Come,' I said taking him by the arm. 'Don't stop here.'

'Aziz, Aziz.' His mother had come to the door and was calling to him impatiently.

'Mother dear, I had not gone anywhere,' he said. 'I was just outside and I was coming home. Munir Sahib will tell you that I was coming home.'

'I will tell her? Aziz, what are you saying?' He had placed me in an embarrassing situation.

'Brother Munir, I was going to come home. I told you that I had to come home whatever happened.' He stopped at the door of the room, staring at me.

'Come in, come and sit down. You should at least have taken your mother to the doctor.'

'Doctor? What doctor?' he burst out angrily. 'What doctor are you talking about? I do not know any doctor. Believe me, I don't know any doctor.' The pupils of Aziz's eyes expanded and it seemed that every hair of his thick bushy eyebrows was in motion. If as an experiment you had looked at these bushy eyebrows through a magnifying glass you would certainly have got the impression that a large number of snakes were writhing in a box. His eyes were burning and he was terrified. He turned round and glanced at the door by which he had just entered, and then went towards the charpoy. There was no sheet on it, or pillow or anything. He sat down on it and, intertwining the fingers of both hands, he placed them under his head and then lay down on his back, not looking at anyone. His mother and I were still standing in the doorway, watching in amazement, because we could not understand the way he had answered me and the manner in which he had spoken about the doctor. His mother seemed upset too, partly because of her head injury and also because she was anxious about him. The head injury was visible, but Aziz himself was a greater wound for her and this wound was in bad shape. Aziz lay on the bed for a few seconds. It seemed as if he had lain down in order to see someone, and when he had surveyed him with care he got up. He went to the small room. After a few steps he stopped and stood there thinking. Suddenly he turned to me and said, 'Which doctor were you talking about? Believe me, I do not want to meet any doctor. I hate them. They are not good people.'

'Aziz, you must try to understand . . .'

'Brother Munir, what are you talking about?' he interrupted. 'Leave such things alone and let me take rest. Munir Sahib, Munir Sahib!' His voice rose to a scream. 'I tell you that I do not know the doctor, so why do you go on insisting I see him?'

'There is no question of knowing or not knowing. You should have gone with your mother to see the doctor.' I spoke angrily. 'She is ill. If you do not go with her, who will?'

'All right, all right; thanks.' He smiled as if he had been relieved of a heavy burden. 'Thank you, I am always prepared to go with Mother, but only to a good doctor.' He was smiling like the remnant of the picture of a smile on a charred piece of paper. It was a smile that could snap under the slightest pressure. He blew off the smile with a heavy sigh and once again went in the direction of the small room.

By now Aziz's mother had sat down on the charpoy and the way she was sitting, together with the fearful silence, made the atmosphere in the room even heavier; it was as if someone had prohibited her movements and speech, and from the expression on her face it seemed that she had been brought before strangers, that she had been deprived of her capacity to determine her rightful place here. There was no sign of Aziz's father. Aziz's maternal grandmother was still in the next room; in fact, we had all forgotten her existence and Aziz's going towards that room reminded me about her.

He was a few steps from the door when the old woman appeared. She peered anxiously at us. She held on to the door with her left hand and stretched out her right, as if she wanted to pat the head of some small child. Aziz went to her quickly and took her outstretched hand and led her to the charpoy. Aziz's mother shifted to one side to make room for her and helped her sit down. The old woman shrank like deflated rubber beside Aziz's mother and sucked her long hanging lips into her mouth. The absence of teeth made her face appear to be more wrinkled.

'Mother, have I caused you any trouble?' Aziz asked, standing beside the charpoy. 'I am sure that I have not, but anyway I ask your forgiveness.'

Sorrowful shadows had enlarged Aziz's mother's eyes and her cheekbones stood out more prominently. She bit her pale yellow lips uncertainly. She was controlling her tears.

'What shall I do?' asked Aziz despondently. 'Tell me what to do, Mother. How can I best ask for forgiveness? Please do not curse me; I know that you curse me in your heart, but please don't. For God's sake, don't. Have pity on my condition. I do not ask you for love, I don't ask you for anything, only forgive me. Everyone hates me, nobody likes me, nobody approves of me. Why is everyone so against me? I don't trouble anyone, I have no right to. I even paid Munir Sahib the money. I will not eat without paying for my food, but the question is, why do I eat? Why do I consume food? I will not be a parasite. I will earn my food by working, and now I assure you that I will do something and show you, and even Father would agree that I must eat something. But first of all, forgive me. This afternoon I slept out in the open and I had a dream that dreams seen while sleeping on the ground can never be false. What is the date today? Munir Sahib, please tell me what date it is today.' He looked intently at me.

'Aziz, what has happened to you? Sit down. Come, let's sit down on this cot.'

'No, no, I'm all right here. Please tell me what the date is today,' he said impatiently.

'The nineteenth,' I said, growing desperate.

'Munir Sahib, that is the date I dreamed. I went to sleep near the old pipe under the trees in the hockey ground and there I saw in the dream that I should do nothing but ask my mother's forgiveness.'

'Aziz . . . my son, what has happened to you, whose evil eye has struck you?' Aziz's mother got up and clasped him in her arms.

'No, mother, I will certainly ask your forgiveness,' Aziz said and, exhausted and restless, moved away from her to the small room. The switch was turned on and the room brightened. Aziz soon returned with what looked like a register in one hand and a fountain-pen in the other. He opened the register and tore off a page, and placing it on the register came towards us. His mother was still sobbing and the old woman was sitting on the charpoy, peering at him. Aziz said to his mother, 'I have brought pen and paper, Mother. Please write on it that you have . . . no I will write that myself, and you can put your thumb mark on it that you have forgiven me . . .' He went hurriedly to the table.

'Aziz, what are you doing? Don't do this,' I shouted angrily at him. 'Come, let's go out.'

'Munir Sahib, you go. All right, you go,' he said, 'and if you wish you may return after fifteen minutes.' He began writing. He did not bother to look to see whether I had gone or not. Aziz worried me; I did not know what to do with him. I was looking at him, thinking of some effective means of stopping him from all this nonsense, when he stood up holding the crude register, the page and the fountain-pen awkwardly in his left hand. The way he held them betrayed the confusion in his mind.

'I have written it down,' he said. 'I have written it all down and solved everything. Munir Sahib, please cast an eye over this, see that nothing has been omitted. Wait, I will read it myself. Mother dear, you listen too and if something has been left out that you think necessary, please tell me. I will alter it as you wish.' Aziz started to read.

'I, Aziz Akram, beg my mother's forgiveness. If she does not forgive me now I will ask whether she ever will.'

After reading this he held up the open register like a torch in his hand, went towards his mother and stood silently beside her. His mother was lying on the charpoy and was sobbing, her face covered with the sheet. I decided to take Aziz from the room by telling him to stop troubling his mother. I was about to say this when the door opened and Aziz's father entered the room, carrying an old bag.

He was in such a state that the poorest of the poor would have pitied him. He was wearing a strange-looking open bush shirt. It was impossible to guess what its original colour had been. One pocket was of a different coloured cloth and there was a large triangular patch, crudely sewn in another coloured thread, where the other pocket should have been and from a distance it looked like stitches around a wound. The trousers were of some dark colour and were made of thick material. The bag he was carrying very much resembled, in colour, his trousers. As he entered the room he looked around as if he had come to the place by mistake. He glanced at the small room and then went over to his stool. He started to undo the laces of his worn-out canvas shoes; he had no socks on.

Without paying any attention to his father, Aziz bent over his mother and exclaimed, 'Mother, I have written it. See, I have finished writing.'

'Aziz, switch off the lights and go into the small room and sleep,' his father ordered him. He ignored me as if I was not present, or perhaps he thought that the darkness of the room would itself expel me.

From his mother's side, Aziz looked at his father with restless eyes, and said, 'I am just switching off this light, but I cannot turn them all off at once.' He went quickly to the small room and, putting out the light, hurried back.

'Father, dear Father, you are everything to me, but in spite of this I do not ask you for everything. I beg you not to turn off the lights so early tonight, let them stay on a little longer. These lights burn but are not burnt up and I will pay something towards the cost. I will go hungry, I will sleep in a bus shelter or the porch of a shop, but I will not cause you any inconvenience. I will keep you happy. Why should you not be happy when money is given to you? Here, take this. Keep it.' He held out a one-rupee note. 'This is just for sleeping here tonight and for leaving the light on for some time. I did not eat here today. I will not be eating anything here in the morning. Now I have to talk to Mother about something important.'

Aziz's father had taken off his shirt and was sitting on the charpoy, lost in thought. He did not answer Aziz but when Aziz approached with the rupee note, he suddenly got up in confusion and knocked it from Aziz's hand; Aziz quickly retrieved it and tried again to hand it to his father, who ignored it and said helplessly, angrily, 'Useless body, useless body.' He went to the small room and was lost in the darkness, but returned a moment later and looked at us with frightened eyes which also showed a thirst for something unknown.

'He will be finished, you'll see, he will be finished,' Aziz's father shouted in an extraordinary voice to his wife. He went back into the small room. The old woman screamed her inhuman scream again and began to wail and lament waving her feeble arms up and down. She made strange sounds with her mouth and lips. Aziz's mother sat up and from the colour of her eyes and the expression on her face, it was obvious that she had been weeping for a long time under the sheet. Aziz stood silent and lost as if he was waiting for something. His lips were pressed tight together and his dark purple eyes looked as if they would boil over out of their sockets. All of a sudden the door opened and the neighbour who had come down the previous day when he was drunk stood there. He was not drunk this time, but had come downstairs in a fury. Behind him I could see the face of the artist. That surprised me. There was a boy with him about the same age as Aziz. The neighbour from upstairs looked at us angrily and shouted, 'I will tie you all up. All this noise, all this disturbance. You people disturb my peace. I will come and sort you out!' He went back upstairs, his threats echoing in the restless atmosphere of the room. We were all silent. The artist was standing near the door. The old woman sat as if any capacity to speak or move had been snatched away from her. Aziz's mother did not look at anyone. Aziz had his hands in his pockets and seemed sunk in thought. The boy who had come in with the fat neighbour and the artist was now standing near Aziz, examining him closely. The silence was at last broken by Aziz, disturbed by the lad's constant stare.

'I understand that the sweetness in the foundation of mankind is very quickly consumed. You are my neighbour and I know why you have come here. Please sit down.' He pointed to a corner of the charpoy that was still free.

'No, Aziz Sahib, I'm fine here,' said the boy, hiding a smile. 'He (pointing to the artist) wished to meet you, and I came to show him the way.'

'Ajmal, you must stay awhile, and have some tea also.'

'No, Aziz, I do not need tea,' said Ajmal. 'Tell me about yourself. How are you? Any particular news?'

'News is always particular and special. Common news cannot be called "news"; it is merely information.'

'Right,' said Ajmal and smiled.

Meanwhile the artist drew nearer to me and now both of us were standing beside the charpoy by the wall. Aziz was about twelve feet away and he sat down next to his mother on the other charpoy. She was wrapped in the sheet, her knees drawn up to her stomach. The old woman was still lying bunched up. She was not much affected by events around her, only revealing her presence by that unexpected inhuman scream which would draw everyone's attention. For the present, she lay silently, her body barely perceptible on the dirty old mattress.

'Aziz, my son, have some food,' his mother entreated him. 'Shall I bring you some?'

'I will eat, but it is not necessary. First of all, forgive me. Here on this paper . . .' He picked up the register again from the charpoy.

'Aziz, what are you doing?' I said, going closer to him. 'For God's sake, have a little consideration. Your mother is old, she is ill and injured.'

'And no one notices my wounds, nobody sees my wounds,' Aziz shouted with pain.

'I would . . .'

'No, Munir Sahib, you know nothing. All you want is for everything to be put right and done correctly. But how can things be put right?'

'Aziz, it is night now and we . . .'

'What does that matter? You can answer me even at night-time. If you want to, you can tell me even in the night how things can be put right.'

'Aziz, do as your mother tells you, and have your food, I must be going. Here are your two rupees,' I said, taking the money from my pocket. 'Keep them. I will come to see you again some other time.'

'Munir Sahib, what are you saying?' Aziz jumped excitedly from the charpoy. 'I will not accept money from you. I told you in your room that I would not take money from you, and I would not worry you.

Please put it back in your pocket and stay a little longer. I have something to show you. When you have seen it you can go.'

'No, Aziz, don't insist now. Keep the money and let me go. I will come back in a few days.'

'Munir Sahib, what are you doing? What are you doing? Believe me, I will fall ill. I am tired and do not wish to say anything more. Ajmal, please ask Munir Sahib to put the money in his pocket and stop frightening me.'

'You will see, he will be finished, he will be finished very soon,' said Aziz's father again, emerging suddenly from the dark room. He snatched up the bush shirt from the table and put it on, tied the strings of his trousers firmly and walked out of the door.

The tension mounted in the room and the dim yellowy light stared in open-eyed wonder at all that was going on.

'We are leaving now,' I said, putting the money in my pocket. I went with the artist towards the door. We opened it and were leaving when Ajmal joined us. Aziz quickly came after us and taking my right hand in both of his said, 'Please stop a while and wait for me.'

'Aziz, you cannot imagine how wrong all this is,' I said helplessly. 'Go and have your food and sleep.'

'No, Munir Sahib, I want to come with you,' he said decisively. 'I will come, whatever happens, though I promise not to stay long. I may accompany you to the hotel and then return home, and tell you everything on the way. I also want to show you what I had promised. I will also tell you why I flung the box of medicines at the doctor. Munir Sahib, I hate doctors. You don't know that the notes are made from blood. I will tell you everything, please wait for me.' He ran to his mother and asked, 'Mother, how long is today?'

Ajmal said in my ear, 'He is mad. Please go. Why are you wasting your time standing here?'

'Mother, please forgive me,' Aziz pleaded pathetically. 'I saw in my dream that it must be done today.'

'Aziz, what can I do for you?' For the first time the artist stepped forward and spoke.

'I want everyone to forgive me, and so get me out of the habit of dreaming,' Aziz said, looking at him sadly. In his eyes were pathos and vision which was far beyond us.

'I want people to grant me freedom of movement,' he said in the same tone, continuing to look at the artist, 'and not let my feet become heavy. I want to meet them and them to meet me. I want to be with Shagufta and everything should be as it was before.'

'Who is Shagufta?' I said involuntarily.

'Shagufta, my own Shagufta.'

'Munir Sahib, let him come with us,' the artist said to me. 'Get his mother's permission and bring him.'

Aziz's mother was leaning behind the door, the old woman behind her, just visible from the corner of her shalwar. How much could she hear? How much could she see? And what did she want to know? There was no answer to these questions. But she was standing there, making her presence known through the little bit of her shalwar that was visible. Aziz's mother asked us to come back inside and sit down. But when the artist and I told her we wanted to take Aziz with us and keep him safe, she was speechless and she just looked at us with tear-soaked eyes. Aziz was very happy to accompany us. His face brightened. We got to the top of the stairs and he stopped. He looked at me and said humbly, 'Munir Sahib, that sign, the thumb mark on that paper . . .'

'Aziz, give me the paper,' I said taking it from him. 'I will give it to your mother to put her thumb print on, and it will be waiting for you when you come back.'

I took the paper from him and went back to the room. Seeing me enter, Aziz's mother stepped aside. I gave her the paper and said, 'Please put your thumb print at the end of this paper and then give it to Aziz.'

'What kind of a print? I do not understand anything,' she called.

'The thumb print of your left hand. It will make no difference,' I said, hurrying to get back to my companions.

We went downstairs carefully, Aziz in the lead, then Ajmal and the artist, and I last.

'Both of them are asleep, both are fast asleep,' Aziz said merrily, as he reached the hall where the two goats slept, tied to the pipe. He sat down on the floor beside the tap and started turning the knob. No water came because the pipe was empty at that hour.

'Munir Sahib, you can see for yourself that the water has gone to sleep too.'

'Yes Aziz, come on. We're going.'

'No one can go where the water is sleeping,' he addressed us seriously. 'The water has stopped somewhere inside these miles of pipe and it is sound asleep.'

We left Aziz's street for a wider one. Aziz talked about one thing and then, without completing one topic, switched to another, leaving the first incomplete, complicated and confused. In his mind ideas wept, and his needs refrained from expressing themselves. It was important for him not to talk too much, to give his fatigued, helpless brain more rest. But whenever he came across something with the remotest connection with some unpleasant experience of his past, the door to his mind opened. We were walking silently and were about to enter a broad road at the end of this street when Aziz said again – and I didn't know what he really meant – 'Ajmal, you are coming with us, and you know that the sweetness in mankind's foundations is quickly consumed?'

'What can I say?' said Ajmal, smiling.

'You know that this is a fact and that is why you are coming with us.'

'You are quite right,' Ajmal said out of politeness, laughing quietly.

'What I am saying is right, but I do not know whether you understand correctly or not. The real thing is to understand correctly. Is that not so, Munir Sahib? We can gain nothing until we understand things properly. I fully understood my dream and I will tell you what else I saw in it.'

'No, Aziz, not now. Let us talk about this later,' I said trying to make him understand. I wanted to know which doctor had aroused Aziz's hatred. Was it the same doctor he had borrowed twenty rupees from? If so, what was the trouble? And who was Shagufta? And why was there such acute sadness when he talked about his pain? Furthermore, what was it that was so important he wanted to show me? Had he got it on him, or had he left it at home? I had a lot to ask him, but now was not the time, in fact it would only cause him more trouble.

We reached the hotel a few minutes after eleven. Ajmal wanted to leave us there, but I brought him upstairs and invited him to a cup of tea which I prepared in my own room on an electric ring.

Aziz drank his tea silently, looking from Ajmal to the tea and back again as he sipped. Aziz was the first to finish. He refused a second cup and sat quietly, examining the room. Suddenly his eyes stopped at my face and he asked, 'If you don't mind, I should like to open the cupboard behind you and see what is inside.'

'Go ahead,' I said smiling.

Aziz got up and opened the wall-cupboard and started examining its contents. It was an ordinary cupboard, with nothing in it worth mentioning; some unwashed clothes on the lower shelf and various other odds and ends on the other two shelves. Aziz soon resumed his seat.

The artist got up quietly and went out, saying that he would come back soon. He returned with a large paper bag that he placed before Aziz. Aziz looked at it and remained sitting silently.

'Please eat, if you like, I have brought these biscuits for you. Eat as much as you need.'

'If you insist, I will eat,' Aziz replied, 'and it was good of you to say that I should eat as much as I need. That is as it should be. It should be like that in hotels. It is right that they take money from us and bring us what we ask for, but they never say that we should eat as much as we need. Munir Sahib, there is so much sincerity and homeliness in this one sentence, that it is difficult to find its equal. And by homeliness, I mean the environment of a good home.'

He had eaten half a biscuit as he was talking.

'Munir Sahib, the place and the surroundings have an influence on people eating. Once I bought some cooked sweet potatoes and went to a bazaar where there were several butchers' shops and I saw large chunks of raw meat hanging. The smell of meat was all around and it made it difficult to walk. I had only taken a few bites of one potato, and then could no longer even look at it. I placed it on the outside platform of a closed stall and walked away. I wondered afterwards why I had done this, and was annoyed with myself. I returned and picked up the sweet potato. Please tell me, why was it like this? How the environment changed me! Yet, Munir Sahib, I myself changed the environment. I did not care about anything and I started to eat again.'

'Aziz, finish your biscuit,' I said. 'They were brought for you, and you are not eating.'

'Munir Sahib, I know they were brought for me and he told me to eat as much as I can. Now you judge for yourself what kind of environment we have here. I don't know what to call it. An environment is always bad. There should be another word for this.'

'Eat freely, they are for you,' the artist said, looking at him kindly.

'Jinab, it is you who have created something contrary to the environment, something very nice and pleasant,' said Aziz and paused while eating. 'You brought the biscuits of your own accord. I did not ask you to bring them.'

'What did you go to the cupboard for?' asked Ajmal.

'The sweetness in your foundations has been consumed, and you cannot obtain it from everywhere,' Aziz answered, annoyed.

'You . . .'

'Let it be,' said the artist with a gesture of his hands.

'No, Jinab, you don't know . . .' Ajmal wanted to say something as if in justification.

'Ajmal, the sweetness in your foundations is consumed and you cannot get it from everywhere.' Aziz spoke again, this time more intensely.

'Sugar? You don't know what you are talking about,' said Ajmal laughing, and left the room.

'Wherever he sees people he will stop and want to neutralize the bitterness of his body with sweetness. I know, he came to obtain sugar.' Aziz had stopped eating. He looked at both of us and said, 'Jinab, I will always remember you.'

'Don't mention it, Aziz. It's all right. Now let's sleep. You sleep here on this charpoy, I will borrow another from Rafiq. There are two charpoys in his room and one of them is spare.'

'No, there is no need,' said the artist getting to his feet. 'It is not proper to trouble anyone at this hour. Aziz will sleep in my room. We'll meet in the morning.'

I decided to accompany Aziz to the artist's room. I did not like the idea of leaving them in the corridor and closing my door on them. The artist unlocked his room. The moment he switched on the light, I stood stock still in amazement.

The room was the same size as most of the others on that floor. What startled me inside was a painting lying to one side close to the easel, obviously just finished. It had given wings to my thoughts and I could not tear my eyes away.

'Please, sit down.' I heard the artist's voice.

'No, thanks, I will go now,' I replied. 'It is late and you should take your rest.'

I came to my room and lay down. I started thinking about the painting which I had just seen in the artist's room. It reminded me of the white coat, the boxroom behind the stairs, and the stranger's actions. Apart from this, it had conceptualized something which passed on after crushing me and all people under foot.

The painting showed the same child in a small cradle, lying in the same position as the dead infant found in the hotel. The cradle was rocking high in the arc of a circle pushed by the child's own hand. The details of the air around the cradle showed that the child had swung it thus several times and would continue to do so. The earth was at the centre of the circle around which the cradle was swinging. One hand of the infant was keeping the cradle in motion while the other had pushed through the cane net that formed the floor of the cradle and was stopping the motion of the earth. Instead of a still picture the artist had painted a living scene in a state of motion. The cradle was rotating round the earth in various changing orbits and wherever the child's outstretched hand touched the earth, the fingers ploughed through its surface destroying anything that came within reach, buildings, houses, railway lines; as the hand touched the ocean and passed on to the land it drew deep channels of water with it. In some places the infant hand raised walls of fire and in others it caused indescribable destruction.

I do not know when sleep came to me, but that night I dreamed a terrible dream, more like a stormy flood of boiling blood and water. In my dream all the rivers had dried up and, helped by that baby, the water of the oceans was trying to enter the rivers. The moment it entered the dry river beds, it was terrified and returned to the ocean in such haste and confusion that it spilled across the land, destroying cities as it went. In some places the hand of the infant tore open graves and dragged out the skeletons and bones of the dead and scattered them on the roads. The air was filled with terrifying screams, and blood started flowing from the bones. The bones searched for other bones that belonged to the same skeleton, and were sucking the pains and troubles of the past. I saw the bones of my relatives and ancestors lying by the road, so exhausted that the blood from their fractures had stopped flowing. When these bones saw me they started wailing and warned me to protect myself from the destruction of the grave and told me to act before I met my death and was buried. Those bones could not walk and they called to me to tell them how to reach me. 'What is the use of asking the way? We cannot even walk,' said one and started weeping. 'Until we have the power to move, how can we walk? You can see all around how rapidly motion is coming to an end. Motion is coming to an end. Motion is coming to an end.' They all shouted together, 'What will happen when motion stops?' and they started laughing. Their laughter was so shrill and loud and abandoned that their wounds opened up and from the cracks blood started flowing again, but when that infant hand came round once again tearing up the earth, the mouths of more graves opened and innumerable hidden graveyards were revealed. The fractured portions of other bones also started to bleed. The blood from these bones flowed into the blood of the other bones and when the two streams of blood mixed there was such a clamour in the skies that it drowned all other sounds, and yet more graves broke open, more bones, soaked in thick and viscous blood and writhing in pain, began to appear. This blood mingled with the blood that was already flowing and the same clamour arose, and every time this happened the same scene was repeated. The newborn hand was tearing the surface of the earth and throwing out the old bones, and so much blood was produced that it flowed into the dry river beds. Now the dry river beds were filled with blood, which was flowing down to the oceans as swiftly as electric current travels down a wire to explode dynamite. The waters of the ocean were made bloody, and soon the whole earth. Then I saw that same infant hand, the hand of the newborn child, rapidly come towards me. The façade of the hotel was shattered and the rooms started to collapse and I woke up with a blood-curdling shriek.

I was soaked in sweat, and I heard the scream once again. This was surely not my own. I sat up fully awake, thinking about the scream, when it came again. I collected my senses and looked at the time and then got up and walked to the door. There was complete silence, no sound of the scream, or any sound of footsteps. I opened the door and came out into the corridor. The artist's room was silent and peaceful; perhaps they were both fast asleep. The other rooms were also quiet. I was still standing at the door when I heard the scream again, and the faint sound of someone scratching the walls. The scream was not as loud as at first, perhaps because I had been drowsier then. I walked slowly towards the bathrooms and heard the sound of someone breathing heavily and again of a wall being scratched. It was the old decrepit man.

'What is the matter? What's going on?' I asked from below.

'Water . . . water . . .' he called, panting.

'How do I get up to you?'

'Water, water . . . The way is closed. Everyone has died.'

His insistence was most strange. I had never been able to find out how to get up to this attic. There was a small window above the bathrooms and that was where the old man's voice was coming from. I decided to try there. I went to my room, folded up my bedding and placed it on the table, picked up the charpoy and hurried back to the old man. I put the charpoy against the wall of the bathroom just below his attic and reached the window. It was pitch dark inside, the darkness of conspiracy. It was impossible to see the old man under such thick cover of darkness. I called him and jumped inside. I heard a sound from him and going towards it, I asked, 'Where are the matches?'

'Water . . . bring water, I am dying,' implored the old man. My eyes were still not used to the darkness. I collected my senses and went in the direction of his voice. I hoped that I might find the match-box under his pillow. The old man was lying quietly as if he had had his drink of water and was now sleeping in peace and comfort. I felt under the pillow and fortunately found a match-box. As the match flared up I was able to glance round the attic. The flame burned my finger and I flung the match away, paralysed. I was chilled to my bones to see the poverty and condition the old man was in. His face shocked me; worse than that, there was a gaping hole just near his charpoy like an open gutter; I was lucky not to have fallen into it. What kind of a hole was it? Curiosity led me to light a lamp that I had noticed nearby and I carefully approached the hole. It was a rectangular opening with steps going down; only the top of the steps was visible, the rest was shrouded in darkness. I was examining these steps when I remembered that the old man needed water. I picked up the lamp and went over to him. He was lying with his eyes closed, covered with a dark sheet. On the ground near his charpoy was an odd-looking aluminium container which had toppled over, spilling the water it had contained. I picked it up and searched for water. There was a bucket in one corner of the room which had no cover of any sort. When I dipped the container into it clouds of mosquitoes and moths flew out. It would not normally have been considered fit for human consumption, but this had to do. I at least carefully examined the water to make sure that it was not further contaminated and went over to the old man who continued to sleep even when I called him.

'Here's water for you,' I said, touching his arm. A sound came from his mouth that sounded like 'Hoon'. I put the container down by the lamp and with both hands helped him to sit up. His intense thirst had made him faint. He sat up in the charpoy, his eyes closed. I brought the container to his lips. At first it just nudged against them, then they moved a little and he began to drink very slowly, his eyes remaining closed. Taking his mouth away from the vessel he took a deep breath and opened his eyes. He looked around and again put his lips to the water. Then he indicated that he wanted to lie down, and I helped him. He looked as if he had left life far behind. He went to sleep after drinking and I could not possibly think he was dead, but, believe me, looking at him lying there was just like watching a corpse. His dirty white beard was tangled and unkempt, at its edge the cheek bones were clearly visible to the temples and the grimy hairs peeped out from his long ears. He was wearing a white cloth cap which seemed to belong more to a shroud than a cap. Every part of his face seemed ashamed of itself, as if it was anxious to escape from the sight of the beholder and to be buried many fathoms under the earth, there to rest in peace and comfort and to plan some dreadful vengeance upon others.

I looked at the room. It had not been constructed for human habitation at all. If during its construction anyone had thought that it could be, then that person would surely have been most despicable. In the darkness I had had no idea of the height of the ceiling, but now I saw that it was only a few inches above my head. If I had stepped on something, or raised myself on tiptoe, my head would have banged against the ceiling. There was no electricity there and the insufficient light of the lamp made the naked brick walls seem terrifying. I was standing near the small window, imprisoned in the tight net of silence. The room was so narrow that there was little space left between the window and the charpoy, which was placed against the wall. At the head of the charpoy a long overcoat hung from a nail, reaching almost to the floor. It was a ragged overcoat with rolls of newspaper in both the outer pockets. Near the coat was an enamel commode, which filled the air with a stench; just three paces from it was the bucket from where I had taken the water. The floor round the bucket was damp, and beyond it was a heap of odds and ends and rubbish, two or three empty cardboard boxes, a torn shirt, dried pieces of bread, and a large iron part of a machine covered in oil. Near the charpoy close to the pillow was an empty wooden packing case, the same kind the bathroom doors had been made from. On the packing case was a straw basket and the lamp that I had lit.

'Put out the light,' I heard the old man whisper.

Although I dimmed the lamp, I could still see that the bedding had not been washed for a long time. It was stained with sweat. I thought that the stain on the pillow might be urine and it had been used to change babies on. The old man reeked of accumulated vomit. It made me retch. The old man's voice came again, 'Put out that light, put out that light and go away.'

As he seemed to want peace and quiet, and to revert to his accustomed darkness, I extinguished the lamp and went back to my position at the window. I could not stop brooding about that hole in the floor which threatened to push me into hell. The silence in the room intensified, asserting its supremacy. I was still holding the lamp with the utmost caution. I groped my way towards those dreadful steps. I wanted to know where they led and how to get up to this room. I was shuffling cautiously across the floor when my left foot felt the gap of the gutter-like hole. I sat on the floor and dangled my feet into it until they touched those frightful steps. I lowered myself carefully to the second step. I was aware of a thick chain on the left, and, holding on to it, I descended another step. There I put down the lamp and lit it again. The chain was fixed to the wall and followed the steps down. Without it there would have been the danger of someone slipping and falling. I continued down, carefully watching my steps, holding on to the chain with my left hand. I was trembling and the shaking light of the lamp as I descended those steep, narrow steps reminded me of my nightmare and seemed to be part of it.

As I descended the darkness slowly lifted. The stairs ended at a closed door with a fine wire screen. There was light in the room the other side of the screen. I pushed the door and entered a storeroom. There was a heap of onions in one corner which looked like a pile of symbolic zeros, and in another corner were sacks of charcoal; near these were large pieces of rock salt placed neatly one on top of the other, and near the salt was a thick-set man asleep on a charpoy. I knew him. He was a hotel employee and it was his duty to fetch vegetables from the market and to do odd jobs around the hotel. He was sound asleep. His slippers lay under the charpoy and a foot away on the floor, drawn in charcoal, was a criss-cross pattern for a 'Baratani' with bits of broken earthenware and chunks of salt near it, used as pieces in the game. There were two more such stores in the hotel, the doors of which opened into the hall. I had not had occasion to enter any of the three rooms, though I had often seen the thick-set servant and the two cooks coming out of them. I had never imagined that the way to the old man's attic lay up dreadful mysterious stairs from the room where the short, stout servant lived. I stood still staring at the person sleeping and then realized I should be going back to my room: I had left the door open and my charpoy was still placed against the wall near the bathrooms. I decided to speak to the ugly manager about the old man as early as possible in the morning. I would ask him who that helpless and abandoned person was who lived in the attic all by himself. I had left my watch behind in my room and it had said two o'clock then. I guessed that it must be about half past two or three by now. The storeroom door was unlocked and I quietly went through the hall to the stairs. There I found that the door leading upstairs was bolted from my side. If I left it open behind me who would close it after I had gone up? It would stay open for the rest of the night and that was not at all proper. Besides, I had something in my hand that I should take back to the old man's room. Carrying the lamp I returned to the storeroom and went towards the stairs. I thought I had better switch off the light in the store which must have been left burning by mistake, but I could find no switch. The electric wire from the bulb came through from the adjoining room so I left the room as I had found it. Upstairs the old man was fast asleep. Putting out the lamp, I left his room by the window using the charpoy as a ladder. I took it back to my room and slept.

I woke late that morning. It was as if I had had two nightmares; one while I was asleep, the other when I was awake about the creature lying in the lonely attic and the dreadful stairs going down from his room. I got up and knocked at the artist's door. He opened it at once. Before I could say anything he told me that Aziz had left without telling him. I was surprised to hear this and had no idea when Aziz might have left. I was still tired from my interrupted night and so I went to the bathrooms. There was no rush there at this hour and I was able to bathe immediately. As I came out, I looked up involuntarily at the small window. I was about to walk towards my room, but Qadir Ali's words stopped me: 'I do not know how the poor old man died.' He was standing talking to Rafiq the dyer, and the office clerk was with them. I drew nearer and heard Qadir Ali say, 'No one knows who he was, or how long he had been living in the attic, but he died this very morning.'

'How did he die?' Rafiq asked unsteadily.

'He had been paralysed for quite some time; people say that this was the cause of his death.'

'The old man is dead, the old man is dead,' the office clerk mumbled to himself and went away.

'Qadir, do you know who the old man was?' I asked, passing my tongue over my dry lips.

'Nothing can be said just yet. The old man's body is in the manager's room and he wants him buried without delay.'

After changing my clothes I went to the hall and, sitting on a chair, started thinking about the old man: a man who could not move and who lived with only a few sounds at his disposal had met death silently. I saw the manager enter, and got up intending to ask him some questions, but he squashed me with one sentence, 'I do not have time.' He sounded utterly helpless. He hurried on, not stopping even for a moment.

I later found out that the old man who had died so miserably, who had screamed for water in the middle of the night, lying alone in that isolation, was the manager's father. I began to detest the hotel. The manager's callousness and the way he had treated his own father was beyond imagination. He was amassing wealth, but to what end? What was he going to do with it? With a heavy heart I went to my room, longing to lose myself in deep sleep. I passed the artist near the bathrooms, looking towards the street. The moment he set eyes on me he said, 'I was coming from your room. I forgot to tell you that last night before going to sleep Aziz told me that he wanted to show us both something, and that if we could, we should come to his house this evening.'

We arranged to see Aziz. At about four o'clock before we left for his house, a man entered the hotel who would commit a brutal murder within half an hour of his arrival. No one had expected Gaman and the two other men with him. They had come searching for Fiazi, but had failed to find him, and hence the murder and a second one too. My plans to go to see Aziz were changed because I met someone who was also looking for Fiazi and seemed to be quite worried.

FIVE

When Gaman entered the hotel he went straight to the counter, opened the glass jar and started eating the biscuits from it. The fat manager started up from his chair behind the counter as if some invisible force had lifted him by the neck. He unscrewed several glass jars and put out a variety of edible things on a plate and stood respectfully aside. Gaman did not deign to look at the plate and continued to eat biscuits from the jar.

'Water!' Gaman commanded.

The manager at once placed his finger on the bell and looked around impatiently.

'You go.' Gaman pushed him out from the counter. 'Hurry.'

The clumsy manager ran to the kitchen, making himself a comic sight. When he had gone Gaman opened the drawer of the counter and took out all the money and laid it out before him on the glass top. He attempted to sweep all the money back into the drawer, but he did this so carelessly that only a few notes fell into it, and the rest of them scattered on the floor. The obese manager soon returned, carefully carrying a glass of milk in both hands.

'I asked you to fetch me water,' Gaman shouted at him, accompanying his words with an obscenity. The five or six people in the hall turned to stare at him in amazement. A waiter quickly brought Gaman a glass of water. He drank it and threw the glass out on the street.

'Any news, any information?' Gaman asked, fixing his gaze on the manager.

'Jinab . . . Jinab . . .'

'You informed the police again that I had come here?'

'No, I swear by God, no. I did not. Who said I had?' he gasped. 'Who told you? I swear that I . . .'

'Run along and send food upstairs. I will talk to you after I have eaten. I have two men with me. Send us enough food and make sure that it's good.' The two men followed Gaman to the stairs. When he reached his room he opened the handcuff-shaped padlock and entered with his companions. It was dirty because the window had been left open and the wind had blown in all sorts of things. A cotton mat spread over the floor was full of dust although it was new. Two suitcases were open in one corner, and there was a chocolate-coloured pedestal fan.

'Turn the mat over,' Gaman ordered gruffly. Underneath it were seven ten-rupee notes, several notes of smaller denominations and two green passports. The two men paid no attention to these things and after shaking the mat out of the window, spread it out again. Gaman was wearing a crimson shirt and shalwar. He took from the pocket of the vest under the shirt a long-barrelled pistol, a flick knife about a span long and several ten-rupee and fifty-rupee notes. These he placed on the mat.

'There is an extra key to this room on the roof,' Gaman told his companions. 'If you scratch around under the loose brick in the corner you will find it.'

'Boss, Fiazi doesn't live here any more. He left the hotel two or three days ago,' one of his companions said.

'Who told you?' asked Gaman sharply.

'The fat manager.'

'Send for him.' Gaman cursed again. One of his companions got up and went out. Gaman said to the other. 'We have to catch this man, catch him and kill him. I've promised. Furthermore, we need money. Ghazanfar is in jail, and that bastard lawyer won't do a thing without his fees. Only yesterday I told him he would get his money – he can keep it for himself or give it to the magistrate, that's up to him – but unless Ghazanfar is released on Saturday, we'll despatch the lawyer to the next world. We need ten thousand rupees urgently, and the only way we can obtain it is from the woman who has asked me to kill that man. It won't be so easy to get the money from other sources. The police are searching for me and it is not safe to stay here these days. I wanted to go away to Dera Ghazi Khan for some weeks. Why hasn't the manager come yet, the son of a pig!' said Gaman getting worked up with anger and impatience. 'Maybe he knows where the man went.'

Just then Gaman's companion brought in the manager.

'Jinab, food is almost ready and will be served in a little while,' the manager said entering the room.

'Sit down,' growled Gaman. The manager sat down at once.

'Where did that man go? Where did . . . what was his name?'

'Fiazi,' one of his companions reminded him.

'Yes, where's Fiazi?' Gaman shouted. 'Look, fat man, you know me well. I want Fiazi; he must have told you where he was going.'

The manager was even more afraid to talk when he saw the pistol and the knife.

'Speak up. Tell me where he went, at once. We have to find him before nightfall.'

'I swear that I know nothing.'

'Then bring me ten thousand rupees immediately.' Gaman opened the flick knife.

'Ten thousand!' the manager was gasping in panic. 'I do not have that much money. I may just have five hundred rupees.'

'Look, fat man, just tell me where I can find him, that's all. He is the equivalent of ten thousand rupees for us. Get that into your head.'

'I don't know. Please believe me, he did not say where he was going. He was so depraved that he never told anyone anything. Jinab, I do not have the money or I would give it to you. I am sorry.'

'Go away. No. Wait. Bring me the five hundred rupees.'

'I don't have the money here. I will give it to you, but at the moment . . .' He was not allowed to finish his sentence, because he received a punch which sent his heavy body reeling to the floor. He started to weep. 'I will bring it. I will bring it, in just a minute.'

'Get out. Don't forget I can kill you whenever I want.'

'Please forgive me,' the manager said amidst his sobs. 'I ask your forgiveness. I will bring the money right now.'

'Go and send up the food. Here take this,' Gaman said, giving him a fifty-rupee note. 'Send whatever has been cooked and don't show your face in here again.'

The manager took the note in his trembling hand. He wanted to say something about returning the fifty-rupee note, but then thought better of it and left. Soon after two bearers appeared with a jug of water, glasses and a large tray laden with food and drink. The manager had prepared a few special dishes for them, and these were followed by more dishes cooked outside the hotel. Gaman and his companions sat a long while eating their food. They ate in silence. After the meal Gaman concealed the pistol in his vest pocket again and stuck the knife in his waistband. All three got up and went to wash their hands. The bathrooms were occupied. One man was standing in a corner waiting for his turn to bathe. Someone was whistling in one of the bathrooms. Gaman knocked on the door. The bather stopped whistling and shouted to him to wait. At that moment the door of the adjoining bathroom opened. Before Gaman or his companions could enter, the man waiting his turn went in. Gaman once again knocked on the door of the bathroom where the bather had resumed his whistling. This time, abusing his mother, the bather told him to go elsewhere and bath with her. Gaman opened the door easily, startling the man inside. He gave him no time to be embarrassed, put his hand over the naked man's mouth, hoisted him on to his shoulders and took him to his room. He told his companions to fetch the man's clothes. He removed his hand from the man's mouth and threw him on the floor as if he was a roll of bedding. The man was pale with fear and did not dare utter a sound.

'Here's your "breakfast"*, Raja. Take care of him,' Gaman said to one of his companions. Raja smiled, looking with pleasure at the frightened man lying naked before him. Gaman took out his flick knife, stuck it point downwards on the wooden tray, and started to deal out cards.

'Jinab, what's going on? What are you doing?' the victim asked through his tears.

'Silence, silence,' Raja whispered ominously, and then tried to repeat the words in a whistle. The man looked piteously to the door, hoping that some unseen power would come to his rescue.

When the cards were dealt, Gaman proposed a blood-curdling bet, but his companion heard it calmly and accepted it. The two played cards while Raja finished his 'breakfast'. Then the naked man wanted to get dressed, but Gaman was sitting on his clothes. He threw down his cards and said to his opponent, 'I've lost the bet, but I've won in a way too.'

'I understand, boss,' replied the other with a smile. 'You lost the game on purpose.'

'Not at all. I wanted to give you a chance.'

'I am still prepared.' He took from his waist a long, sharp dagger, which glittered in the dim light of the room. He stuck it on the tray next to Gaman's flick knife, but Gaman returned it to him saying, 'Two knives should never be in the same place side by side.'

Their victim huddled up behind the suitcases. He no longer knew where he was, only conscious of being trapped and of his desperate need to get out of the room.

'Jinab, give me back my clothes. I want to go.' He was terrified. Gaman threw him his clothes and tossed his knife over too.

'You wanted to send me somewhere with my mother. Why?' Gaman asked coldly.

'Jinab . . . Jinab.' The man was shaking.

'Wait!'

The man was wrapping his loincloth around him when Gaman's

* In this context, it means sexual intercourse.

voice lashed out. The flick knife still lay where Gaman had thrown it.

'Pick up that knife and press the small button on the handle. The blade will disappear. If you press the button again the blade will shoot out. You can repeat this operation any number of times but if I give an order to the knife the blade will not shoot out even with your finger on the button.' Gaman stopped. Their victim did not dare speak. Raja was examining the passports, and Gaman's other companion was unconcernedly playing with the cards.

'Jinab, I beg your forgiveness, I . . .'

'Pick up the knife and cut your loincloth and shirt into shreds.'

The man just looked tearfully at Gaman and did not move. Gaman went over and picked up the shirt and cut it in two himself and then slashed the two pieces into four; he did the same with the loincloth. Tears welled from the victim's eyes. Gaman leapt on him at lightning speed, laid him flat on the mat and sat on his chest. Without wasting any time, he took pieces of the torn material and stuffed them into the man's mouth and tied the wad round with a bit of loincloth. Then he bound the man's legs and arms.

'If there had been a tank of acid somewhere I'd have pushed him into it and killed him,' said one of Gaman's companions, gathering up the cards.

This was Jida Qulfi and he was as long in shape as the ice cream he was named after. He was extremely loyal to Gaman and his loyalty had frequently been put to the test. He had been lashed many times and his back was full of scars to prove it. It is remarkable that though he fainted on the third or fourth lash he never cried. Probably it was his physical defect which stopped him from crying. Sometimes it seemed as if his bones were made of steel and the flesh was a mixture of iron filings and some kind of rubber that he had no feeling of pain. He was a skilled pick pocket, an expert sharper, and unequalled at cards. His real name was Javaid, but Gaman and his companions called him Jida Qulfi, and so did police records.

The companion who was known as Raja really did look like the ruler of a state. He had a dark, attractive face. He was well built but not obese and his face was fleshy, creased in places, particularly around the jowls. He was prepared to perpetrate any sort of evil. He had a smouldering cigarette in his left hand, while he used a matchstick to pick at his teeth with the other.

Gaman's arms were placed on his knees and he was looking fiercely at his victim. Gaman had no equal in the world of crime. He enjoyed being in combat with the police and was their sworn enemy. The most prominent feature of his face was his long, drooping moustache which entirely hid his upper lip. His face had cruelty written all over it and anyone looking at him, no matter how carefree, at once grew silent and apprehensive. His eyes were hooded, like those of a wild animal about to pounce. His nose was misshapen through constant injury. There was a scar under his right eye with the marks of old stitches along it. The way he walked and his habit of suddenly stopping and calling someone to him was aggressive in the extreme. Long before he spoke Gaman appeared to have decided the fate of any victim and seemed only to be waiting to carry it out.

The prostrate man was staring at him in terror, tears gushing from his eyes, and his stomach convulsed with jerks. Gaman stood up as if he was waiting to see the full effect of the man's agony. He picked up the flick knife lying beside the man and pressed the white button and closed it, and then pressed it again, shooting out the shining blade. Keeping his finger on the button, he moved slowly towards his victim. He depressed the blade and stood near the man's head. A thin film of water was spreading across his cold, angry eyes and his jaws were clenched. He placed the knife on the man's throat and, his vision blurred by the watery film, firmly pressed the white button. The blade shot easily into the soft flesh of the victim's throat and the blood gushed out. The man's body twitched and then lay still. Gaman wiped his knife on the rags before cutting the bands tying the man's hands. The hand jerked with the result that the dead man's wrist was cut too. Jida Qulfi and Raja watched all this quietly.

'You said you would have drowned him in acid,' said Gaman to Jida. 'I have drowned him in his own acid.'

'How was it, Boss?' Jida Qulfi asked.

'Salty.'

'Good,' said Jida shaking his head. 'That is why salt is becoming scarce in the world.' He casually picked up the cards, shuffled them and went out to urinate.

Gaman looked at the water in the jug where he had washed his bloodied hands and threw it out of the window. When Jida returned they discussed how to dispose of the dead body. Gaman liked Jida's proposal very much and shouted happily, 'Excellent, very good. Long live Jida Qulfi, two ice creams.'*

'Foreign ice creams?' Jida asked smiling.

* Ice cream in their gangster jargon means a bottle of liquor.

'Foreign, real foreign ice creams,' Gaman agreed, taking out all the money he had in his pocket; nearly four hundred rupees.

'Boss, the liquor should be brought soon,' said Jida, 'or my blood will stop flowing.'

'Look, there's the money in front of you,' said Gaman smiling.

'Come along then. What are we waiting for?' Jida got up.

'Let's go. We'll drink in the large room. Raja, cover the corpse with the mat. You will have to dispose of it this evening as Jida suggested.'

Raja was covering the corpse with the mat when there was a knock on the door. They froze. Gaman looked at the window ready to jump out and Raja and Jida prepared to follow him.

'Who is it?' asked Gaman in an authoritative tone.

'Jinab, it is me, your servant. Shall I send some tea?'

'Go away, you son of a pig,' roared Gaman going towards the door. 'When we need tea we will squeeze it from your mother's breast.'

'Boss, the manager is a terrible "thing",' Raja said, resuming his job of covering the dead body.

'One day I'll kill him too,' said Gaman. 'He always comes at the most inappropriate moments.'

'Does he also own the hotel?'

'Curse him. Talk about something else. Ghazanfar is on my mind, I keep hearing him asking me how much longer he has to remain in gaol.'

'How are we going to find Fiazi?' asked Raja, when he had finished covering the dead body. 'He is a very good prescription,* for ten thousand rupees. We have to find him.'

'If it was his dead flesh here instead of this man's we wouldn't have any problem,' Jida said to Raja.

Their banter was interrupted by a more peremptory knock on the door. Gaman and his companions were startled. They were sure the manager would not dare come back so soon after his curt dismissal. The knock was repeated and someone called out, 'Open the door, open the door.' Gaman went over and asked who was outside. The caller did not give his name but only said, 'It is me, open the door.' Gaman glanced at the wrapped up corpse and then let the visitor in. Gaman was surprised to see that it was Bashir, who came up to him and said, 'Where's Fiazi? I'm looking for him.'

'Fiazi? Who gave you his address?' Gaman asked him sharply.

* Gangster jargon for a solution.

'The people I thought were my parents.'

Gaman was puzzled by Bashir's reference to Fiazi. He had never imagined that Bashir would come searching for the same person.

'Do you know Fiazi?' Gaman suddenly shot the question at him in a tone which demanded a straight answer. Bashir shook his head regretfully. 'No, I don't. I came here to meet him.'

'If you don't find him here, where will you look for him?'

'He must be here.'

'He isn't. He doesn't live here any more. Anyway, who told you that you would find Fiazi in this room?'

'A fat man sitting behind the counter downstairs. I did not know you would be here.'

'A fat man!'

'Yes, he told me that . . .'

'I thought he might perhaps be of some use to you . . .' The door was opened by the manager. It was quite clear that he had been standing outside eavesdropping so that he could enter when necessary. 'He wanted to meet Fiazi and I thought he might help . . . I swear by God . . .'

'All right, go away.' Gaman waved him out of the room, and the manager scurried off.

'I'll be right back,' Gaman said as he quickly got up and left the room, throwing Raja and Jida Qulfi a warning look. He overtook the manager outside the bathrooms. He took his arm and said threateningly, 'Look here, fat man, I don't need your help, got it? You should have come yourself and told us that there was a man looking for Fiazi. And why were you standing so close to the door?' He slammed him up against the wall.

'Jinab, you were angry with me. You had forbidden . . .'

'Listen to what I have to say.' Gaman held the flick knife at an angle close to the manager's stomach. 'No one must know anything about my coming here. And never stand outside my door or else . . .' He pressed the white button and the sharp blade flashed out to within half an inch of the manager's stomach. The fat man screamed in terror. Gaman closed the knife, returned to his room and said to Bashir, 'Now you can go, but meet me outside the hotel at nine o'clock and I will tell you where Fiazi lives.' He picked up the padlock and walked to the door, glancing at the lumpy mat.

'I'll come with you,' Bashir said. 'Just tell me where he lives.'

'Go away,' said Gaman angrily. It was clear that he would have hit him if Bashir had persisted. They came out of the hotel together.

Gaman and his companions walked away rapidly. Bashir was no longer inclined to follow them. He went back inside.

Bashir had been adopted from a hospital shortly after Kausar had given birth to him. Farzana and Safdar, her husband, had gone there to visit a relative. On their way out Farzana saw a nurse carrying a newly born baby. Hearing her say how beautiful the child was, the nurse stopped and told her she could have him if she wanted. Once the necessary formalities had been cleared, they left the hospital with Bashir.

Farzana had been married for five years, but had remained childless. Her husband Safdar had taken her to several doctors, and had consulted many hakims, without result. When his wife suggested that he should marry another woman he had refused, saying that he needed Farzana more than a child. Now they had a son on whom to concentrate all their love and care.

Bashir was sent to primary school for five years and then to a secondary school with a good reputation. He did quite well. When he finished at secondary school, he announced that he wanted to go to college in a nearby town. The town where Safdar lived was small and had only two colleges, both of which Bashir spurned. He was sent to the college of his choice, where he stayed in a hostel. For five or six months Bashir came home every weekend, then the visits became monthly and then even less frequent. By the time he finished at college and returned home Farzana and Safdar found it difficult to communicate with him, possibly because they could not forget that he was not their real son and this affected their attitude towards him. Bashir seldom talked to them now and never adopted the familiar affectionate tone normal between blood relations when he did. Conversation at home was as distant as between a customer and a salesman in a department store. After about three months Bashir found a job at an experimental farm in a small town quite far away.

Bashir had been away from home for only a few months when his parents were visited by Goli, one of Gaman's cronies, who had brought a note from Bashir asking for a small box from his room. Gaman had happened to meet Bashir outside his farm and, on learning that Bashir had some foreign currency in his parents' house, immediately asked him to change it. With Bashir's consent he had sent Goli to fetch it. Goli was so impressed by the kindness and courtesy of Bashir's parents that he told Safdar an exaggerated version of his conversation with Bashir: that he was going around with girls of loose character and doing other odd things. Safdar went to Farzana in the next room and told her that the adopted Bashir had not proved himself their son, even though they had given him the love of true parents. Goli overheard it. He didn't think this was of any consequence; he was only concerned with the box of money he had come to collect. He caught a bus back to Gaman and told him briefly about his journey, mentioning that the hapless Bashir was not really the son of the couple he had visited.

While they were talking, Bashir came over to say goodbye. As he shook Gaman's hand, Gaman said, 'I should like to shake hands with your father too.' When Bashir asked him why, Gaman explained what his friend had heard. Bashir felt numb when they had gone. He brooded for a long time. He remembered small incidents showing his 'parents'' indifference to him, and other things came to his mind. Several times he decided to go to the town and ask them who his real parents were. Yet he hesitated. At last he wrote a letter to his 'mother' and posted it. This was the letter that Farzana had given Kausar.

After the last of Fiazi's visits, Kausar thought seriously of suicide but was checked by the desire to see her son. In the morning she went to Farzana's and once again changed her mind about disclosing her identity. She did not tell her that she was Bashir's mother, just that she knew someone who could tell Bashir who his parents were. She gave Farzana Fiazi's name and address at the hotel and returned home overwrought. She became convinced that both Fiazi and she should die and that only her son should remain alive. She commissioned Gaman to kill Fiazi. If he succeeded within twenty-four hours, she would pay him ten thousand rupees. Gaman was in dire need of money and agreed. He smiled when he heard Fiazi's address and took two of his companions to the hotel that afternoon.

'Boss, why did you tell that man you would meet him at nine o'clock? How will you get Fiazi to meet him?' Raja asked Gaman as they walked away from Bashir.

'I cannot say anything now. There is plenty of time.'

'So we will go back to the hotel at nine o'clock?'

'*Zeroor*, certainly.' Gaman placed so much stress on the word that it sounded like a motor-bike being revved up.

Jida Qulfi returned with the liquor and in the large room of an old house which was their other hide-out, the three sat down and started drinking, and while they drank they talked heatedly. Goli turned up unexpectedly early. He had been out of town and had planned to meet Gaman at nine outside the hotel. Gaman had given Bashir the same rendezvous so that if Goli were detained, rather than tell Bashir Fiazi's address, he would ask him for his so-called parents' address and find out Fiazi's present address from them. So when Goli returned earlier than expected Gaman jumped up from his seat and said to Raja, 'We no longer need to be at the hotel at nine. I am going with Goli, you sit with Jida and enjoy your drinks, you have two bottles, keep more than half for Goli. The two of you can go and remove the corpse. Come on, Goli,' said Gaman, taking him to the door. 'We have to hurry to the house from where you brought that box.'

'Yes, Boss. They live quite close, in Munshi Gunj.'

'Quick. Point the house out to me when we reach it.'

Gaman and Goli strode rapidly to Munshi Gunj. Safdar was at home and he opened the door to Gaman's knock. Gaman had told Goli to stand away from the door because he did not want to waste time on introductions and the usual chit chat. He told Safdar that Fiazi was not living at the Bara Dari Hotel and asked him where he now was. A worried-looking Safdar said that he did not know. Gaman asked how he knew that Fiazi would be able to tell Bashir who his real parents were. Safdar started to relate the story of some woman who used to visit them but who had suddenly stopped coming, and he did not even know where that woman lived. This drove Gaman into a towering rage, and he hit Safdar with all his force, sending him reeling against the wall. Gaman left quickly, his jaws clenched and his brain seething. Goli wisely did not try to talk to him or ask him any questions. They returned to the room where they had left Raja and Jida Qulfi. It was empty. A finished bottle of liquor lay on the ground. Gaman sent Goli to fetch some food and when he returned with it they sat and ate and drank from the remaining bottle. Gaman did not drink more than two pegs and was soon satisfied with his fish. Goli was too busy drinking to eat anything. When Gaman returned from washing his hands he told Goli he might drink as much as he liked as long as he did not fall asleep. He was to wake Gaman up at half past twelve in the morning.

'Boss, liquor fills my stomach with fire and who can sleep while burning? You go to sleep and don't worry, I will wake you.'

'All right,' said Gaman running his tongue along the inside of his top lip. 'Let the fire of liquor smoulder inside you and see to it that the fire is not extinguished before half past twelve.'

Goli laughed. 'Boss, go to sleep. Goli is near you and has understood what he has to do.'

Goli woke Gaman at the right time. Raja and Jida were nowhere to be seen. Gaman had a drink of water and got up. He put his hands in his pockets searching for something and then he picked up a piece of cloth and wiped his face and eyes.

'Wait for me here, Goli. I'll be back soon.'

'OK, Boss,' said Goli, accompanying him to the door. 'I'll be here. Any other orders?'

Gaman did not reply. He left the room and after walking a few paces stood for a while examining the knife and the long-barrelled pistol which he then carefully put back in his waistcoat pocket. It took him only seven minutes to reach Kausar's house. He entered silently from the roof. He saw two doors. One of them gave easily when Gaman pushed it. He went in stealthily, pistol in hand. He stood and listened but could not hear anything, not even the sound of someone breathing. He then switched on his small torch and found that he was in the same room as before, with its sofa, tables and plang. He undid the bolt on the outside door so that in an emergency he could easily escape. He switched off the torch and cautiously went out to try the other door. This was firmly secured and did not yield to his pressure. He switched on the torch and went to examine the rest of the house. He looked at the kitchen, the bathroom, the stairs and the largish courtyard. He returned to the closed door and again tried to force it open. Failing in his efforts, he knocked. He heard Kausar's frightened voice. Gaman at once switched off the torch and put it with the pistol in his pocket. For some time there was silence and then Kausar came close to the door and asked, 'Who's there? Who's there?'

Gaman knocked again and called out her name whereupon Kausar opened the door, her hair dishevelled. Gaman stepped into the room. It was a little larger than the other and, like it, its windows opened on to the street.

'Don't you close your door before going to sleep?' asked Gaman, sitting on a chair near the plang. 'The outside door was open. You should close it at night.'

'Where is he? Where is Fiazi? Did you find him?' Kausar asked agitatedly, standing before him.

'Where's the money?' asked Gaman in a changed tone. And, more fiercely, 'Give me the money. I have to go back.'

'Have you killed him? You must have killed him,' said Kausar, terrified. 'Why did you kill him? You are a beast, you are a murderer, a killer.' Her voice choked in her throat.

'Where is the money? Give it to me and let me go.'

'That means you have killed him? Why did you kill him? You . . . you are a scoundrel, a bloody scoundrel. I did not ask you to kill him outright, not actually to kill him.' She was entreating him now.

Gaman controlled his voice and said as coolly as he could, 'Kausar, show me the money. I have to return. I can kill people, but I cannot bring them back to life.'

'You cannot have really killed him. I'm sure that you haven't,' Kausar screamed hysterically.

Gaman whipped out the pistol and pointed it at Kausar: 'Fetch the money.'

'Oh . . .'

'Fetch it,' he prodded the barrel into her side, 'or I may kill you too.'

'You . . . you must have been sent by Fiazi. Of course, he must have sent you. Tell me, how much did he pay you? His money is mine too.' Kausar looked at Gaman with frightened eyes. She stood up, but before she could utter another word Gaman said, 'Where is the money kept, you wicked woman?'

'I do not have it with me. Why did you murder him?'

'Hand it over,' Gaman insisted. He had the feeling that Kausar wanted to detain him as long as possible. Why? Gaman could not work it out; at any rate, he felt that he should not stay longer in the house. More fiercely he repeated, 'Kausar, give me the money and let me go. Where is it kept?'

Kausar got up and went towards the only cupboard in the room, but before she reached it she turned round and with a sad, depressed look said, 'I have returned the money and now I have nothing left, nothing whatever.' She stayed where she was. Gaman was growing more apprehensive and he began to think it would be better to leave while the going was good. Kausar had moved again towards the cupboard and had opened one of the doors. Suspicious of her delays, Gaman gave her no time to turn round. He threw her to the floor, clamped her mouth shut and stabbed her several times. Kausar writhed for a few minutes and then lay still, bathed in her own blood. Gaman went quickly to the cupboard and rummaged inside, throwing out everything on to Kausar's dead body. He searched every nook and cranny for the money, but he found none. On top of Kausar's body were a broken table lamp, bottles of medicine, rolls of newar, and shoe boxes containing odds and ends. One of the rolls of newar had fallen against the wall, the other had landed on Kausar's stomach from where it fell to the floor and started to soak up the blood around her dead body.

Gaman was livid at not finding any money. He was about to check under the newspapers lining the shelves, even though it was obvious that ten thousand rupees could not have been placed there without showing, but before he could do so there was a click and the light went out.

Gaman immediately sat down and then moved away a little as if there was a mechanical connection between the extinguishing of the light and his sitting down and moving away. While he was sitting a door banged loudly and then for a long time there was no sound. Gaman could not make out who had closed the door, nor was he sure whether the person was inside the room with him, or whether that person had seen everything and had then turned off the light and gone out, closing the door behind him. Black silence was all around, pinching him. He had been confronted by many strange situations in his thirty-two years. Once when he had been caught by the police, he had been tied to a block of ice and had become numb and had fainted. On another occasion, he had been caught by five of his rival gang who had locked him in a room and beaten him up brutally; they had broken the bridge of his nose with a hammer and had stabbed him in the stomach and sides several times and as a result he had been in hospital for a long period, fighting for his life. But he had never been in this sort of situation before. It was like being hung down a blind well. His torch was in his pocket. He dared not put it on in case a bullet sealed his fate. He was sure that someone who dared come into this room and witness a murder could not be unarmed.

A few minutes passed and still there was no sound. Gaman moved along a bit further because the blood on the floor was sticking to his hand. He bumped into something and shrank back. Someone told him to sit on the plang. The voice was clear and quite sympathetic. Gaman did not move and tried to locate the sound of the voice. The room was silent once more and he began to think that he had imagined the voice. Now another idea struck him. His pistol in his hand, he edged towards the switch. He found it quite easily. He aimed in the direction where he expected to see the intruder and switched it on. It clicked, but the room remained in darkness. Someone had removed the bulb from the holder. The silence was broken by a laugh. Gaman fired two shots in the direction. The room echoed with the reports and when the noise died down again, the laughter returned from another direction. Gaman fired again. This time there was return fire and a bullet ripped through his calf. He fell down on the floor.

'Put the pistol in your pocket and sit down comfortably,' the voice said a little more sternly. 'I know where you are and I can kill you whenever I want to.'

'Who are you?' Gaman asked.

'I did not come here to answer your questions. Listen to me. Why did you murder this woman? Did you hope to steal her money?'

'Were you eavesdropping?'

'Certainly. I must say, I did not expect that you would really kill her. I could easily inform the police, or kill you with one shot. However, neither of these suits my plans. I came here for a special reason, but when I found you in the room I stayed outside.'

Gaman thought that he should fire another shot in the direction of the voice, but his target was not visible, and what would happen if he missed again?

'I am going now,' the man said. 'Come out five minutes after I leave. Do not do anything hastily; just remember my pistol.'

Gaman was provoked almost to the point of firing again. 'Who are you?' He repeated his question.

'Ask Fiazi,' the man replied with a slight laugh.

'Fiazi?' Gaman was startled.

'You know, Fiazi, the same Fiazi that you are supposed to have murdered? I gather that you have not actually done so.'

'Who are you? Who are you?'

'Come out five minutes after me.' The man spoke with assurance as if words were all he had, just words and determination.

Because of his wound, it took Gaman two hours to struggle back to his hide-out. Jida, Goli and Raja were indignant to see him in such a condition. They wanted to do something about it at once but Gaman stopped them and told them to go to sleep. 'Now,' he said, 'it is even more important to find Fiazi.' In fact, Fiazi had become of secondary importance; his prime task was to search for the assailant who had told him that he should ask Fiazi to discover his identity. The problem of ten thousand rupees was still not solved and his failure to obtain it made him a seething volcano of rage.

Arif had gone to Kausar at one in the morning because of a misunderstanding the previous night. When Fiazi had parted from him he used the word 'morning' which Arif probably didn't hear; apart from that, the night had been unusually dark and he must have misunderstood, thinking that Fiazi meant twelve at night. He waited impatiently outside his house. When it turned a quarter to one and Fiazi had still not arrived, he decided to go to Kausar's thinking that Fiazi might have gone there or that she might be able to give him his new address.

SIX

After sleeping I felt better. I went to the artist's room, to take him with me to visit Aziz. He was out. I came down to the hall and sat on a chair to wait for him. I was only there for a few minutes when a man approached me and asked: 'Do you live here?'

I had no reason to hide anything so I said that I did and gave him my name.

'Munir Sahib, I am Bashir. I should like to know where I can find Fiazi.'

'Well, he left here about two days ago,' I answered.

'Where did he go?' Bashir asked. He seemed very agitated.

'I can't tell you anything . . .'

'Doesn't Fiazi live with Gaman?' he interrupted.

'Gaman?' I asked, unnerved by the sound of the name. 'No, he doesn't. Who told you about Gaman? Do you know him?'

'He was in his room just now and he went out with friends a short while ago.'

'Really?' I asked in amazement. Gaman interested me very much and I was curious to have a look at the man about whom I had heard so much from the waiters and others.

'Can you tell me, where is Fiazi likely to be now?' Bashir asked again.

'I've already told you, Fiazi has left the hotel.'

'Could you at least show me the room where he lived?'

Even when I told him it was locked, and that there was no point in his seeing it, he insisted. So I went upstairs with him and stopped at the door to Fiazi's old room.

'Fiazi lived here?' he said as if to himself. I watched him intently. All I knew was his name, that he was searching for Fiazi, and that he wanted me to show him his room, which I thought was an extraordinary request.

'The door is locked,' said Bashir, looking at me.

'I told you that downstairs,' I said, aware of his sense of helplessness and anxiety. I wanted to know more of this man and to find out what was causing him such anxiety. Why was he keen to meet a reticent man like Fiazi? I took him into my room and offered him a chair and myself sat down on the charpoy.

'You must know Fiazi,' he said. 'What kind of person is he?'

Bashir's anxiety and restlessness were growing all the time. He was swallowing nervously. He did not wait for an answer and addressed me again, 'What kind of relations could Fiazi have with Gaman?'

I told him that Fiazi stayed aloof, that he was very intelligent and that there was no question of his having anything to do with Gaman, whom I had never seen in my life.

Bashir listened to me in silence.

'What business have you with Fiazi?' I asked. 'Please tell me. Perhaps I can be of some help.'

'No, no, it's nothing like that; nothing like that.' The words 'like that' came out of his mouth as if they had been ground out under his tongue. He suddenly got up and entreated, 'Please come with me, if you have no work to do at the moment.'

It was clear that he was in need of sympathy. I was not busy so I postponed my visit to Aziz and got ready to accompany him.

'Will you not have a cup of tea first?' I asked, having forgotten during our conversation to offer him something to drink, but he answered in a changed tone, 'Never mind about tea, let's go to my hotel.'

Within fifteen minutes we reached his hotel. It was decent and clean. The glass was draped with a fine net curtain. Inside, the entrance hall was carpeted and there were pots of palms. There was a telephone on the counter and a wall clock ticked away behind it. He took his key from reception and we went upstairs to the first floor. He opened the door to his room and went in without saying anything to me. I could not make out his apparent indifference.

'Come in, Munir,' he said, returning to me. 'Why are you standing at the door? Please sit down and make yourself comfortable.' He then went out of the room. I was a little surprised and wondered where he had gone. He was soon back. Five minutes later a uniformed waiter came with a tray on which were a glass bowl filled with ice, and a full bottle of liquor. The waiter entered silently and as silently went out. I recognized the liquor bottle, though I had never seen one from such close quarters. Bashir took two glasses from a corner table and poured a generous peg in each and brought me one.

'Bashir Sahib, I don't drink alcohol. I never have. I will leave you now.' I got up, fully intending to go away.

'You don't drink?' he said examining me with surprise, smiling.

'I ought to leave. I think I have already told you that I do not know Fiazi.' I found his smile detestable.

'Please wait a moment. Munir Sahib, if you are my friend, stay with me for a while.' This time he spoke with persuasive gentleness. He poured the contents of both glasses into one glass and then back into the bottle and put the stopper on it, and placed it under the bed. I was not interested in his drinking. His words restored a trace of my earlier sympathy which compelled me to sit a while with him.

'You hate liquor, Munir Sahib.' He looked earnestly at me. 'Yes, alcohol is not a good thing, nobody should drink it. Tell me, did Fiazi ever speak to you about me? Did he ever say that he knew me?'

'I never heard him mention your name. Anyway, I have told you before that he was not intimate with anyone.'

At this, Bashir got up and gave me a disapproving look. He wanted me to go. He did not see me out or shake my hand and the moment I left the room he slammed the door shut.

When Munir had gone, Bashir took the whisky bottle. He poured some out, added a little ice-cold water and emptied the glass in one gulp. He poured himself another peg but added less water. This time it took him about six minutes to empty the glass. He drank steadily and within about twenty minutes finished more than a quarter of the bottle. He went to the bathroom and washed his face. For a few minutes he smelt of soap and whisky. The smell of soap soon disappeared as the intoxication from the whisky increased. He stretched out on the easy chair to relax. As soon as he felt refreshed Bashir got up and went downstairs to tell the receptionist he would not be in for dinner. Then he went out. He reached the Bara Dari Hotel a little before nine and waited restlessly for Gaman until half past. Gaman did not come in. The futile wait destroyed Bashir's intoxication. He felt like shutting Gaman in a large cage. At about ten o'clock he entered the hotel once again and, finding Gaman's room locked, went to Munir's but stopped when he saw the padlock on the door. He tested it, then returned downstairs lost in thought and stood a while on the road, just soaking up the atmosphere.

After a time he walked away. He came to a lonely road with tall trees growing on either side. He stopped and looked up to see an electric pole on top of which was a lighted bulb. The light made the leaves of the nearby tree seem to glitter in green blood. They seemed happy in their good fortune. Looking at the bulb, they seemed to be saying that if they were extinguished the bulb too would be darkened. Bashir was lost in their magic beauty and forgot his own troubles.

Then, quite suddenly his awareness of himself returned with great intensity. He stood watching the lonely road. Not a ray of light had ever brightened his being, his individuality had no special colour, and despite the fact that he lived in the lights of the whole universe he was still in darkness. He could not recognize his true self, he only knew the shadow, a shadow that amounted to nothing. What kind of world was this that gave a shadow the status of personality? He remembered all the months and years, the moments and incidents when people had tried to exploit him for their own profit, when he was considered a lottery ticket. He felt that whenever he laughed he laughed alone; others would join in only so as not to hurt his feelings.

Those who called themselves his friends were not really that at all. They were nothing to him. He felt it was all a lie and people thought that the lie was the truth and, thinking that, came to see him. If they had learnt that this was not the truth but a lie, would they have continued to meet him? He was actually introducing people he met to a falsehood, an anonymous shadow. He was the sole owner of a nameless island – himself – and what caused him pain was that he had suddenly been made aware of the isolation of this island.

Who were his real parents? It was as though he had fallen from their pocket like a coin onto the public highway. How had it happened? Was he the common offspring of Negro slaves, or was he the child of weary ice-breakers who had left him to freeze in some lonely spot? Has rain ever stayed in the air, or the slopes refused to accept it? Water flows down slopes to join other drops of rain released by the tyrannical clouds. Drops mingle with other drops, but who was that drop which had fallen by the wayside as a tear?

After a while Bashir came to a crossing brightly lit by electric lights from shops. He stopped and watched the shoppers emerging, talking to each other. He was like a small boy trying to understand the bustle of the bazaar. He was assailed by a great thirst, which caused him pain; his tongue was not dry but he had a feeling of emptiness in his breast. He hailed a tonga to take him to the Bara Dari Hotel again.

Qadir Ali was in his room, talking to friends; their voices could easily be heard from the corridor. I heard a knock on my door as I was turning the pages of a magazine before going to sleep. The knock startled me. I got up and opened the door. After what had happened between us, I was surprised to see Bashir. His eyes expressed deep regret and he stood silently as if he had come to apologize for his earlier behaviour. I made room for him to enter and quietly came back to the charpoy and sat down. At first Bashir did not move. I gestured, inviting him to sit on the chair, and he did so, not speaking or even looking at me. He looked tired and seemed lost in thought. He took out a cigarette and lit it, but still did not speak. He glanced at the wall and then at the floor and then started examining his hands. I did not think it proper to say anything either, and started to fiddle with some loose threads in the corner of the sheet, just to have something to do, trying to give him the impression that I was not worried about his silence and his deep preoccupations. I wanted him to feel that he had plenty of time to continue to think his thoughts. He went to the window to throw out the cigarette butt and stayed there, staring into the darkness outside. When at last he spoke, it seemed to be the result of long deliberation. He still had his back to me.

'Do you think that I am a very bad person?' His voice shook. I was about to give him a suitable reply when he turned round and, returning to his chair, stood there and said, 'Munir Sahib, I want to talk to you as a friend. I want to be able to confide in you but I'm afraid you do not think well of me.'

He gave me no chance to answer. 'Today, Munir, when I talked to you downstairs in the hall I felt that you were a very good friend. I don't live here. If you agree I'll come and see you sometimes. Can we go out somewhere now?'

The circumstances in which I had to leave his hotel earlier made me feel reluctant to go anywhere with him, but he sounded so sincere that I found it difficult to refuse. I sensed that he was in serious trouble and badly needed a companion. I put on my shoes and stood up. We did not speak as we walked. After a while Bashir hailed a rickshaw and took me to a beautiful spacious restaurant in a busy street. He ordered tea and remained silent. I began to feel uncomfortable.

'How did you come to know Fiazi?' I asked, trying to start a conversation. 'Do you have important business with him?'

'No, I just want to meet him,' he said surprisingly calmly.

'And what are your plans now? How will you search for Fiazi when you do not live in this town?'

'I would rather not discuss it, Munir my friend. Please don't mention it again,' he said, as if he was disgusted with the whole subject. 'Have your tea. I am ashamed of myself, sending for alcohol for you.'

'That doesn't matter,' I said, smiling. 'It happens sometimes.'

'I think you understand me. I think you have come to understand me.' He became serious again. His mood kept changing and I was finding it difficult to keep up with him. I could not make out what pain he was struggling against. After tea he asked me to accompany him to his hotel. I felt I could not refuse him and went along with him.

'Munir, tomorrow morning I have to return, but you must come to see me, you must,' he insisted.

'Bashir Sahib, you appear to be worried. Please tell me what is the matter . . .'

'Munir, I think well of you,' he interrupted. 'Just for today do not think of yourself as Munir, but simply as my friend.'

'What can I do for you?'

'I want to have a drink of whisky,' he said, looking straight into my eyes. 'I know that you do not drink, and that's fine. I will ask you something and then you must tell me how I can meet him. Please make yourself comfortable.'

He pressed the bell to summon the waiter and ordered iced water. Before the waiter could return he had poured himself a large double peg and drunk it up. Vapours from the liquor filled the room. I saw from the bottle that he had been drinking from it after I had left. It was now about eleven o'clock and I wanted to go to sleep and, besides, I did not like the smell of alcohol. I thought I would stay for ten or fifteen minutes. I sat carefully watching him.

'Let me tell you one thing, Munir. You think that I am worried, but I am not.'

'No, that's not it, I just . . .' At that moment came a knock on the door and the waiter entered with a jug of cold water and ice in a bowl. Bashir gave him a five-rupee note and the waiter went out thanking him respectfully. Bashir had a smile on his face which remained after the waiter had gone out, and then it melted away to be replaced by his previous serious expression. He picked up a piece of ice and let it fall again.

'Munir Sahib, don't drink whisky at all if you don't want to, but if you do drink, then eat some ice afterwards. Ice is hard and if you take it in your hand you cannot squeeze all the water out of it at once, but in your mouth, drops of water ooze out and fall in the courtyard of your mind waking up the parents sleeping there. Eat some ice, Munir Sahib.'

He picked up a piece of ice and started eating it. I felt uncomfortable as I sat there. I realized that he was lonely; but I was alone too. I had no one. I remembered my father; how had he died? He had slipped away so silently from this world. My mother, my sister, where were they now? Bashir was making me uneasy. The bitterness in my heart increased so much that it started to flow out. I looked helplessly at him and without a word or a sign got up and walked sadly out of the room, down the stairs and back to my hotel.

When Bashir got up in the morning he was assailed by painful, bitter thoughts. He quickly dressed, breakfasted and left the hotel. Instead of going to his so-called parents' house, he went to the office where his 'father' worked. There he learnt that Safdar Sahib was on two days' leave. So now Bashir had no choice. He went 'home', to the place where he had spent so many years. He remembered everything about this house and the previous ones they had rented. He was nervous and excited. He knocked on the door and stood aside. Safdar Sahib himself came in answer to his knock; he looked in a pitiful state.

'I could not find Fiazi Sahib,' Bashir said with downcast eyes, trying to hide his feelings.

Safdar stared at him and did not answer. He was trying to hold back his tears. 'Come in, let's sit inside,' he said hoarsely.

'Fiazi had left the hotel and gone away,' said Bashir after a pause during which he had managed to look at Safdar.

'My son, come in and sit down.' Safdar took a step towards him.

'No,' Bashir almost shrieked. He was trembling. 'Where is Fiazi? No, never mind Fiazi, I do not want to know his address. Please tell me where you got me from. Who are my real parents? I want to meet them.'

'Come inside. For God's sake, Bashir,' said Farzana appearing at the door. 'Come in, and I will tell you everything.'

Bashir suddenly went in and said, 'I will return every penny you spent on me, I will give you back all that money, but I want the names of my real parents.'

'We don't know them. We brought you from a hospital when you were very small,' said Safdar. He briefly told Bashir how Kausar had visited them and revealed the name of Fiazi. He told him that he himself had never set eyes on Fiazi and that the woman had only told them that Fiazi would be able to tell them everything about Bashir's real parents.

'Where is that woman? Who is she?' Bashir asked.

'She came here to see us. The last time she came she took away your letter. She told us that a man called Fiazi lived in that hotel and that he could tell us a great deal about your real parents.'

'Who is this elusive Fiazi, and who was that woman?' Bashir got up agitatedly from his chair. 'Please tell me exactly who abandoned me in the hospital.'

'We went to the hospital to visit someone and we saw you there and brought you home with us. That is all we know. Bashir, why will you not accept us as your parents? Where did we fail you?'

'You do not know, you do not understand,' Bashir interrupted Farzana. 'Safdar Sahib, please give me the woman's address and help me to meet my parents.'

'We know nothing, no more than that.'

'How can that be possible!' retorted Bashir angrily.

'Really, we know nothing.' Farzana got up and came over to him. 'Bashir, you are my child, I have . . .'

'No . . .' screamed Bashir closing his eyes. 'I am not your child, I am not your son.'

Safdar moved to Farzana. He led her to the plang with the lacquered legs and helped the weeping woman to sit down.

'Safdar Sahib, you are not my father,' Bashir said tensely, 'I beg you to tell me who my parents are. You know the answer and are hiding it from me. Am I a bastard?'

'My child,' said Farzana once again getting up. Her dopatta slid to the floor. She paid no attention and took two steps from the plang and stopped. She was unable to go on. She looked dully at Bashir, who was standing holding on to the back of another plang; he felt as if all the vitality of his body and soul were under immense pressure. Farzana suddenly sat down on the floor and burst out weeping again, her face in her hands. Safdar did not move. He did not seem to be able to see anyone or hear anything.

'Son, your parents were poor and that is why they left you and went away,' he said. 'And since we had no children we took you from the hospital and brought you up as our own. You are our son and we are your parents.'

Bashir looked at Safdar with the eyes of a beggar and then lowering his gaze he seemed to speak to himself. 'Did I have no one to call my own?' He slowly raised his eyes to him. 'You should have told me this from the beginning. When I was old enough you should have told me everything. I am going now and . . . I shall never come back, never.' He stopped abruptly in the doorway. 'Safdar Sahib, at least tell me who that woman was . . . that woman who told you about Fiazi.'

'She . . . she used to come to see Farzana but she never told us where she lived.'

'What was her name?' Bashir asked loudly.

'Kausar . . . She is about forty, neither fat nor thin. She has dark brown eyes and there is a mole above one eye.'

'Which one?' Bashir asked quickly but with apparent indifference. Then, without waiting for an answer, he hurried from the room.

Bashir wanted to go to sleep for a long while, to get away from everything, from these roads, from hotel tables, taxi seats, the green fields of the farm, bare plains, hard rocks, railway lines, the blue sky, shining leaves, dark shadows, from sharp pricking thoughts and from mysterious contorted imagination. His heart seemed to have been extinguished and from it all around rose poisonous smoke which hurt him and numbed him.

'Why did they have to leave me in hospital? Did my mother abandon my brothers and sisters there too? Who knows? They were left on a hospital doorstep or at the edge of a manhole perhaps!'

Bashir drank a glass of water from a sweet shop, trying to dispel the smoke that was clouding his throat and brain. Then he took a rickshaw to his hotel, but just before they arrived, he asked the driver to turn down a street which took him to where Munir lived. He was uneasy; the smoke which he had wanted to dispel had settled somewhere inside him.

When Bashir entered my room it was difficult for me to understand the state of his mind from the series of expressions flitting across his face. He sat down and closed his eyes. Then suddenly he opened them again and asked, 'Do you want to drink liquor?'

I was baffled. He knew I did not drink alcohol.

'No, thank you,' I said. 'Drinking isn't good for you. People don't approve of it.'

'Who doesn't approve?'

'People, people . . .' I tried to make him understand.

'To hell with them. Forget these tuppenny ha'penny people. I don't compel you to drink with me but if you yourself wish to have a drink then I shan't stop you. You can call that the revenge of a drunkard if you like.'

I did not know what revenge he was talking about but I repeated what I had said about drinking alcohol. He smiled and said, 'All right, if people want to condemn other people, I have no objection to their getting pleasure that way.'

'I only meant . . .'

'Forget it. Alcohol should only be discussed when it has been brought before you. That is the third rule of drinking.' He smiled. His mood seemed to be lifting. I was pleased to see this and began to show an interest in what he was saying. I asked, 'What is the first rule of drinking?'

He did not answer at once. He looked at me and said, 'That means you are not acquainted with the seven golden rules of drinking?'

'No,' I admitted.

'The first is that you must make sure that the liquor is good. Never drink or even touch inferior liquor or rough, home-made stuff.'

'Very good,' I said, taking greater interest. 'What is the second rule?'

'The second rule is that a man should drink whenever he wants to. This is why I told you that if you wanted to drink I would not stop you, nor would I compel you to drink if you did not want to.'

'And the third?' I wanted to hear all seven.

'I have already told you the third rule,' he said, picking up an empty glass from the table and setting it down elsewhere. 'Liquor should be discussed only when it is in front of you. Hollow talk about liquor, trying to get drunk on such talk is a futile activity.'

'Bashir Sahib, these are excellent rules,' I said. 'They seem to have been formulated by a veteran tippler. Please tell me the fourth rule of drinking?'

This conversation had brought about a welcome change in him and I wanted to continue it. He asked me for water and I gave him some. Placing the empty glass on the table he said, 'The fourth rule is that one should not have sexual intercourse in a state of drunkenness. Most people get drunk and then go in search of a woman and that is quite wrong. Woman has her own place and liquor its own, and the two should never be mixed. Woman and liquor are rivals to one another; if a man makes the mistake of trying to get both pleasures at the same time he will be in serious trouble, as often happens.'

'What is the fifth rule of drinking?' I asked.

'The fifth is that one should not drink with a stranger. One should drink alone or with old friends. If you break this rule there is every chance that the results will be troublesome. Let me tell you of an incident to illustrate the rule.

'Once there was a man who bought a bottle of liquor, wrapped in paper. He was holding the bottle in his hand and waiting at the side of the road for a taxi. No taxi came. At long last a tonga appeared in which there was only one person sitting in the back seat. The man signalled to the tonga to stop and asked the driver to be taken along. The person in the tonga had hired the whole tonga but seeing the man's need had invited him to share it.

'The first passenger asked the man with the bottle what he did for a living. The man answered: "I catch fish from the river and then let them free in the river again."

'"What do you mean?" asked the first man with surprise.

'The man holding the bottle smiled and his smile seemed to embody absolute reality standing as a barrier to all questions. The other man could not understand it and said, "If you catch fish, why do you need to throw them back in?"

'"Are you free at the moment?" the other asked, as if he was getting ready to dismount from the tonga. "If you like, let's sit down somewhere at leisure."

'"I don't have anything to do just now, but where will we go and what shall we do?"

'"We will go to my place and drink," he said, again smiling his peculiar smile.

'"Surely you are joking," the man said laughing. "You are a very interesting person."

'"Whether I am an interesting person or not is another matter, but at the moment I am in no mood for joking. In fact, I catch and free a special kind of fish."

'"I suppose these fish supply you with liquor?"

'"That is correct."

'They alighted from the tonga. The first man was a retired civil servant. He was not particularly fond of drinking, but had gone with the other man out of curiosity. "How do you obtain liquor from fish?" he asked as they walked.

'"In the same way as people obtain milk from goats."

'"You mean that there are fish which give alcohol?" The man was amazed. "I can't believe that fish produce alcohol, just as goats, cows and buffaloes give milk."

'"And women," the other added and laughed.

'"I mean that goats, cows and buffaloes give milk, but I never heard of fish yielding liquor."

'"It took years for people to find out that these creatures gave milk." Then he asked the other man what he did for a living.

'"Strangely enough, I do something similar, but unlike you, I do not get liquor from butterflies. I catch them and photograph them."

'"Oh," said the other man as he stopped before a closed door. He opened the door and both of them entered a small and untidy room. It did not seem much lived in. There was a charpoy with thick legs, two metal folding chairs and a cheap table, with some dirty dishes and glasses, a few stale chapatties, an aluminium jug with a cover and an electric fan on it. In one of the corners of the room were lying four brand new motor-car tyres on top of one another. The man placed the bottle on the table, opened up the folding chairs and switched on the fan. They both sat down and started drinking.

'"I am interested to know how do you get liquor from fish?" the guest asked his host.

'"Have you not heard that you should eat mangoes and not go around counting mango trees? The liquor obtained from the fish is here, enjoy it."

'"Well, whatever the fish are, they seem to be most generous."

'"Much depends on the person catching them. Not everyone can obtain liquor from these fish."

'"What kind of fish do you catch? You cannot obtain liquor from them."

'"Yes I can, you foolish old man," the man retorted angrily. "In this net," he pointed to the four walls surrounding them, "one more fish with an attractive body is about to come. If you want to meet her you can wait. But . . . you are not in need of fish. You only want butterflies which you can photograph. Go . . . go, you have had your drink. Let me wait for my fish."

'"A fish will come here? You are dead drunk," the retired civil servant said with a smile. "It seems as if today these fish put some small fish in the bottle and sent it to you and now they have entered your stomach and are churning you up inside."

'"You are a stupid old man who would not know a fish if he saw one." The man drained his glass. "I catch fish and obtain liquor from them. You catch butterflies and obtain pictures from them."

'"What kind of fish are you talking about?"

'"Immoral and vagabond fish," the man said in a sharp voice. "Bad charactered fish wandering on the roads, libertine fish who sell their bodies."

'"What is your profession?" asked the retired civil servant more quietly.

'"I am a policeman and I catch fish. I stop them wandering about on the streets. I also hold up those that are pickpockets and I do not let them go until they have paid me my share, what I need for my liquor."

'"What is your job in the police? What is your name?"

'"Whoever I may be, all the fish in the town are known to me and the moment they see me they automatically give me my share for liquor. I know this is forbidden, but I spend it on liquor which is also forbidden."

'"You should not drink liquor," the retired civil servant said, rising. "The way you drink is wrong. It is not proper to drink so much in one sitting."

'"Are you telling me how to drink?" Angrily he took his handkerchief from his pocket and wiped his lips, and went on, "You are an old butterfly catcher. When I brought you with me I thought you were a sympathetic stranger but now you start advising me."

'" I am not advising you. I just want to show you how things really are."

'"Whom do you want to show me to?" the other asked curiously. "I don't need to be shown to anyone." He looked dazed and shouted, "Go away, get out."

'The retired civil servant got up and went out, taking with him an odd impression of the evening. He had only had one peg and it felt as if he had drunk the menstrual blood of a prostitute. He went home but could not sleep. He phoned his younger brother, a senior police officer, and asked how an official department could protect people when it was itself corrupt. The retired civil servant told his brother all that he had experienced that evening and advised him to resign. It is better to pimp secretly than in a particular uniform. The younger brother at once rang up the officers concerned, who took prompt action and ordered their subordinate officers to apprehend the culprit. The policeman who had laid the foundation of the fifth rule of drinking was caught red-handed, and dealt with severely.'

'Has every rule a story behind it or is it only the fifth rule?'

'Every rule was born out of some event, though not all these events can be told. Now you're going to ask me the sixth rule. Let me tell you this: many people who drink liquor ignore it, thereby bringing disgrace upon themselves. If it is rightly observed then liquor gives herself to the drinker whose pleasure is greatly increased. People usually treat their liquor badly and try to squeeze everything from it. Liquor does not yield to such an approach, and when crushed under a stony slab of compulsion, only her unclean tears fall which we drink, thinking that they are liquor. One should not rape liquor. If one does, one faces unavoidable ignominy. It is vital to bear in mind the sixth rule, but a lot of people knowing it still remain unsuccessful. I shall not tell you yet about this strange, mysterious rule, or about the seventh, because there is a kind of by-rule attached to the sixth; that one should not disclose all seven to anyone in one sitting.'

I would have insisted but the door opened slowly and Aziz came in, in very bad shape. He could hardly stand. He squatted near the door, not saying a word. I went across to him to bring him to the bed. Bashir got up too.

'Aziz, what is the matter? Where have you been?' I asked, bending over him.

His eyes had a tragic look. He raised them tiredly to me and said, 'Munir Sahib, you . . . you . . .' The words seemed to drown in his throat. The few words he did manage to speak cost him a great deal of pain. He was in urgent need of medical attention. I put him over my shoulder and hurried along the corridor. The artist's door was closed. I told a bearer to tell the artist that we had gone to such and such a hospital. Bashir said nothing as we went down the steps to the road. A taxi took us quickly to the hospital where doctors examined Aziz and told me that he was to be admitted. Bashir had come with me but then he disappeared. I asked a nurse to take care of Aziz and with a trembling heart set off to tell his mother about him. I had also to lock my room which in my hurry I had left unlocked. I reached the hotel. The artist was not yet back. I went alone to Aziz's house.

It was three o'clock by the time I arrived there. The sun shone brightly, but in the street where Aziz lived tall buildings cast their shadows. I passed the goats and climbed the steps. The door to Aziz's place was closed and there was no sign of anyone inside. I knocked lightly and then a little louder, whereupon the door opened at once. To my utter amazement, it was Aziz. On seeing me he paused. He still looked weak and exhausted, but at least he was able to stand. He looked back into the room and quickly closed the door in my face.

'Aziz, open the door,' I called, knocking on it. 'Open the door, it is me.'

'Go away, go away . . . for God's sake, go away,' I heard him say feebly from just inside the room. I stood there indecisively, worried. I was about to knock again when I heard his voice. 'Munir Sahib, please go away now, I am ill and cannot do anything.'

'Why did you leave the hospital? What has happened to you? Aziz, I want to talk to you. If you are my friend, then open the door.'

'I cannot open it, Munir Sahib, please go away.' He choked on a scream. He was sobbing, sitting somewhere near the door. I was unable to speak and I was not in a position to compel him to open the door. I stood just outside and in this way several minutes passed. No one came up or down the stairs. The sound of Aziz's sobs ceased. There was complete silence. I tried to peep into the room through a crack in the door, but all I could see was part of the wall. My heart began to sink. I could not stay much longer in this tragic situation. I was being tormented, yet I was sure that if I slipped away and went downstairs and out into the street my torment would increase. I again ventured to knock but said nothing. I knocked a second time and begged him to open the door. I was thinking of going away when I heard him repeat, 'Munir Sahib, please go away now. I will meet you again some other time.'

'When?' I asked, putting my mouth to the door.

'In two weeks, maybe three,' he said shrilly.

What else was there for me to say? I was troubled and the dank darkness hemmed me in. Slowly I left. When I came to the main road I saw Aziz's father coming in my direction on the other side. I turned my face away and stood still. I decided to follow him and knock on the door when he had got home. I had a suspicion that he would be displeased if I greeted him now and if he noticed me following him would probably change his mind about going home. He passed me in his dirty old clothes, carrying the same cloth bag as before, wrapped round his fist. He walked slowly, his feet dragging. I followed and stopped at the water pipe to have a drink as he went upstairs. Then I went up and found the door ajar. Before I could knock I heard the same terrifying scream of Aziz followed by the sound of Aziz's father flinging something heavy on the floor, shouting violently, 'Some day I will discover the den of scoundrels.'

'I know nothing,' Aziz said in a scared voice. He appeared at the side of the table. I watched. Aziz had some notes in his hand, four or five ten-rupee notes.

'How much money is there?' Aziz's father asked, sitting down on the stool.

'I will pay for my stay here. I am fully aware that I cannot stay without paying. Whatever happens, I will pay.'

'How much money have you got altogether?' Aziz's father said in one breath. 'The rent must be paid. You said you would bring the full amount, now tell me, how much is there?'

'That's right. I understand. I know I have to pay to stay here. I will continue to give you money,' Aziz said in a hoarse voice. 'But . . . but . . .' he stopped and stood there looking at his father.

'Come here, and tell me . . .'

'Yesterday you beat her again,' he said looking at his father in fear. 'I had gone to bring money and here I am with it, but why do you beat her every day?'

Aziz's father didn't say anything and gazed at the floor, and Aziz watched him. Aziz's right arm hung down with the notes in his hand, his left arm rested on the wall. Aziz's father quietly got up from the stool and walked in my direction. I was about to knock on the door and let my presence be known, when he veered off to the left and went out of sight. I could see only Aziz now. Then Aziz's father came back with a cardboard packing box which he put on the table.

'Here, take this money,' said Aziz, 'but why do you beat her? I know you pushed her downstairs. Don't you know that you could have seriously hurt her?'

'She's a whore,' Aziz's father yelled. 'You'll see, even now she has gone on her evil mission. One day I will discover the place where she carries out her trade. I know her . . . I have known her from the time you were not even born. I caught her once with another man. I'm not even sure whose child you are.' The old man tried to say these words as quickly as he could. Aziz sat hunched over the charpoy.

After some moments' silence, Aziz's father burst out again with the same bitterness, 'You're all bad and yet you stay here. You send me out and then carry on your evil work. Leave this place, all of you, I don't need anyone. I will not keep thieves and pill freaks with me. You're a thief. I am certain this money is stolen.'

Aziz got up and said, 'The money is not stolen. It's true that I haven't worked, but I have not stolen this money. This is my blood. Go and ask Dr Yakub and he will tell you that I sold my blood for money. I thought that I'd give you back your blood, but how? Only in the form of money.' Aziz was leaning against the wall. 'Push me too,' he said, looking at his father, 'I will stand somewhere and then you may push me, and perhaps I will reach some destination. There are a few things that require a few pushes.'

He was so exhausted that if I had not come in to support him he would have fallen to the charpoy and then rolled to the floor. Aziz's father did not seem surprised at my sudden entry. I helped Aziz lie down and brushed back the hair from his forehead.

'I don't tell lies,' said Aziz's father loudly. He placed the cardboard box on the floor near the charpoy and started to open it with impatient fingers. I was anxious about his state of mind. He took a new, woman's blouse wrapped in newspaper from the box and flung it at my feet.

'Where did this come from? How did she get it? The same thing happened some months ago and she said she had received the dopatta from a house where she worked. Good clothes can be obtained only from well-to-do homes. Do you know who the people are who give such clothes? I do. They are the sort who drive cars. I swear she is not a good woman and I will tell the whole world so.'

I had stopped listening to his nonsense. Aziz lay motionless as a corpse, staring at the roof. The old man had gone back to his stool, had placed the box on the table, and was busy closing it, with the blouse in it. I started looking intently at Aziz and the thought suddenly occurred to me that this boy, who was less than twenty, would die soon. A cold wave swept through my body and left me shivering. I closed my eyes, took a deep breath and tried to forget everything.

Aziz's father had meanwhile returned the box to the small room. He came back holding a key which he put into his pocket. He sat down on the stool.

'Brother Munir, I want to sleep.' Aziz looked at me pathetically.

'Aziz, try to sleep. Your mother will come soon. Go to sleep. Don't worry.'

'Brother Munir, brother Munir,' he said, sobbing. 'You know I am not a thief, and I am not bad. You know that I have never stolen anything from you.'

'Aziz, go to sleep. We'll see about all this tomorrow,' I said holding back my tears. 'Sleep. We'll talk later.'

'Where is food?' Aziz's father spoke to remind us of his existence. He could not ask me about it since I was not responsible for such things in this house. Aziz was ill and there was no question of asking him anything. Aziz's mother was not in the house, so his speaking like this was nothing but an assertion of his presence. He kept looking at us. Just then Aziz's mother and her aged mother entered the room. The atmosphere became charged. Aziz's mother still had the bandage on her head and the old woman leaned against the wall as if the door had detained her for a while, breathing heavily through her mouth. The moment Aziz's mother saw her son lying on the charpoy she hurried over as fast as her weak condition allowed her and sat down on the floor. Aziz saw her but did not move.

'There are far too many thieves, and bad people.' Aziz's father got up from the stool, opened the door and went out. The old woman screamed in her usual inhuman manner. I went towards her but she gestured to me not to go close. It was a very gloomy atmosphere. I wished something would happen, some miracle to make the people in this house happy and well.

Aziz's mother took the old woman over to the empty charpoy. I wondered how the old woman had ever managed to climb the stairs.

'Munir Sahib, tell me one thing,' said Aziz from the charpoy. 'How can I get the power of acceptance for my prayers?'

I moved towards him as he spoke. Aziz's mother was staring at him, as if she wanted to preserve him in her eyes. Aziz looked at each of us and then, speaking like a man who was rapidly passing the last moments of his life, said, 'I desire, brother Munir, that in one sip of water should be gathered the maximum chilliness possible and that this should reach to the stomachs of all the cruel people and become a foul vapour that can never be digested.'

Aziz's condition was rapidly deteriorating. It was becoming difficult for me to stay in this room any longer. I looked at Aziz's mother, silently seeking her permission to leave. Without waiting I nodded goodbye and went towards the door. I had hardly reached it when I heard Aziz's mournful voice, 'Come back.' I stopped and turned round to find that Aziz had sat up and was placing his feet on the floor. Before I could reach him he had put on his worn out slippers and stood up.

'Look, Aziz, stay here with your mother. You need rest and sleep.'

'Brother Munir, please take me with you. I will stay with you for a while and then I will return. I will explain why the doctor used to tell me to sell blood, and why I did so today.' He glanced at his mother and then said to me, 'I agreed to do what Dr Yakub asked, but why did you take me to the hospital? The doctors there said they would have to give me blood, but whose? Liquid notes of money. They gave me an injection and two pills and then I slipped away.'

Hearing mention of blood and doctors Aziz's mother looked at us with wide open eyes. The references also caused a chill cold crack in my brain. I wanted to talk with him on the subject, only not now when he needed rest.

'I am sure that you dislike me,' he said, holding my hand, 'but Aziz doesn't dislike you, he can never hate.'

'All right, come along then,' I said and caught his hand and, nodding goodbye to his mother, left the room. Downstairs where the goats were tied Aziz drank water from the pipe and sprinkled some on the goats. 'You will see that this water will be absorbed into their bodies. Where drops of sweat can come out water can enter through the same pores,' he said.

'You're quite right, Aziz,' I pretended to be in full agreement. Every four or five steps he paused to push at some litter with his foot. 'Come along, Aziz. If you find a small piece of stone, an empty cigarette packet or any such thing lying in the road, why do you think it your duty to move it from its place?'

'Munir Sahib, things get tired lying in the same place.'

I had not the slightest doubt that Aziz's mind was not normal and that it was getting worse by the day. Poverty and deprivation had sown poisonous thorns in his home, and these thorns pricked him. He did not cry in pain, or try to uproot them; instead he was trying to find ways of getting used to walking on them. The way he mentioned the word tiredness gave it an involved and complex meaning about which I wanted to ask him. However, I realized that if I asked him one question it would lead to many others. The moment we reached the hotel I prayed that the artist would be in his room. As we entered through the main door, I saw Bashir sitting in the hall.

'Where have you been?' Bashir asked before I could say anything. 'I searched for you all over the place. How is he?' He looked at Aziz, and ordered the waiter to bring pastries, milk and tea.

After tea, Bashir said he had to go somewhere. We could accompany him if we wanted to. I asked Bashir to wait with Aziz for a moment and went upstairs to the artist's room to consult him about Aziz. The door was still locked. I decided to take Aziz with us. I hoped that the artist would be in his room when we returned.

Since there seemed to be no taxis, we decided to take the bus. Not many people were waiting at the bus stop: a peasant with a large turban on his head, sitting by the roadside with a child beside him and a few labourers, taking long pulls from their cigarettes, laughing and joking among themselves. When the bus came the peasant, his child and the three of us got on; there was plenty of room inside and we all found seats. The labourers must have been waiting for another bus, because they did not get on. I sat with Aziz, and Bashir found a seat two rows in front. Aziz looked closely at some women sitting in the front seat of the ladies' section. When he saw that I had noticed he was staring at the women in the bus he whispered in my ear, 'Brother Munir, that girl wearing the pink, flowered blouse, I knew her when she was very small.'

I paid no attention since he was in the habit of making disjointed critical comments on things and objects that he saw.

'Brother Munir, it's her all right. Her nose was like that and both her eyes were exactly the same,' he went on speaking while he studied the girl. 'Every feature is similar. It is as if she has suddenly been made to grow up and has run away from home to sit on this bus.'

'All right. There's nothing to get so excited about, Aziz.' I wanted to put an end to this futile talk.

'But, I wanted to tell her that there is a child exactly like her in this world. How strange it is, that someone may die and then later become young again.'

I decided that the best thing was not to respond. After a while he got up and stood in the aisle between the seats, looking at the girl with questioning eyes. Aziz was far too wretched in his green striped shirt and loose khaki trousers to attract the attention of any girl. Besides, he was staring at her in the most objectionable way. He then tried to attract her attention by moving his hand, and when she looked at him he raised it to his forehead in salute. Several passengers in the bus noted his actions and heard his voice clearly, as I did: 'I know a small girl just like you, she lives near our house.'

The girl only heard part of his words and turned away to look out of the window. Fortunately, after that Aziz did not feel the need to say anything further and stood quietly. I wanted to call him to me, I might even have dragged him back, when the bus stopped and the girl got up from her seat and, passing close to Aziz, left the bus. I heaved a sigh of relief, but then as the bus pulled out again, Aziz moved quickly to the door and got off too.

It was too late for me to alight as well; my actions were slower than my thoughts. I was very worried on account of Aziz. Before the next stop I asked Bashir to excuse me and I got off the bus and walked back. I wanted to find Aziz and take him with me. There was no sign of him, or of the girl.

I had not been back in my room for more than fifteen or twenty minutes when there came an impatient knock on the door and I heard Aziz calling my name. I opened the door. He came in and said, 'Brother Munir, I have found out where she lives. I will go and tell her everything.'

'Aziz, give this up. There is no point meeting her and telling her anything.' I tried to make him understand. 'Those people may resent your going there and they may not meet you with the same feeling as you expect.'

'I will persuade her somehow or other to listen to me, and then I promise I will do whatever she tells me.'

'Aziz, what is happening to you? This is not a world of promises. It is better not to go.'

'I will go,' he said passionately. 'You do not understand how important this is to me. I will meet her and tell her that Shagufta herself told me to keep meeting the child who exactly resembles her.'

'What?' I asked in astonishment. He had mentioned the name Shagufta before. Now when he said it again, linking it with a child, I realized that I should find out what all this was about. 'Who is Shagufta? Tell me all about her,' I said, sitting complacently on the charpoy.

'Shagufta is the name of a girl, Munir Sahib. I love this girl and I used to meet her,' Aziz began. 'She lived nearby and six or seven years ago when I was small, something happened to my heart when I saw her. I will tell you the truth: I loved her from the very beginning. For many years I was not aware of this love and perhaps I never would have been if Shagufta had not heard what I said. It was a cold day in February. Mother had gone out to our neighbours and my father had come home unexpectedly. He sent me off to fetch her. Munir Sahib, Shagufta was sitting there and she asked whether I wanted tea. I said I did not but if she wanted some she should make it for herself.

'"Wait," she said, "I will bring tea for you and your mother and I hope you will like it."

'The tea was delicious. It tasted like the warm juice of fruits. I praised it and asked her where she had bought it. Then, that small girl whose face resembles the girl in the bus arrived on some errand. Shagufta told me that the tea came from the shop of this girl's father. The tea leaves were gathered high up in the mountains, and she laughed. I liked her laughter. I wanted to take it away with me so that I could hear it again whenever I liked. My mother had finished her tea and it was time for us to leave. I wanted to talk to Shagufta, but what could I say to her?

'Munir Sahib, all these memories belong to the past. There are many cracks in them now where blood-sucking mosquitoes live who want to suck the few remaining drops of my blood. Tell me first, what do you think of me?' Aziz suddenly turned his eyes under their bushy eyebrows in my direction.

'What do I think of you?' I looked at him in confusion.

'Yes, brother Munir.' He stood up. 'Just imagine that someone came to visit you in my absence and asked you what you thought of me, what would you say?'

Aziz had been talking about his relations with Shagufta without any hesitation. He had not contradicted himself, or been sidetracked into irrelevancies, and so when he wanted to know my opinion about himself I could only heave a sigh.

'Aziz, you are good and your . . .'

'No, Munir Sahib, please talk frankly, because I know that my love for Shagufta is true, and I want you to tell me what I am. When I saw her lips move, I did not think of anything dirty or obscene. I did not want to lie with her, or with any girl. It was at that exact moment that I realized I loved Shagufta truly and she would respond in the same way and that I would get proof of this by itself, but I was wrong.

'The next day I went to the bazaar with the three and a half rupees I had saved for several weeks. I asked many shopkeepers whether they had the tea from the mountains. Most of them were surprised to hear about this mountain tea and none of them had any. I asked at the shop of the little girl's father. He told me that their stock was finished, but that they would be getting more in a few days. I went to other parts of the town asking for it, and at last found a little at a very small shop. I went to Shagufta's home with the tea and said to her mother, "Look, Auntie, how is this?"

'Shagufta's mother opened the packet and after examining the leaves said that it was all right. She closed the packet and returned it to me. Shagufta was not at home and I waited quite a long while for her to return, but still she did not come.

'Munir Sahib, I am tired and want to sleep,' he said, huddled in the chair.

'Yes, come to the charpoy and lie down,' I said, getting up from it. 'You should not mind what people say. When you have slept, I will go to your house with you, and to see that small girl, if possible. Please go to sleep. If you are hungry I will fetch something for you from the restaurant downstairs.'

'No thank you, Munir Sahib, I don't need anything to eat. I am not hungry, and now I do not even need to sleep,' he said, firmly sitting in the chair. 'I will sleep at night and the night is still far off. First I have many things to tell you.'

'Aziz, come and lie down,' I implored. He was not at all well, and anyone seeing him would feel that he needed rest.

He was annoyed. 'You don't have a good opinion of me either; you think I am not obeying you. I will sleep, but not just yet. I will sleep in half an hour, and I am sure that I cannot die before then.' He went on with his tale.

'I left the packet of tea there, imagining the tea kissing her lips, and passing down her soft and delicate throat. Shagufta's mother called out to me not to forget the tea, but I told her that I had brought it for them. She asked me to sit down. She said Shagufta would soon return and then we could drink tea together. It was a warm invitation. She made me sit beside her and we chatted until Shagufta returned. She saw me and went inside and then when she came out she said that she was going to see a girl friend who lived close by. When her mother asked her to make tea and drink with us first, she ignored her, as if she had not heard. I stood at the door and watched her walk away. I said to Shagufta's mother, "Auntie, I am also going. I will come some other day." The next day I went there and found Shagufta. The moment she saw me she said, "You brought very dirty tea. Where did you get it?" I told her it was mountain tea and that it required much labour. "You call that stuff mountain tea?" she said and laughed out loud. "The tea we gave you to drink was the real mountain tea, not that."

'Then her mother came out on to the verandah too. When I asked her about the tea she did not express any definite opinion, just said that it was all right. In my mind I started mixing emotions with colours. Shagufta did not seem to want to ask any more questions. I got up to go home, because my continuing to sit there seemed to me without real purpose. Besides, it was time for Shagufta's brothers to return home from the flour mill where they worked. They did not like my coming to their house and the younger brother particularly; he detested me and when he saw me leaving he would often say something nasty which made me burn up inside. I was thinking of going when Shagufta went into the kitchen. I followed her and stood in the doorway. Shagufta was looking at me questioningly and I was embarrassed. Despite this I said, "Shagufta, I want to do something for you. Please tell me what."

'"My brothers are about to return and they don't like my talking to others," she said hurriedly, turning her face away.

'Munir Sahib, Shagufta's hair was lovely, and when she laughed it was as if her laughter was praising her hair. I am not talking nonsense. I may not be able to pick up a weight of two maunds, or to run very fast, I know this and yet I can recognize praise, and it is a fact that her hair was being praised when she laughed. You have not seen her hair.' He suddenly put out his hands and spread the fingers. They came within a few inches of my face, and I drew back. His eyes flashed, his desolate face was pale and white foamy saliva was gathering at the corners of his lips. It looked almost impossible for him to go on speaking so much in his present weak condition, but all his old sorrows seemed to have drained from his body and he went on speaking.

'Munir Sahib, you do not know what kind of hair that was,' he said, licking his lips with his tongue. 'It was the kind of hair that could listen to you, and it could hear the sound of laughter, and could also see the comb crawling over it. I have never heard hair talking to the comb. Yet its beauty told me everything.' He got up abruptly and holding the back of the chair said, 'All this should not have happened in this way. It should not have been like this. You have no idea what was happening to me before yesterday, what my body has been thinking. Munir Sahib, is my body really mine?' He came close. His eyes were searching me to find out what was going on and what the meaning was of what he was saying.

'Munir Sahib, my body is not really mine. I went to Dr Yakub and sold it and came to you with all the money I obtained. Now I ask you to take me home and tell my father that Aziz's body is not really his body.'

Although his excitability worried me, I did not know how to calm him. He should have gone to sleep, but he was not prepared to. I wanted him to realize how sympathetically I was thinking about him so I put my hand on his shoulder. The moment I touched him he jerked away and said, 'Munir Sahib, Aziz will die and he will take the thought with him that his body was not his own.' He walked to the open window and stood there, lost in thought. Then he rushed to the door, violently tugged it open and closed it with a loud bang which could be heard all down the corridor. He stood still, facing the door. Then he went and stood firmly in the corner between the door and the side wall. He was breathing heavily, his eyes closed. I led him to the charpoy and he sat down on it, looking at his left hand with extraordinary care.

'Munir Sahib, this room is not the same,' he said, gently raising his head. 'Let me tell you. In that room two charpoys were placed straight and even then there was plenty of space. It was bigger than this and near the two charpoys was a small cot where Shagufta was sitting. I looked at her, came closer and said, "Shagufta, I love you." It was all I was able to say because she got up and said angrily, "You should not say such things." I told her once again that I loved her, to which she replied that I was mad and that she could not love a madman.

'She was about to go out when that child entered. Shagufta caught her hand and led her to me saying, "If you want to love someone, then love her," and saying this went out of the room. The face of that eight or nine-year-old child was exactly like the girl's face which we saw in the bus. Munir Sahib, how did Shagufta know that the small girl would enter the room and I would see the girl in the bus today? Was the girl in the bus a friend of Shagufta? Why was all this done in this manner? Why did Shagufta want me to love the girl I saw in the bus? I cannot love that girl. I love only Shagufta, and I will always love her.'

Aziz looked vacantly at me. His whole being was helpless and his presence seemed to be a mirage in the surroundings. I got up and went out intending to ask a waiter to bring refreshments. The artist's room was still locked and the corridor was deserted. As I reached the stairs, Aziz opened the door and peeped out. I signalled him to stay in the room, but he followed me. Perhaps, I thought, we could sit in the hall; he might feel more comfortable there than in my room. I locked my door and accompanied him downstairs. Instead of going to sit in the hall Aziz went out on to the road. I invited him back inside, but he did not answer and proceeded down the road. I followed him a few steps and asked him if he was leaving. He kept quiet. I shouted after him, 'Aziz, listen; I will come to your house tomorrow.'

SEVEN

The young men of the town were cowards as regards their emotions. All their desires and sexual urges were suppressed. They were energetic at work, and would somehow or other fulfil their duties, but they stood passive and silent as beggars before their sexual needs, hoping that some day a helping hand would miraculously appear and lead them to a closed room where there would be beautiful virgins clad scantily in diaphanous clothes. Their frustration turned them into day-dreamers. When they talked to one another about their fantasies, though interesting, it was like toy cardboard houses soaked in water; flabby and pathetic. They would climb the stinking staircase of their conversation as if crawling on their bellies, and not restraining the open display of desires born of their early, premature experiences.

These young men had devised various strange pastimes for themselves. They had woven a hateful net of the dirty, stinking fibre of words which trapped and yet falsely consoled them. If some momentary pain happened to find its way into their conversation, they would avoid giving expression to it. Until they were fortunate enough to experience the harmony of necessity, they tried hard not to drown in the gyrations of words and sentences. The sexual emotions of these young men had not become atrophied, but blocked off; their minds and personalities could only be saved if their sexual needs obtained a natural and proper outlet. This seldom happened. Usually they found themselves in an unhealthy environment where uncleanness sullied their desires. When they had such an opportunity, they became anxious to run away from it, taking their dirty bodies and thoughts with them, but the new situation which they then created was worse than the previous one.

The boys and girls were equal participants in the dashing concourse of youth. Although aware of one another's deprivations, they hesitated to give clear expression to their frustration, and their fantasies and desires were hidden behind closed doors which they themselves jealously guarded. Consequently their desires and dreams were imprisoned within the closed rooms of their minds, and as in dirty ponds the green scum accumulates and breaks at the surface, their suppressed desires used to rise and burst. Only they could hear the sound of the bubbles bursting, and knew that the poison from these bubbles would be absorbed in their bodies and join other accumulated dirt to become the impotent, wounded, crippled expression of frustration and failure.

The most popular pastime among these young people was listening to the songs broadcast over the radio, even though they were incapable of acting out the implications of these love lyrics. The lyrics helped them forget their emotional deprivations and supported their individuality with which they wandered about the town like a cloud of dirt in which their expectations could be seen as countless dust particles.

Fiazi was sitting on a bench outside a shabby, wooden tea shop drinking tea, trying to understand the meaning of the song being sung on the radio. Before broadcasting it, the announcer had read out a long list of names of boys and girls who had made the request. It sounded like a gathering of people licking the feet of useless dreamers. Then the singer sang about the most horrifying, unacceptable forms of longing and desire. The prevailing fashion was such that instead of being introduced to beauty directly, people embarked on improper paths, long and difficult, to satisfy their physical and emotional needs.

It was now three days since Fiazi had left the Bara Dari Hotel and two days earlier he had left Khan's quarters. He had found a suitable room at a reasonable rent. Its only drawback was that it was further away from the place where he had eaten for the last two years. He read about Kausar's murder in the newspaper, as well as news of the horrible murder of two people in the Bara Dari Hotel. The dead body of the hotel manager had been found in the attic; he had been murdered about fourteen hours after the first man, and they had probably been killed by the same person. The first body had only one large wound on the neck, whereas the manager's had many wounds, indicating that the murderer had been in a frenzy when he killed him.

The next day, after breakfast, Fiazi went to see Arif. He had no particular reason for going except that Arif intrigued him. Fiazi pushed open the main gate and went in and reaching the verandah pushed the bell. Arif opened the door, looking at Fiazi intently as he stood aside for him to come in. Fiazi sat down on the broad-backed chair. Arif sat down near him. He had barely been seated for three seconds when he jumped up and went inside through the curtained door. Fiazi glanced round the room. It was the same room though it seemed emptier in daylight than at night. Arif soon returned and sat down again.

'That day you went off somewhere,' Fiazi said politely to him, 'I came, but found the gate locked.'

Arif did not answer. He did not even look at him, he seemed to be trying to bore a hole in the table in front of him with his eyes. Before Fiazi could say anything else or Arif alter his posture, that same old servant, whom Fiazi had seen earlier, entered the room. Arif got up a second time and went out with him. He was away a little longer and when he returned he looked solemn and grave.

'Do you think that she actually resembles some child?' he said sitting down in the chair. 'Do you know any such child whose face resembles hers?'

Fiazi had not fully understood the meaning of his questions, when Arif asked, 'Do you know this child? Who is she?'

'I don't know any child. What are you talking about?'

'Riffat told me that a boy followed her to this house, trying to convince her that her face resembled that of a child. I suspected that you must have sent him after her and instructed him what to say.'

'I know nothing about this.'

'You do. Don't pretend.'

'Arif, I don't know you very well, and I am not concerned with what you are, but your life is so complicated, with so many twists and turns, that you will have to experience sorrows and grief. All I can say is ask whatever you want and give up trying to make matters worse than they are.'

'Who was that boy? That is all I want to ask.'

'I don't know of any boy who followed Riffat.'

'How did you come to know about Riffat?' Arif asked in a harsh biting tone. 'You said before that she loved me truly, but she did not know my real character. What made you say that?'

'I know nothing at all about Riffat and Azra, but despite this I can tell a great deal about your relations with them. What I will tell you I have gathered from you, although you have not told me all that I know.'

'Nonsense, utter nonsense. How did you get to know about Riffat, how did you find out all this?' Arif was speaking excitedly.

'I saw a note signed by her, and I saw Azra from the hotel window. I do not know why I smiled when I saw her.'

'Why, how did all this happen? What note are you talking about?' Arif looked at him sharply.

'The note was not in an envelope. I was leafing through a book and happened to find it. I thought that it was just a chit used as a book-mark. I did not think that anything of importance would be written on a page torn from a rough copy book, so I read it. What I read added fuel to my burning thought, and I could not help telling you that the girl was innocent and that what you were doing to her was wrong.'

'What do you mean?' Arif asked seriously.

'It is wrong for you to meet Riffat, and more so to go to bed with her. It will do you no harm, but will be harmful for her, and she has probably become aware of that. Certain things are harmful for other things and their effect can lead on to other unrelated things being affected. If a series of harmful effects continues unchecked by another positive force which determines the proper use of things, if this positive force does not intervene quickly to break the continuity and expansion of harm, then the death of the senses will follow without end.'

'I don't understand. What do you want to tell me?'

'That girl is not like the girls you consort with, so why force her to become like them?' Fiazi went on in his calm even tenor. 'If she herself wants it, then by all means continue to meet her, but do not compel her. Compulsion is a curse, a painful existence, dividing human beings into master and subject. In the master's mind it breeds sin, which comes subtly to wake dormant desires and stirs up the timid love of pleasures. To the mind of the subjects it injects helplessness, whereupon they become imprisoned within themselves and their deprivations and needs throw a heavy burden upon their breathing, and as a result the blood flowing in their veins turns in terror and coagulates and burns.'

'I don't have to listen to all this. Tell me, why did you go to that prostitute when you know that prostitutes do not really want to be kept busy in sexual intercourse? Did you not coerce Kausar?'

'When I went to Kausar I gave her money and she accepted it. We both consented to it. I never compelled her. I know that most prostitutes do not really desire that any man should come and have intercourse with them, yet they do want to be visited and paid. If the truth be told, quite a number of men do not want to pay them, yet they do want to have sexual intercourse. This is the meeting point of these two awful conditions. In fact it is because the environment is artificial and defective that such conditions continue.'

'You used to see Kausar: are you not the father of some child by her?'

'I do not know why you have opened this subject. She was ill. How could I admit something to her that was incorrect merely to support her delusions?'

'It is possible that you fathered a child.'

'Yes, I am the father of a son, but he is not here, he is abroad.'

'All right . . .' Arif wanted to say something but changed his mind.

'What is all right?' Fiazi looked at him attentively.

'Tell me, what made you start going to prostitutes?'

'I understand what you really want to ask. I was married, but my wife died two years after our wedding. After that I did not feel the need for regular marriage. I am not saying that marriage is not necessary. It is more important though to understand its purpose; without such understanding, marriage amounts to bringing helpless victims into this world.'

'Do you not feel any sorrow for the woman's death? Kausar's, I mean.'

'I am not sorry she died, I would not be sorry for my own death. In her circumstances, she should have died. If she had not, circumstances would not have remained the same. When he is in the grip of sorrow, man seeks to burrow deep into holes where he can feel safe and secure. At the same time he is frightened of these holes. As long as we do not know the proper place for fear and sorrow, our paths will never be clear. We should keep them in perspective. What is fear? Fear comes from ignorance and sorrow from losing knowledge of what we once knew.'

'Hmm,' muttered Arif. He looked away. A thought occurred to Fiazi, and he asked, 'Please tell me, why did you abandon that child in the hotel, and then come back later for it?'

'I would rather not discuss that.'

'Fine.' Fiazi was convinced that he would not be able to get any information about the affair from him now. A little later he asked another question. 'There is one thing I would like to ask you. What kind of a woman was it who was asleep in here that day?'

'Oh, a useless woman, an altogether useless woman,' replied Arif contemptuously. His lips were thinner than ever.

'But you told me she was your wife.'

'One needs a woman, but God knows where this one was brought up that she finds it difficult to understand anything.'

'She is your wife, isn't she?'

'Forget it,' Arif said, waving his cigarette resentfully in the air. 'I see no need to discuss this subject. Besides, I am busy and have to leave.' He looked uneasily at Fiazi.

At this moment there came a knock on the door leading inside at the same time as the outside door bell rang. Arif rushed to answer the knock. A few seconds later he returned to answer the door bell. He came in with the lad who, a few days earlier, had asked Fiazi for ten rupees' change outside the Bara Dari Hotel.

Aziz sat in the chair with his legs together, his hands in his lap. He looked from Arif to Fiazi and back.

'Have you just stopped talking about something important?' he asked, as if his life depended upon the answer.

Although Arif was a little surprised at the question, he did not show it and answered calmly, 'No. Tell us what important thing you have come to talk about.'

When Arif had begun to speak, Aziz lowered his gaze to the carpet. It was as if Arif was on the other side of a thin glass floor. It made Arif feel uneasy and he pressed his thin lips even tighter. Fiazi observed Arif and Aziz in silence.

'Should I go?' Aziz asked suddenly, raising his eyes from the floor. He stood up. 'If you wish, I will go.'

'Please sit down. You have come to say something,' Arif said, amused.

'All right, if you give me permission, may I ask one question?' Aziz's arms hung straight from the shoulders. He had the demeanour of a servant.

'Who is it you wish to meet?' Arif spoke in a harsh tone without even waiting for Aziz's question.

Aziz was nonplussed and trembled. It looked as if he wanted to take some weighty problem from his heavy moral and cultural overcoat. Arif stood up, waiting for Aziz to say something important. Aziz passed his tongue over his lips, shifted slightly and said, 'I want to meet the girl, I have come to meet her.'

Arif took a deep breath and slowly sat down again. Aziz looked anxiously at him.

'I will go, I promise. If you do not want me to see her, then please just go in and ask her whether Shagufta knows her.'

'Sit down.' Arif waved in the direction of the chair and took a cigarette from the packet. 'Tell me, why did you follow her to this house?'

'The moment I saw her I realized that her face was exactly the same as the child's to whom Shagufta had introduced me, and so now please go and ask her if she knows Shagufta.'

'Who is Shagufta?'

'She told me that I should see the child whose face . . .'

'Which child? What child are you talking about?' Arif interrupted him.

'She is very innocent. You do not know her, but I do and I also know that if you let me meet that girl once, I would ask her this particular question. Please call her out, I want to talk to her and then I will leave.'

Arif did not speak. Aziz went on: 'All right, then let it be. I will go away without asking her, what is the use of calling her, I am leaving, and it does not matter if I do not see her.' Aziz looked questioningly at Arif, seeking permission to leave, then took a step back and sat down, resting his head on his right hand. Fiazi remained seated in the same position. He had been on duty the previous night and had not slept and his eyes were aching with tiredness. Arif smoked his cigarette and silently examined the lad.

'Dear brother, I respect you sincerely,' Aziz said, 'but I do not know what you think of me. If I say that you think I am a coward and this is not correct, then I disgrace myself. You may think this or that of me, whatever you like. The only thing I wish you to understand is that I cannot say anything. What can I say, what can I say . . .'

'Shut up, shut up!' Arif shouted and banged the ashtray on the table. Fiazi was startled and sat up straight. Aziz's mouth had fallen open. He was held as if in a vice by Arif's eyes.

'Do you know what you are saying?' Arif curled his lips contemptuously. 'You are young and you are not in good health. If it had been someone else who had followed her as you did, I would have had him locked up.'

'But I respect you, as I respect all the people who are here.'

Arif glanced briefly at Fiazi, and asked Aziz in surprise, 'All the people? Who else is here?'

'The people who live here, I respect them with all my heart.'

Arif heaved a deep sigh. His mind was in turmoil. He wanted to examine Aziz carefully, then decided this would be futile and turned his attention to the packet of cigarettes in his hand instead.

'What is the most respect one man can have for another?' Aziz flung out. 'That is the amount of respect I want to give you. I am Aziz* myself, but your good name is much dearer to me. You people live in this house and the perfume of words is not sold here. I am certain of this, and that is why I respect all of you.'

Arif and Fiazi looked attentively at him as he continued, 'In a ship there are many people and many small and big things. These things and these people are further divided into numerous parts. Great as all

* Aziz means 'dear' in Urdu.

the parts contained in an ocean-going steamer are, my respect for you people is even greater.'

'Which people are you talking about?' Arif lit another cigarette. 'What in particular do you want to talk about?'

'I want to let desires and wishes lie undisturbed like clothes placed in drawers with mothballs, but you must at least do something too.'

'What do you mean?' Arif blew out smoke. 'Speak up frankly, so that we can understand what you are saying.'

'Things that are understood lose their power and it slips down to the dirty drains of our bodies.'

'What are you saying? Why don't you speak plainly? Until you can make other people grasp what you are saying, nothing will happen. All right, if the girl you have been following is brought to meet you, what will you say to her?' asked Arif with obvious interest.

'I . . . I . . . will say nothing. I will look at her.'

'Why will you look at her?' Arif was getting annoyed.

'I will just look at her. I will not let any "why's" come near.'

By now Arif had come to the conclusion that it was useless to talk any more to the boy, so he looked away and concentrated upon smoking his cigarette. Aziz got up quietly from his chair and started looking around as if he wanted to take in the whole room with his restless eyes. Suddenly he stopped, and going close to Fiazi, started examining his hair. Fiazi remained seated and looked straight ahead. Aziz stood beside him for some time, completely ignoring Arif. Then he collapsed on to the carpet at Fiazi's feet and began to weep. Both men in the room were startled. When Aziz had walked to visit Fiazi, Arif had had a suspicion that Fiazi knew this boy and that he had followed Riffat at his instigation, but now these suspicions were dispelled. Arif felt he should console the boy and stop him weeping in this pathetic manner. Before he could move, Fiazi tried to get Aziz to stand up and said, 'Come on, let's go.' Aziz continued to weep. Just then came a knock on the door somewhere inside the house, an odd kind of knocking. After a little while the noise ceased. Aziz stopped weeping and got up. He did not pay any attention to Fiazi and went towards the door that opened out on to the verandah. Before reaching it he turned and looked straight into Arif's eyes. He held his gaze steady and then slowly walked up to him and said, 'It looks as if all the girls have come here.'

Arif saw Fiazi getting up, he stood too and, placing his hand on Aziz's shoulder, said, 'Sit down, I will bring you tea.'

Aziz acted as if he had heard nothing and he spoke again. 'When all the girls come to one place then what happens?'

'Aziz, stop this and let's go.' Fiazi caught Aziz by the arm.

'But girls have started disappearing after coming here.'

Arif sprang towards Aziz but managed to say calmly enough, 'What is this about girls? Tell me.'

'Jinab, all girls who come here disappear,' Aziz replied in the same tone as before.

'Who is Shagufta? Tell me about her.'

'No,' Fiazi interrupted quickly. 'Don't ask about anybody, Arif. I will not permit it.'

'Why not?' Arif's lips returned to their thin line.

'Why do all girls disappear after they have come to one place?' Aziz was staring ahead vacantly as he repeated his question.

'Fiazi Sahib, don't be taken in by this,' Arif spoke sternly to Fiazi in a voice that was like the snapping of several wooden planks. 'If you want to go, you may, and this boy will follow. I want to ask him something important.'

'Arif, I beg of you, restrain yourself. I also advise you to give up all thoughts of Riffat, to sever your relations with Azra whose dead child's body you left in the hotel, and to try to give satisfaction and happiness to that woman who is your wife.'

'As you gave happiness and satisfaction to Kausar,' Arif replied ironically.

'That was different. Quite another matter. I tried to save her to the last, whereas this woman who is your wife is trying to save you.'

'Save me?' Arif said with a smile. 'Am I being threatened by floods?'

'You are a flood yourself, a destructive flood contained within a small space and spilling out to destroy life and its prosperity.'

'What do you mean?' Arif asked angrily.

'Jinab, tell me why all the girls who come here have disappeared,' Aziz said yet again.

Arif looked at him as though he wanted to crush him and said, 'I cannot say what you are and what the best way is of talking to you.' Then he turned to Fiazi and, pointing to Aziz, said, 'Fiazi Sahib, remove this thing from here. You are welcome to come whenever you wish, but please take this creature away now. I have an important matter to discuss with you but unfortunately our time has been wasted because of him.'

'Does this mean that I will never be able to meet her?' Aziz said going up so close that Arif could have slapped him.

'Listen carefully,' Arif said, his eyes blazing hatred and anger. 'Get out of this room immediately and go far away. Never try to come again.'

'Why?' asked Aziz in all innocence, drawing back. Arif might have thrown him out had not Riffat slipped into the room.

She had arrived earlier than they had arranged and she was completely taken aback to see Aziz. She could not understand what that boy was doing here.

Arif and Riffat had known one another for three months. He liked the girl very much and he made a vow to see only her, and not to treat her as another version of Nayyara, Saima Akhtar, Azra or Kulsoom.

Nayyara had been a student at a local college and had been fond of beautiful clothes. She used to tell Arif that she was not really accepting money from him, that what she took hardly covered the cost of sewing her clothes. Arif would hand her some notes, silently thinking that if instead of paying for the sewing of her clothes she spent this money on sewing 'something else' up it would be far better. A few months previously Nayyara had got married and had stopped coming to Arif for money. Saima Akhtar had been the wife of a bookseller. She still came to Arif, but she never asked him for money, only for loans; without repaying them, she kept her balance clear. She had a strong body and Arif gladly gave her loans, smiling at her and saying, 'How strange that this loan will not be entered in any book'. She would return his smile and say, 'Who reads books these days? If people were fonder of reading, I should not have needed to come here.' There had been other girls in Arif's life who had not left any deep impression on him. Then he had married. The head of the family into which he had married was an idle man, an inveterate gambler constantly in need of money. Once Arif lent him some money and he returned it. Gamblers, especially that kind, do not return loans. This one thought he should, as he might need to borrow again one day. The man had come to return the loan in person. Arif had refused to accept the money since he had considered it a gift. When the gambler insisted, Arif took it and invited him for tea. Over tea the man asked him about his private life, about why he did not marry. Arif replied that he was in no hurry, he was young and had plenty of time. The gambler's tone had changed and he began to argue that Arif was the right age for marriage, and that if he did not marry now he would be sorry later. This touched a chord in Arif. He replied that he would marry, but that it was difficult to get a good match nowadays. Upon this the man became silent. He stared at the floor and then said in a strange voice that he had a daughter of marriageable age and was prepared to swear that she was a virgin, and if Arif wished, then . . .

Arif asked for the man's address and said that he would call on him. This embarrassed the gambler. They were poor people, he said and smiled unhappily.

'What does that matter?' Arif had said. 'Wealth and poverty are not values, it all depends on one's thinking. Give me your address and I will certainly come and call on you.'

Arif found the man's house with difficulty. He consoled himself with the thought that he would not have to come often. He was given a seat and the girl came and sat down in front of him. The room became oppressive in the presence of her humility.

The man had three daughters and a son, each of whom had suffered some physical defect from birth. Arif noticed the defect of the eldest girl at once and it seemed to be a good quality to him. For the kind of marriage he was contemplating, he might not be able to find a more suitable woman. He quickly finished his tea and told the girl's father that he accepted the match. The man tried hard to hide his happiness. Then he said sadly, 'I have to make preparations for the wedding, but I have nothing. If I can get five hundred rupees, the necessary arrangements can be made.' Arif would not have refused a thousand rupees. He placed a hand on the man's shoulder and said, 'There is no need for any arrangements, everything shall be done simply and quietly. Keep these five hundred rupees for yourself.' The man was surprised and tried, unsuccessfully this time, to hide his happiness.

Arif married the girl and brought her home. After this formal marriage he stopped meeting Nayyara, Saima Akhtar and girls like them. Once he was married he did not feel the need to visit his wife's people or to encourage them to visit him. They came two or three times, but he did not give them a warm welcome and excused himself, saying that he was busy. When the man asked for another loan later, Arif refused it, saying that his carpet export business had almost dried up and he was unable to help. Then Arif, following up a suspicion he had had for a while, forbade his wife's people to come to his house ever again. The woman who lived with him was a kind of wife to him; she was physically all right and gave every satisfaction in bed. After a while Arif realized that she was changing. These changes were inevitable, because she felt that Arif was not treating her as his wife. Arif had to find a solution to this problem, and should have explained things to her, had he not in the meanwhile seen Riffat and fallen in love with her on first sight.

Riffat was angry to see Aziz in the room. She turned towards Arif but before she could say anything Aziz came forward, and looking straight at her, said, 'This is the girl, I swear by God that this is the one I saw in the bus.'

'Arif,' cried Riffat in a voice that was extraordinarily intense. Arif could not believe that Riffat could utter his name in such a manner. He wanted to find out instantly what was the matter with her, but meanwhile Aziz had come very close to him. He said, 'Please listen to me, I will . . .'

'Fiazi Sahib, take him out of here!' Arif said turning to Fiazi. 'Explain to him that what he was doing was not right.'

'But I did not bring him,' replied Fiazi.

'Then let me ask you this as a favour.'

'How can I force him to come with me? I don't think it is right.'

Arif did not want any unpleasantness between himself and Fiazi or Aziz lest it create a bad impression on Riffat. If she had not been there, he would have caught hold of Aziz with both hands and literally thrown him out on the street not thinking that the one he was waiting for would enter by the same gate and that Aziz would go on pestering her or start telling her exaggerated tales of Arif's cruelty.

'I will go nowhere,' said Aziz as he looked at both of them fearfully. 'Every girl who comes here disappears. I want to know why she comes here and why she wants to disappear.'

'All right, now go,' said Arif, still in control of himself. 'I will see you tomorrow. Fiazi Sahib, please take him away.' He gave Fiazi a look and then turned to Riffat.

For the last few minutes Arif had not been able to pay much attention to Riffat, because he had wanted to get rid of Fiazi and Aziz. He wanted to sit down in peace with Riffat and make amends for what had happened in her presence, and assure her that he had just met that boy for the first time and had real difficulty in understanding him. Arif moved towards her but Aziz caught his attention once again, 'You were talking to me! Very well, I will go.'

'Fine. I will be in all day tomorrow,' Arif replied with a smile.

'He is lying, lying.' Suddenly Fiazi's voice was heard in a strange tone. He moved to the door.

Arif did not pay any attention to Fiazi's words, all he wanted was for him to leave as soon as possible. Then he would somehow get Aziz outside the house, but Aziz quickly moved forward and stopped Fiazi and wheedled, 'Please stop, don't go.' Fiazi stopped where he was and glanced at Arif, then gazed down at the carpet.

'Come, Riffat, let's go to another room.' Arif reached for her hand, but instead it rose with the speed of electricity and arched through the air on to Arif's face.

It would be wrong to suppose that Riffat slapped Arif because of what Aziz was saying. That had only further strengthened her resolve to slap Arif. The real reason was, that before entering the room she had gone to the back of the bungalow and had met a woman standing behind the iron bars of a window.

Riffat had arrived earlier than the appointed time. The gate opened easily. She had only taken a few steps when she heard someone crying. She walked towards the sound. A paved path which had not been cleared of its dry leaves and bird droppings led her to the back of the house and she reached a window with iron bars. A woman was holding on to the bars from inside, weeping. When she saw Riffat, the rhythm and pitch of her crying did not change. Her cheeks were wet and some strands of hair clung to them.

'Why are you weeping?' Riffat asked her sympathetically.

The woman gave her no answer and kept weeping in the same way. Riffat reached out her hand to her through the bars and tried to console her. Arif had told Riffat that there were other people living there so she assumed that this woman was someone's wife or sister.

'Please stop,' Riffat gently touched her.

The woman began to dry her tears with the palm of her hand. She went back to her charpoy and lay down, her face to the wall. Riffat called to her and after a while again tried to attract her attention but got no response. After about two minutes the woman turned to the window and seeing that Riffat was still standing there, quickly faced the wall again. Riffat called her softly and waited for her to respond. She was standing there quite perplexed, when the woman got up and came towards her.

'Can't you hear me?' Riffat asked and made gestures towards her tongue, asking whether she could speak. The woman replied by signs that she could not. Riffat shuddered in pity. She made signs to her asking why she was crying. The woman broke out again, then suddenly stopped and, pointing to her private parts, made signs as if someone was having intercourse with her. Riffat was disgusted. She asked more questions with her hands. The woman's lips moved, yet no sound came from her mouth. Then she closed her eyes and kissed an imaginary mouth in the air and, opening her eyes, again made the same abominable sign towards her private parts.

'Can you hear me?' asked Riffat pointing to her own ears, to which the woman shook her head.

'Who does this to you? Who are you talking about?'

The woman did not answer. Then Riffat asked the same question through signs. In reply, the woman turned her face towards the door and pointed to it and, shaping her lips in a circle, started looking back and forth from the door to Riffat.

'Arif?' Riffat asked at once and tried to describe him through signs. The woman nodded in agreement.

'Arif, Arif,' Riffat repeated without pausing and rushed to the sitting room. The woman's gestures had filled her with revulsion. She thought of going away and never again returning, but she wanted to meet Arif in order to retrieve her letters. Riffat slapped Arif's face with all her might. 'You, you are the most . . .' Riffat stopped, searching for an appropriate word, and then completed the sentence,' . . . contemptible person.'

'This is exactly what I told him once before,' Fiazi said calmly.

'I will kill you, you swine.' Arif leapt towards the door then suddenly stopped and stood with his back to them. The presence of others in the house had prevented him from doing anything drastic.

'Listen, Arif,' Fiazi said to him. 'You have no standards, and those you think you have are incomplete – their foundations are weak. You are journeying in the dark and in the darkness are searching for darkness. It is most important to know the reality of things and to be guided in life by this knowledge. Only by the light of truth can one find the safe and sure ways of living. Dirty, indecent truth is better than a beautiful lie. You are on the wrong path and are not ready to admit your faults and weaknesses. You appropriate to your own use whatever you set eyes on.'

Although Arif listened, he did not understand. The only thought in his mind was how to get rid of Fiazi and Aziz and then to ask Riffat why she had slapped his face. He was not angry with her nor was there any thought of revenge in his heart.

'Arif,' said Fiazi, 'you are part of the abhorrent environment which prevails here. I do not name individuals, but those without proper standards are all tiny parts of a corrupt and filthy society.'

'Fiazi Sahib, please go away. I do not know what you are saying. All this . . .'

'Arif, who is that woman?' Riffat interrupted.

'Which woman, whom are you talking about?' he asked.

'You never told me you were a married man.' Riffat spoke with great intensity. 'What kind of a wife do you have and what kind of man are you? You're her husband, and yet in a sense you are not. What do you do with women? And why does every woman who comes here disappear as that boy says?'

'Who told you about her?' Arif looked closely at her.

'She may not be able to talk but I have eyes.'

'You have seen Kulsoom! You have met her!' Arif uttered these words as rapidly as a man could.

Fiazi was smiling quietly to himself without looking at anyone. Arif's lips were drawn thin, his arms folded, and he was staring at the floor. Aziz was standing silent, lost in thought, his thick dark eyebrows were lowered and he looked like a faded photograph.

'Arif, please return my letters,' said Riffat with trembling lips. 'Give them to me and let me go. I am not that kind of a girl.'

'Do you know Shagufta?' Aziz suddenly addressed Riffat innocently and went near to her. This acted as a trigger. Arif jumped at him and gave the poor boy such a violent push that Aziz crashed back into the chair and then struck the door some four feet away and lay still. It all happened so quickly and unexpectedly that no one could come between Arif and the weak, tubercular-looking boy. Fiazi reached him at once and found that his forehead was bleeding. There was no doubt that he had fainted. Fiazi laid him on the carpet and took a handkerchief from his pocket which he pressed against Aziz's forehead, then he picked him up in his arms and went out of the house. Arif was obviously worried and followed them. Fiazi stopped an approaching car and told the driver that the boy had been injured and had to be taken to the hospital. The man in the car opened the door without delay. Fiazi placed Aziz on the seat and got in beside him. Arif hesitated for a second and then, looking at Riffat, opened the front door of the car and got in.

There was a deep wound on Aziz's forehead. The moment the doctor in the hospital saw him he said that he was suffering from anaemia. His wound was stitched. There was a blue bruise on the arm near the shoulder which hurt Aziz more. They came out of the hospital, Fiazi supporting Aziz while Arif walked alongside, not speaking. He took out his purse to give Aziz twenty rupees but Aziz ignored him.

'Put them away,' said Fiazi to Arif. 'Twenty rupees is quite expensive for such a push.'

Arif said nothing and put the money back. On the way Fiazi took Aziz to a cheap wayside eating house and told him to order whatever he liked. Aziz said softly that he had no money. Fiazi said comfortingly that he would pay.

After Aziz had eaten, Fiazi escorted him home. While Arif waited outside. Fiazi went upstairs and watched Aziz go in. It looked as if Aziz had alighted from a train where no water or food was available. The moment Fiazi started downstairs, Aziz's mother called him with tears in her eyes and asked him to go in for a little. When he finally came downstairs he was very sad indeed.

Fiazi and Arif walked out of the narrow street and came out on to the road. Both remained silent and walked along together until they came to another road where they stopped in order to cross. Arif looked at Fiazi and said, 'I love her truly, believe me.'

'True love and true hatred, intense love and intense hatred. Which do you like?'

'What do you mean?'

'What I mean is that there is true love on the one hand and true hatred on the other. Which would you like when you are the source of both?'

'Love,' Arif answered. 'Obviously I prefer true love.'

'And hate? If you know whom you hate and why you hate and you consider yourself justified in hating, then in that case will you not be in favour of hating?'

'When I hate a person I will hate him and believe that I should.'

'This means that you know that you are treating that person quite correctly and your hating him is altogether right.'

'Yes,' Arif replied, looking at Fiazi.

'Now there is true love and true hatred. Why prefer one to the other?'

By now they had come to a 'garden', an open plot of land hemmed in by a barbed wire fence, where grass was allowed to grow. There were a few trees and benches. They sat on a vacant bench.

'Fiazi, I do not understand what you are trying to say,' said Arif, getting confused.

'In the grip of a moment of intense hatred you pushed that poor boy and you accept this as true as well as correct and yet you dislike it. This is something strange. After all, how can you dislike something of your own which you consider correct?'

'I did not push him knowingly.'

'Arif, you are an educated person, please talk sensibly. If you did not push him knowingly, then you pushed him unknowingly. Why do a thing when you know nothing about it?'

'I did push him, but did not know that he would be so badly hurt.'

'You are saying odd things, that the murderer does not know the victim will die when he fires a bullet at him. How strangely you talk. You should have known that there was every probability of his getting hurt. You talk and meanwhile lap up the cruel pleasures hidden in the consequences of your actions.'

'Fiazi, I really do not understand what you are trying to say. I cannot make out what is going on in your mind.'

'What I am thinking is of no consequence to you. Just tell me why you pushed him.'

'I was angry and could not bear it any longer. I tried to give him money afterwards, it is another matter that he did not accept it. I am sorry.'

'Are you really sorry?' Fiazi asked, giving him a searching look. 'Do you consider it bad to push the boy so hard that he banged into the chair and the door and then fell?'

'I think it is extremely bad. I should not have done it.'

'Arif,' Fiazi said after a pause, 'you felt intense hatred for the boy and sought catharsis by pushing him. Now you hate what you did. You hate the fact that you hated him. It means that you are destroying one hate with another. I feel, however, that out of hatred love is now arising. That is to say that the real hatred you had for that boy has been transformed into real concern and love. I now want to ask you, which do you think is more lasting, this true love or your true love for Riffat?'

'What do you mean?'

'You do not try to understand. You fling these words at me. Leaving aside what you like or dislike, what I am asking is, of the two loves, which do you think is more lasting? Which will be transformed into hatred, and which will remain in your heart as true love?'

'But I can also call this love a "non-love". When I hate a person and then stop hating him, I do not necessarily have to start loving him. I can forget that person. To say that I have true love for him seems to me absurd.'

'When you started hating this person your hatred went on increasing until it reached its maximum intensity and you expressed this by giving him a violent push. Your hatred for him ceased when you noted Riffat's reaction and also because of something in you. When your hatred ceased, you did not want merely to forget him. You have said that you hate this act of yours and, remember, that when you consciously come to express detestation for some hatred then it means that love has begun. It is a strong love which soon dies since we do not understand it. You do not believe in this love, but once we understand the psychology of the destruction of hatred by hatred, and this is strengthened by our power, it could prove to be an eternal emotion of love.'

'I really love that girl, Fiazi, I do not understand the rest.' Arif looked earnestly at Fiazi. 'You may not believe this, but I am willing to do everything for her.'

'And she slapped you in front of everyone. Do you know why?'

'I know nothing. I love her and shall meet her, despite your opposition.'

'Meet her?' Fiazi said in surprise. 'If you meet her, no harm is done to us. However, she has come to understand what is harmful for her, and has decided herself never to see you again.'

'You have met her before, I am sure you have. I want to tell you that you will never be able to delude her,' Arif retorted with some heat.

'Arif, I will not say anything more to you about this girl or any other girl. You are following a most complicated path in search of your own lost shadow. Instead of asking about what you have lost, you start harshly cross-questioning all you meet on the way about their presence there.'

'I may have given the boy a push, but I also wanted to give him some money. I wanted to give him even more.' Arif changed the subject.

'How much more? Thirty, forty or fifty? If you gave him some more pushes you could easily buy his life. Listen to me, Arif, you say that you love that girl. She's probably the same girl whose note I found in your book. You make much noise about being in love. Why don't you say rather that you want to meet her every day, to lie with her naked and want to see her naked? What you call love is your selfishness. Love does not desire to reach its goal by hurting anyone, it does not compel any girl to forget everything and to risk every danger and all kinds of disgrace to meet a person who merely announces his love. Love cannot bear the thought that the beloved should be made cheap and no "riffat"* be left behind afterwards. Your love is nothing but the stench of your dead desires.'

'But . . .' Arif wanted to interrupt.

'We cannot understand love like this, therefore we cannot see it expressed, and, not experiencing it in the right way, we merely

* Riffat is Urdu for grace.

recognize it through inferior signs. When the dust of our love is dispelled, when this fever subsides, we want to trouble and humiliate and disgrace those very people for whom we professed love, for whom we made love the subject of our songs. Love is greater than all other emotions; all other feelings and emotions die but love never dies, it lives even after a person dies. Through love doors of knowledge are opened that are beyond the reach of intellect. Love is not merely the name of a feeling; it is an organized and disciplined way of life, which gives out the scent of flowers which never wither and which preserves their fragrance with their everlasting shape and beauty. Love teaches selflessness and to those who spiritually understand its depth, love returns its very essence and brings them those incredible moments where the wings of angels begin to flutter.'

'Do you think then that my love for this girl is not pure and true?' asked Arif.

'It is not love. You don't love any girl, you merely want to purchase them in instalments with your charming ways and your capitalistic mentality. Love which is introduced in such a way, which is bought with money, which wants the satisfaction of physical desires, and engages in the trade of emotional bodies, is never successful. It proves never to be lasting. When the time comes it turns like sour milk.'

'I don't understand why you are saying all this. That night when I went with you to see Kausar, you talked in the same way. The truth is that I am becoming afraid of your words. I have never loved anyone except this girl. She slapped my face, and I should not have minded if she had done anything worse. I love her. In her presence I am not the Arif Nawaz who goes about with other girls. This is the real truth about me.'

Fiazi smiled and gazed at a large patch of grass which was being watered not far from them in the shadow of the trees. The water gave the grass a melancholy look. He kept staring at it and smiling.

'I talk to you seriously and you just smile,' said Arif, looking deeply at him. 'I am telling you the everlasting truth.'

'Everlasting truth?' Fiazi repeated, as if he were impressed.

'Try to understand my words. Keeping in mind all that you have said, I say again that I love her and always will.'

'Your philosophy of love is very strange. You will be angry at me, but I still say that you don't love her. In fact you are incapable of it. You want to meet all sorts of different women and have an odd sexual relationship with them. I asked you before, and you did not reply: tell me, what is Azra's existence in the mirror of reality? You were not the father of her child, and you did not kill it, you say; then who did kill the child? Why, if you were not responsible for bringing the baby into this world or for its death, were you carrying it around the hotel?'

Abruptly Arif got up from the bench.

'Arif, why do you do such things? Once you stopped me on the road at half past eleven at night and took me with you,' Fiazi continued, as they walked out of the garden. 'What did you want to ask, what did you want to find out? Tell me, who is this Azra and why did my smiling at her the one time I saw her, disturb you so much?'

'Oh, do please go away now,' Arif said and lit a cigarette. Fiazi realized that Arif would not tell him anything. They shook hands without warmth and Arif went his way.

I remembered how Aziz had left me, how silently he had gone downstairs from my hotel and walked away with weary and lifeless steps. I had told him I would go to his house, and intended to go that evening, but by noon I was worried about him and decided to go at once. Half way down the stairs I met Bashir.

'Are you going out?' he asked.

'Yes, to Aziz. It's important.'

Bashir stood silent. I went on: 'Come, if you like.'

He started walking with me. 'You know Aziz. Tell me what kind of boy he is. I have not been able to understand him. Who is he, what does he do?'

'Aziz is . . .' I began and faltered. 'Aziz cannot be described in a few words.'

When we reached Aziz's house the door was opened by his mother. She moved aside to let us in. It was obvious that something bad had happened to Aziz. He was sitting on a charpoy spooning up rusks soaked in milk, his left arm in a sling and his head bandaged. He took no notice of us. I went and sat next to him. Aziz's father and the old woman were not there. Aziz's mother sat down on the other charpoy, and she seemed as motionless as the charpoy itself. Aziz put the bowl to his mouth and drank up the last of the milk. Then he put it on the floor. How had he got hurt? I wanted to find out as soon as possible. Bashir walked over to us and stood close to Aziz. Although there was room on the charpoy for another person, he did not sit down.

'If you wish, we will get up,' Aziz said, looking despairingly at Bashir. 'Please sit down and make yourself comfortable.'

As he said this he tried to put both his feet on the floor. I stopped him and said, 'Aziz, stay where you are. Bashir Sahib, if you . . .'

'Yes, yes, I will find a seat somewhere. My sitting down is no problem,' and saying this Bashir joined us on the charpoy.

'Aziz, how have you hurt yourself?' I asked him.

'Brother Munir, do you know what wounding oneself means?' He paused, as if expecting an answer. He repeated the question and then answered it himself. 'It is a way of preventing an act of suicide. If it is prevented then the tears of a wounded person are shed, and these can be recognized by their reddish colour.'

'What do you mean, Aziz?' I asked, worried.

'I don't know what has happened to Aziz,' his mother said sadly. Aziz did not look at her and remained silent.

'Why don't you speak?' I said. 'How did you come by this injury?'

'I did not want to wound myself. I had only asked about Shagufta, that was all.'

'Aziz, tell me plainly, how did you get this hurt?' His mother wiped her eyes with the corner of her dopatta and told us what she had learned from Fiazi about the incident.

'Aziz, when I stopped you going there, why did you still go?'

'Brother Munir, brother Munir,' was all he could answer, then his jaws worked silently, as if chewing the air.

'You should not do such things,' I said to him. 'Why did you need to go back to that house? In fact, you are obstinate with your own self too and remember the consequences of it are not good.'

'Is it likely that when a person is forbidden by his own self to do something, that he would persist in doing it just the same?' asked Bashir, placing his hand on my shoulder.

I was about to answer when Aziz's mother got up from her cot, probably to come nearer, but Aziz yelled, 'Stay where you are, why are you coming close to frighten my thoughts? If you are a mother, then listen to your son and stay there.'

Aziz's mother stopped in mid-track. Without changing his expression, Aziz said to her, 'I had wished to hear you say that you had forgiven me and that you would put your thumb mark on that statement. Nothing is left, everything has been taken away from me. No one forgives me, no, everybody wants to kick me out. Munir Sahib, please tell me whether even God will kick a sinner out of his Hell.'

'Aziz, keep quiet. For God's sake, don't say such things.'

'No, Munir Sahib, please tell me where a man goes who is turned out of Hell, and tell me whether it is a fact that I have been expelled from there. I know that I am not fit even for Hell and that is why I am here.'

Aziz looked at me fiercely. I did not know what to answer. He droned on loudly, 'Please, tell me, when night comes, does a person in his grave feel it? And how does night descend upon total darkness?'

Bashir addressed me, 'Listen, can't you take me to that person's house where Aziz was hurt?'

'Who told you I was hurt?' said Aziz looking at him. 'Who knows whether that hurt might not itself have been a cure?'

'Munir Sahib, let's go to that man and ask him why he had to assault this boy so cruelly,' Bashir again said to me.

'If you want twenty rupees you can go there,' Aziz said. It was a strange remark, I could not understand what he meant. He lapsed into a dull silence.

'Aziz, go to sleep. We are leaving. If you like, we can come another day and we can all go to that man and find out everything.' I was not actually sure that I should be saying this and thought I should check with Bashir. Just then Aziz spoke. 'When you go to that place take me along. Never go there alone, and don't bother about those twenty rupees.'

Bashir and I got up. I was surprised that Aziz did not insist on coming with us. His mother rose in a state of agitation and hurried to him and took his face in both her hands, to kiss him on the forehead. Aziz wriggled away and said, 'There is only a little time until everything happens. It will happen rapidly, and what will be left then? What will remain? Nothing, nothing . . .' He spoke vehemently, looking at me. Again I wondered what was best for him, how to bring about a normal balance between his thoughts and feelings. All I knew was that whatever he said had a vague shadow of what was in his mind, he was unable to communicate his full meaning to others, and this meant that he was in a state of perpetual frustration.

'Why don't you leave? Go away, Munir Sahib, you, too, need rest. It is the right of every good man to get rest, and every good man should use this right.'

'Yes, we are going. If you need anything, please tell me.'

'All I need is for you to go and find a place to rest.' Aziz was still seated on his charpoy. 'When you go something will happen, but in fact nothing will happen, nothing at all.'

'What do you mean? Aziz, I don't understand.'

'When you go away, nothing will happen here, Munir Sahib.' He lay back and, placing his wounded arm on his chest, closed his eyes. I was about to say goodbye and had only got as far as 'Aziz . . .' when he suddenly opened his eyes and sat up and said, 'Sleep is the right of every fortunate man, and I tell you once more I will not be doing anything.'

'Aziz, lie down and rest.'

'How can I, when I know that sleep is a right only enjoyed by fortunate people?' A mixture of expressions crossed Aziz's face. Looking at him I really felt I was a long way from understanding his words.

'I will go to sleep. What will you do?' He addressed both of us. 'I tell you what to do, on condition that you really want to do something.'

'What's the matter? What are you saying? Stop this, do not destroy yourself for nothing.'

'Munir Sahib, there is something you have to do apart from listening to me. Only then can I rest.'

'What?' I asked quickly.

He did not notice my eagerness and went on, 'When nothing happens, should I believe that in the future nothing will happen?' He got up and came towards us. His mother looked from us to him, her mouth hanging open. She was shrouded in anxiety which seemed to cast its shadow over everything. Aziz gave his mother a glance and then took me to a corner of the room.

'Listen, Munir Sahib,' Aziz said very seriously, and so softly that only I could hear. 'I want to tell you one thing, and then you may go. Put my mother to sleep; until she sleeps nothing can be done, and I want to do something.'

'What do you mean? What do you want to do?' I asked, raising my voice a little.

'Death . . .' he said, fixing his gaze on my face. So I found the key to all that he had been saying. I was bathed in sweat and my heart beat unevenly. I went to Aziz's mother and was about to suggest that Aziz come along with me, when someone called him from below. I looked at him to see how he would respond, but he merely sat down on the charpoy as if he had heard nothing. The caller shouted again in a still louder voice. Even this evoked no response from Aziz, who sat impassively, his eyes closed. Aziz was called a third time, this time the voice coming through the staircase. I went to the door and opened it. It was the man who had walked away with the baby's corpse from the counter of the Bara Dari Hotel. He said in a clear voice that he wanted to see Aziz. I remembered his well-chiselled, thin lips.

'Please tell me your name, I will inform him.'

His lips moved slightly. 'Arif Nawaz.'

I went inside and informed Aziz that Arif Nawaz had come to see him. He didn't answer me at first, then, staring at the floor, he said, 'I don't need twenty rupees. Tell him that if I wanted the money I would have taken it when he first offered it.'

This made me realize that Arif must have been the man who had wounded Aziz. Just then came a polite knock on the door. Aziz jumped up, bolted the door and then shouted with all his might, 'I don't want twenty rupees,' and returned to his charpoy. We were all dumbfounded. I did not dare say a thing. Aziz's shout must have been heard on the street below, and I was afraid that the wound on his head might have opened again. There was another knock on the door and this time Aziz said in a normal voice, 'I don't need the money and will not accept any from you.'

'Please open the door, I have come to talk about something else.' The voice was confident and assured. Aziz went to the door, but paused before at last sliding open the bolt.

Arif came in. He made quite an impression. He was certainly worried and yet managed to maintain his dignity. His glance swept over us all and then he turned to Aziz. Aziz did not ask him to sit down. In order to overcome the embarrassing situation Arif took a few paces towards him and said, 'I am sorry that you were hurt so badly because of me. I have not come to give you money. Money is nothing. I have come here to ask your forgiveness.'

Aziz's mother could no longer control her tears. She sat down on the small charpoy and started to weep. Arif went over and tried to console her; he said that he was ashamed of himself, that he did not know what he should do.

'What should be done?' said Aziz looking at a spot on the floor near his foot. After a while he looked thoughtfully up at me and said, 'Munir, remember my words that in the end nothing will happen.'

'We should leave now. We have been here quite a long time,' said Bashir, sighing heavily.

'Do you live here?' Arif asked Bashir, staring at him.

Bashir was about to answer when Aziz's mother came over and in a heartrending voice pleaded, 'Please go away, all of you, no one lives here.' She was talking more to Arif than to us.

'What would you think if you were convinced that the girl's face resembles that child's?' Aziz was completely ignoring what his mother had said. Arif glanced at him and looked out of the window.

'Munir Sahib, we must leave. I can no longer justify my presence in this room,' said Bashir.

I hesitated, then said, 'Aziz, we are leaving.' I walked a few steps towards the door. Arif wanted to leave too. He told Aziz that he would come again some day to assure him on all counts.

Aziz did not reply. Ignoring the fact that Aziz's mother had asked us to leave, I went to him and said, 'Aziz, my friend, keep a hold over yourself, everything will soon be all right.' It did not seem proper to stay any longer then and I went out. Sadness enfolded my heart. As we went downstairs, Arif asked Bashir whether he knew the child Aziz had just mentioned.

'No, but I have seen the girl Aziz followed once.'

Arif was startled. 'Where have you seen her?'

'We were in the bus with Aziz when it happened.'

'And she . . . Well it does not matter.' Arif checked himself. Then he asked Bashir where he was going.

'Why do you ask? What is your programme?'

'No, you tell me yours,' Arif responded.

'I want to drink and enjoy myself.'

'Come, I invite you to a small drinking party. I want to drink today too.'

'Tell me just one thing, where did you take the dead body of the baby that day?' I asked Arif before parting from them.

'What is your name?' he asked me, annoyed.

'I am Munir, and I live in that hotel. Why did you take away that dead body and why did you not answer that man who said that he knew the child as well as its father?'

'It was a strange business. Someone had placed the corpse behind the stairs and then thought about fetching it again to bury it decently.'

'But why leave the body there in the first place?' I wanted a satisfactory answer.

'I don't know the details of the case.' Arif turned towards Bashir.

They discussed alcohol. It was not a subject that interested me and I did not want to listen. Bashir was breaking his fifth principle. I did not remind him of this breach and made my way back to the hotel.

Bashir and Arif walked along until they came to the main road, and there Bashir said that he no longer felt the desire for a drink.

'What is the harm? I am not an addict, but when I heard you say that you intended to drink, I prepared myself to drink as well.'

'Forget about it. Tell me, did you go regularly to that hotel?'

'Which hotel?' Arif asked.

'The hotel where Munir lives, the man who was with us just now. Does a friend of yours live there?'

'No. I just happened to pass the hotel and that is how I met the fellow who asked me to do that job.'

'Do you know Fiazi? He used to live there.'

Arif chewed his lip. He at once concluded that this must be the same Bashir whose name Kausar had repeated, insisting that he was Fiazi's son. He remembered Kausar's death, the murderer, and all the scenes of that night in a flash and did not know now how to answer him.

As Arif did not reply, Bashir asked him once again, 'Do you know of anyone who has lived in that hotel and has left it now to go and live somewhere else?'

'Why do you want to meet him?' Arif answered as flippantly as he could.

'Oh, it isn't important. I just thought, you might be acquainted with Fiazi.'

'I know him,' said Arif promptly.

Bashir stopped in his tracks and stared at Arif. 'You know Fiazi?'

'Yes. We have been meeting for the past four or five days, but I do not know where he lives.'

'You know him and yet you don't . . . tell me, where can one meet him then?' Bashir was deeply anxious.

'I've already told you, I do not have his address. Once or twice I asked him where he lived, and he refused to answer.'

'Do you know a woman of about forty with brown eyes? Or has Fiazi talked to you about her?'

Arif did not like to go into details. All he said was that Fiazi had once told him about her and said that her name was Kausar. She had been murdered by someone at dead of night; it had been in the papers a few days previously.

Now Bashir remembered reading about her and seeing her photograph.

'Look, here is the liquor shop,' Arif said. 'I want a drink, and if you feel like it too, I will buy enough for both of us.'

'No, I don't want any. Buy it for yourself only. I will sit with you and watch you drink.' Bashir decided to go to Arif's house, hoping that he might somehow meet Fiazi, or that he might have left a message in Arif's absence.

Arif bought a quarter bottle of alcohol and some roasted peanuts. Bashir also bought some liquor and told Arif that he would take it to his farm. They went by taxi to Arif's house. Bashir asked Arif to inquire whether anyone had called while he was away. Arif replied that they were going inside and if anybody had been, the servant would certainly inform him.

Arif pushed open the sitting-room door. He asked Bashir to sit down and left for some glasses and a bottle of iced water which he placed on the centre table.

'No one called while we were out. I have asked the servant.' Arif opened the bottle of water.

'What kind of a person is Fiazi? What do you think of him?' asked Bashir.

'He knows how to communicate with others. His words and ideas pour out in such a flood that they sweep away the thoughts and ideas of others like so much chaff and straw.'

'What should I do?' asked Bashir, shifting uneasily in his chair.

'You have still not told me why you are so anxious to meet him,' said Arif. 'Let me tell you one thing: he is not the kind of man who will consent to have even the most casual relationship with a person of whom he does not approve. Forget him, have some whisky.'

'It may not be enough for both of us. Don't you worry about a thing; just enjoy yourself.'

'A man is always haunted by a worry when he is drinking, and many people drink just to get rid of this worry.' Arif opened the bottle and started pouring out the drinks.

'But the worry doesn't go; it stays there.' Bashir indicated that there was enough in his glass. 'I am going to drink alcohol, and what I feel before it is an unforgettable dream.'

'Drink up, then we will talk about other things.' said Arif to him.

The quarter bottle did not last long. Bashir stretched out his right hand towards the bottle that he had bought for himself. He took it and started looking thirstily at its square shape. Arif smiled.

'These glasses look new,' said Bashir. 'I do not enjoy alcohol when it is served in an old, used glass. How much shall I pour you?' He removed the cap and placed it on the table.

'As much as you like,' replied Arif. The two small pegs of whisky seemed to have made him very cheerful.

Bashir poured them both double pegs and asked Arif to bring some ice. The ice cubes looked very innocent, like young girls handed over to the wrong people. Bashir put some cubes in his glass and some into Arif's. Arif looked at his and said, 'How "farhat angase".'*

* Farhat angase means delightful. Farhat is also widely used as a girl's name in Pakistan.

'Farhat! Who is Farhat?'

'No, no,' said Arif laughing. 'I am not talking about any girl named Farhat.'

'Then does that mean that Farhat cannot be delightful?' asked Bashir seriously.

'She can be, she can be,' said Arif, still laughing. 'I don't know why, but looking at dry gin reminds me of the tears of flowers.'

'And I am reminded of flowing mirrors.'

'Flowing mirrors, very good, very good.' Arif said happily. They drained their glasses, then Bashir poured out a peg each and put the glasses on the table and started looking intently at Arif's lips.

'You have surprisingly well-shaped lips, my friend. To which race do such chiselled lips belong? Lips may be thin or well shaped, but the beauty of your ruby lips is undeniable. What would happen if your lips were on my face and my lips on yours?'

'What would happen?'

'This was my question and you must not steal it.'

'I am no thief, but you have certainly been stolen from somewhere,' said Arif taking a sip. 'No, I did not mean to offend you, Bashir. You are my friend.'

'I didn't tell Munir the last two principles of drinking, but I will tell you,' Bashir said seriously.

'Bashir, what I said was a joke, nothing else.' Arif laughed.

'Do you live here alone?' Bashir's tone was back to normal.

'Yes, quite alone and far from everything. Do you think I should or should not live like this?' Arif began to feel deeply serious.

A little later, the old servant brought hot food, with plenty of meat. Arif and Bashir did not talk about anything in particular as they ate. After the meal they were silent, then someone knocked at the main gate.

'It sounds like the knock of the waves of the sea. I wonder who has landed on the shore,' Arif said in an alcoholic haze.

'Perhaps that boy again.'

'He was indeed a strange boy. I will go and see.' Arif got up carefully and was almost at the door when the old servant entered and said, 'The man who came this morning has come again.'

'Man, what man?' Arif went out, followed by the servant. Bashir stood up. He heard Arif inviting someone in.

'Who wants to meet me?' the visitor asked in response to a question by Arif. They entered. Bashir knew at once that the man before him could be none other than Fiazi.

'Arif, I think you may be drunk,' Fiazi said. 'I must go back. I only came to tell you to wait for me tomorrow at four o'clock in the afternoon. It is important.'

'I realize that is important, but here is someone who wants to talk to you about some important matters,' said Arif. He pointed to Bashir and sat down on a chair.

'What do you mean?' Fiazi examined Bashir intently and they both took their seats too.

Arif did not speak. He was being as aloof and indifferent as the day he had been present at the scene between Fiazi and Kausar, except that this time his eyes were misty with some happy thoughts, like a solitary traveller resting under a shady tree in some lonely spot recalling pleasant memories. Bashir, too, sat quietly, trying to keep control of himself, but the effort was like building a house with bricks of ice.

'I have some things I want to talk to you about,' Bashir raised his head and addressed Fiazi.

'Go ahead,' said Fiazi laconically.

'Do you know me? Or have you seen me before?'

'No, I am afraid not. Please introduce yourself. Only then can we talk comfortably.'

'Do you know of a woman with brown eyes who used to go to Safdar Sahib's house?'

'Safdar Sahib? A woman who used to go to his house? I really don't know who you are talking about.'

'I want to ask you, whether you know . . .' Bashir broke off in mid-sentence, glanced for a moment at Arif and then began looking at the wall clock. Instead of getting up and leaving the two to talk in private, Arif withdrew by closing his eyes, now assuming the pose of the solitary traveller who has closed his eyes to rest for a while.

'Please feel free to talk. I will answer you correctly,' Fiazi tried to reassure Bashir.

'Fiazi Sahib . . .' Arif said with closed eyes. 'This is Bashir. He is asking about Kausar who was murdered a few days ago, her name was in the papers.'

'Bashir . . .' Fiazi said the name slowly, emphasizing it. 'How did you come here? Well, never mind. Briefly, let me tell you that I have no knowledge of your real parents. Kausar used to claim that you were her son, but I could not bring myself to believe her.'

'How did you know her? Who was she?'

'Let me just say that you should think of her as a victim of cruel circumstance. She suffered much and was mentally disturbed by the time of her murder.'

'Mentally disturbed? What do you mean? Please come with me.' Bashir stood up with a jerk. He was somewhat intoxicated by the whisky and gin but his alacrity was remarkable. Fiazi got up too and followed him out. When they left Arif reckoned with detachment that there were three possibilities: one, that Bashir was the common child of Fiazi and Kausar, two, that Bashir may have been Kausar's son but not Fiazi's, and, three, that Bashir's parents were other people and Kausar had obtained him from somewhere just like that other small boy. Where had Bashir been all these years? Who had brought him up? Arif did not know the answer to all these questions, his brain was too befuddled. He stretched out his legs and again closed his eyes.

They walked in silence. After a while Bashir opened the conversation, saying, 'I should like to ask you some questions. Please answer me, fully.'

Fiazi remained quiet. Bashir started talking again. 'Did Safdar Sahib . . . no, first tell me whether you know Safdar Sahib. He lives in Munshi Gunj and his wife's name is Farzana.'

'I'm sorry, I know nothing about them. Both their names are unknown to me,' Fiazi said to him.

'You knew Kausar. What was the nature of your relationship with her? Why did she tell you that I was her son? Why did she make such a claim? Is it true that I was her son, or was I the son of someone else? Please tell me all that you know about me.'

Fiazi did not answer immediately. After a while he looked at Bashir and said, 'You have raised many questions. However, the last was the most comprehensive and, in my opinion, this is the only one you should have asked. Your name was mentioned to me by a prostitute. Don't be scared by the word 'prostitute', form an opinion after I have had my say. I started visiting this woman years ago. After a long time she told me that she had a son and she wanted to make me his father. I had never imagined that this might be possible. I told her that you cannot have ready-made parents, and sons are not made like this. They have to be moulded. Nevertheless she insisted that I should accept the fatherhood of a boy.'

'I don't understand any of this,' Bashir said aggressively.

'The fact is that such women suffer from a strong sense of deprivation. Kausar was one of them and terribly conscious of it and on one occasion she even tried to commit suicide. I was there and was able to prevent it. Then she was murdered. I think now that if she had not been murdered she would have attempted to commit suicide again and would have succeeded.'

'Who knows? Perhaps you murdered her,' Bashir blurted out.

Fiazi stared at him.

'Who are you anyway?' Bashir asked with slow deliberation.

'You might ask me more politely to introduce myself.'

Bashir gave him a long look and went on walking.

'Whatever I may be, I can be of no use to you,' Fiazi said in a calm, steady voice. 'I go right here. Which road will you take?'

'I shall stay with you and go nowhere.' Bashir's tone was cold and determined, as if he had reached some inner resolve.

'With me? What will you gain by staying with me? It is night. You should go and rest.'

'Rest?' Bashir said in a strange tone.

'If you are not in the mood for rest, then you should decide for yourself what to do. I no longer wish you to follow me.'

'I will not follow you, but Fiazi Sahib, please tell me who my parents were.' Bashir was wheedling now. 'Safdar Sahib said you could give me the information I needed, and so did that woman . . . Who was she? Where did she come from?'

'I advise you not to waste time and energy searching for mythical parents. You would be occupied more profitably in starting a search for children of your own. That would bring new parents into being and then you would not need your parents so much.'

'I want to meet my parents. That is just my problem.'

'When you marry, this problem will go and then, in time, you will receive all that you are now searching for.'

'Please tell me what I should do.'

'Rather than forget everything, acquire the power to forget some things, pay heed to time and let it solve your problems. Give up trying to find those things that have been lost in the past.'

'Did I not have parents?'

'No child comes into the world without parents,' Fiazi answered him.

'What should I do? What should I do?' Bashir ignored what Fiazi had said.

'You must give your inner powers a chance to recover. Everything is possible, limbs can be amputated and rejoined, feeling too can be killed and new feelings can be aroused. No operation is needed, because man has within him a well filled with virtue and power, and we often do not realize that we have this unlimited store within us. Go down into this well, unlock the doors of new emotions and feelings. Do not escape from yourself in your sleep, but go closer so that you can arrange things in some order and when the sun rises or night falls, things should be able to communicate to you and provide you with a sense of direction. Stop wandering about causing trouble wherever you go.' Fiazi held out his hand. 'I want to go now, perhaps we'll meet again. Until then, permit me to leave.'

Bashir parted from Fiazi in a strange mood. He felt as if he was travelling inside himself. He wanted to go to the Bara Dari Hotel to see Munir. He hailed a motor rickshaw, then told the driver instead to take him to Arif's house.

The clock stood at a quarter past ten when Bashir entered the room. Arif was still sitting in the same chair. He had had no more gin. He had had enough for one evening and felt slightly drunk.

'Where did Fiazi take you?' Arif asked when Bashir was seated. 'What did he talk about?'

Bashir did not answer. Arif got up, and came over. 'Anything he said about you is incorrect. However, I don't want to discuss these matters with you. Fiazi is an intelligent person, but he is difficult to understand and that is what I like about him.'

Bashir still did not say a word. He was staring gravely at the carpet, his legs crossed. Then he slowly got up and went to the window and said, 'I do not know why I have come here.' He was lost in his thoughts and did not look at Arif.

'You have met Fiazi now. What did he say?'

'Arif, what do you do?' Bashir caught the handle of the window. 'You live here and this place is so quiet. Don't you get bored with this silence?'

Arif only smiled.

'I want to meet a girl,' Bashir suddenly said. 'It is an odd kind of request, but I want to talk to a girl.'

'Talk?' Arif said laughing. 'What will be the nature of your conversation?'

'I will watch the reflections of my words on her body. Then I will either wipe out those reflections or will take them for sketches and start colouring them in as I like.'

'Very good, very good.' Arif laughed out loud.

'Arif Nawaz, saying your name gives me a lot of pleasure. I am not flattering you, just expressing what I feel at the moment. Your name sounds as if it is made of twisted ropes. It has many layers of sound and it seems very firm and strong. When I say it, the image of a rope stretched tight between two trees comes to mind. Tell me, what do you feel when you pronounce my name? Let us talk frankly to one another.'

'What is your name?' Arif looked at him. 'Before I hear it and tell you what I think of it, listen to this. While asking "what is your name?" I felt as if small tin cans were being thrown downstairs. Now tell me what you want to ask. You want to know what I feel when I pronounce your name. Bashir. This is your name, isn't it? It sounds like one of one's own bones being scratched with a knife, a sound few people can hear.'

Arif turned very serious. It was as if he could actually hear the sound of the knife scratching one of his bones.

'Bashir . . .' Arif looked at him with narrowed eyes. 'You are sad and worried, but there was a time when I was more sad and worried than you.'

'Yes, I am sad. I cannot find the reason for this sadness and this is what causes me so much pain. Perhaps you were sadder than I am, and your worries have come full circle to where they started. Yet my worries are not really worries, rather frightening delusions that haunt me and which I cannot understand. We have dreams when we sleep and when we wake up we are certain that we are out of the world of dreams. I feel that for the last twenty-four years I have been seeing a continuous dream. Arif, I want to get out of it, but I cannot find the way. Before my eyes there is one dream and it paralyses me. You are outside this dream and cannot imagine the torture I endure. I am sick of it and it seems to me that I am a prisoner bound in ropes. It is an old dream, yet it is also the sum total of the contradictions of the present, and it has the power to sustain itself. This is my situation. When will this dream disappear, when will it . . . vanish?' He became more and more excited as he spoke and by the end of his outburst he was exhausted and sat down on the chair.

'Have you ever truly loved?' Arif asked him.

'All loves and all the partisans of loves have left me, and the feelings through which I claimed to recognize things and people have gone to unknown destinations. What can I say when all memories became deceptive? Whatever I say will be based on ignorance, will express the pain of frustration, and will be a part of the never-ending dream. Arif, I told you that on hearing your name I thought of a strong rope, one that is fixed between two trees. Each strand of the rope is firmly bound to other strands and, most important, it links two large trees into one relationship. Where am I, though? What am I? I am nothing but the victim of cruel dreams. My dream told me the name of two trees and the rope tied between them, yet nothing about myself. If I am not released from this dream, I will never be free. You live here without worry. If you have to go somewhere you do not carry your worries with you, and if you stay here, you are not plagued by them. You are free to do as you please, and that is why I asked what you did and how you lived.'

'I sleep with pregnant women, and foster dumb sins,' Arif replied matter-of-factly.

Bashir kept quiet, not understanding what he heard. Arif had not realized that he would say what he did, but there was no sign of regret on his face. He sat there calmly, not giving a clue to what he was thinking. He remembered the dead baby which he had taken from Azra, the corpse which he had picked up from the counter of the Bara Dari Hotel and had taken away.

The woman had been about twenty-two and Arif had seen her sitting in the hospital garden. At her side there was a large handkerchief with food in it. An older woman was with her. Arif went up to them and asked sympathetically, 'Have you found the doctor?' The older woman's eyes filled with tears and she looked at him half in hope, half in despair and said, 'Yes, we met the doctor. We have just come from him. He says that no place is available unless we take a private room, and if we don't want to be admitted then the medicines can be used at home.'

'Where is the prescription?' Arif spoke in the tone of a doctor.

'Who cares for the poor? Everyone is cruel and callous. We could buy a month's food with the expensive medicines that doctor prescribed.' She gave him the prescription.

Arif looked at it. There was a long list of medicines on it. The old woman had folded it several times which had left creases in the paper.

It is easy to trap women in hospitals. Arif was convinced of this and had never doubted his ability in picking them up there. He had happened to be passing the general hospital and had spotted these two women, one of whom was pregnant. The sight of the pregnant woman aroused him and he yielded at once to the temptation.

Some months previously he had met a beggar woman wearing a threadbare black burqa on the pavement. Through the fine gauze veil over her eyes he had noted that she was not too old. When she approached him he asked her why she did not work, and got no reply.

He then asked her to come along with him and he would get her some work in a household. The beggar woman understood the kind of work she would have to do and quietly told him that it would cost him ten rupees. Arif laughed at this and made up his mind then and there not to do any such thing with her, that he would only look at her naked body. He signed to the woman to follow him and took her to a friend's room. Before entering, the beggar woman looked around to satisfy herself that there was no one else there. Arif paid her and then told her to take off her clothes. She asked him to put out the light which he did. He took off his shirt and vest. If he had not, the woman might have been suspicious. She took off her shalwar and threw it on the floor under the charpoy. Arif asked her why she threw it on the floor. She lay down quietly and gave no answer. Arif got up and switched on the light. She crooked her knees and legs over her body and clasped her hands over her breasts and asked him to put out the light. Her body was rather corpulent, and had swallowed many one anna and four anna coins. Arif caressed her soft neck where the skin was still firm.

'A woman's neck is the last part of the body to show age,' he thought as he gently pressed his palm over her neck. The woman's lips were dark, and although her teeth had never been cleaned, no unpleasant smell came from them when he bent down. His eyes caressed her body for some time. Somehow he had persuaded her to stay like this with the light on. Then he gave her another five rupees and asked her to show herself walking around the room. During these few minutes his eyes were drawn to her body like magnets. He felt the urge to get his money's worth, but since he had decided to refrain at the start, he got up and put on his vest and shirt and asked what her father did. She told him that he was a tailor, and Arif thought all at once that this woman was an enemy of tailors and vilifying them. He had come to the conclusion that she was not a professional beggar and that she was doing this on the side; why then was she selling herself so cheaply? Even now she could, if she wished, get more than ten rupees. Perhaps she came from somewhere outside town and did not know the local rates? The woman was dressed and had put on her burqa and was ready to leave the room when Arif told her, 'If you got a decent burqa and bought light sandals, you would be able to ask for thirty or forty rupees instead of only ten.'

'Afterwards they would still pay ten and say that was all they had.'

He remembered that incident now, just as he remembered the woman's light brown body. He examined the prescription and found that nothing was written on the reverse. 'Have you asked the chemist about these medicines?' he asked.

'Son, this prescription is for three days and the shopkeeper says that the medicines cost forty-five rupees.'

'Forty-five rupees is too much.' Arif said. 'Where do you live? Why didn't you bring some man from your house with you?'

'I am a servant in a house. She used to have pain in her chest, and her eyes smarted, and when I went to work, there was no one to look after her. A neighbour used to come to look after her, and she told me to bring her to hospital.'

The pregnant woman had half hidden her face with her veil and was looking the other way. She had thick black hair around a fair forehead. The way her legs were placed as she was sitting on the grass lawn looked very suggestive. Her belly was swollen and the fold in the lower part was visible even through the shalwar. Arif would have paid no attention to the woman, if he had not noticed her swollen belly and felt drawn to her. The loveliness of her state aroused deep desires in him. She was about to give birth to a child, perhaps her first, and the expected arrival of the new guest had added a blush of modesty to her beautiful fair face.

'Do you feel pain?' Arif asked the pregnant woman.

'No Jinab, only my heart feels discomfort and dull, and sometimes my eyes burn.'

'This is usual and will go away in time. Rest and care are needed.'

'Are you a doctor in this hospital too?' asked the older woman as she helped the pregnant woman to get up. 'There are yet some good people in this world.'

'I will buy you the medicines. You should have her admitted to some other hospital.'

'Son, now that we have met you, do something for us, please,' the older woman begged sadly.

'Come with me, let us first buy the medicines. Then we shall see about getting her a place in hospital.'

Arif bought them the three medicines and twelve analgesic tablets to alleviate the pain. The old woman took the packets and asked when the younger woman would be admitted. Arif told them to wait. He hurried to the chemist and bought himself a tonic and when he came back he told the women that he had phoned somewhere and had been told that there was no place available. He said he would take them to their home and would try to get her a place quickly.

Arif took the two women to their place behind the Bara Dari Hotel, at the back of the compound of a dilapidated building. They lived in one of a row of four similar rooms. The room was shabby and poor. Arif assured them again that he would return as soon as he had settled things.

The old woman blessed him and thanked him profusely and the pregnant woman looked at him with grateful eyes. It was then he learnt that her name was Azra.

Arif was back by eight that evening. His servant had come in the taxi with him, mainly for appearances. The old woman opened the door to his knock and Arif told her briefly that a room had been arranged for the patient, and for the time being, there was no need for her to come to the hospital. He would see her in the morning.

Arif had already told the driver to take a circuitous route to his place to make it difficult to identify where they were going. Darkness was falling and that helped. When they got to Arif's place, he and the servant helped Azra upstairs to the room which had been prepared for her. Arif told her to lie down and he felt her pulse. 'You are quite all right now. There is no need to worry. You have the packet of medicines and I will send some more in the morning. Go to sleep. Try to be cheerful as long as you are here.'

'How many days will I have to stay, doctor?' she asked.

'Not long. Your child will be born within two days and then you can go home,' replied Arif and, giving her a smile, left the room.

The first thing he did in the morning was to go to the old woman to reassure her lest she should search for Azra in the General Hospital and by evening report the matter to the police. Arif was offered tea in a comparatively clean cup which the woman had washed several times in front of him. He did not want any tea, yet he sipped it. There was too much sugar in it.

'I have admitted your daughter to a small hospital where she will get food and all the necessary medicines. All we doctors agree that the child will be born within two days.'

The woman was happy to hear this and was profuse in her prayers for him. He said, 'The patient is in hospital and the doctor will not let anyone see her for two or three days. Stay here and tomorrow or the next day I will take you to her.'

After putting the mind of the old woman at rest, he went home. When he entered the room, Azra was lying down and her long hair was spread out on the pillow. When she tried to get up. Arif gestured to her to stay as she was. He sat down on the chair beside the bed and began to read the labels on the bottles of medicine.

'How are you feeling now?' he asked, putting back the medicine bottles on the table.

'I am all right, Jinab, quite all right.'

'Do you need anything?' As he said this, he reached for her pulse and sat there for some time holding her arm.

'Just pull your shirt up a little bit,' Arif told her, letting go of her arm.

She turned her face to the wall and Arif pulled aside the sheet and slowly started to pull up the shirt which was clinging to her belly. He felt as if he was slowly slipping his sex organ into her. He pulled the shirt up to about an inch below her breasts and with intense desire and concentration examined the tight skin which was stretched like the bladder of a football. He liked the swelling roundness. Her shalwar was tied loosely, but she was holding on to its cord quite firmly. She had a fair complexion. Arif wanted to lick her body. He gently started to caress her belly with his hands. The woman pressed her tongue between her teeth and closed her eyes. His hands touched her hands and from there passed over her belly. As he caressed it, he felt indescribable sensual enjoyment. He thought that he had never before got so much pleasure from anyone. Suddenly he covered her body with the sheet and sat down on the chair.

'You need a massage. Here is the balm with which you must massage twice a day.' He took the jar of balm from the table and said, 'Take a little of this and rub it on your belly, especially the lower part. If you like, I can send the old servant to do this.'

'No, no. There is no need,' she said promptly. 'I will do it myself, it is very kind of you.'

'We are taking special care of you because we want your child to be healthy in all respects.'

He went back upstairs after one hour. Azra had not yet gone to sleep; she was looking through an English magazine which had pictures of women in various kinds of modern dresses. Arif had placed it on her table earlier. As he entered, she closed the magazine and put it down and, despite his gesture, sat up. Arif sat down on the chair beside her bed.

'Don't you feel tired?' Arif asked. 'If you feel any heaviness, then you should take deep breaths.'

'Hasn't my mother come?' she asked with her dry caked lips. 'I want to see my mother.'

'Your mother was here downstairs a little while ago, talking to me and another doctor about you. We forbade her to see you, because, for the time being, it is not good. Take your medicines on time and remain cheerful.' Arif asked her to lie down. He then put his hand on her belly and pressed gently at various points.

'Take off your shirt,' he said suddenly, lifting his hand from her body. 'I will turn my face away and you can cover yourself with the sheet.'

Arif's words had been well thought out. In due course he would strip her and lie beside her naked too. He was proceeding towards this gradually, according to a plan he had made in advance. Azra gave a light cough and Arif turned his attention to her. He drew up his chair close to the bed and pulled back the sheet and, examining the naked belly, said, 'Yes, it is all right now. Face the ceiling and take deep breaths.' She followed his instructions. After making her do this unnecessary exercise he started to caress her taut belly with deep satisfaction.

'Did you massage yourself?' he asked. Before she could answer, he found the cream beside her medicine bottles and began to rub some on gently. It gave him immense pleasure. After a while he removed the sheet, saying that it was very hot. Now Azra was only wearing her red shalwar and a white home-made brassière which emphasized her swollen belly even more. Arif used very little cream and his hands touched gently the area around her breasts and around her waist. Once he wanted to take his hands lower and his hand touched the hair below her navel; she made a hissing sound in fear. He came on to the bed and told her not to be afraid, he would not do anything; saying this he switched off the table lamp, whereupon she groaned, but Arif dispelled her fears with some medical talk.

'Just lie still, I shan't do anything to you.'

'Please put on the light. I will massage myself.'

'It's all right, it's all right,' he said more sternly. He felt that sternness was necessary at this point. If he had requested her gently she would have become cross and have insisted that he leave her bed.

Arif turned his face to her and said, 'I like you very much, my dear, and I will marry you.' He kissed her neck and licked her. She was sobbing helplessly. Now Arif was wearing only his trousers and underwear. He took off his trousers and threw them under the bed. He was suddenly reminded of the beggar woman. Cautiously, he turned towards Azra and put his arms around her and bent over her breasts. Only his wrists were touching her belly, the rest of his weight was on his hands on the bed on either side of her.

'What am I to do . . . what am I to do?' Azra said amid sobs.

Arif did not answer her. He pushed his hands under her body and easily undid her brassière and took it off. He had Azra's breasts in his hands. He was treating her body as if it was made of glass which would break with only slight pressure.

'Don't do this. For God's sake don't,' Azra gasped. Arif put his hand inside her loosely tied shalwar and reached for her thighs. He was feeling some discomfort because of his underpants and he wanted to take them off so as to be quite free. Now his underpants and her brassière were lying together, and he himself was lying with this pregnant woman. He kissed her lips wildly. Azra's lips were insipid and would have been unattractive to any other man, but he sucked them with great pleasure. His lips were on the top of hers and this way he was also stopping her from saying anything. After some time he started to lick her cheeks and neck, and it seemed that he could make her whole body moist with his tongue. Azra persistently tried to stop him, but he was not to be checked by anyone. From the neck he moved towards her breasts and placed his lips between them, then he cautiously moved down her body and placed his face on the tight belly. He was breathing deeply. He had no thought of anything, only that this woman had borne nine month's pregnancy just to be with him for this night. His weight was resting on his hands and knees as he squatted above her. If he had been caught in this position, the next day's papers would have carried a strange story. He moved slowly downwards and sat to one side and started to draw lines on her belly with his fingers. Again he brought his lips to her belly and began to breathe heavily.

'Please stop it, please stop it, you are hurting me,' Azra begged, biting her lips. She started to cough. Arif paid no heed and kept licking her, not minding the taste of cream in his mouth. He placed himself more comfortably on the bed and started drawing long lines with his tongue. After a while he passed down to her right side where the tension of the skin was so great that he was scared. He returned to his previous position and then moved towards her lower belly. From here arose an unpleasant smell which would have repelled any other man, but it did not seem to put him off. He continued to lick the belly just where the pubic hair started, which gave him much pleasure. He brought his face down to her legs and had reached her knees. He lifted up her legs. Now his sexual desires were fully aroused and his penis was hard. Suddenly his knees struck the woman's belly and her scream seemed to come from a dreadful cave of pain and fear. Arif ignored this scream and did not even try to console her with words. He put his hands inside her shalwar and then, feeling uneasy, slowly pulled it down into a heap beside him and started to caress her legs, especially behind her knees. He noticed that the woman's head was resting on its side, quite still. This brought him to his senses and he got off the bed and put on his underpants. He switched on the light and covered her body with the sheet. He quickly finished dressing, told her that he was going and asked her to put on her clothes. She did not answer and lay there motionless. He raised the corner of the sheet to look at her face and found that although her lips were moving a little, her eyes were closed. She had fainted. Arif gently shook her head and gave her some water to drink with a spoon. Azra opened her eyes and looked at him with great fear. The white sheet stretched over her body and the protuberant stomach made her look like a grave.* The silence in the room was like that of a graveyard too. Arif put the glass to her lips. She drank, a little water spilled over and ran down her neck. She covered her face with the sheet and began sobbing and crying. Arif gave her two analgesic tablets and told her to swallow them. She did not uncover her face, but continued to weep.

The next morning Azra's condition was serious. Arif went out saying that he would bring a lady doctor. He brought an experienced nurse from the maternity ward of a nearby hospital. Azra was groaning in pain. At a quarter past nine she gave birth to a stillborn child. Arif paid the nurse and sent her away. Then he called for a taxi and carried Azra downstairs in his arms and took her home. On parting he condoled with Azra's mother and advised her to be patient and to bear the loss with fortitude. The old woman took the dead body of the child in her arms and started to weep. She said, 'Please do something about this, how can we poor people bury her? Let us console ourselves with the thought that she was not born at all.'

Arif was surprised to hear this. He had no idea that the old woman would hand him back the dead body. Suddenly he thought of the nearby hotel where he had once been. He looked at Azra who, finding his eyes on her, turned her face away. He took the wrapped dead body from the old woman and carried it to the second storey of the hotel and left it in the small room behind the stairs.

'Bashir, it was a night like this when I left her alone in the room upstairs and came down. But let's forget all this, today you will see a dream within a dream.' Arif suddenly got up from his chair. 'Come with me and I will lead you to a bedroom.'

Bashir remained sitting and looked at Arif with surprise.

* In Pakistan, most graves are mounds, about one foot high.

'I do not deny that I am married to her and that she came here as my wife, yet she is not my wife. She is a shirt that one wears at home occasionally. Come with me and I will take you to her.' Arif was slurring his words. He wanted to convey his very peculiar desire to Bashir.

'Who is she?'

'She is the battlefield of dumb sins and I am fostering her.'

'Fostering?' asked Bashir in amazement.

'All that is of no matter.' Seeing that Bashir remained seated, Arif sat down again too. 'What's the harm in staying with her tonight? You know, you grow tired of a shirt after a while. My shirt will be yours for tonight. Use her and in the morning leave her on the bed and go away. Do not think that I will ask for anything in return. Go and use her.'

'Who is she? And you . . . and you?'

'Bashir, I don't want to hide anything from you. I will tell you whatever you want to ask me.'

'Are you married formally to this woman?' Bashir interrupted. 'If she is your wife, why do you not consider her as such? I am certain that you are not so very drunk.'

Arif laughed lightly and clasped his hands together on his right knee. His laugh turned into a smile and the smile was disappearing when he again burst out, shaking his head from side to side. 'A marriage certificate is nothing more than a receipt for a thing you have bought. Everyone knows that the real value of the thing is never mentioned on the receipt. I met a man and decided to marry his daughter. I brought her home after the wedding exactly as I would bring home a piece of furniture from a shop for domestic use.'

'Does that mean that you do not consider her your wife?' Bashir asked once again.

'No, I don't. If this answer pleases you, well and good. Now you will ask why I don't consider her as my wife, and what my opinions are on the subject. I think no further explanation is needed. I am satisfied with my attitude and that is enough.'

'Arif Nawaz . . .'

'My friend, I am going to tell you the greatest truth of my life. Bashir, I have been through strange experiences. Love was altogether unknown to me, it was like a place in some foreign land, but now I know that I am in love. Fiazi does not call it love, but I swear that I love her.'

'This is indeed strange. You do not consider her your wife and yet you claim that you love her.'

'No, no, I am talking about another love. I am talking about a pure, true love.'

'What do you mean?' Bashir looked searchingly at him. 'I do not understand.'

'I love a girl and this girl slapped my face. She was the girl that boy saw in the bus and followed.'

'You love her?'

'Intensely. I know that one does not talk about love; one only feels it. Love is in the heart and is not held up for exhibition. Love should always remain with you. Bashir, I tell you honestly, my love for her is infinite.'

'You did not love the woman you married, and you still do not, so why did you marry her? And having married her, why do you not honour your commitment to her?'

'You don't understand. She is merely a shirt that I sometimes wear. I have never loved her, I have never loved anyone, until the moment I saw this girl and heard her voice. I realized at once that I had always been unknowingly in love with her. The absence of love was like a vacuum within me, slowly eating me up.'

'What should I do? Arif, you have not been listening to me. Tell me how I can look upon the falling walls of a dream.'

'Bashir, listen to me. Am I not capable of loving anyone? To love someone it is necessary to feel it and I can swear by all the sacred things that I have a great love for her.'

'Will you marry her?'

'At the moment I cannot say. All I know is that I love her.'

'That boy also says something about loving her. Perhaps he was trying to tell us that. When you pushed him she was enraged and slapped you with all her might.'

'Nonsense, utter nonsense. She cannot love him. He is the sort of boy who must be at other people's beck and call and I pushed him after she slapped me.'

'Who is he? I do not know much about him.'

'He is a "body" that shadows you. Yes, that is what he is.'

'You went to his house to console him?'

'Don't talk about him any more, Bashir. I can deal with him by myself.' Arif's voice was harsh. 'If you want to find your parents, then go into that room.'

'What . . . ?' Bashir started. 'I'm not sure I understood what you said.'

'Go to that room and spend the night with that dumb body, in a dumb, quiet atmosphere.'

'How will that help me to meet my parents?'

'You were separated from your parents while very young. How can you look for them now? Even if your search is successful, what can you demand from them?'

'I will demand them to make demands on me.'

'What should they demand from you?' asked Arif in a thoughtful tone.

'Arif, I don't wish to marry anyone, I don't want to declare my love to anyone. All I want is to meet my parents.'

'Tonight you will sleep here, and colour your shattered dreams in that bedroom as you please. She is healthy and worthy of attention, and you will have to give her that attention.'

'I don't want to. Please let me go,' Bashir said and got up.

'No,' said Arif and stood up quickly and asked Bashir to sit down again. Arif's thin lips were twisted tightly inward. After Bashir was seated, Arif remained standing; although he had calmed down a little, the manner in which he stood there showed that he was determined to do what he intended, and could pose a challenge to the other person. Bashir stared at him, then lowered his eyes. When he looked up again, he found Arif staring fixedly at him.

'What is the matter?' Bashir asked him.

'Nothing, nothing,' Arif answered and sat down too. 'Bashir, you will stay here with me for some time.'

Arif seemed to be trying to make Bashir understand his purpose affectionately. Bashir noticed the changed tone. Arif's eyes were half-closed. He looked at the table in front of him, and spoke persuasively. 'I don't demand anything from you, I only wish you to stay here. She has a nice body, you will have nothing to complain of when you go to her. You are worried at present and I want your worry to be melted away tonight.'

'Who is she?' Bashir asked.

'Whoever she is, you have to go to her and spend the night in her room,' Arif said. 'I will not come into the room. Believe me, I will stay away.'

'Have you before . . . I mean, has someone done this before?'

'Go, I tell you. Go in without hesitation.'

'And what will you do?'

'I will sit outside,' Arif answered.

'Sit outside? What will you do sitting outside?' asked Bashir in surprise.

'You just go inside. A friend of mine from Lyallpur used to come and stay the night and when I gave him permission, he would sleep in that room. Before him I never thought about it.'

'Arif, you . . .'

'You do as I tell you,' Arif interrupted him. 'It is my desire that you spend tonight here.'

'Don't you have any children?' Bashir asked him suddenly.

Arif burst out laughing in a strange way. 'Bashir, forget all this, sometimes you are concerned about parents, and sometimes the idea of children haunts you. I have no child of my own, I take precautionary measures and give her birth-control pills. She is merely a shirt, I told you.'

'Yet she is your wife.'

'Who says?' Arif looked intently at him.

'But . . .'

'She is all right physically and you will feel refreshed in the morning. Go to her. I will sit outside.'

'What do you mean, sit outside?' Bashir could not understand why Arif wanted to sit outside.

'Just that. No one will notice. You will undress her near the door and have intercourse with her standing there. I want to see you coupling, I want to have a good look at how it is done.'

Bashir was disgusted beyond endurance. He could not understand how to deal with this man. He was not prepared even to think of doing as he was asked. He did not know the woman, or what her attitude would be when he went to her. Why was Arif compelling him to do this? Why was he obstinately urging him to do something utterly wrong? Once again he stood up and, assuming an air of detachment, moved towards the door.

'Bashir . . .' Arif called him in a voice filled with entreaty and passionate desire.

Bashir was nearly at the door, when he suddenly came to a decision and stopped. He decided that he would spend the night here. He needed a woman, and he had earlier told Arif of his need. He thought, if a friend from Lyallpur could stay a night with her, why should not he? He went back to his chair. Holding on to its back, he said, 'I also want to say something. I too have a desire.'

'What is that?' Arif stood up.

'I agree to stay here tonight,' Bashir said, 'but I will not leave the door open. I will bolt it from inside and about two hours before dawn or whatever time you suggest, you can see whatever you wish.'

'It is half past eleven now,' Arif said, pointing to his wrist-watch, 'at four o'clock I will knock on the door, and then you can open it. Be prepared to show me then.'

Arif took Bashir to Kulsoom's room which was bolted from the outside. He gestured to Bashir to enter. Bashir hesitated, looked back at Arif, and then went in. He switched on the light and closed the door behind him.

It was a small room. A woman was lying on a charpoy with her face to the wall. Bashir could see only part of her face and hair, the rest of her body was under the sheet. He went closer and saw the two black lines of eyelashes on her closed eyes. It seemed she was fast asleep. Her face was fair and bright and she was about twenty-three years old. He did not know how to wake her up. He sat down on the settee beside the charpoy and gently lifted the hair from her forehead, as if he was removing dirt from a glass. The woman heaved a deep sigh and woke up and then sat up with a start. She wrapped the sheet around her and moved to one side of the charpoy. Finding that there was no one else in the room, she got up and went to the door. Bashir approached her, but made no attempt to touch her or take any other liberty with her. He was about to bolt the door from the inside so that no one could enter without warning when a thought suddenly struck him. He tried to open the door, and as he had expected, it was already fastened on the outside. He returned to the settee. He had his back to her, wondering how this woman, whose face, features, and body were all right, had fallen into the clutches of Arif. After a while he turned his face towards the woman and found her in an odd position.

She was sitting on the floor against the wall, chin on one hand and the other resting on the floor. What surprised him most was that her eyes were closed. Bashir got up and, without disturbing her, sat down on the floor close to her.

'Listen . . .' he said and then asked her name. The woman did not react. Had she fallen asleep where she sat? He thought of shaking her, and had hardly touched her when she opened her eyes. Seeing him close by she stood up quickly and moved back until she struck against the charpoy and sat down on it and started looking about on the floor.

'Please listen to me. I am not your enemy.' Bashir spoke in a friendly manner. 'I am here for the night. I have to leave in the morning, so why not relax and be comfortable.'

The woman made no response and went on examining the floor.

'Why don't you answer?' Bashir said, holding her arm. 'I am speaking to you, not to the things in the room.'

The woman looked at him in alarm, but she did not try to free herself from Bashir's grip.

'At least tell me something, then I will leave if you wish.' Bashir wanted to win her co-operation by gentle means and to find out what she was thinking. He was preparing himself to sleep with this woman and to have a rapport between their two bodies, but seeing her attitude he began to feel there was little chance of this occurring.

'Should I leave? If you wish, I will leave.'

She said nothing. Bashir let her arm go and went over to the window. He opened it and looked outside. The light from the room flooded onto the low wall four feet away and the shadows of the bars of the window fell on it. Near it were trees whose leaves rustled joyfully in the fresh, cool air. Above the thick cluster of leaves was the black curtain of the sky. The stars twinkled mysteriously like the lights of some far distant city. The fluttering leaves asked him whether he liked their sky. They told Bashir that the relationship between the tree and sky was very old. The secret of the beauty of the trees was that they derived their beauty directly from that of the sky. It told them things that they preserved in their leaves and branches. It sent them rain and dew and the message contained within these shining drops could only be understood by trees.

The atmosphere was dancing with happiness. The woman was dancing too and Bashir watched her, entranced. Her dance was full of ecstasy, sometimes she appeared to fall and then she would steady herself and come near him, and then she would gyrate and sway in beautiful curves. It was a wonderful dance, that he had never seen before. Then there was a sudden knock on the door and the woman stopped. Bashir did not like her stopping. He thought that he would forbid Arif to come and knock before the stipulated time. As he was thinking this, the woman went to the door, opened it and quickly went out, and someone bolted the door from the outside. What was all this? What was happening? Where had she gone? Why did Arif go away after closing him in this room? He had said that he would come at four in the morning, and he should not have come at this time. Why had he, Bashir, not stopped the woman from leaving? He could have done; she had looked at him before opening the door as if seeking his consent, and Bashir had stood passively by the barred window watching her go. If he had wished, he could have prevented her going to the door, and told Arif to go away and come back at the agreed time. Suddenly he left the window and turned round.

The woman was still sitting on the charpoy, lost in her own

thoughts. Bashir shook his head free of his imaginings. He closed the window and went to sit beside her.

'If you are not prepared to talk to me, then what is the point of my being here? You can well imagine what I might . . .'

The woman showed no sign of imagining anything and continued to sit in the same position.

'I am talking to you,' Bashir said, catching her hand. 'Will you never answer me?'

The woman tried to hide her pain and surprise and looked at him with helpless eyes. Then opening her lips a little she gasped and began to cry. Seeing this, Bashir caressed her cheek lovingly and said, 'What is there to cry about? Please don't cry, all I will do is talk; nothing else.'

Her sobs slowly ceased, she passed her tongue over her lips and grew silent. Bashir was perplexed. He was thinking about what to do when she suddenly turned towards him and gave him a most pathetic look. He could not understand it. He was unable to find a way to deal with her. What kind of communication could he have with a woman who would not speak to him?

'Will you not answer me at all?' he asked. The woman opened her mouth in a strange way and tried to speak. It was only then that Bashir realized that the unfortunate woman was deaf and dumb. He bent his head and sat silent and felt very deeply for this woman to whom he had been sent for the night and who would at four o'clock in the morning be the means of fulfilment for the peculiar desires of another person. She was in fact very lonely, imprisoned within herself. Where had Arif obtained her? He had told him that she was like a piece of furniture bought from a shop and for which he had paid the price. Arif had also said that she was a shirt which he wore sometimes. He began to recall things that Arif had told him. 'She is the battlefield of dumb sins' he had said and other odd things which now clearly applied to this deaf and dumb woman, which he had not understood at the time.

This knowledge had a profound effect on Bashir. The desires which had been in his heart disappeared, leaving no traces. What should he tell her, how should he behave with her? Whatever he had to do did not involve asking questions.

'Whose son are you?' he chided himself. 'What will you do if you lie with her? Even if she is naked and you have your will, what will you leave behind for this helpless woman to think about? You should not do this, you should not even think of it. When a thought passing through the valley of sin returns unfulfilled, it curses itself and those companion impotent feelings that supervise it. But, to see, one must have clear vision; unless this happens, thought wanders about aimlessly, and in some small room, on some old and rickety bed, or in some well furnished office with the door locked, your body against a wall will always search for such thoughts.'

Bashir got up from the charpoy and aimlessly walked a couple of steps. What should he do here? Instead of chasing the thought he came to the woman and made signs for her to sleep.

Kulsoom stared at him with wide open eyes, hiding her fears. Feeling deeply for her Bashir came close and asked her to sleep. She looked at him with doubt on her face and, maintaining the modesty of her looks, remained sitting as she was.

'How should I behave with her, how can I explain to her, make her understand that I want her to go to sleep in peace?' Bashir discovered a new self within. He felt that his shadow had spread out on the floor, had become alive and had passed through him and gone back to the floor. Turning away from his own worries, he started walking about the room. He was a man suspended in mid air. Today a door inside him had opened up and he was now able to enter this door and get to know this hitherto unknown world within himself.

'I am sitting here.' Realizing that she could not hear him he immediately became quiet. He sat there for almost a minute, then got up and went and stood beside her. Very gently he placed his hand on her shoulder and made signs to her to go to sleep if she wished to. Kulsoom understood him and showed surprise on her face. She looked back at Bashir who again made her understand that she should lie down and cover herself with a sheet and go to sleep.

Kulsoom got up from her charpoy and sat down at his feet. Bashir quickly raised her up. He told her by signs that she should not sit on the floor. Tears gushed out of Kulsoom's eyes.

'Don't cry . . . for God's sake, don't cry.' While trying to make her understand, his own tears welled up. He wiped them away with the palm of his hand and then, holding her arm, led her to her charpoy and told her to lie down and sleep. She told him by signs that she would lie on the settee, and she sat there. Bashir shook his head and pointed to the charpoy. She got up and resolutely sat down again at Bashir's feet. This time she was so determined that Bashir had not the courage to draw her back and he was forced to observe her in silence. Kulsoom touched his feet with both her hands and, taking her fingers to her lips, kissed them. She was again about to touch his feet when Bashir quickly raised her up and placed his lips on her hair. He wet her hair with his tears. He took hold of her shoulders, looked straight into her eyes and said, 'I did not know you, I was not acquainted with you. Where did I see you? Where did I find you? Have you ever met me before this? I don't know the answers to these questions. All I know is that you are the woman who has become a symbol of honour for me. I will do all I can do for you and provide you all happiness and comfort. You are not able to hear my words, but the time will come when the air and space will tell you what I have said. And all the feelings in my heart for you, which remain unexpressed, not moulded into words, will come close to you and will dispel your loneliness. You don't speak. If you did, then the barbarous treatment you have received from people would have come down before them like a dense fog, and in this black mirror they would have seen the corpses of their own crippled and stinking desires.'

Aware that the man sitting beside her was talking, Kulsoom looked intently at him, captivated by his eyes. She closed her half-opened mouth and started shaking her head from side to side, trying to make Bashir see that she could not understand a word he was saying, that he should give up this method and try some other way of communicating with her. Bashir understood and at once stopped speaking. He found the flow of his thoughts falling deep down in him like a waterfall.

Kulsoom again made signs for him to lie down on the charpoy and she got up from it. Bashir stood up from the settee and tried to make her understand that she should stay there and sleep in peace.

Here were two people making sacrifices for each other at two o'clock in the morning. One could not hear or speak, the other was unable to make her understand what he said. Far above them the wind blew and in this little room they each tried to persuade the other to go to sleep. What a night was this? When had such a night come to Kulsoom, when had such a night come to Bashir? Bashir caught Kulsoom's hand and pressed it to his lips. When after a while he removed her hand, his eyes glowed with deep happiness, shone in positive assertion. Kulsoom was in ecstasy too and once again placed her head on his chest and clasped him to her with all her might. Bashir kissed her hair and led her to the charpoy.

Bashir's eyes suddenly fell on the ludo board lying on the settee. He picked it up and brought it to the charpoy. He spread out the board to start a game. Kulsoom turned it over and wanted to play snakes and ladders. Bashir began the game and was the first to throw a six and his piece started moving on the squares. By the time Kulsoom threw a six, Bashir's piece was on number twenty-four. Several times Bashir was brought down by the snakes and then again moved upwards. At last Kulsoom won, and this made her very happy. Bashir was also pleased and said to himself that he wanted her to win so that he could see her happy. They played three more games and Bashir only won once. At the end of the games Bashir again made signs for Kulsoom to lie down, but she looked uneasily at him and remained seated. All at once she laughed and spread out the board for another game. She picked up Bashir's piece and placed it at a hundred and with a movement of her hands told him to lie down on the charpoy. Then she placed her own piece at a hundred and closing her eyes, she tried to say that, if she won, she would sleep. Bashir understood and agreed. He saw that she was looking at the ceiling, praying to God. They started the game. Kulsoom was the first to throw a six. By the time she was at eighty-six, Bashir was only at twenty-seven. In the very next turn Kulsoom had to come down to twelve, while Bashir went on advancing. When Kulsoom was at twenty-one she climbed a ladder which took her to forty while Bashir was at eighty-three and now there were only two snakes ahead of him: one at eighty-five and the other at ninety. At his next turn Bashir was at eighty-six and Kulsoom at forty-seven. When Bashir came to ninety-one, Kulsoom climbed another ladder and reached eighty-three; now Bashir had no snakes in the way and only needed nine to win, and if he won he would have to sleep on the charpoy. He tried to place his piece on ninety, but Kulsoom was watching him carefully. Bashir got to ninety-eight and only needed two to win; when Kulsoom reached eighty-six Bashir threw a five which he did not need and therefore did not move. At the next throw Kulsoom reached ninety-two. Bashir threw a one and moved his piece to ninety-nine, he was in danger of winning. Kulsoom reached ninety-eight. Bashir threw a five, Kulsoom threw a four; neither moved. Bashir threw a six and then a five which he did not need, and in her next move Kulsoom threw a two.

'Even if I had won I would have sat on the floor, while you were awake I would not have slept,' Bashir said to himself and went to the settee. Kulsoom looked at him with regret and lay down on the charpoy. She pulled the sheet over herself and apparently went to sleep, though in fact she had no intention of sleeping. How could she when the person who had wept on her hair and who had given her a place of honour in his heart was awake? She thought that after a while she would get up and indicate that she had had her sleep and then would ask him to sleep. By then, though, she was fast asleep.

Bashir remained seated on the settee. He had put out the light so that Kulsoom would not be disturbed by it. The whole of his life passed before him. He recalled all the important incidents in it, all his journeys, short and long, new meetings, old friendships, quarrels, promises, broken promises, victories and defeats, all the vicissitudes of his life. He recalled his childhood, his life in the hostel, his education. Then he remembered his life on the farm, and Gaman, and Gaman's companion who had gone to his house to fetch the wooden box. Although Bashir had not discovered his destination, at least he had found something, which was a deep realization in the journey of life. This woman who was sleeping a few feet away from him had given him the means whereby he could identify himself. For a long time he sat there and thought about different things. His musings were interrupted by a knock on the door. It was still dark everywhere. The knocking came again and Arif calling out. Arif knew that only Bashir could hear his knocking, so his second knock was louder than the first. Bashir was wondering whether to get up or not, when the light in the room was switched on and off, and then on again. Bashir realized that there must be a switch outside the room too. There came another knock and Arif's impatient voice.

'Bashir, open the door, what are you doing? It is three minutes past four.'

Bashir remained seated. He did not know what to do.

'Open the door, open the door,' Arif said knocking. 'Have you become dumb too?'

Bashir opened the door and Arif rushed in.

'Why didn't you open the door?' asked Arif, glancing at the sleeping Kulsoom. 'Had you gone to sleep?'

'No, I have woken up,' answered Bashir calmly.

Ignoring his tone. Arif asked, 'So, how was she?'

Bashir gave him a sharp look and went to the settee.

'All right, wake her up now and keep the light on. I shall go out and will leave the door open a little. Remember to take off all her clothes.'

Bashir sat down on the settee and stared at the closed window.

'How many times did you do it? I knew that you would be pleased, and that is why . . .'

'Arif Nawaz . . .' Bashir stopped and went on staring at the window.

'Well, get up, get up. Take off all her clothes and when I knock, get in position by the door. I am going. Try to wake her.'

'Arif Nawaz . . .' Bashir again called and stopped.

'Stop talking. Arif Nawaz will stay with you,' Arif said standing near the door. 'Explain to her that there is more pleasure doing it while standing. Anyway, I tell you, doing it standing keeps a man young longer. There is a close relationship between the bed and a sick patient;

the bed is the place of sick people, and the wide floor is the field for youth. Remember there is someone outside the door while you are doing it, and that the real purpose of your doing it is because of that person. I want to see everything in detail.'

Bashir did not say anything.

'Come on. Get up. I had set the alarm for a quarter to four, but I came to you at exactly four o'clock,' Arif said, looking at his watch. 'She is usually upset when you touch her, so you should be fully prepared for the act.'

Quick as lightning Bashir jumped up and struck Arif a violent blow with his fist just below the neck. The blow was so hard that Arif rolled back and struck the window. He was stunned. Bashir gave him no chance to recover and picked him up and flung him on to the floor and then pinned him down. Arif tried to push Bashir aside, but Bashir's hold on him was very strong. Bashir found an opportunity to get one hand free and gave Arif a fierce blow with the fist just above his left eye. Arif caught Bashir by the waist and flung him with all his might against the wall. Bashir hurt his shoulder and head. Arif sprang upon him and tried to get hold of his head and bang it against the wall. Bashir managed to step back and get free from his grip and aimed his boot at Arif's face. Arif dodged the blow and Bashir kicked the wall instead. Arif got to his feet and picked up a glass from the table. He broke it against the wall, leaving him with a jagged weapon. He advanced savagely on Bashir.

'I didn't murder her, but I will certainly kill you,' Arif cried. When he was within striking range he swiftly swung his hand. Bashir crouched down to avoid the blow and grabbed Arif's legs. Arif lost his balance and fell flat on the floor. The broken glass fell from his hand. Bashir jumped on top of him and held him down firmly. He was breathing heavily and after a short while when he controlled his breathing, he pressed one of Arif's arms under his knee and with his right fist struck him a fierce blow to the mouth followed by a rain of blows on his face.

They fought like savages for about twenty minutes. Sometimes they stood and confronted each other and then one of them would spring upon the other. Once Bashir gave Arif a severe blow to his stomach which winded him. He went over to Kulsoom who was sleeping undisturbed, and woke her up. When she saw the blood flowing from his jaw, she opened her mouth as if to scream. Bashir was about to take Kulsoom out with him, when Arif recovered, and picked up a metal can and threw it at him. Bashir ducked and signalled to Kulsoom to leave the room. He grappled with Arif, picked him up and flung him on the charpoy. It was obvious Arif could no longer get up. Bashir left the room, bolting the door behind him.

EIGHT

After some effort, Arif failed to open the door. His dazed mind realized that Bashir had bolted it from outside and that it was futile to go on trying. He went to the barred window and called to his servant and then gave that up too. He knew that Bashir and Kulsoom must be far away by now. He held his right-hand finger tightly; it had been cut by the broken glass, There was also blood on his thin lips. He sat for an hour and when he saw signs of the dawn he called his servant again. The old man was astonished to find Arif in the room, and was even more astonished to see his injuries.

Arif did not explain what had happened. He went to his room and dressed his wounds. He thought about going to Aziz's house. It was likely that Bashir lived in the same street and he might be able to find out his address from Aziz. But Arif changed his mind and decided to go to the Bara Dari Hotel to see Munir and ask him where to find Bashir. Then he changed his mind again, which was just as well, because he would not have found Munir at the hotel.

I was out for a morning walk when I saw a beautiful little girl playing on the lawn of a bungalow. Her hair was golden and soft and was tied at the back of her head. Her frock was light pink, her socks were white, and she was wearing dark red shoes. She added gaiety to the smiling flowers all around her. She looked so sweet and innocent. I went up to her and said, 'Hello, what are you doing here?'

'I'm playing,' she said looking at me with mischief in her eyes.

'What are you playing?'

'There was a butterfly here a moment ago and I don't know where it's gone.'

'It's still here.'

'Where?' she said as if she did not believe me.

'It's here but you cannot see it.'

'Why can't I see it? I have eyes, haven't I? Her eyes were bright and eloquent.

'Yes, you have, but you cannot see the butterfly.'

'All right, then you catch it for me,' she said getting tired of this game. She made the request in such a manner that I forgot everything else and was prepared to fulfil her wish. On the other hand I was in a mood for playing with her and said, 'Should I really catch it?'

'Yes, yes, but please do it quickly.'

'All right,' and saying this I caught her hand. She freed herself at once and said, 'Tell me where it is.'

'I don't know,' I said admitting defeat.

'Look, it's here, here!'

I turned round and saw a beautiful orange butterfly flit past. I ran after it. The flight of the butterfly was charming and its wings twinkled like quicksilver. I ran after it a long way, until I passed some trees and came out into wide open fields. I was running as fast as I could, trying hard to catch the butterfly, but it flew over blue waters and disappeared. I stood near the large pools of rainwater and watched it go. On my right were wild plants. The area was very green and fertile. I was about to go back when I caught sight of another small girl, feeding chickens behind a hedge. The girl was as tall as the height of three hens, and a red ribbon was tied to her hair. She was wearing fine, well-cut clothes. She had an olive-coloured complexion and bright eyes. There were grains of wheat in her hands and she was calling the chickens to her, clucking like a hen. I went close to her, enjoying the gentle heat of the sun.

'These are our hens.'

'Good.' I laughed and asked, 'Do you go to school?'

'Not yet . . . I play.'

'What else do you do?'

'I eat, sleep and play with my hens. We also have a white dog, who runs very fast.' She turned aside and said that she was going; she had to fetch flowers. I said I would go with her.

'Where?' she asked and her eyes shone brightly at me. 'Where will you go? I have to gather many flowers.'

'What of it? I will go with you.'

She did not answer and we went to the garden which was one of those children's parks provided by the municipality on new estates. The local residents had equipped it with facilities for children to play. On one side was a large wooden bench, which had not been firmly fixed in the ground and was now askew, one side lower than the other. There were bare patches in the grass. The plants had been planted only recently and not many flowers were in bloom. Seeing this, I asked her: 'What kind of flowers will you look for?'

'Haven't you been here before?'

'No, never.'

'Then how will you be able to find flowers?'

'I will find them. I can give you one straight away.'

'What colour is it?' Her voice was sweetly impetuous and happy.

'It is olive-coloured and its leaves are black.' I brushed back her fine black hair.

'Where is it?' she cried with joy.

'I cannot show it to you, because you don't need it.'

'I do!' Suddenly, as if she had weighed me and found me wanting, she said, 'No, I don't want any flowers. I will find them myself.'

I was upset and said, 'I am going, I will bring flowers for you.' In front of me was a wide open space. The only sound was a bird singing a melodious song as it flew high overhead. I needed beautiful flowers and pretty butterflies. Walking along a broad road lined with thick sheesham trees I saw small girls going sedately to school, satchels on their backs. Their uniforms were neat and clean and well pressed as if giving a promise of the future. Two girls walking side by side and holding a picture book, passed me. They were looking attentively at the coloured pictures. I caught up with them and listened to their conversation.

'Look, how beautiful this European child's dress is,' one of the girls said. 'I like these pictures.'

'So do I,' her companion replied. 'Oh! What a beautiful garden.'

'Look at the picture of the singing bird.'

'Yes. Do you think they really sing?'

'Of course, why not?'

'And dancing nightingales?'

'Yes, but this . . .'

'And a cunning fox?'

'That too, but look at this, in this picture you can see fish swimming in the water.'

'Let's see.' Her friend bent over the book. 'May I have this book for a day?'

'No, I'm sorry. What if everyone wanted to borrow it?'

She had hardly spoken when some other girls came up and all of them wanted to see the pictures in the book.

'That's it. I shan't show it to anyone else,' she said, closing the book and going through the school gate.

I got on a bus and went into town. I bought some coloured picture postcards and put them in an envelope. Then I went to a garden where I picked flowers of beautiful colours. They were blooming there unnoticed, and I took them from the frontiers of their loneliness to the world of love. The noon-day sun was overhead and the dryness in the air did not suit me. Where was I to search for butterfly wings? If I did not take them, then the little girl would be displeased. I decided to give her some of the pictures instead.

I set out to the school, but I arrived too late. With a sad heart and heavy steps I returned to the route for my usual morning walk. Though it was unlikely that the girl would still be there, there was no harm in trying. I reached her bungalow and found the gate open. There was no sign of her. I was holding the pictures as if they were exiled corpses, and the flowers in my hand looked like innocent people being exposed to public ridicule. Time was passing like a mysterious mirror into which heaps of staggering confusions and dreams were falling. Then I heard the sound of footsteps. The girl was running towards the gate, where a fruit seller was standing. I was very pleased to see her. Looking at her I smiled, but she ignored me.

'Listen, do you like these pictures?' The girl's glance contained surprise and fear.

'What is your name?' I tried again. Just then an old man appeared from inside the bungalow. The girl ran to him and looked at me with suspicion. This old man had the crown of age on his head and fetters of leisure on his feet. He gave me a stony look and when I saw him approaching my smile disappeared. He shouted at me, 'What is the matter? Who are you?'

'Four annas a pao, four annas a pao,' the fruit seller shouted seeing me coming towards him.

After a while I reached the children's park. Some children were on the swings and a few were watching the water flowing among the plants. One child was standing on the bench about to jump off it. I went to a group of children whose clothes showed that they came from well-to-do families. Two of the boys were wearing wrist-watches. Another little girl had on ear rings and her arms glittered with bangles. After a little while the girl who fed her hens in the morning came out. I called her to me and said, 'Look, I have brought you some flowers.'

'Give them to me!' Before I could offer them to her she snatched them from me and, throwing them away, shouted, 'Are these flowers, dead and two years old? Why didn't you bring me fresh flowers?'

'I have very good pictures. You may keep them if you like.' The other children in the park also ran to get them. One of the boys with a wrist-watch turned a picture upside down and said, 'What kind of a picture is this? There's no building in it, or palace.'

Two other children made boats of my pictures to float on the water. I took one back from a boy who had rolled it into a cigarette. I took all the cards I could and left, hurt inside.

Evening was drawing in as I came to an area where the mud huts of the poor lined the road on both sides. Pools of dirty water, dust and rubbish lay here and there and everywhere stank. There were peals of loud laughter, but as one came closer this noise turned out to be the howling of stray dogs. The atmosphere was repugnant and polluted with smoke. The women here were weak, and evidently in dire need of clothes and good food. They were engaged impassively in domestic chores in their open yards. Some houses did have doors, but no way of closing them, and it was left to the doors themselves to close or to remain open. There were a few hand pumps for general use. The men were sitting smoking hookah and talking in loud voices. These people were as useless and common as the dust particles burnt in the rays of the sun. I could not fully study the conditions of this area and was anxious to get to my hotel. The day had passed in a strange way. I wanted to see the artist, he might have some news for me. I was impatient to get out of this God-forsaken place as quickly as possible, when I saw a little girl weeping bitterly. On her dirty cheeks the lines traced by the tears appeared to be the cancellation marks on Nature's futile handiwork. In the fading light of the evening her frail body looked like the outline of an oppressed victim. If this spectacle had been presented on the stage or had occurred in the programme of some cultured society it would undoubtedly have been entertaining. But in this suffocating atmosphere of real life, the poverty-stricken body of the little child seemed a foul insult. I drew closer. She was a child of about eight but she was weeping as if she had been tortured continuously for many years. Her swollen lips made her beautiful, shining teeth ugly. Her hair was matted and unkempt and her face showed indescribable bitterness, which could not be washed away by her tears. I bent down and tried to console her and affectionately tried to raise her up from where she lay. My hand made no contact and touched the ground instead. Her left arm was missing. She was wearing a tattered dirty frock, which seemed to belong more to the dust and dirt than to her. Even if I wanted to, I would not be able to describe the anguish that seemed to be concentrated within the body of this crippled girl who was slowly being annihilated. I sat down beside her and my hand wiped away the saliva dribbling from her trembling lips, and said, 'Munny, why are you crying? What is the matter?' I was unable to use the formal pronoun 'aap' for her since she would never have understood the respect I wished to convey. When I showed her my pictures, she stopped sobbing and a faint, lifeless smile began to glimmer on her lips, the kind of smile that appears on a person's face after death.

'Why were you crying?' I asked. 'What happened? Tell me.' Her face was becoming more and more indistinct in the fading light, and the gathering darkness was bent upon wiping it out altogether. I gave her the pictures and the flowers and said, 'These are good and beautiful pictures, keep them. These flowers are for you too.'

All of a sudden she got up, looked fearfully at me and walked away with small steps. The flowers and pictures were left abandoned on the ground and with each step the girl became darker like a sinful blot.

On my return to the hotel I ate nothing and talked to nobody. I lay down on my charpoy as I was, not even taking off my shoes. My eyes grew heavier. After some time the same girl came to visit me, in the same old tattered frock and with those poverty-stricken eyes. Holding my hand she came closer and said, 'You forgot all these flowers and the pictures. They are yours, keep them. Beauty has no meaning when the stomach is empty.'

I took the pictures and put them aside and said with an effort, 'How did you manage to come here so . . .'

'I came to meet you. You brought me flowers and beautiful pictures, when all I had were tears and dust. My tears would have ruined the colours of these pictures, and the dust have dimmed the brightness of these flowers, so I thought I would return them to you.' Her voice rustled like leaves. 'I am only one of many girls living down there. The colour of our tears is the same and so is the colour of our blood. Give these bright pictures to those who wear coloured socks, and on whose delicate wrists are glittering bangles. These pictures will be well placed in such hands. If you want to give me anything, bring me food to eat. What good are these pictures and flowers to me?' For the first time I noticed an eternal smile on her lips.

'How much food should I bring you?' I asked quietly.

She laughed aloud. The noise of her laughter was enough to break the heavens. When the echoes died away, she turned around and said angrily, 'Today my father beat my mother and broke the vessel from which we all drank water. He cursed everyone and then himself and went out. Afterwards my mother beat me cruelly and threw me violently in the dust and left. We need a lot of food. Last night my friend cried with hunger. Her little brother was ill and he, too, needed food. There they are in need, there they are in need, there they are . . .'

I opened my eyes at four in the morning. I was still wearing my shoes, and I was lying partly on the charpoy and partly on the floor.

In the evening Arif became restless again and began to pace his room. He sat down in an easy-chair, lit a cigarette and started thinking about what he should do. He wanted to go and search for Bashir with a pistol in his pocket, determined to return with one bullet less.

He did not know when he slept, but early next morning he left to see Aziz, hoping to find out Bashir's address. Aziz's father answered his knock. Arif first inquired about Aziz and then added, 'Do you know where I can find Bashir?' Aziz's father gave no answer and quietly went back inside. Then Aziz himself came to the door.

'Shut the door, shut the door,' the old man shouted. Aziz looked anxiously at Arif, and Arif closed the door at once.

Aziz was wearing a dirty shirt and coarse blue trousers. There was still a bandage on his head, but now his left arm was not in a sling. Arif asked him where Bashir lived.

'At the moment Bashir can do nothing for anyone,' Aziz answered calmly.

'I must see him, please give me his address.'

'He will not be able to meet anyone. He took an oath yesterday to be cautious in dealing with people in future.'

'What kind of oath?'

'He swore not to meet people. People talk to him and he listens attentively, which is not good for him. Actually he has not sworn an oath, but it sounded like an oath.'

'Just take me to his house and leave me at the door,' said Arif, ignoring what Aziz had said.

'You are the man who pushed me,' Aziz said moving away. 'I cannot go towards those stairs with you. Someone else has been pushed down them already.'

'A taxi is waiting below, I will bring you back. Don't be afraid, come and show me where Bashir lives.'

'I am sure that you will push the taxi when you reach some particular place. A table, chair or a man are pushed from outside, but I know a taxi can be pushed from inside.'

At first Arif thought he would force this crazy boy to come and show him Bashir's house at pistol-point. Then he gave up the idea and said, 'I am ashamed of the way I treated you, Aziz, believe me, what happened was not done by me deliberately. I am . . .'

'So what? I was only injured, but I have met Riffat and she told me . . .'

'What did you say? You have met her? How?'

'I have met her and have talked about many things with her. She told me that she will surely slap your face again before the year is out.'

Arif managed to control himself with difficulty. Yesterday's incident had been far from ordinary and now here was someone else talking to him in the same tone. Luckily for Aziz, Arif realized that he was not really balanced and that one should not mind what he said. The point was, how had he managed to meet Riffat and what had they talked about? He had wanted to track down Bashir, and now he also had to find out how Aziz had met Riffat.

'Aziz, I consider you as my brother. When you met Riffat, you did not say anything against me to her, I am sure of this. Please come with me.' Arif stretched out his hand to him. 'Come on, your father may get angry, it is not proper to talk here.'

Aziz looked at the closed door and went reluctantly towards the stairs. Arif followed. When they were in the street Aziz asked where they were going.

'Not far, we will remain in this town,' Arif answered.

'I want to eat. Instead of going on a pleasure trip, give me food. I am afraid the morning will go quickly today.'

Arif thought it proper to take Aziz first of all to a restaurant and give him a good breakfast. During the meal he would ask him to relate all the details of his meeting with Riffat and get Bashir's address from him.

The taxi took them to a restaurant. Arif ordered a good, full breakfast. Aziz ate it as though it was his lunch as well. When he stopped, Arif asked him if he wanted anything more. Aziz said nothing and passed his tongue over his lips.

'Aziz, you are my friend, you may think whatever you like about me, I only want to ask, what did Riffat say to you and where did you meet her?'

'Do you want the truth?'

'Yes, the truth.'

'I will tell you, I will tell you one day.'

'Tell me now. I swear that I consider you my friend.'

'Bashir swore an oath too. He wanted to swear a great oath, and I, too, am prepared to swear a great oath.'

Arif was again frustrated. He did not know whether first to try to get Bashir's address out of him, or get him to speak about Riffat. He was afraid that if Aziz spoke about one of them, he would not say anything about the other.

'What shall I tell you?' Aziz asked Arif.

'What did you talk to Riffat about, and what did she say about me?'

'I did not pluck flowers, because I found out that Riffat did not want me to. I looked questioningly at her and she understood my looks and she went quite near the plant where the flowers were blooming.'

'Where? Where?' Arif asked quickly.

'Arif Sahib, have you ever been to that place? There are many flowers there, and lovely grass, but the best plant was the one we were standing beside.'

'What did she say about me?'

'She said that she would certainly slap your face again before the year was out. I am telling you the truth, because you told me to.'

'Why did she say that?' Arif glanced at the people sitting at the nearby tables.

'I don't know. It was her answer and then she started to play with the flowers on a plant. I told her that the flowers were saying that she should take them. Despite this, she did not pluck them. She told me that one should never break anyone's heart, or break flowers.'*

'Aziz . . .' Arif wanted to say something, but decided otherwise and heaved a deep sigh.

'Riffat told me that the two of us could meet. I was very happy talking to her and thought that if I could get five more such happy days, I would again begin to trust the friendship of strangers.'

'Aziz, listen to me . . .'

'Arif Sahib, you listen to me too. I was telling you about Riffat. I told her: "You cannot see the air, still it exists and is necessary for you. Likewise, I cannot see your love, but it exists and is necessary for me. But I am not in love with you." Yes, I told her: "Knowing that I feel your love, and that it is necessary for me, I cannot bring myself to love you. In the same way that I know I feel the need to breathe and that it is necessary for me, I don't want to live merely for the sake of breathing." Arif Sahib, I love her, but I don't want to. This is my trouble, the cause of all my pain. How can I love Riffat? I know that I cannot. I told her about the girl I love and will always love. She is the girl who said to me to love that child whose face resembles Riffat's. At this, Riffat became sad and my tears gushed out. She had a small handkerchief in her hand. She turned her face aside, gave me the handkerchief and went away. I

* In Urdu flowers are broken, not plucked.

put it in my pocket, I swear that I did. I can tell you its colour. It was white with small pink roses. I remember putting it carefully in my pocket, but when I got up from sleep, it was gone.'

Arif heaved a sigh. He was not at all worried about Riffat now, because he had come to believe that Aziz had not met Riffat at all. It was all a dream. Arif thought there was no need to ask any further questions about it. He asked Aziz the question that interested him now.

'How can we get to Bashir?'

'Arif Sahib, I was wearing this shirt, everything was the same, but the handkerchief was not in my pocket. I searched all round the charpoy, thinking that someone had hidden it, but it was nowhere to be found.'

'Don't worry, you will find it. Where do we go to meet Bashir?'

'Granted that it is important to meet Bashir, finding the handkerchief is also important. She gave it to me to look after, and I have not been able to keep it safe.' Aziz touched the vase on the table and said, 'I cannot take care of anything. Perhaps that is why people get angry with me. Arif Sahib, you tell me, if, for some reason, Riffat asks me to return her handkerchief, what shall I do?'

'She will not ask for it, and even if she does, I will give it to her.'

'You will give it to her?' Aziz said, almost jumping up from his seat. 'Why will you give it? She does not want to meet you under any circumstances and if you send it through anyone else, she will know that you sent it.'

Aziz looked very odd. Seeing this, Arif got up. He had already paid the bill. He pushed open the door, and went out on to the road with him.

'Arif Sahib, if you like, I will tell you something.' Aziz stopped on the pavement.

'Certainly.'

'What I want to tell you is that you are a thief.' Aziz looked straight into his eyes.

'What was that you said?' Arif flared up. Only his preoccupation with Bashir stopped him from hitting Aziz.

'I cannot prove that you are a thief, but I am very sure that you are.' Arif did not understand. Aziz continued, looking intently at him, 'You must have stolen that handkerchief and now you are thinking of sending it to her yourself.'

'Aziz, tell me Bashir's address. That is all I want from you.'

'You cannot meet him. He told me himself that he will be most cautious in future about meeting people, and he will not trust them.'

'I will not tell him that you sent me to him. I will not even mention your name.'

'I want a drink of water,' Aziz said, altogether ignoring what Arif was saying.

Arif decided to go back to Aziz's neighbourhood and ask people if Bashir lived there. No one knew. He came with Aziz to the main road and they started walking again.

'Aziz, tell me where Bashir lives.' Arif caught hold of his arm and stopped. Suddenly finding his arm in Arif's grip did not worry Aziz. On the contrary, it looked as if he was being held by a sympathetic friend who was stopping him for his own good to let the traffic pass.

'Listen to me.' Arif jerked his arm sharply.

'Hmm,' Aziz mumbled softly. Then he shook his head violently and screamed, 'Let me go, for God's sake, let me go.'

Arif was afraid of a crowd gathering, but luckily no one heard. He released his grip on Aziz and said, 'Aziz, you are my friend, my brother. How can I hurt you? If you say that I should not send Riffat the handkerchief, then I shan't. I will not meet her, or even think of her. Just tell me one thing: where will Bashir be now?'

Aziz walked on in silence. It would be wrong to say that he was with Arif. He was walking on his own and Arif was beside him.

Suddenly Aziz said, 'You will never meet Riffat?'

'I will never meet her,' Arif replied, understanding Aziz's tone. 'Why should I? I will not even think of her.'

'And you will not send her the handkerchief?'

'No.'

'All right, I will tell you Bashir's address, I will take you to him, but you must not tell him that I told you.'

'I shan't tell him. Why should I?'

'It is not a matter of why you should. Sometimes the compulsion driving a man can reduce him to helplessness.'

'I promise you I will not tell him.'

'All right, from now on you will never meet Riffat . . .' Aziz left the sentence incomplete and went on, 'Where is that handkerchief? Return it to me and I will send it to her myself. It was given to me to look after.'

'I will search for it,' Arif said, trying to reassure him. 'I put it somewhere and I will have to search for it. It is difficult in such a short time.'

'That's all right, you overcome your difficulty and then I will go with you and leave you near the cement bags.'

'Cement bags?' Arif asked in surprise.

'Yes, Bashir lives there,' Aziz said seriously. 'That's where I met him yesterday, where he told me that in future he would not meet people. I will act as if I am just happening to pass that way and someone asked me about him and thinking that the person might be his good friend, I am bringing him with me. But fetch me that handkerchief. Only then will I take you there.'

'Listen Aziz, I promise you, whatever happens, I will bring you the handkerchief by this evening,' said Arif, feeling himself checkmated. 'I also promise that I will never meet Riffat again.'

'Not even once?'

'Not even once. Now come on, let's go,' Arif said impatiently. If Aziz prevaricated any more he thought he would shoot him.

Both were walking silently. They had covered about a mile and a half by now. Arif was feeling uneasy. He had told Aziz that they would take a tonga or rickshaw, but had got no reply. They were in a neglected-looking road with single and double-storeyed houses on either side. A cattle-fodder market was close by, a large open space with some horses and bullock carts. Aziz led Arif across this open space and then through a narrow passage behind the houses. There were some new houses under construction here and building material lay scattered around. Aziz went to one of these houses which had a temporary room made of plain bricks without any kind of mortar and a rough roof of wood and straw. The door to this room was open. Inside were piles of cement bags, a kerosene oil stove, some tin cans, an aluminium pot and, spread out on the floor, a large handkerchief of the sort used by country people to carry things. No one was in the room. Before Arif could ask Aziz about finding Bashir here, a man of about thirty entered wearing a loose shirt and a cloth wrapped round his loins. Aziz went forward and greeted him with the usual Asalam Alaikum, calling him uncle and shaking his hand.

'How are you, friend?' the 'uncle' said with a smile.

'I am all right. Did you trace that man?'

'No, I have found nothing out yet. But then such people don't come a second time.'

The man, whose room this was, sat down on the mat on the floor and taking out the stub of a pencil, started writing in a copy book. Arif was fuming with impatience. When he had finished his accounts, the man asked Arif and Aziz to sit.

'It's all right, we are fine here,' Aziz said, looking at Arif. 'In fact, he has come to see you . . .'

'See him? What nonsense!' Arif burst out roughly.

Aziz ignored Arif. 'You told me that you would seldom meet people now. This man seemed different. I thought that he might be one of your friends.'

'I don't know him at all,' the man said, picking up his handkerchief and rubbing his neck with it. 'I have never seen him before.'

Arif glared at Aziz as if he wanted to punish him cruelly. His thin lips opened and he drew a deep breath.

'This is Bashir. Last night . . .' Aziz wanted to continue, but Arif did not wait to hear him out and left the room. He was very confused. He had wasted three whole hours with that boy, and did not know how to compensate himself for the loss. Aziz had caused him much anxiety and at times had reduced him to a state of utter helplessness, but he had kept quiet in the hope that he would lead him to Bashir. Now he had two plans; one was to go to the Bara Dari Hotel and ask Munir about Bashir, and the other was to go to the house of Kulsoom's parents. Perhaps Bashir had left her there. He decided to go to Dilawar's house first which was not far away. It was a really poor area without proper paths and streets. The single-storeyed houses were made of clay bricks, some baked and some not. These houses had been built at random and the passages between them were often blocked by heaps of dirt. He had crossed one such lane and was entering another when he suddenly caught sight of the man he had intended to visit at the Bara Dari Hotel. He was surprised to see him here and so far from the hotel.

When I had woken I unlaced my shoes and put out the light. For some time I lay still in the bed and then slept. When I woke up again the day was quite bright. It was about two hours later than I usually got up. I had breakfast and went back to where I had seen the girl crying the previous evening.

No one seemed to know her, no one could tell me where she lived. Labourers and their children had gone to work. At this time of the day very few people were around. On one side of the path I saw a lot of sugar-cane peelings which were removed to make sugar-cane pieces for sale, and nearby two joined legs of a plastic doll, an old army boot, half a cycle tyre, old rags used by women during menstruation, and other rubbish scattered about. Three boys were gambling with cards on a charpoy, watched by two small urchins. When I stopped and tried to speak to the boys about a very young girl, they ignored me and continued their game. I stood a while listening to them and then again asked them about a little girl with one arm missing.

'She must be in some hospital. Your turn, friend,' one of them said in a bored tone.

I moved away and had not gone far when I spotted Arif. He was wearing a slate-coloured bush jacket. His trousers were dark blue and both his hands were in his pockets. He came up to me and asked imperatively, 'Where can I find Bashir? I mean the Bashir who was with you in Aziz's house the day before yesterday.'

'I don't know his address,' I replied.

'You must do. You seemed well acquainted.'

Arif looked as if he might resort to violence and would do anything to get what he wanted. Realizing this, I grew wary and politely told him that I had not seen Bashir for the last two days, that I had not known him long and did not know where he lived.

'How can that be?' he asked, without changing his tone.

'Now what can I say to you? Believe me, I don't know where you can find Bashir.' Saying this I tried to move on.

'All right, tell me what kind of man he is,' Arif asked somewhat more gently. 'It is very important that I meet him.'

'What is the matter? Maybe I could help you.'

'I don't need help. I need Bashir.'

'He was with you the evening before last. Where did he go?'

Instead of giving me an answer he questioned me. 'Whom did you come to see here?'

I was about to tell him about that armless girl, when he turned aside and walked away. I was surprised at his behaviour. After his departure I asked a bunch of boys about the girl I had come here for, but they looked on me as a stranger and ran away. I questioned an old pedlar who was carrying overripe and rotten fruit in a basket to sell to the poor here. He lifted his weak eyes to me, but before he could answer, a little girl who had come to buy some of his fruit asked whether I was looking for Seema. 'Yes, yes,' I replied, 'she is about your age, she has only one arm.'

'Come with me,' she said, after she had bought what she wanted, and led me down a lane. Now the day had advanced and I felt the warmth of the sun. Three or four children came out of a house. A woman, wearing a loose shirt without a brassière, followed them to the door and watched them run off.

'Come back soon!' she shouted at them and, without looking at us, stayed there. A little farther two or three stray dogs were rolling about on the ground. Soon we reached the end of the lane which was almost flooded with stinking water. I had to walk cautiously so as not to slip. Clouds of mosquitoes rose into the air as we passed. A little later on, the girl stopped at a door hung with a crude curtain made of cement gunny bags sewn together. She pointed to the house opposite and said that was Seema's.

I went over to it. It was more or less like all the others here. Someone had used the white-wash brush to paint a large ship on the exterior wall. The door was of used corrugated iron sheets with holes in it where nuts and bolts had been driven through. I knocked softly. The door rattled and a man of about fifty appeared. He looked tired.

'Seema is your daughter?' I asked, avoiding his look. His eyes were strange.

'Yes, Jinab.' He nodded slightly as he answered. Suddenly, ignoring me altogether, he turned his attention to an old man who was collecting waste paper from the ground.

Once again I looked at his eyes. The shape of the eyes did not match the rest of his face. I have never seen such eyes anywhere. They seemed older than him, as if several people had lived with them. Another thing which was remarkable about him were his ears. They were large and bent forward. His whole expression was exhausted and defeated.

'I met Seema yesterday evening.' I reminded him of my presence, emerging from the still cover of silence. 'I saw her weeping and . . .'

'Please come in,' he answered without waiting to hear any more and pushed back the iron door.

I entered a small yard. At the end was a plain brick wall with a passage and no door. The wall had been built with used bricks, older than the house itself. Looking at it, I immediately thought of the man who had brought me in, as if two old bricks were placed on his face.

A heap of firewood lay to one side of the yard. Nearby was a newly made clay fireplace and beside it an earthenware pot with dirty water and a hammer caked in mud. There were other trivial things scattered around which I didn't pay attention to. I entered with the man. It was a medium sized room. Several wooden and metal suitcases were in a pile; on top of them was a black office paper bin. The presence of the bin gave an odd impression. One did not know for what purpose these people used it, but whatever it was, it must have been very strange, and if they really used it as a dustbin, then it was most incongruous in view of the surroundings. Beside the suitcases was a charpoy; someone was lying on it, covered with a black sheet. On the right-hand side of the room were two unoccupied charpoys. Near them was a roll of thick rope and on top of that some spades were visible. Aluminium pots, a few pairs of worn out shoes, a large straw platter for bread, and radish leaves lay scattered around the floor. There was no window in the room. The cheap door facing the entrance was painted roughly in dark and light blue.

I was offered a seat on one of the empty charpoys. Before I could sit down, the man suddenly took me out of the room and went back himself. After a short while he returned. Just then the iron door opened and a woman of the same age as the man entered, holding the one-armed girl by her hand. I knew her at once. I looked at her, but she showed no sign of recognition. In order to remind her, I went towards her, stretched out my arm and called her name. The girl was surprised and looked at me with frightened eyes. The man came over and asked harshly, 'What do you want anyway? Whom do you want to see?'

'I would like to help you people. Please consider me your friend, I want to give this child something,' I said with some hesitation.

'What . . .' he said with astonishment.

'I simply want to give you some money. Call it sympathy, or anything you choose to name it.'

'We are not beggars, and . . .'

'Keep quiet,' the man scolded his wife. I caught a whiff of alcohol on his breath. 'Come in, Jinab, please come in,' he said politely. 'We will sit inside.' He said to his wife, 'You are not fit to talk to respectable, civilized people. I don't know who made you a woman.'

We entered the room where I had been before. I simply could not understand why he had taken me out and gone back in alone.

The person I had seen lying on the charpoy was still there covered with the sheet. The blue door was closed as before. Seema came into the room with her mother, who took a small box from the table at the head of the sleeping person's charpoy and went out again with the girl.

'Actually I came to see that girl. It hurt me to see her crying yesterday evening.' I sat down beside him on the charpoy and asked, 'What happened to her arm? Did she lose it in an accident?'

'Yes, you could call it that,' he said.

'What kind of accident? Where did it happen?'

'It must have been an accident, and it took place in her mother's womb.'

'Was she born a cripple?' I wanted to be certain.

'Yes, when she was born, her arm was left somewhere in her

mother's womb. I don't understand what is wrong with this woman, this happens every time.'

His wife re-entered the room with Seema. They sat down on the other charpoy. The man turned all his attention to the woman and said to me, 'Whatever you wish to give, please let me have it, don't give anything to her.'

'We are not beggars,' she repeated, looking at me. 'We don't want anything, we are not in need of anything.'

The man looked at her angrily and said, 'Why not? Afterwards you will say we have no money. If you don't need money, I do.'

'You are doing something very wrong.'

'What?' the man shouted angrily. 'Is it not wrong that from a defective body I have been given other defective bodies?'

The woman got up and turned to the charpoy against the wall.

'Let her sleep, let her sleep,' the man shouted at his wife.

The woman walked back heavily and sat down. 'That's what you said to the other man. You . . .'

'I will beat you!' screamed the man. 'Go and sit outside. All you have is a defective body. Get out, get out.' It was clear that if she did not obey him at once, he would beat her. She went out to the yard and Seema followed, looking frightened. They had not been gone long, when someone knocked on the outside door. The man went quickly to answer it. I could see the iron door clearly from where I was sitting. He opened it and Arif entered without saying a word to the man, or even looking at him.

I was amazed to see Arif. He began to talk to the woman who was squatting on the ground. She stood up. I could not hear what he said to her and what she answered. The next moment the man with the old eyes, his wife, Seema and Arif entered the room. When I saw him, I got up involuntarily.

Arif stood stock-still. He gave me one look and then turned to the man and asked angrily, 'What is he doing here?'

'Oh, I was about to ask him that myself.'

He had asked me to come in and was prepared to accept money from me, but the way he changed his tune now, and his servile manner in front of Arif made me believe that he would adjust according to environment and circumstance.

'Arif Sahib, I had to come to this house and this is the girl I wanted to meet,' I said, pointing to her. 'I saw her yesterday evening . . .'

'Shut up!' he said, calling me an obscene name. He turned to the man and said, 'Dilawar, show him outside immediately.'

Dilawar hesitated, perhaps thinking of the money I had promised. Seeing him hesitate, Arif grabbed me by the arm and demanded, 'Where is Kulsoom? You know about Bashir, so you must know where Kulsoom is and now you have come here to snoop.'

Then Arif checked himself and tried to cover up by saying, 'Dilawar, this man knows where Kulsoom is. Bashir is his friend and he has taken Kulsoom away.'

'Who?' screamed the woman standing beside Seema. She went up to Arif and stared accusingly at him.

'I know nothing and the person who does is standing right here,' Arif replied in his own defence.

I was quite perplexed. I knew they suspected me of complicity with Bashir but I had no idea what he had done or what to do about it. There was silence. Dilawar was not looking at anyone. The woman with the 'defective body' was still staring at Arif. The one-armed girl's condition was most pitiable. She was standing with her only arm across her chest. Perhaps she was used to doing this, but it looked very strange to see it there without the companion arm. Her eyes were lifeless, despairing. Dressed in good clothes and taken to school by a servant carrying her books in a satchel, she would have looked beautiful, but now she had no shoes, not even a cheap pair of slippers. Her tiny feet were filthy, because of dust, mud, wind and all kinds of weather, and resembled more the feet of some animal than those of a human being. The woman standing beside her, wanted to say something to her husband, but again Arif spoke, not looking at anyone in particular. 'I came here to inquire about Kulsoom. I thought that man might have brought her here.'

'I don't know any Kulsoom, and I don't know what you are talking about. What do you mean by saying all this?' I retorted.

'You know everything. Whatever has happened, you and Bashir are both involved.'

I did not answer. I could not think what to say in response to his accusation. At that moment the person asleep on the charpoy took off the sheet and sat up. She was about twenty, dark complexioned and with beautiful features. She moved to get off the charpoy, then remained seated and asked, 'Who is there? Who has come?'

Her face had an innocent look and the voice seemed to come from the sky. She was looking in the same direction, blinking rapidly. I realized at once that she was blind. Not receiving an answer, she got up and groped her way along the wall to the other room through the blue door. As she opened it, I caught a glimpse of slight brightness, indicating that it had some kind of window or ventilator. Dilawar and his wife followed her, leaving Arif, Seema and myself alone.

'Why were you talking to me like that?' I asked Arif when Dilawar and his wife had left the room.

'What?' he replied, looking at me angrily. 'Don't you know where Bashir has taken the girl?'

'No. I have already told you that I know nothing about all this.'

'You must at least know where he is.'

'I have no idea where he might be. I only know that he stayed at a hotel, but he is no longer there.'

'Rubbish!' he said harshly. 'You cannot convince me. If he stayed at a hotel, he must have told you where he was going afterwards.'

At that moment Dilawar and his wife returned. Dilawar asked Arif, 'Who is Bashir, and why has Kulsoom gone from your house?'

'She may have run away somewhere.' As Arif told him this, the blind girl came noiselessly back in. Seema went over to her and sat down beside her.

'Since when has Kulsoom been missing?' Dilawar asked Arif. Before he could get an answer, his wife asked, 'Where has she gone? And who is Bashir?'

Arif answered neither of them, just bit his lip. I was looking at him when Dilawar suddenly jumped up and rushed over to the two girls. I realized immediately that something serious was going to happen. He caught the blind girl roughly by her hair, dragged her violently to the blue door and pushed her against it. He started shouting all sorts of things at her. The girl managed to save herself from falling and cried out, 'What is it? Now what has happened?' and started crying. Her father was stopped now by the pathetic tears of Seema. I rushed to her and, putting my hand on her shoulder, brought her back with me to the charpoy. The blind girl was standing near the small table and her father was shouting loudly. 'Look at her. She cannot sit properly. She cannot even sit properly.'

The girl stood leaning against the wall. It was pitiful to see her. Seema was sobbing and I was trying my best to make her stop crying. While all this had been going on, Dilawar's wife had gone up to Arif and caught hold of him by the collar of his bush jacket, and asked him something. My attention was diverted from this to the crying of Seema and when I sat down beside her I saw that Arif was unruffled by the woman's appalling behaviour. He did not try to escape from her clutches, but took his lighter, pressed the button and brought the flame to the woman's wrist. She quickly released his collar and jumped aside, screaming and shouting. Holding the burn on her arm, she went to the blue door. Before she reached it, a strange creature came through it into the room. To tell the truth, my growing hatred for Arif was forgotten as I saw the boy.

He was about eighteen years old and his head looked as if it had been shaved recently. The surprising and remarkable thing about him was that he entered the room walking on arms and legs, like a quadruped. Dilawar did not react to the boy's entry. He went over to Arif who moved his lighter to his left hand and then put his right hand into his jacket pocket and said quite indifferently, 'Go and sit on the charpoy.' Dilawar stopped where he was and stared at the ground near Arif's feet. The emotions in the room were in constant turmoil. I watched dumbfounded, not being able to make up my mind as to what my own responsibility in this situation was. I attended to Seema and placed my hand on her head to console her, and watched the strange boy crawling on all fours. Now he was sitting on the floor near the charpoy, looking for something in the heap of coiled rope lying there. Arif seemed quite detached. He lit a cigarette. Blowing out the smoke in a fine stream through his pursed lips, he spoke to the woman. 'You should not have done that. You caught hold of my jacket as if I had Kulsoom in my pocket. I don't know where she is. If I knew, I would not have come here.'

'How it is . . .'

Her husband scolded her at once. 'Be quiet. All this is happening because of you. You are a woman of defective body and defective brain.'

'I wanted . . .'

'Why don't you sit inside,' Dilawar said without listening. 'I told you to remain there and you come out. What do you want?'

'She only wants to . . .' Arif broke off and, looking at me, said, 'What do you mean by sitting here?'

'I came to see Dilawar Sahib,' I said calmly.

'Well, Dilawar?' Arif asked, seeking confirmation.

Dilawar gave me a look and then loudly said to Arif, 'Yes.'

Arif stood up. He went on smoking a bit longer and then threw the rest of the cigarette outside. Looking where it had fallen, he said, 'In reality you have no sympathy with your children.' He turned back to Dilawar, 'Kulsoom has left my house and you showed no reaction when you heard. It is true that she can't hear or speak, but God created her also. If you treat all your children like this, then they will soon go back to their Maker. I wondered what you might do when you learned that Kulsoom was no longer with me, but I am sorry to see that you have no interest in your children. Why is this? Why?' He shook his head and continued, 'Your hatred and disgust for your own children will only bring harm on you. They are yours and just as you have your rights, they too have a claim upon you.'

'Where is Kulsoom?' the woman asked him.

'Kulsoom is with me and this evening we are going away to another city for some days. I thought I would come to you so that you could meet her, but your hatred for her will turn her heart against you.'

'My child, my child, I will come with you,' said the woman, quickly forgetting all her troubles and pain. The grief for her daughter smouldered more than the pain of her burnt wrist.

'I will bring Kulsoom to you when we return. I tell you again, you people should change your thinking a little. Just now Dilawar pushed this poor girl savagely. She is blind and sometimes causes trouble. Nevertheless, her care is your responsibility. And when your son, Mando, entered the room, no one gave him a helping hand. I saw your callousness. Seema was crying and no one consoled her except a stranger. You may resent my speaking like this, but I am saying this for your own good. I want you to treat your children well, so that they get an opportunity to grow to be good citizens.'

Arif's words again upset me. I did not know him too well, neither had I met the deaf-and-dumb woman Arif spoke about as his wife. I had never been to his house, nor had Bashir or anyone else told me anything about him. I therefore had no clear picture of his character. From what I heard him say to these people I concluded that he was not a bad person. I then recalled what Seema had told me in her tears the previous evening about her father. I could not break through the fact that this had been in a dream. My mind was confused. All forms of truth were mingling promiscuously with fantasy and illusion.

After saying all he had to say, Arif looked at his wrist-watch and said to Dilawar: 'All right, I am leaving now. I will bring Kulsoom back to visit you when we return.' He took thirty rupees from his jacket and put the money near Seema on the charpoy.

I had brought some money, for all these people, not specially for Seema. When that woman had said they were not beggars I had not wished to annoy her, and so, unperceived by any of them, I had put the money under the pillow on the charpoy. The amount I had placed there was less than what Arif gave them.

Arif replaced his purse and, bowing to the two of them, went out with a peculiar smile on his lips. I wanted to go too. The unpleasant incidents that had taken place here had been partly eased by Arif's remarks and what had followed. I looked at them, seeking their leave to depart, and followed Arif out.

He had not gone far. I thought we should both walk together for a little while, so that I could ask him about some things that were troubling me. I politely called out to him. He turned round and waited for me to catch up. At about three paces from him, I heard him heave a sigh. He left it for me to initiate the conversation.

'Which way are you going?' I asked respectfully.

Arif did not answer. He looked at me intently, but the next moment turned and walked away. I did not think it proper to call him again, or to follow him. He turned to the right and was soon out of sight.

'It would be better if you did not come here,' Arif said, as he opened the main gate and saw Fiazi standing there.

Fiazi showed no resentment and said nothing. Just then a thought occurred to Arif. He led Fiazi into the sitting room. When they had both sat down, Arif said, 'Fiazi Sahib, I should like to ask you one thing: did Bashir give you his address?'

'No, he did not.' Fiazi uttered these words with such finality that Arif could not pursue the topic.

'Fiazi Sahib, your words are fairly tolerable to me, but you are not. What is the reason for this?'

'Since I don't think I can agree with you, how can I give you a reason? I do not understand what you mean.'

'Oh, it's not important,' Arif said in a different tone. 'I just want to know certain things but I have no idea how to get hold of them.'

'You may do whatever you want only don't harm other people in the blind continuation of your activities. You know what happened in this room a few days ago. Due to your own peculiar reasons you chose to react to it in the worst possible way, by giving that poor boy a violent push.'

'Fiazi Sahib, you don't realize, he is mad. You don't know him as well as I do. He consists of the leftover blood of all mad people.'

'I don't want to go into a discussion as to whether he is congenitally mad or a mad illusion. We can talk about that later, and perhaps arrive at an agreed conclusion. At the moment your choice of action is considerable. Let me tell you, however much in the wrong someone may be, even if he is altogether insane, there is no justification for another person to do as he pleases with him. If he does this he will prove himself to be mad.'

'Fiazi Sahib, what kind of life should a man live? Please tell me.'

'Arif, you are worried and you are unable to find the cause of your worries. You throw a question at me, but you don't even care whether you get an answer or not. Forget what a good life is or a bad life for the moment, and tell me what your real problem is.'

'I need your consent about something,' Arif said after a pause. 'I have some plans. It seems to me that if I implement them then I will live in peace for some time.'

'It may also happen that something appears to us to be good, whereas in fact it is not good, only its shadow. Let me tell you one thing, the shadow of everything is always good, and we should examine everything in the light of its shadow.'

'I want to put a problem to you, and ask you whether it will lead to difficulties later on.'

Fiazi remained quiet, waiting for Arif to continue: 'A few days ago Bashir came here with me and we had a talk. Then you arrived and he went away with you. I don't know what you two discussed, and I accept your statement that you don't know his address. The day before yesterday, in the morning, he took away the woman you once saw sleeping in this room. At that time it was not possible to follow him. Yesterday morning I went to her parents' house, thinking that Bashir might have left her there. They live a long way away. Their two other daughters were also born cripples; one has no left arm and the other is blind. Kulsoom wasn't there. I told them that she had gone away somewhere. They all got worried. I thought that might result in further troubles for me. Therefore I said that I had just been testing them, because I knew how indifferent they were towards their children. I told them that I was taking Kulsoom to another city for a while and I would bring her to see them when we got back. The fact is, Kulsoom has gone off with Bashir and I don't know where they are and in what condition. I am really quite . . .'

'You are really quite detached . . .' Fiazi completed his sentence for him.

'No, it's not that, Fiazi Sahib. Well, you say whatever you like, but the problem I want to discuss with you is more important and I want your candid opinion about it.'

Fiazi was listening attentively.

'I want to go to the house of Kulsoom's parents to tell them that Kulsoom has been killed, in a traffic accident or by a fall down a cliff. In this way she will be erased from their mind, and this will clear the ground for the second important event to take place. I am sure that my plan will be successful because I find no opprobrium in it.'

'What do you mean?'

'I want to go to their house and tell them this and the rest will straighten out itself. I have already told them that I was leaving town. I hope in this way all will be set right.'

'What will be set right?' Fiazi asked him.

'Kulsoom was living with me. She was unable to speak, but I had no complaint about this disability. I never felt the need for conversation with her. In the same way that blind girl cannot see anything, nevertheless she is something to be seen.'

'So you want to bring their other daughter here?'

'You don't understand. They are poor people and daughters are a burden for such parents. I will, in a way, be helping them. First I will go and offer my condolences and later when the situation is favourable I will speak to them about the other girl. I am sure that nobody else will marry her.'

Fiazi was silent.

'I want your opinion about this matter.'

'Will you accept my advice?' Fiazi asked.

Arif watched him attentively.

'Arif, you should commit suicide,' said Fiazi, giving him a fixed look.

'What did you say?' He half got to his feet, then sat down again.

'The kind of life you are living will most probably lead to a disastrous and painful end. Poison does not know how dangerous it can be for people, it remains in a bottle, but alas, there is no bottle around you. You should commit suicide and then you will probably find a better way ahead.'

'I do not understand. What are you trying to tell me?'

'You cannot immediately understand what I am telling you. When you do it, you will. Think about a suitable method and then practise it.'

'Practise it? What nonsense!' Arif was again incapable of recognizing things. In his mind was a kind of whirlpool in which he thought that whatever he was doing was correct and all else was being done to cause him harm.

'Why don't you marry Riffat? You're always proclaiming your love for her. I know that she will not accept you, it's strange that you haven't mentioned her once in connection with this. Arif, you think I'm your enemy, that I'm always creating problems for you, but I tell you again, you have no standards. Unless you start living according to some standard, you will go on having problems and difficulties. The path you are following now, will not end, but will gradually narrow. You will not be able to retrace your steps, because the way will have been destroyed by your own actions.'

While Fiazi was speaking the old servant, whom Fiazi had seen here before, came into the room. Arif was very angry to see him. The servant stood at the door and only dared to say that someone had come.

'Go and say I am not at home,' Arif replied harshly.

The servant disappeared and when he had gone, Fiazi got up and said, 'Wait, I'll see who is there.'

'No, it is not important, please remain seated,' Arif said. 'Whoever it is will go away.'

'Maybe it's Riffat.'

Arif stared at Fiazi. He got up and went out by the door that opened on to the verandah, leaving Fiazi alone in the room.

With all the beauty and ugliness, all the good and evil, all the distance and directions, all the possibilities and limitations, all the holiness and profanity on this wide earth, and in the unlimited space of existence and non-existence – what can a man do, how far can he go, how much wonder can he create, and how can he arrange to introduce a wonder to another wonder? We are imprisoned within walls and have forgotten that we built them. The foundation of the walls is a liquid that flows from the flaws in our thoughts and ideas. Man will make skylights higher than his own reach, and as a result he continues to grope about in the feeble and flickering light of the everyday world.

Arif soon returned. He closed the door behind him and sat down.

'Who was it?' Fiazi asked.

'Oh, I don't know. When I reached the door whoever it was had gone away.'

'Arif, you told me earlier that it would be better if I did not come here. I was thinking how sensibly you spoke.'

'Forget it, Fiazi Sahib. What are you saying? You mustn't mind what I said.'

'Tell me, are you worried?'

'Yes, I am,' Arif said seriously. 'You think I am worried on account of Kulsoom. I am uneasy about her only because Bashir has taken her away. After she went I felt the need for the blind girl, but she is not the real cause of my worry. I am worried because of Riffat. Believe me, I love her . . .'

'You don't,' Fiazi interrupted. 'I have told you before, it is just your fantasy. You don't understand the meaning of love. How can you make an assertion about something the meaning of which is not known to you? What you call love is more the accumulation of your loathsome desires which you have not yet been able to satisfy. Once they are satisfied, this love will seem to you to be like the soot that gathers inside a glass chimney and which you want to scrape away.'

'Why will you not believe that I love her?'

'Arif, each of us at some time or other thinks that he has fallen in love. In fact it is not love, merely the expression of our erotic desires, which are not a true reflection of our real selves. Then what do we do? We pawn the emotion of love to our lust and prostitute this emotion in the most shameful manner.'

'If I love her, what should I do?'

'Forget her. This will be a humble proof of your love.'

'Forget her?'

'With the firm resolve that you will never try to meet her again.'

'How can I do that?' said Arif, shifting uneasily.

'Arif, two kinds of love are very poisonous and endanger all the senses. The first compels a man to love a dreadful God on condition that he will be rewarded for doing so or else be prepared for eternal torture. This is the worst form of love which is based on the commercial principle of doing something for reward. The word love should never be used in this context. The second kind of bad love is that of a human being for himself, when he begins to recognize everything in terms of his own ego. Just as love cannot be commercial, so it cannot be confined to the four walls of one's ego. This is the total exposure of selfishness, the crude nakedness of which we cover up when we use the pronoun "I".'

'I only want to ask, would I be able to persuade this girl to love me?' Arif, who had been thinking about this for the last few minutes, wanted an answer.

'What kind of love? The use of this word does not suit you. That girl slapped your face and I think any person who received such a slap should feel the pain of it all his life.'

Arif pursed his lips and sighed. His thin wiry hair was drooping over his right eye. He brushed it back with his hand and said, 'Fiazi Sahib, please go now. I have a bad headache.'

'Arif, I know a person who, when he lies down in bed, feels that his head is heavy on the pillow. Can you tell me who this person is?'

One cannot say what answer Arif would have given or whether he had understood the question or not, for just then there was a gentle knock on the door. Arif looked at Fiazi, went to the door and jerked it open. His thoughts and feelings vanished like drops of water sizzling off a hot iron, because standing there were Dilawar's wife and Seema, the armless girl. Arif went out on to the verandah, closing the door behind him.

'How is my daughter?' the woman asked. 'Where is she? I want to see her.' She was wearing a faded black burqa and on her feet were a pair of old slippers coated with dust and dirt. It was obvious that she had walked a long way. Seema was standing by her side, watching everything carefully.

'You cannot see her,' Arif told the woman. 'She didn't come back with me. I only returned for a couple of hours because I had forgotten some things I had to take with me.'

'Where is she?'

'There's no need for you to ask so many questions,' Arif told her. 'Don't worry about her, go home and rest.'

The woman bent her head. Seema looked from Arif to her mother and back again.

'Very well, come in. Have something to eat and drink.' Arif changed his tone and attitude with amazing speed and opened the door. 'I sincerely apologize for my rudeness. Because of my base act your wrist was burnt.'

'When will you and Kulsoom return?' Instead of talking about herself, she asked about her daughter. The three of them came into the room.

Fiazi got up and said he would leave. Arif with a wave of his hand politely requested him to stay.

'Do you think I like these words of yours?' Fiazi asked pleasantly with a smile in his eyes.

'Please be seated, these are visitors, they will soon be leaving. Anyway, I shall be returning to Peshawar and I don't know when we shall meet again.'

'Peshawar?' Fiazi asked with astonishment.

'Yes, Peshawar, Peshawar,' Arif repeated with remarkable emphasis. His expression was serious, as if he was busy dealing with various important matters at the same time. 'I'm coming,' he called, not looking at anyone and hurriedly walking from the room.

He went to his own room, glanced quickly over it and then went to the window and called the servant, asking him to bring tea and whatever there was to eat for the visitors. Then Arif asked him whether the man who had called a little earlier had left his name.

'No, Jinab, he did not give his name. He said there was no need, he might come back.'

'Who could it have been?' Arif muttered to himself. He looked at the servant and asked, 'Was there a burqa-clad woman and small child with him?'

'No, Jinab, he was alone and not very young.'

'All right. Bring the tea to the sitting room. In future, whenever anyone calls, ask them their name first.'

Arif strode back to the sitting room. Fiazi was sitting, the woman and Seema were still standing. Looking utterly pathetic, the woman said to Arif, 'Please come again some time to our house. We shall leave now.'

'At least have some tea.' Arif thought for a second that he would let her go and nod his head and smile, but then he felt a whim to detain her for tea.

'No thank you, we have just had tea. When will you be returning from Peshawar?'

'At the moment I cannot say, but I will come to visit you when I get back.' He spoke gently to the woman and placed his hand on Seema's shoulder. The little girl shrank away immediately and looked resentfully up at him.

'Come to me, come here,' Arif smiled at her.

'No, I won't, I am all right here,' she replied.

'Seema, go to him, there's a good girl,' said her mother, pushing her towards Arif.

'Come on, why won't you come to me?' Arif tried to get hold of her by her only arm, but she slipped away from his grasp.

'No, I don't like you. I won't come to you.'

'Seema, you . . .' her mother said, aghast. She caught the girl by the hair and pulled it.

Fiazi quickly came over to them, took the girl by the arm and affectionately placed his hand on her head. Once again Arif thought he should ask Fiazi to leave. He was trying to catch Fiazi's eye to convey this to him, when the servant brought tea and food.

'Fiazi Sahib, let her go and have your tea.' Arif spoke peremptorily.

The servant was setting out the tea things on the oval table. Tension in the room was mounting and Fiazi was aware of it. He made Seema sit on one of the four broad-backed chairs and studied her with care. The girl was silent and scared, yet still seemed prepared to speak out. She looked helplessly at Fiazi and then turned her face away and looked around the room, her eyes moist. Fiazi offered her a pastry.

'What are you doing, Fiazi Sahib? Please remain seated comfortably,' Arif said, and then turning to Seema's mother asked, 'Why is the child so frightened?'

'She is a naughty girl. That is why I don't like to take her anywhere with me,' she answered and then, turning to Seema, said harshly, 'Sit quietly. Now why don't you eat?' She looked at Arif and said, 'Please don't mind what she said, she is ignorant and is often ill, therefore . . .'

'That's all right. You have your tea,' Arif said, laughing.

Fiazi was silent, he felt as if he was listening to the whispering of the objects in the room. The servant placed a cup of tea before him. Fiazi watched the steam coming from it.

'Fiazi Sahib, have your tea,' said Arif with a pleasant smile. Fiazi took up his cup and started drinking.

Arif sometimes addressed Fiazi as 'Fiazi Sahib', using the formal pronoun and at other times called him 'Fiazi', using the familiar form. This he did because of his own changing attitudes towards Fiazi. He would change his manners and behaviour according to the situation, and his voice, too, would then be modulated accordingly; sometimes it was gentle, sometimes harsh and he would clench his fists and make his hands express his feelings too. Fiazi had noticed this several times. He was wondering about it when an incident occurred which took all his attention.

Arif and Fiazi were sitting facing each other and Seema was beside Fiazi. When she placed the cup of tea on the table, she accidentally knocked it over. The cup was about half full and the tea spilled over the table and down on to Arif's trouser-leg and sock. He jumped up in anger, spilling a glass of water too. He was enraged and swore at the miserable girl, who shrank in fear. God knows what Arif thought he was doing. These people were his guests and spilling the tea was an accident. Hearing his abuse, the woman started to curse her daughter too. Fiazi felt his heart sink.

Arif went to the door and called the servant. He must have been standing just outside waiting for Arif's call, because he entered immediately. Arif pointed out the mess near the table. The servant quickly picked up the fallen cup and glass, and rushed to fetch a rag to sponge the carpet.

'She has no manners. Why did you bring her with you when she cannot sit properly?' Arif asked the woman.

'Arif, she is a small girl,' Fiazi interrupted. 'She did not deliberately spill the tea.'

'Fiazi Sahib, you don't know, you have no idea how spoilt she is.'

'Arif, small children are not capable by themselves of being spoilt or trained; they are influenced by grown-ups and learn their manners accordingly. When children are precocious beyond their years, then you should understand that their elders have neglected their duty to bring them up properly.'

'Fiazi Sahib, I will discuss this with you at length some other day and then try to arrive at some conclusion.'

'If you already have the conclusion in your mind, I assure you, you will have little difficulty in reaching it!'

Both mother and daughter stood up. Seema's lone arm hung down limply as if on a peg. Arif and Fiazi also got up. Arif went to see them off at the gate, keen to be rid of them.

'I will come to your house when I return,' Arif said at the gate, and added, 'I don't know when that will be.'

He came back to the sitting room. Fiazi was seated, looking towards the door. Only seconds had passed when the servant reappeared and, with some trepidation, informed Arif that the man who had said there was no need for him to leave his name, had returned and wanted to see him briefly.

Arif went to the door opening on to the verandah and found a stranger standing there.

Fiazi recognized the visitor at once as the artist who lived at the Bara Dari Hotel. The artist greeted Fiazi as soon as he saw him and asked, 'Is that boy here? He told me that he would be coming.'

'Which boy? Whom are you talking about?' Arif asked.

'The boy's name is Aziz, he . . .'

'Aziz,' Arif ground the name between his teeth. 'No, he has not come here. If you meet him, tell him on no account to come.'

'Arif, let me speak to him. I know him,' said Fiazi. 'He is a very good artist and lives in the hotel where I used to live.'

'Fiazi Sahib, before saying or listening to anything, I want to tell you that the boy is mad and eating up his days. He does not realize what he says, and whatever he does say is so complicated and enigmatic that one can hardly tolerate it.'

'Where did he meet you?' Fiazi asked the artist, ignoring Arif.

'In my room. There was a girl with him.'

'Girl? What sort of girl?' Arif asked with a smile.

'I don't know. They came to my room, and spent a long time looking at the paintings. Then Aziz told her he had found something he thought he had lost. When the girl asked what it was, he answered that he would soon be back and would tell her everything. He took me aside and whispered that he was going to your place to tell you that the thing had been found.'

'What did the girl look like? Did you not find out her name?' asked Arif eagerly.

'I cannot explain what she looked like. Her name was Riffat, that was the name he . . .'

'Riffat! Are you sure?' Arif spoke excitedly.

'What do you mean by "sure"? I saw both of them in my room looking at paintings.'

Fiazi sat silent in the broad-backed chair. It seemed as if he had left his body in the chair and had gone himself in search of Aziz.

'Fiazi Sahib, you call this boy innocent and so on. Now you can see for yourself what he is doing. He is crazy and hell-bent on getting others into trouble.'

'Everyone is crazy about something or other,' Fiazi answered. 'Some people's craziness is approved of by the majority, that of others is rejected; it is a game of choice, and we are all involved.'

'But he is mad, quite mad. He wanted to take a handkerchief from me which he in fact had never given me. He saw it in his stupid dream and then wanted to obtain it from me.'

'Why from you? He must have given some reason.'

'Fiazi Sahib, don't bother about these things. You know yourself that he is mad and his condition is pitiable.'

'Pitiable? You admit that he deserves pity and yet you did not give him any?'

'Fiazi Sahib,' Arif said with disgust, 'I meant that one should not believe what he says.'

Fiazi laughed and said, 'It is strange. You say that he is pitiable, and by this you mean that one should not believe what he says. Arif, your words are surprising. One understands what the boy says despite his personality, but sometimes what you say is baffling even when the listener tries his best to understand.'

Arif heaved a sigh and took a packet of cigarettes from his pocket and lit one. 'Did the girl say anything to you?' he asked the artist.

'She talked about several things,' the artist answered gravely.

Arif examined the artist critically and then offered him a cigarette. The old man said that he did not smoke.

'Where would she be now?'

'I don't know,' the artist said briefly.

'Any guess?'

'It was my guess that brought me here. Aziz should have come here. I don't know where he is now.'

'If he comes here, I'll lock him up in an empty room. He follows you around like a shadow. I don't wish him to come here.' Arif turned to Fiazi and said, 'Fiazi Sahib, maybe you think that I am bad, but I am not.'

'How good those people are who do not try to make other people think well of them.'

'I love Riffat. I really love her.'

'Don't give me all that again,' said Fiazi with disgust.

'Do you love that girl?' the artist asked Arif, who looked witheringly at him and took out another cigarette. He was not a chain-smoker, though it seemed now as if he was determined to finish the packet quickly. He placed the cigarette between his lips and did an odd thing. He lit the lighter and brought the flame to the middle of the cigarette, burning it into two equal halves. One part fell on the table while the other remained in his mouth. He took a pull at the piece in his mouth and then put it in the ashtray, as well as the other piece which was lying on the table. The artist was watching attentively. Fiazi was trying to interpret Arif's action, wondering how this act could indicate his future course of life.

'Fiazi Sahib,' Arif said, taking a seat, 'I want to know what kind of woman one should marry. Please don't ask me whether I want to marry or not. Just answer my question.'

'I shall not ask you whether you intend to marry or not. This is entirely your own problem. As regards the question the most important thing is that she should be a virgin. Girls are adept in the art of polite conversation and if a person asks them about social and current moral values, they can answer on the basis of their bought education and received knowledge yet they will not be able to say in which age and which culture they were seduced into losing their virginity. In a society where a ten-year-old girl sees such programmes on television that she starts sucking her own lips, and hears such erotic songs on the radio that she stands before the mirror, spreading her hair to the right shoulder and then to the left to see the effect, and then goes out and people in the neighbourhood stare lasciviously at her, how can she do anything but succumb? Woman has so much beauty within her that if she restrains herself before marriage, then many beautiful realities, of which she never even dreamed, will come to her of themselves. Perhaps one should marry an illiterate village girl; there is no use in marrying a girl who has been to a co-educational school where she has played carom board and other indoor games with boys. If such a girl is asked, "How are you?" and replies, "I am all right", she is talking nonsense, telling lies. She may bring a fridge and a car as dowry, but she will also bring with her, somewhere in her body, eyes that have stopped being formed, and on the blackboard of her brain she will carry a list of birth-control pills. She will know different ways to kiss and she will also remember names in her eyes. On the other hand we should also unveil those eyes that go about in bazaars in search of lechery. Respect should be created in all our social relationships. Once we can accept that this is my mother, this my sister, we can extend that to a brother's wife, a friend's sister, a neighbour's mother, a nurse in a hospital and a lonely woman waiting for a bus. Until we respect our near and distant relationships, we will never make any progress and to know the sanctity of human relationships is the only acceptable form of respect.'

'Rubbish!' Arif retorted angrily.

'This may seem difficult, but it is possible,' Fiazi continued unperturbed. 'The whole of society needs to be changed. A car which has defective brakes, clutch, gears, lighting, speedometer, steering wheel, doors, wheels, tyres and tubes can hardly be expected to move. Almost everything here is defective and useless, but we think it is all right. We shall have to introduce a healthy way of life and live confidently. This means speaking the truth. When truthfulness becomes the rule in life for all, we shall have confidence in each other, and when this mutual confidence becomes the characteristic of society, then sanctity of relationships and their protection will follow automatically. Truth should be promoted in every department of life and there should also be ample opportunities to practise it. Just suppose that a man is sitting at an ordinary table. On the table is a dish of rice, and a bowl of soup, but no water. He will eat, thinking that he can find the water afterwards. After he has eaten, he feels more thirst. The only door in the room is closed from the outside and above it is an open ventilator. He knocks on the door and, failing to get any response, peeps through the cracks in the door and sees that on the other side there is a jug full of water. He eventually reaches the water by placing the chair on top of the table and climbing through the ventilator. In this situation the man was able to get at the jug of water only after overcoming many hurdles. If there had been no ventilator, he would have had to lick his saliva to quench his thirst.

'We, too, are licking our saliva, and have got into the habit of it. We tell lies and have got into the habit of it. We are no longer acquainted with the taste of clean water, and do not know how much freshness there is in it, and how it gives peace of mind. We are telling lies or licking saliva. We have grown to like the taste of the tiny bubbles, and the layers of moist filth that we find to absorb in our mouths. But when a man has water to drink, he does not need to swallow his own spittle. To provide greater opportunities to speak the truth, the means for development should be made available equally to all. No one should be envious or desire to steal from others. We should all feel we can obtain what we need through our own efforts and strength.'

When Fiazi stopped Arif remained still. It was difficult to say whether he was listening to him or not.

'Once desires become rusty, people start avoiding truth,' the artist said, shaking his head.

'Desires,' said Fiazi, as if he was sweeping aside the fragments of a shattered interpretation. 'Man and desires, these two go together, and somewhere between them is death.'

The artist looked thoughtfully at Fiazi. He wanted to say something, but started to cough and went out for a while and returned wiping his mouth with his handkerchief. He sat down on his chair and said, 'Love can wait for this old cough.'

'Arif, you should stand before the artist's door and knock in the air,' Fiazi said.

'What do you mean?' Arif asked, puzzled.

'That sentence is devoid of all meaning; you go there and you will come to know, if love can wait, how long it can wait for.'

'But I will not permit him to come near my door,' the artist said, looking at Arif as if he was a painting.

'Oh!' said Arif, jumping up from his seat. 'What are you saying?'

'I will not allow you to come near my door. Your kind of person should never come there.'

'I never expressed any wish to meet you,' said Arif, looking daggers at him. 'Do you know in whose house you are at the moment?'

'Then I should leave,' said the artist and got up. 'I only came to ask about that boy and girl, because the girl was really lovely, and I wanted to meet her again.'

'Shut up, you idiot!' Arif screamed with all his might, pushing him towards the door. 'Get out of here!' He opened the door.

'Arif Nawaz,' Fiazi's voice followed him, 'he is old and an artist, don't harm him in any way.' Arif stopped. Fiazi thought that his words had had some effect. He realized his misunderstanding, however, when he reached him, for Aziz was standing against the wall on the left, looking down at the ground.

'Aziz!' said Fiazi in surprise.

'I came only to say that the handkerchief has been found,' Aziz said, not raising his eyes.

Arif released the artist's arm and turned his full attention to Aziz. 'Fiazi Sahib, you see, this boy has been standing outside eavesdropping.'

'Arif Sahib, I would not have come here, but I came just to tell you that the handkerchief has been found.'

'Where is it?' Arif asked calmly.

'No, I don't have to show you.' Saying this Aziz looked at the artist and Fiazi and said to them, 'Come, let's go.'

The three of them moved to leave.

'Aziz,' Arif called. 'Listen to me, I want to discuss certain things with you, only a few things and then you can go.'

'Riffat told me that there was no need to go anywhere. If you have found something . . .'

'So you did not tell her that it was the handkerchief?'

'What was the need? She knew she had given me the handkerchief,' said Aziz, heading for the gate.

'Wait,' said Arif, stopping him with a hand on his shoulder. 'Come, let's go inside and sit down.'

'No, no.' Aziz shrank from him in fear.

'Come in, you are my friend. Come Fiazi Sahib, you too, please.' Arif invited the artist as well.

Aziz went up to the verandah with Arif. Fiazi followed and, after a little hesitation, the artist also came after them, taking small steps. Arif took Aziz inside and Fiazi made room for the old man to enter.

'Will you have something to drink?' Arif addressed Aziz.

'May I leave if I wish?' Aziz asked innocently.

'Of course. Why don't we talk first. Riffat gave you a handkerchief, and you told me that you would return it to her. Now you have found it, why are you not returning it?'

'I told Riffat that I had a very beautiful handkerchief and asked her whether I could keep it and she said yes. Now this handkerchief is with me and will stay with me till the day Shagufta tells me why she told me to love that child. When she tells me that, I will return this handkerchief to Riffat.'

'Where did you find it?' asked Arif after a pause.

'I was climbing upstairs and found it lying there. But why did you say that you had the handkerchief and that you would give it to me? Why do you tell such lies?'

Arif had to restrain himself.

'Now please let me go. I want to sleep.'

'So early? Why do you want to sleep now?'

Aziz gave him no reply and started opening and closing his fingers. Arif had nothing further to ask, yet he wanted Aziz to stay there and not go until he could get something important out of him. He soon felt that if he remained silent any longer the people in the room would get up and leave. He was about to ask some meaningless question just to keep the conversation going, when a sentence from the artist drew his whole attention. Even Fiazi looked at the old man in astonishment.

'I want to give you another Arif Nawaz,' the artist said. Arif gazed at him scornfully. The artist spoke again. 'I will bury him in one place and will tell Fiazi Sahib what condition must be fulfilled before opening it.'

'I don't understand your words. Stop this talk. If you wish to leave, you may go,' Arif said with some heat. 'What silly people they are,' he muttered to himself.

'It doesn't matter,' said the artist and got up and went to the door. Fiazi followed him.

'Stop meeting Riffat, Aziz,' said Arif. 'It is not at all proper for you to meet her when you yourself . . .'

'When do I meet her? She gave me the handkerchief to look after.'

Aziz had just finished speaking when the artist and Fiazi re-entered the room. Arif ignored them and, expecting a quick answer, asked Aziz, 'Show me the handkerchief.'

'If I don't give it to you, will you push me again?' Aziz asked defiantly.

'I want to see the handkerchief. I promise before these people that I will return it to you.'

'No, I won't give it to you.'

'Aziz, show him the handkerchief. I will get it back for you,' Fiazi said.

'Fiazi Sahib, it has a fragrance which will change, which will be finished.'

'What rot this boy is talking.' Arif got up and, clasping his hands on his breast, walked with small steps to one side of the room. His lips were tight and his jaws fiercely clenched. No one knew what his intentions were. As Aziz saw him return, he stood up and took out from his pocket a handkerchief with small flowers and tiny stars. He went to Arif and spreading it on the palms of his hands, said nothing. Arif picked up the handkerchief.

'Where did you get this?' Arif asked looking fiercely at him. 'I am sure that it cannot be Riffat's.' He returned the handkerchief to him. Fiazi and the artist stood up and, nodding goodbye to Arif, began to walk out of the room, accompanied by Aziz.

'Fiazi Sahib, I want to tell you that this handkerchief is a fake,' Arif said as they were leaving. 'I feel sorry for the boy, but the fact is that Riffat gave him no handkerchief.'

As Arif spoke, Aziz pushed against Fiazi and returned to the room. He went up to Arif and stood so close that Arif had to take a step back.

'What's the matter?' Arif asked in a harsh tone.

'This handkerchief is not a fake. It is Riffat's.'

'Fiazi Sahib, you are older and wiser, you can see that this boy will create many problems for himself.'

'This handkerchief is not a fake, and there are many days before the end of the year.'

Arif's eyes flashed with a mixture of many emotions. He controlled himself with great difficulty and catching hold of Aziz's arm said, 'I cannot understand what justification there is for you to go on consuming food. You will die soon, until then don't create so much trouble for yourself and everyone else.'

'That handkerchief is not a fake, nor are people and everybody knows that the year will not end all at once,' Aziz said, crushing something between his teeth.

The artist had not come back inside. Fiazi was the first to become aware of his absence. He went out to look for him, but when he could not see him anywhere, he returned and said to Aziz, 'Aziz, let us go.'

Aziz looked utterly dejected. Fiazi caught him by the arm and led him away.

'Fiazi Sahib, even this portion of the wall knows that there are still many days before the year ends,' Aziz said, placing his hand on the wall. 'In all the layers of the wall, among all the bricks joined together, it is written that the year will not end soon, and that before it does, something can easily be done.'

Arif started laughing and the sound of his laughter rolled ruthlessly over them. He came to the door, and stood there laughing. Fiazi pulled the gate open and went out with Aziz. They saw the artist farther along the road.

He would give me a new Arif Nawaz. What nonsense! What kind of Arif Nawaz? What did he mean? Arif set off to call on the artist at the Bara Dari Hotel. He was still a long way off when he also remembered Fiazi's words about standing before the artist's room and knocking in the air. He hurried now, impatient to reach the hotel and unravel what Fiazi had meant.

When he reached the artist's room, he found that the door was closed. He read the red letters on the board: LOVE CAN WAIT, BUT LUST CANNOT. He stood stock-still. His body and mind clashed in turmoil. Standing there contemplating it, he forgot why he had come to meet this 'ordinary' artist as he had thought him.

After a while, Arif knocked on the door. From inside the artist asked who was there. Arif answered, 'It's me; I have come to see you.'

'I am busy,' the artist said.

Arif drew a deep breath and knocked once again humbly requesting to be let in, adding that he would only stay for a few minutes.

'I'm busy,' the artist repeated. 'I cannot see anyone.'

'Please open the door. If I offended you, I am sorry.'

'That's all right. Now please go away, I am working.'

'It's very important that I see you. You said you would give me . . . a new Arif Nawaz. What did you mean? I am ready to accept any condition you impose.'

'I will tell Fiazi when it can be seen. Now leave me alone. I wish to work.'

'Very well. When will you be free? I can wait.'

'I don't know. I may not be free until tomorrow evening. Go away.'

'Please let me ask you one thing,' pleaded Arif, helpless before the closed door. 'Did Riffat tell you that she would come back here?'

Arif heard the sound of a chair or table being dragged across the room. Then the artist came to the other side of the door and unbolted it. Arif stood for a moment in the doorway and then entered the room. As soon as he saw the paintings on the floor and against the walls, he recognized the old man's talents.

'Will you have a cigarette?' Arif said, taking the packet from his pocket. He realized at once that he had made a mistake.

'I have already told you that I don't smoke. I would never have opened the door, but you mentioned a name that I could not ignore and so I let you in.'

'Thank you,' Arif smiled.

'That's all right. What do you want?'

'I came here to find out two things, or rather three. Firstly, did Riffat say when she would come to see you again? Secondly, what did you mean by saying that you would give me a new Arif Nawaz?'

'And thirdly?' the artist prompted.

'Thirdly, I want to know how that sentence "Love can wait, but lust cannot" occurred to you.'

The artist got up and went to the window and gazed at the tin roof below. Arif sat quietly, hoping that he would take notice of him and would answer his questions. The artist came back to his chair, still not speaking. He looked intently instead at a painting on the wall. Arif also turned to look at it. It was of three children sitting on a bed, playing a game. Only the backs of their heads were visible, and the other details were so fine, that he could not make them out from where he was sitting.

'Riffat told you that she would come back,' said Arif, taking his eyes off the painting. 'I should like to see her for a short while.'

'Arif Sahib,' said the artist, ignoring what Arif had just said. 'Riffat came here. I did not talk much to her, and, yes, she did promise to find time to come back some day.'

'Didn't she give a definite date and time?'

'No. Even if she had, I would not tell you when. In my opinion, you are not fit even to look upon her face.'

'What do you mean?' Arif asked quickly.

'I do not think you should see her. Think about that as much as you like.'

'Will you forbid her to meet me?'

'If she knows that I have met you, she will forbid me to see you again.'

'I don't know your name,' Arif said to the artist, 'but this much I want to tell you, No one, no matter how much he tries, will succeed in keeping me and Riffat apart.'

'How can you break a glass that is already shattered?' the artist asked Arif.

'What is your relationship with her? Why do you want to meet her?'

'I love her. She is the first girl I have loved.'

'What!' Arif screamed, jumping up from his chair.

'Yes, it is true. When I saw her I felt that she was the girl I had been thinking about all my life. I never married. I never paid attention to that side of things. I always thought about my art. If Riffat asked me to set fire to all my paintings I would, for the sake of one small smile of hers. I was not acquainted with love, now I know how precious, how permanent and superior it is. Arif, love is the most beautiful truth. All we do is nothing compared to this emotion. When I paint a picture, some people say: 'you are the god of paintings, you do not put colours in them, but soul'. I must have created many paintings, but I sincerely feel that I have been wasting my time. If I had died this morning I would have died a mean, unfortunate death, but having seen Riffat, I consider myself the most fortunate man in the world. As I was returning from your house, I saw new colours descend, and the harmony of those colours formed a rainbow around me and gave me an incomparable awareness of myself. Arif, you may be my friend or my enemy, my countryman or a foreigner, a relative or a stranger, you may be living nearby or far away. Whoever you are, whatever you may be, I want to tell you in full confidence, that I am at present very happy indeed. People say that a man can die of great happiness. I hope that will not happen to me! I love that girl. Even if all the colours came to me by themselves, I should not be able to express what love is. I feel love and this is enough, more than enough.' The artist became silent and sat looking at the blue sky through the window.

'Sixty years. I wasted sixty years.' The artist spoke again in a calm voice. 'I did not realize that I was like an ordinary pebble lying uselessly. Arif, if I had realized that love had not been given to me, if I had been aware that I was deprived of it, then I would have ended my life. I can find no words for the dimensions of feeling that the girl has given me. I have found something of which I had not the least idea. Today I have been perfected.'

'What kind of love do you have for her? You are an old man, she is a girl of eighteen or nineteen.'

'You measure love by days and years. This is where you make a mistake and it only proves how jaded you are. All my perceptions are devoted to this girl.'

'What do you think about her?' Arif bent forward a little as he spoke. 'All right, tell me, if I bring Riffat here will you be prepared to say to her face all that you have been saying to me?'

'Arif, you don't know. You don't know because you are a worm, crawling inside a tree and have no idea what beautiful flowers and fruit are on it. You cannot see the colours of the flowers, nor can you realize what memories of the past or promise of the future are conveyed by the taste of the fruit.'

'You are used up, and your business is the transmission of deceitful and contemptible ideas,' Arif said harshly. 'Riffat is not for a decrepit old man like you. You are certainly a good artist, but your mind is filled with disgusting thoughts. You artists are all like this. You'll see for yourself whom Riffat prefers. I have her letters which are mementoes of her love.'

'And you have another memento on your cheek. If you take this tone with me, I would start reminding you of many things around you, but I don't care a damn for such things and want to stay far from the air you breathe.'

'Listen . . .' Arif only got that far, when the artist began again:

'What a long time it has been. What was the use of selecting colours, squeezing out various shades from my mind and reflecting them on paper? Scattered colours and trembling shadows always shun one another, I had been thinking that it was not possible to combine them. There is a colour, different from all others, which is washed by my inner rain, close to the colour of the rainbow and this put an end to my seclusion. You could not have seen the dew drops on the lawns, dividing themselves in mid-air to go back to their different colours. You cannot even tell me the colour of the dawn, all you have is a mixture of different ideas, whereas I have an everlasting fondness for her.'

'Stop! Stop!' Arif suddenly got up in anger. 'You are venerable regarding your art, but your words are strange. I cannot tolerate some of the things you have said.'

The artist also got up and gazed shakily at Arif.

'Just look at your beard, consider the blood crawling under your dirty skin, and if you succeed in recognizing this reality, then think further.'

The old man laughed strangely. He walked to a painting and standing beside it kept laughing.

'What is there to laugh about? Your laughter is like the earth falling from a grave.'

The artist stopped laughing. He looked at Arif and said, 'You don't believe in my love, but I can tell you, it does not depend on anyone's belief. It may be that I do not love Riffat, but my love is in love with her. You will not be able to understand this, because you live in a world of calculations, and are unable to recognize the reflections created by drizzling colours.'

'I want to ask you only one thing, and I want a quick answer; what are your intentions regarding Riffat?'

'Arif, inside your mind, details are clashing with details; you can never give birth to an eternal feeling.'

'You old dog,' said Arif, gritting his teeth in frustration. 'I am going, but remember this, if you say anything to the girl, or give any occasion for complaint, I will consign you to eternal darkness.'

The artist only laughed at this. His reaction took Arif aback.

'You seem to laugh in a most despicable manner. Although I have a little respect for you because you are a good artist, you arouse my hatred laughing in this way.'

'Arif, I know that you hate me. If there is respect for me in any corner of your heart, I should like you to put it in a box and drown it in the river. Forget that I make good paintings. All you should remember is that I am a man who loves.'

'Tell me truthfully, did Fiazi ask you to say all this?'

'Arif Sahib, fresh ideas have ceased to come to you. Why should Fiazi have asked me to say it?'

'I thought Fiazi might have told you this. Anyway, tell me truthfully . . .'

'Arif, your saying each time: "tell me truthfully" implies that I have been guilty of telling lies,' the artist said resentfully. 'I don't like that.'

'No. I just meant that you should talk freely.'

'I cannot talk freely,' said the artist and got up. 'I will have to be careful about what I say. I never used to speak at all, and that is why I did not care. Now what I say will be said with care.'

'Do you really love her?' Arif stood up too.

'What do you mean by "really"? I have only one feeling, and it keeps me alive. If anyone takes it away, I will cease to live. This is the love of an old man, who had never seen the tree of love.'

'Suppose . . .'

'Arif Sahib, my love is a concept,' the artist interrupted again. 'I am sure that I can keep this concept alive for ever. I want to see her happy under all circumstances, and from there my love becomes limitless. You think that I am old, that my blood is cold, my hair grey, and my eyes like two gobs of spittle from a sick man on a dirty floor. My face is hateful, and no old man of sixty should want to love a girl of eighteen. Arif, my love will not interfere with others. If you wish, it will go far away from all of you. Then you will believe that the old man's love is finished. But I want to tell you that you can bury me under the earth, but you cannot place my love under even the flimsiest piece of paper. Arif, why do you try to expel love from this dilapidated old body where it is housed? Why are you wasting your time trying to make an old man utterly lonely, when he has nothing left in this world but his love?'

'If Riffat asked you not to see her and to stop loving her, what would you do?'

'I would love even this idea of hers. I would continue to love her, no matter what.'

'Don't you understand that this love of yours could create numerous problems for her? Her good name will be tarnished by the fact that an old man is in love with her.'

'She will understand my love and will never think as you do. Her slanderers will themselves be disgraced and people seeing them sitting laughing alone will give them food.'

'You . . .'

'My love for her is silent and secure,' the artist said, not waiting to hear what Arif had to say. 'My love will not arouse the slightest suspicion in the minds of good people, and bad people will be too busy laughing and eating to bother suspecting others.'

There came a knock on the door. The artist asked who it was. A woman of about thirty, dressed in the modern fashion, came in, followed by a man who seemed to be her servant. Arif nodded in greeting and then started looking at the sketch on the easel.

'Perhaps you are busy,' the woman said to the artist, smiling. 'I hope I haven't disturbed you.'

'Please sit down,' the artist said, offering her a chair.

'Thank you. Have you completed those paintings?'

'I have completed four, I was working on the last one.'

'When will that be ready?'

'I cannot say. I have something else in my mind which I want to work on first.'

'May I see the others?' asked the woman.

The artist brought out three paintings of different sizes from behind the picture leaning against the wall. Arif drew nearer. They were water colours. The scene in all three was the same, though the size was different. They were examples of excellent art. The artist passed the fourth picture to the woman. She examined it and leaned it with the front against the table. She took out her chequebook and respectfully asked the artist, 'Will five and a half be all right?'

The artist looked vacantly at the floor and did not answer. She gave him the cheque which he carelessly placed on the crowded table. Arif thought five hundred and fifty rupees quite sufficient for an artist, who did not seem to have many expenses since he lived alone. He only had the rent to pay and some food, and he must be getting more money from others. Arif glanced at the cheque and saw his mistake: the amount was for five thousand five hundred. He looked from the woman to the artist. What did the artist do with all that money? Why was he living like a beggar? If he made a few more such paintings, he could afford a small car. He should keep a servant, and instead of this room have a proper house.

When the woman left, Arif went over to the painting he had noticed earlier from across the room. Now that he had a closer look, something in it sparked his consciousness. It was a mirror reflecting the faces of the three boys who were sitting with their backs to the spectator. Arif held his breath. The room was painted in fine details, even the fourth wall, seen in the mirror. At the bottom of the painting was written in small letters, 'Observe with convex lens'. Arif found the lens lying on the table and took it across to the picture. He saw a world depicted in the painting. Details were inside details and through the lens these came into range and made his head swim. He closed his eyes and slumped down on the chair. For a moment he was terrified of the artist's superhuman powers. He replaced the lens on the table and finding the artist standing beside him, said, 'Please sit down.'

The artist's face was expressionless. He glanced at Arif and then his gaze wandered all over the room.

'You are an accomplished artist,' Arif said admiringly. 'I may not be a connoisseur, but this painting is undoubtedly a masterpiece.' Arif remembered with remorse calling the artist an 'old dog'.

'I wish to sleep,' the artist said. 'Please go and wash away the dust in your mind.'

'All right, I am going. I have been rude, please forgive me. I only want to ask, if Riffat comes here, will you bring her to me? I can wait. I can wait many days.'

'Riffat did not come into this world to meet you, nor should you meet her. If by chance you see her, you should avoid her.'

'Why? Why? I will meet Riffat. No one can forbid that.'

'What if Riffat herself forbids you?' the artist asked.

'Riffat cannot refuse to meet me. I love her truly. She knows that.'

'Tell me one thing and then you can go,' the artist said. 'What did Aziz mean by saying that there were many days before the year ends? I tried to get him to explain, but he just kept on repeating the same words.'

'He is an ignorant boy, don't talk about him. You are a responsible, intelligent person, and should not bother with such nonsense.'

'Perhaps what you call nonsense is, in fact, sense. I should really like to know what he meant by it.'

'Jinab, these things are not important. Again I ask you to bring Riffat to my place. This is an invitation to both of you.'

'No.'

Arif felt this 'no' as a slap on the face. The moment he heard it, Aziz's words about the many days before the year ended echoed in his mind. He asked the artist another question, hoping to learn something.

'When you meet Riffat, what will you tell her?'

'I will ask her whether Aziz has told her anything about there being so many days before the year ends. Perhaps she knows something about this.'

Arif stood amazed. He felt as if the artist had offered him dirty brush-water to drink. He retorted, 'You will do no such thing.'

There was another knock. Arif looked from the door to the artist. The artist said to him, 'Please go now. I do not desire your company any more.'

'Is anyone in?' the visitor called out, knocking again.

'Who is it? Please wait.' It was Arif who answered.

The artist went to the door. He was about three paces from it, when he turned and warned Arif that if he did not leave at once, he would go and phone the police.

Arif did not respond. He wanted to see who had knocked. The artist opened the door and two people came in. One was a middle-aged man, greying at the temples, his face grave and dignified; the other was about thirty-five years old. Behind his glasses his eyes darted round the room. There was dust on his shoes, showing that he had walked a long way. His lips were thick in the round face and he had an air of suppressed anger about him. He looked tired. They both greeted the artist respectfully.

'I did not think you would be in,' said the younger man.

'Excuse me, he was about to go to sleep, and I myself was just leaving,' Arif said. 'I think he should be allowed to go to bed.'

Arif spoke with unbounded confidence, as if the two strangers were his subordinates. He did not know what their relationship was with the artist, or why they had come to see him, nor could he make out what the man with restless eyes was trying to conceal. The older man was dumbfounded and on his expressionless face there appeared a desire to know Arif better and also an awareness that whatever he did he should consider his reaction.

'We have come to see him,' the older man said, indicating the artist. Then he turned to Arif and asked politely, 'And may I ask who you are, Jinab? I have not met you before.'

'Nor I you. It would be better if we went out and talked elsewhere.' Arif waited for them to leave the room. The artist seemed totally unconcerned. He put the cheque into a drawer, and began scraping layers of paint off thick cardboard with the end of a brush. Arif watched the artist for a while and then spoke again to the two visitors, this time peremptorily.

'Come, I have something to say outside.'

The two men hesitated and then got up, as if compelled by Arif.

Remarkably, the artist still showed no reaction. As Arif reached the stairs, he said, 'The old man needs rest. What I wanted to tell you, was that if you had not come out with me, he himself would have told you to go away.' He shook hands with them and left. He was about a hundred yards away from the hotel when he thought of a dangerous plan and hurried home as fast as he could.

'He certainly seemed very determined,' the older man said to his companion.

'Who was he?'

'I don't know, he did not give us a chance to speak.'

'And where is the man we came to meet? He should have come by now.'

'Look . . . he's coming.'

The two men had come to meet Fiazi. When Fiazi, Aziz and the artist had reached the Bara Dari Hotel earlier, after visiting Arif, they had sat in the hall to drink tea. Someone standing nearby with his friend overheard Fiazi say to the artist, 'How helpless God is, living so far away', and had contradicted him. Fiazi learnt that this man was a Christian and that his younger companion, who was wearing glasses, was a recent convert from Islam to Christianity. He arranged to meet them again within the hour after he had taken Aziz home, in order to explain why he believed God was forced to keep such a distance. When he returned Fiazi apologized for keeping them waiting.

'Truth stays in one place and does not mind waiting,' said the man wearing glasses.

'Something unexpected cropped up.'

'You said earlier "How helpless God is, living so far away",' said the older man. 'This means that you do at least acknowledge the existence of God.'

'I was referring to your helpless God. He has the same existence as other false, impracticable and incomprehensible concepts in the world. The words "flying mountain" exist, but whether they point to a reality or not can be decided by oneself. Anyhow, we can discuss all this later. I have come back only to say that I cannot stay. Can we fix another date? Tell me the time and place and I will come.'

'May I ask why you are in such a hurry?' the man with glasses had hardly asked when an auto-rickshaw came and stopped near them. I had seen Fiazi from a distance and had asked the driver to stop beside him. 'Fiazi Sahib, please hurry, those people are calling for you.'

As Fiazi was getting into the rickshaw he said, 'I have to go now.'

'All right,' said the elder, coming nearer. 'Please come to my house the day after tomorrow at four o'clock. Here's my card. It has my name and address on it.'

'Has the dispute still not been settled?' Fiazi asked me as the rickshaw started.

'No, Jinab, the fat man came down again. He tried to drag Aziz's father out by the collar and threatened to hand him over to the police. I managed to persuade him to wait a little, that his money would be returned and he would not need to go to the police station.'

Earlier, when Fiazi had escorted Aziz to his house, he had found that the neighbour from upstairs was accusing Aziz's father of stealing ten rupees from his room. Fiazi had introduced himself as an acquaintance of Aziz and had told the people there that he had been here once or twice and felt sympathy for the boy. They all liked the way he talked and took him for a respectable person. The fat man also thought that a gentleman was telling him to forget the matter and therefore had agreed to overlook it. Nevertheless, Fiazi had felt that the old man had not taken the money. Unfortunately, when Fiazi left, Aziz's father had accused the fat man himself of being a thief and a liar and the whole row had started up again. The fat man had liked the idea of my bringing back Fiazi, thinking that he would disgrace this wretched old man before him.

Fiazi and I soon reached Aziz's house. Everybody was there. Aziz's father was sitting alone on the charpoy next to the wall. The stool which was usually beside the big table was now close to this charpoy and the fat man was sitting on it, smoking. He was wearing a ring with a dark green stone, which he looked at from time to time, as if it was his wrist-watch. A few local people were on the other charpoy, one was middle-aged, wearing a shirt and loincloth, and a loose turban around his head. He had a serious, dignified look about him; obviously no decisions would be taken without his consent. Beside him sat a man dressed in a shirt and loose trousers. He was very weak. He looked more like a patient waiting on a hospital bench for his turn to see the doctor. There were two other persons sitting beside him on the left. One of them bore marks of leucoderma on his face and both his hands were covered in white blotches. His hair was also white. Next to him was Ajmal. Another young boy leaned against the wall, dressed in liver-coloured shalwar and shirt. His clothes were marked with grease and dirt and he looked like a garage-hand, come straight from work. Aziz was also there, staring at the big table with great concentration.

As we entered the room, the fat man announced impatiently, 'They've come.'

Fiazi went to sit beside Aziz's father on the charpoy.

'Jinab, I accepted your proposal and let this stupid old man go, but after you left he started saying I was guilty myself. He has stolen my money. I was convinced of it before but now I will not let him go under any circumstances. Either he returns it, or he cools his heels in jail. If he needs money, he should work for it. He could clear drains, dig and carry earth or beg. But this is theft and from me of all people!'

'If I had committed theft, the money would have been found on me,' Aziz's father said to Fiazi. 'He is lying, he has spent it somewhere.'

'Where have I spent it? I could have cursed you. Respect for these people restrained me, otherwise I could have extracted the money from you within seconds.'

'How could you get it from me, when I do not have it?'

'When I put my hand on your neck, then you will confess everything.'

'In what condition was he when you met him?' the man with the turban asked the fat man.

'I went down to the street to buy cigarettes. Khwaja, the shopkeeper, sent a boy to get change for five rupees, because he did not have any. I told him it did not matter, he could write it down and I would pay in the evening. I took half a packet of cigarettes and came upstairs and found the old man hurrying down from the third floor. I paid no attention to him, but when I entered my room I found that my ten-rupee note had disappeared from the table. I searched everywhere; under the table, on the charpoy, under the bedding, and could not find it. Why had he come upstairs? Just to get into the open? How childishly he talks. As if he has placed something up there with an open hole.'

'Had he stolen money from you before?' Fiazi asked him.

'I do not know. But I used to keep losing money. He is the only one who could have done such things. Jinab, he is a thief, and a thief should get the punishment he deserves.'

'If I am a thief, I should be punished for it, yet you take women upstairs and have no consideration for the neighbours. And I know what sort of relationship you have with those women you call your relatives.'

'Shut up, you son of a thief!'

'Please look again, the money must be there somewhere,' a feminine voice came from behind a closed door. It was the third time Aziz's mother had asked the fat man this.

'I have searched thoroughly. Do you think that I should spend all week searching for the money?'

'I have not taken it. You talk to me.' Aziz's father's voice trembled.

'What should I say to you? You . . .'

'All right, whatever you are, I don't care; I tell you again that I know nothing about your ten rupees.'

'I asked you whether he had stolen money from you before or was today the first time that this happened?' Fiazi asked the fat man.

'I did not steal any money.' Suddenly the old man stood up. 'I have stated that I didn't take it, so why is it being said that I did?'

'All right,' Fiazi tried to calm him. 'Please sit down and give me a chance to speak.' He turned to the fat man and repeated his question.

'Jinab, he has never been caught before, but I know that he is a thief.'

'How bad theft is, it disgraces and ruins a man's prestige,' commented the weak-looking man.

'How do you know that he is a thief?'

'Jinab, whenever I see him, he only seems to ask for money.'

'I have never asked him for money in my life,' said the old man.

'I know that the old gentleman is not a thief,' said the man with white hair, whose voice was not as old as his hair might have suggested.

'You are yourself a thief, how can you say that he is not one?'

'Unlike you, I do not take woman sweepers and low-caste women to my room. You may have lit a cigarette with the note when you were drunk, and now you are accusing this poor innocent man of theft, and that too of a paltry sum of ten rupees. May you be cursed.'

'Shut up. Who asked you to come here? Go away.'

'You shut your mouth or I will tear out your guts. You know very well who I am. Please let us go, all of us,' the white-haired man said, turning to those gathered there. 'He is a fraud, come on, uncle, let's go,' he said to the man with the turban.

'Quiet, Siddiq, you have no business to say anything here,' the man with the turban said angrily. 'You go home, I will come soon.'

'Fiazi Sahib, there should be rain in this room.' Suddenly Aziz's voice was heard. 'There is no shortage of water in rain and it should rain soon here.' He went into the small inner room where his mother was.

'He isn't a thief either, I suppose,' said the fat man ironically to the man with the turban. 'I am surprised that Ashraf let them this house. I don't know how these people manage to make ends meet.'

'Well, what do you want?' Fiazi asked him. 'Your money may have been stolen, but I can assure you that this man is not the thief.'

'That is my opinion too. The old man can do a lot of things, but not steal,' said Siddiq, the white-haired man.

'Have you ever seen him going up or coming downstairs before and asked him why?' Fiazi addressed the fat man. 'I think you are not the owner of the roof. If someone wants to go there for a while, you have no right to be suspicious. He may have gone to search for his cat, or a hundred other reasons. Someone coming downstairs does not have to be coming from your room. It was coincidence that, when you discovered the loss of your money, the old man was coming down past your door. If you had not lost the money and had seen him coming down, you would never have jumped to the conclusion that he had been to your room.'

'He is a thief, I am convinced of it. He has stolen my money, and he will have to return it.'

'I don't have the money, so how can I return it?' the old man asked tearfully.

'What a bad thing is theft. Oh, theft is really very bad. It ruins a man's prestige,' the weak man chimed in again feebly.

'This isn't the first time,' said the fat man. 'My beautiful blue glass has gone astray and even the electric bulb on the landing has been removed, and some time ago I missed forty rupees. Where is everything going, who is the thief who keeps coming up here? This man has to return my money or I will report it to the police.'

As he was talking, the door to the small room opened and Aziz came out, his eyes vacant. For some time he stood behind the people sitting on the charpoy and then he walked calmly over to Fiazi and said, 'Fiazi Sahib, have you got sixty paisas, please?'

Fiazi took out a fifty and a twenty-five paisa coin and gave these to him. Aziz put the money in his pocket and went out. After he had gone, Ajmal left too. Now there were eight people in the room, including the young boy who looked like a mechanic.

The man wearing the turban was about the same age as Fiazi. He had taken off one shoe and was sitting with his legs crossed. He was following all that was being said with close attention. Next to him was the weak man, sitting like a straw hanging in a cobweb. Whenever he said that theft ruins a man's prestige, he did not seem to care whether anyone was speaking or not, or whether anyone was prepared to listen. Siddiq, who was sitting next to him, aroused my curiosity most, firstly because his features were quite uncommon and secondly because of his absolutely white hair. I had thought he was old, but when he spoke his voice made it clear that his age had nothing to do with his white hair. The style of his speech was strongest of all those present. He spoke in a carefree manner as if nothing could ruffle his calmness. As he sat, he spread out his legs and rested his wrists on them and clasped the fingers of both hands as he leaned forward, or else he would lean back and rest the palms of his hands on the charpoy behind him and look up at the ceiling. At present he was sitting relaxed in the lotus position. Since Ajmal had got up, he had more room on the charpoy for this. Be that as it may, this person always remained in my sight and whenever Fiazi, the fat man or anyone else stopped speaking, I would glance over at him. The boy mechanic was paying close attention to all that was being said, particularly by the fat man. He also often looked at Siddiq sitting near him.

The fat man took out a packet of cigarettes and said, 'What is to be done now? I am a hundred per cent sure that no one except him could have taken the money. God damn it, I went down for a minute and when I returned, it had disappeared.'

'You are a hundred per cent sure, yet I say he did not take the money.' Fiazi spoke humbly.

'Jinab, what strange things you are saying. If he had taken it, do you think he would admit it? Not without torture. Unless third degree methods are used, he will not confess his guilt.'

'Please go away, somehow or other we will give you the money,' Aziz's mother said from the small room.

'Why will you?' Aziz's father said in a voice that shook with rage. 'There is no money. Go, go wherever you like. You may fetch the police. I will receive a beating. If there is no money, how can I return it? Latif, (addressing the man wearing the turban) do you think I can commit theft?'

'Sit down, sit down. Why are you shouting if you have not stolen the money?' the fat man asked.

'I have abducted your mother, I have carried away your sister, but I have not taken the money,' Aziz's father shouted in rage. I managed to catch his arms and restrained him. He struggled to free himself from my hold and looking at the fat man said, 'Beat me as much as you want, but how can I give you the money if I do not have it? You drink liquor and bring back women, we hear the noise of laughter from upstairs . . . voices . . .'

'Please, stop this kind of talk,' said Fiazi, moving towards him.

'You see for yourself what he is saying. Now if I smash his head, people will say that he was poor. He is a thief and that is why he is talking nonsense. I will send his whole family to jail,' the fat man retorted. Everyone except for the weak man stood up and gathered around the fat man and Aziz's father.

'Theft is a curse. How it disgraces a man's prestige.' I heard the weak man's voice again.

'The old gentleman is not a thief, I know he is not,' Siddiq said, addressing us all.

'How do you know that he is not a thief ? You yourself steal iron. Get out, you swindler.'

'Uncle, please stand aside, let me deal with him,' Siddiq said to Latif. 'I will tell him in this very room who is a swindler.'

'No, no, no. We will return the money,' Aziz's mother screamed from behind the door of the small room. 'Don't fight, there is no need to fight.'

Aziz's mother's voice was drowned in the hubbub. The fat man was standing close to Fiazi, saying something to him. Siddiq was just behind Latif who was telling him to leave the room. Aziz's father was struggling with me. He broke free and rushed at the fat man intending to hit him or be hit. I quickly sprang and pulled him back.

'If you are such a staunch supporter of his, then give me ten rupees. Everywhere you try to establish your leadership.' The fat man looked balefully at Siddiq.

'You're a fraud, trying to get money from this poor man. You should be ashamed of yourself.'

'It is you who should be ashamed, the police are always looking for you.'

'All right, I am a thief, but I don't use my home as a brothel. I am bold enough to steal iron, and you look greedily at the house of the poor. If you had accused me or said these things to me, I would have flung you out of the window.'

'Latif Sahib, I respect you, otherwise I would fix this white pig right now.'

'I am prepared to swear that I didn't take any money,' said the old man and began to recite Qalima Taieba.

'He is just reciting. It means nothing,' the fat man said and turned to Siddiq. 'Go, why are you standing here? Go and attend to your business, stealing wire and iron.'

'I intend to do other work today.' Saying this, Siddiq went quickly up to the fat man and punched him. He was about to punch him again, when the fat man stepped back and Fiazi intervened. The fat man was cursing Siddiq. Getting away from Fiazi, he picked up a copper cooking pot and threw it at Siddiq. Now these two were standing facing one another, shouting obscenities. Aziz's mother came out of the room and picked the copper pot up from the floor. She quickly collected all the cooking pots and other breakable things scattered about in the room and took them back with her into the small room. The boy mechanic still stood in one corner. He seemed very pleased with the commotion. I had not paid much attention to him, but I remember that I had noticed him applauding someone, saying 'very good, excellent' above the din of curses. The old man's condition was most pitiable. He had ceased struggling in my hands and had gone silent and limp. I released my hold on him. This was my biggest mistake. As quick as lightning, the old man leaped on to the table and was at the open window. He would certainly have jumped, if the boy mechanic had not caught hold of his leg. I ran over too and dragged him back into the room. This incident with its frozen sea of sorrow and affliction shook everybody. It was obvious that the old man had intended suicide.

'Now tell us, are your ten rupees more valuable than a man's life?' Siddiq asked the fat man.

'All this is drama, no more,' the fat man said, avoiding everyone's gaze.

'You are very mean,' said Siddiq, gritting his teeth.

'All right, he may not have stolen my money, but why go on the window sill? And if he really wanted to jump, then why didn't he?'

The old man was as dangerously quiet as before, so I held on to him firmly. He was blinking rapidly. This may have been an old habit but I had just noticed it. The weak man went to the window and looked down, shuddering.

'People like you are without conscience,' Siddiq said to the fat man.

'It is all just drama, and you are as much an actor as he is,' retorted the fat man. 'If he had not stolen anything, why did he want to jump?'

'That is to say, if he had stolen your money, he should have jumped?' Fiazi asked him. 'That does not make sense. You have some very odd principles.'

'Jinab, you do not know these people. Siddiq, who stands before you, his brother deliberately stabbed himself.'

'He stabbed your mother between her legs! If these people were not here, by God, I would have thrown you out,' Siddiq said, breaking away from Latif. 'No, Uncle. You do not know what a scoundrel he is. It was on his instigation that Rauf filled a bottle with acid. Go and tell him that I am not afraid of his mother's lover.'

'That is why you were asking his forgiveness in the street! Keep cool. I can pick you up and throw you down, you thief and friend of thieves.'

'Mind your language, take a hold of yourself,' Siddiq said angrily.

'I want to ask only one thing, if he did not mean to steal, then what was he doing up there?'

'You are the son of a pig, and your mother was a prostitute,' the old man said, breaking his silence, not caring about the consequences. This, too, was a kind of suicide, because he made no attempt to step back and stood his ground, looking defiantly at the fat man. He had uttered the obscenities before, but the way he spoke now showed that some secret had been revealed.

The fat man's lips trembled. He could not understand what had happened, how this weak old man could talk to him like this before all these people. His mouth hung open in amazement.

'He is quite right,' Siddiq whispered to the boy mechanic who was nearest.

The fat man did not hear. He was still dazed. The old man relapsed into his former listless state, disappointed that the naked electric wire he had just touched had been without any current.

'I would ask you not to take notice of his words,' Fiazi said to the fat man. 'The best thing would be to leave him alone and, as for your money, I promise you will get it from me in the morning.'

'No, Jinab, why should you pay? It's not the money I need . . .'

'Please don't concern yourself any more,' Fiazi said, leading him by the arm to the door. The weak-looking man and Latif also left the room. Fiazi soon returned and said to the old man, 'You should not have said such things. I know that you did not take the money . . .'

'No, Jinab, that is the way to treat such people,' Siddiq disagreed. 'You do not know how mean he is. He is a drunkard and has no consideration for the good name of others.' During this conversation Aziz's mother came out into the room, looking at her husband with trepidation.

'I did not have the money. I never have any, so how could I give it to him? I will try to put an end to my life. What is there for me to live for except starvation and troubles?'

'One should have courage, one should be patient,' Siddiq said, looking sympathetically at him.

'Courage, patience, how patient should one be? There are limits. What is to be done when a man's patience is exhausted?'

'Don't take things so seriously. You must not mind what people say. They are . . .'

'It's not a question of minding, my friend, my master, my lord,' replied the old man. 'The mind starts boiling. When I spend my life cleaning wheels of cars, blowing on windscreens to make them shine and only get eight annas, I am filled with rage, I feel accursed. The mind of a man like me wants to be released. Kill it or keep it alive, and if you keep it alive then don't give a man a mere eight annas; nothing can be done with eight annas.' He spoke the last sentence rapidly as if answering some unseen power.

Fiazi led him to the charpoy and said, 'Nothing can be done without patience and patience is the only inferior thing which can be of any use to us.'

'Let me bring you something to eat,' Siddiq said to the old man and got up to go.

'No, no. He had said that I would become a beggar. I am not a beggar, nor do I want to become a thief. There is no need to bring me anything.'

'Please eat something,' Aziz's mother said.

'I don't need food. I want no share in ill-gotten gains, or in alms.' The old man looked at a corner of the room. 'I have no need for such tainted money, I spit on it.'

Aziz's mother got up and went back into the small room.

'I know where this money comes from, by what devious routes it has reached here. It has passed through evil places. All right, do as you please. I can't prevent it, but I can at least spit on it.'

'For God's sake stop it. I will go nowhere,' said Aziz's mother from the small room, opening the door a little. 'If you like, I will not go out to work. I will stay at home all day, only don't say things like this.' She started to cry and her voice choked as she closed the door again.

'I have eyes and can see, and I see all that is going on. I don't approve of begging, I will not permit anyone to beg for alms.'

The new tone which the old man was trying to create in his voice, pushing back the brimful desire of inquisitiveness, was so ragged, torn and bleeding that it revealed all the hidden wounds. In his eyes was gathered the pain of days gone by, and in them were woven the bad moments of the past like barbed wire. Misery sat on his face as if lamenting its own loneliness and wanting to leave this abode for some other.

'Fiazi Sahib, tell me whether I said anything wrong,' said the old man. 'Is not asking for alms a bad thing? Mother and son do it. Everything that is done here is wrong, how can I tolerate it?'

'Begging for alms is not good, but sometimes a man can be eaten up by his needs.'

'It is better to go somewhere. I can also stay quiet and not open my mouth.'

I could not understand all the old man was saying. His mumbled conversation became more and more disjointed. He looked here and there and then started gazing at the floor.

'First of all, I think that . . .' Siddiq did not get the opportunity to complete his sentence when the door opened with a noise and I was startled to see Arif Nawaz.

Arif had a decisive air about him and his restless eyes surveyed the room. Suddenly he went to the small room and, calling out Aziz's name, pushed open the door. An involuntary 'oh' came from his lips and he turned back apologetically. All of us sat still, watching him. He approached us and the expression on his face changed. He sat down on the stool and said to Fiazi, 'So you are here. You must have come straightaway.'

'Yes, I had some work and had to return.'

'Nobody else is here? Where is Aziz? I have come specially to meet him.'

Arif ignored my presence altogether, thinking me of no importance, and started to examine the rest of the people. No one answered his question about Aziz, and he did not seem to notice, he was too sunk in his own thoughts.

'And how are you, Fiazi Sahib? You left in a hurry. I felt afterwards that I might have said something that Aziz did not like. I came to make amends for all that happened, and to make him feel that he is among friends.'

'He did not say anything afterwards to show that he was displeased with you. Anyway, I will convey your feelings to him.'

'Where is he? It would be good if I could meet him. I will assure him that we will never misunderstand him in future. But the question is, where is he now?'

'He didn't say where he was going. I think he will return soon.'

'Did he go on his own?' Arif asked.

'No, there was someone else with him.'

'Who? Who?' Arif asked impatiently.

'Ajmal, a boy who lives around here, was with him,' said Siddiq.

'Perhaps you were in a hurry that day and that was why you left,' I said, trying to create an opening to speak to Arif, wondering at the same time what answer he would give. He had a good look at me and then only said, 'Yes.'

I bore this condescension and said pleasantly, 'You did well that day to give them some money. I liked that.'

'Thank you.' Saying this, he immediately turned to Fiazi and asked, 'Did the artist tell you anything on the way, something which you felt?'

'Felt? What do you mean? Obviously whenever another person speaks, a man feels what has been said.'

'No, that's not what I mean,' Arif said and smiled. 'I wondered whether he had said something that surprised you.'

'I am not in the habit of being surprised at what is said, in a way I expect it.'

'Of course,' Arif laughed, 'and do you know that near the borders of Alaska, America and Russia are stock-piling atomic missiles to be used against one another?'

'I hate atomic missiles,' Fiazi answered.

'Are you satisfied with America's war preparations?'

'What significance can there be in whether or not I am satisfied with America's war preparations? I am not the American defence minister.'

'Jinab, you said you had to go out of town. Did you go?' I suddenly remembered what he had said his plans were.

Arif looked at me with restless eyes and after a pause said with some severity, 'I went.' It was clear that he did not want any more questions.

Fiazi scanned Arif's face and started to stare at an old shoe under the charpoy. The shoe had no laces and had been repaired in several places. He was unconcerned about the rest of the room and did not care whether Arif was looking at him or not. Siddiq, sitting beside Fiazi, was examining Arif with great interest, ready to look elsewhere if Arif caught his eye. The boy mechanic was next to Siddiq, watching everyone there. Aziz's father was also on this charpoy, silent, perhaps making amends for the nasty things he had said earlier. His loose-rooted hair was so dishevelled that it was as if the hairs had announced their own death before the death of the body. He had taken out some change, which amounted to no more than a few annas, from the pocket of his old, second-hand, army shirt. He stood up, holding it. I stiffened in case he went to the window again, but he went to the small inner room where Aziz's mother was. Arif bent towards Fiazi and asked curiously, 'What's the matter with him?'

'Nothing. What brings you here?' Fiazi asked. 'Who told you we were here?'

'I didn't come to see you. I wanted to meet Aziz, and now I don't know when he will be back.'

'Jinab, he will come soon, he has gone somewhere close by,' said Siddiq.

'Was he alone?' Arif asked. He immediately realized that he had already asked this question, so he quickly added, 'I mean except for that boy?'

'No, Jinab, they went out after each other. It is difficult to say whether they were going to the same place or whether they parted once they were out.'

'I see. You live somewhere here too?' Arif asked him with a smile.

'Yes, quite close. The old man is our neighbour.'

'I see, and what is your name?'

'Siddiq Bawa. I am a scrap-metal dealer. The fact is, there was a hubbub here a little while ago.' He seemed keen to give information, partly because he wanted to avoid further questions about himself.

'Hubbub, what kind of a hubbub?' Arif asked with interest.

'The man who lives upstairs and who's a fraud, accused the old man of stealing ten rupees from his room. The old man was so troubled, his heart was so pained, that he tried to jump out of the window.'

'Ah, that is indeed terrible.'

'Then on top of this, he said that the old man was making a drama – he was making a child with his sister,'* Siddiq added angrily.

While Siddiq was speaking, the sound of whispering came from the inner room. I was listening to Siddiq, but my ears were also tuned to the inner room. I was anxious that nothing else serious would develop.

'I would have beaten him up, if the people here hadn't intervened,' said Siddiq, gratefully accepting a cigarette from Arif.

'Who stopped the old man jumping from the window?'

Siddiq looked at the boy mechanic and said, 'He did, this son of a lion.'

Arif looked at the boy mechanic and said with surprise, 'This boy? He is no more than nine or ten.'

'Jinab, he is a super-hit mechanic, you don't know him, he earns nine rupees a day.'

'Very good. What is your name, friend?' Arif asked him. 'What work do you do?'

'I am a motor mechanic, and I can drive a car,' the boy said with pride.

'Really?' Arif was astonished. 'Congratulations. How fast can you drive?'

* Urdu metaphor.

'One should drive according to the condition of the road. If you drive too fast, you ruin the engine.'

'But you're not old enough.'

'Jinab, he was born in the workshop,' Siddiq said with a laugh. 'He started working when he was very small. He is a very brave boy.'

'How did he save the old man from jumping?'

'I caught hold of his tie rod,' the boy mechanic answered.

'Tie rod?' Siddiq asked in amazement, amused. I noticed that the boy mechanic winked at Siddiq, hiding his embarrassment. Arif also laughed. All three were chatting pleasantly, Arif occasionally glancing at the outer door. While they were talking, the old man came out of the small room and, without looking at anybody, left the house. Arif asked the boy mechanic, 'Do you live around here?'

'Jinab, I live three houses away. I came here when I heard the noise.'

'It seems you do not bathe. On your neck and hands, there is . . .'

'Jinab, he bathes once a month,' Siddiq broke in. 'He hates soap. People like him think that soap is their sworn enemy.'

'Siddiq, you are disgracing me for nothing. Work is work, and play is play. My boss says work during working hours and play in leisure hours.'

'What do you play?' Arif asked him.

Fiazi, who had been aloof from this conversation, got up and slowly walked out of the door. I thought of following him to ask his impressions of the scene he had just witnessed, but before I could move from my chair the boy mechanic asked me what things I thought were amusing.

'Don't count on his opinion,' Arif said, looking at me scornfully. 'He is like a broken trunk. Tell me what you like to do.'

I was not able to understand Arif's irony, nor did Siddiq show any reaction, but the boy mechanic laughed out loud and said, 'Very good, excellent.' He paused and then answered Arif, 'I go to see films, and . . .'

'And what else? Speak up, speak up.'

'Sometimes I play a few hands.'* He had a sly smile on his face. 'That is all. I manage to pass the time.'

Once again I thought of Fiazi and got up. I had expected Siddiq to ask me to remain seated, and had a suitable answer ready, but he got up too

* Jargon for gambling.

and followed me to the door. I was about to push the door when it opened from the other side. It was Fiazi. I stepped aside to let him enter. Siddiq started humming a popular love song 'This intoxicating evening is making me drunk' and went out. After he left, Fiazi said to Arif, 'I am leaving. It is not important that you meet Aziz just now. Everybody is going and you should too.'

The boy mechanic heard and at once got up and left. Arif rose from his stool and came to Fiazi.

'Please wait a little,' he said in a persuasive manner. 'I will leave with you. Did Aziz go out alone?' he repeated the same question. Fiazi did not respond, did not even look at him. Arif got ready to leave and we all came out of the door. Arif led the way down, followed by Fiazi, I brought up the rear. Downstairs, the two goats had gone and the water tap was dripping as usual. We were approaching the main entrance when Aziz staggered in. He looked at us with dazed eyes and said with some difficulty, 'He . . . he . . . is coming . . .' He seemed to be addressing us from a great distance.

'Who is coming, Aziz?' I asked, coming close. There was a strange smell on his breath, stale, like wet lime that has been lying about for a long time.

'Who is it?' Arif asked impatiently and was about to go out of the main entrance when Bashir came inside and stopped, dumbfounded.

Seeing Bashir, Arif took out a small pistol.

'Come here, come here, or I will shoot you right now,' Arif told Bashir, gesturing with his pistol. Bashir approached, looking at Arif in fear and anger.

'Sit down,' Arif said, pointing to the earth, which was quite unfit for anyone to sit on. It was unpleasant even to stand there. Goat droppings and urine, old feathers, bits of waste paper, cigarette butts, and broom twigs were scattered around. Water from the tap had made the place even damper. Arif looked at Bashir with blood-shot eyes, it seemed possible that he would shoot him there and then. Bashir realized this and, looking helplessly at us, sat down.

'Arif, listen, I want to . . .' Bashir tried to talk, but Arif refused to listen to him. He made a swift movement of his hand and said ferociously, 'Just sit still.'

Fiazi was standing near the stairs, watching Arif with concentration. Aziz had sat down near the door behind us. Now the nature of the smell from his mouth was revealed; the odour of wet lime was obviously the smell of some cheap drug, beginning to have its effect.

'Arif, what are you doing?' Fiazi took a step towards him. Arif did not answer. He went to the door and closed it in such a way that no one passing in the street could see what was going on inside the entrance, but still some light came in from outside.

'Arif, you have no idea what you are doing. A little while ago something quite serious happened here and . . .'

'Fiazi Sahib, keep quiet,' Arif said, looking at him angrily. He turned to watch Bashir.

'Arif, you are doing something very wrong,' Fiazi said, trying to make him understand.

'He is your son, and that is why you cannot keep your mouth closed. I tell you with all responsibility, that you should keep quiet.' It was difficult to know what he meant by 'responsibility'.

'Arif, you . . .'

'Wait,' he said, rudely interrupting Fiazi, and to Bashir, 'Pick up this boy (pointing to Aziz) in your arms and walk upstairs. Remember, if you try to be clever, you will answer for the consequences. The bullet that is aimed at your arm can also pierce your chest.'

Bashir went to Aziz who was reluctant to be moved.

'Be quick,' Arif ordered Bashir, then he remarked, 'Fiazi Sahib, how strange it is that the bullet which left home for one person is now destined for someone else.'

'Arif, I tell you again, you are doing wrong. How can he be my son? You are suffering from a delusion, and you are surrounding yourself with more delusions.'

'Fiazi Sahib, stop this talk,' Arif scolded. 'Bashir, carry this boy right up to the roof. I will speak to you there.'

Bashir picked Aziz up in his arms. Arif led the way, climbing the stairs backwards, watching us all. He asked Bashir and then me to follow and, when he had climbed a few stairs, motioned Fiazi to come up also.

After some steps, Bashir stopped and said, 'Look, Arif, don't take the law in your hands. You know . . .'

'Bashir, I am giving you a last warning, do not stop and do not try to speak. I will talk to you when we get to the roof.'

Bashir gave Arif a searching look and continued climbing again. Now we had started the climb to the second floor where the fat man lived. His door was padlocked. There was a strange, dead kind of silence in this part of the house. We went to the third staircase. These stairs were in better condition than the previous ones and it was obvious that they were not much used. They were brighter, too, from the light coming directly from the roof, though the twilight made them seem sad and forlorn. Arif took us out on to the roof and told us all to stand on one side.

There were a couple of bamboo poles which had been discoloured by weathering and near them some planks and beams, a portable water heater and the wooden frame of a charpoy. There was very little else on the roof. Arif told us to sit close to a high wall where the bamboo poles and planks were lying. He sat on a brick a bit away from us.

Bashir placed Aziz gently on one of the planks and let him rest his back on the wall behind. Aziz was quite senseless, and would not have been able to sit without the support of the wall. Seeing his condition I suddenly remembered what the old man had once said: that there was no room in his house for pill freaks. I had a vague recollection of having once before seen Aziz when he was under the influence of drugs, though I could not recall the exact occasion. Anyhow, he looked pathetic. He had blocked all possibilities of getting better with the remnants of his own flesh and blood. His eyes were half open, but he was in no condition to see anyone. His long legs sprawled out awkwardly and looked like the bamboos lying beside him. The situation was very uncertain. Arif held the small black pistol in his hand and from the start I noticed that his mood was such that if anything was done contrary to his wishes, he would open fire. Quite apart from this, I was convinced now that whoever among us was destined to die could not escape, but that Aziz would die anyway in the days to come.

'Look, Arif, put away your pistol, this is . . .'

'Fiazi Sahib, do you think I am a child? I know that he is your son. All right, you refuse to own him as your son. So much the better for me. I will, however, ask you to remain absolutely silent.'

Fiazi did not speak and it looked as if he would not for some time. Bashir was sitting next to me and that made me feel quite frightened.

'Bashir, where is Kulsoom?' Arif asked him calmly.

'Arif Sahib, I want to discuss this with you myself. Please put your pistol away.'

'Shut up. Answer my question. You took Kulsoom and went away. Did you pick her up alone in a jungle or in some boat that you were so unmindful of the consequences of your action? Answer me.'

'Arif Sahib, what answer shall I give you?'

'If you do not answer, I will wait a few moments and I shall shoot you, that is why I brought you to the roof. Kulsoom is not as important to me as your answers. Do not tell lies. The moment I find you lying, you will be dead. Why did you take Kulsoom away with you? What was in your mind at the time?'

'If you want truthful answers, put your pistol in your pocket. I cannot tell you anything while you are holding it.'

Arif gave him a piercing look. He did not put the pistol in his pocket, but placed it in his lap, and looked at Bashir, waiting for an answer.

'Arif, I loathe and detest you. That is my complete answer,' Bashir said.

'What do you mean?' Arif's hand went involuntarily to the pistol, but he controlled himself in time.

'Arif, you did not consider her to be a woman. It is true that she cannot speak, but that is no reason to give her such severe punishment. I don't know what you are. I am not able to understand you. You treated her disgracefully.'

'Why did you take her away with you?' Arif asked, his voice controlled. 'You are not her guardian. You should have gone away without her.'

'I want to marry her.'

'Marry?' exclaimed Arif in a tone expressive of his anger and scorn. 'What do you mean by that, how can you marry her?'

'Whatever the nature of your marriage was with her, it must be ended. Then I will marry her in the correct manner, respecting all her rights. I wish to make her my wife.'

'And what is her reaction to this?'

'She will marry me. She is certain that I will keep her as a wife.'

'As a wife? Bashir, get up.' Arif's voice was icily monotonous, as if it came from the wall behind. 'Get up, be quick and stand there,' he said, gesturing with the pistol.

There was the silence of death all around, or the silence which creeps below a flowing river. Bashir watched Arif carefully, surprised. He went over to the wall overlooking the street and stood there. He seemed aware that if he disobeyed, Arif would definitely kill him.

'Bashir, listen carefully. Look, I have three more bullets,' Arif said, taking them out from the pocket of his bush jacket. 'There are six in the pistol, but I assure you that one will be enough for you. The price of a bullet is five and a half rupees. Remember, if you agree to do what I ask, I will not waste the money. You have two alternatives and you have to choose one: either give me the occasion to use a bullet or else jump down from this three-storeyed house.'

I could not believe my ears. I shrank in fear and sat very still, thinking that even the slightest movement might make me the target of his anger. Bashir looked terrified.

'Hurry up. If you do not obey me, your death is certain. I have given you the chance to choose one of two alternatives.'

'But why should you be after my life? I have merely saved an innocent woman from a situation in which her mind and body were rotting. You cannot punish me like this.'

'Bashir, I count up to fifty in my head, and I will not tell you how fast I am counting. Only the sound of the bullet will announce that I have reached fifty, and that will be the last moment of your life.'

'Arif, you will not kill him,' Fiazi said, looking him in the eye.

'I know that he is your son, but if you show the least bit of irresponsibility, then you will pay for it. Perhaps you have no idea of what loss you will suffer. Keep quiet. See all this as a dream.'

'How? How can I?'

'Fiazi Sahib, just keep your mouth shut and try to absorb all you are seeing. Why should you grieve at his death when you do not acknowledge him as your son?'

'Arif, I cannot keep quiet. He is not my son, I don't know whose son he is, yet I will not let him die. You have gone off your head. I will stop you . . .'

'Fiazi Sahib, I do not want to hear your voice again. If you became silent for ever, then the responsibility would be yours. I have decided that Bashir will jump from here. He will probably be killed or he might escape with serious injuries.'

'Listen to one thing I have to say, and maybe you will change your mind,' Bashir said in a frightened voice. Arif did not speak, it was obvious that he had started counting.

'What are you doing? You . . .' Fiazi tried to speak. He was interrupted by Arif: 'Thirty-seven, thirty-eight, thirty-nine . . .' The numbers seemed like drops dripping steadily. He let us hear them to prove that he was actually counting. Arif must have reached somewhere near forty-five when Bashir looked at him appealingly and asked, 'Can you not count up to seventy-five?' Arif nodded. 'All right. You still have to choose one of the two alternatives. Forty-nine, fifty, fifty-one, fifty-two . . .'

He was counting mentally, even as he spoke, so that the counting did not stop. Bashir realized this and therefore did not try to buy time by asking questions. He went to the wall and looked down. Fiazi joined him. I was breathing very slowly, and felt as if I was hardly present. Aziz slumped, senseless.

'Sixty-seven, sixty-eight, sixty-nine . . .' The numbers started dripping again.

'Arif Nawaz.' Suddenly Fiazi spoke, as he returned from the wall. 'I promise to arrange a meeting between you and Riffat. You may talk to her for an hour. I give you my word, trust me.'

Arif heaved a deep sigh. He looked at the barrel of the pistol, at Bashir, Fiazi, and back at Bashir. 'Bashir, I will save up a worse punishment for you. I will tell you what it is when I next meet you.' He then said, 'We are leaving. Stay here, the rest of you, and come down shortly.' To Fiazi he said, 'Come on, Jinab.'

The two went towards the stairs, Arif looking at Bashir and still holding the pistol. He went downstairs with Fiazi, closing the door behind them. Despite the closed door we could hear the sound of their footsteps on the stairs. We were all quiet. I did not have the courage to say anything to Bashir. We both looked over the wall. After a while we saw Arif and Fiazi emerge from the main gate, walk down the narrow street and turn right at the end.

'I will have to do something about him. It has become imperative,' Bashir said to himself.

I was looking down. Three storeys, nearly fifty feet high. In the dim twilight there were many colours, many scenes and movements. There were shades above windows, and electric wires hung loosely across the street. It was so narrow that anything the size of a human body dropped, no matter how carefully, would certainly strike these wires. Further below was a balcony projecting out from the first floor of the house opposite, surrounded by iron railings with pointed spikes. The thought of falling on them was so horrible that it made me shiver. I was afraid just looking at them. I did not say much to Bashir. What could I have said, anyway? I was forced to think about Arif and his strange character. I recalled him burning the old woman's wrist and I felt convinced that if Bashir had not jumped, Arif would certainly have shot him. I trembled. Where had Fiazi taken him? And Riffat? Who was she?

We had to call a small boy from below to come up and open the door. We carried Aziz down. We laid him on a charpoy and all I told his mother was that he was not well and was a bit tired and that was why he had had to be carried. I could not stay there long and respectfully took my leave of Aziz's mother, whose eyes were heavy with sorrows. Bashir had left the room before me. I searched for him in the street and in the bazaar, but failed to find him. I was feeling depressed, so out of sorts and sad that I could not even walk properly.

'Let's sit somewhere.'

'Certainly,' said Arif. His hands were in his pockets.

'I won't go to your place. Let's go somewhere else.'

'All right.'

They found a restaurant and went inside. As usual, it was called a hotel, but only food and drinks were available. There were a few family cabins. Arif and Fiazi entered one.

'Well?' Arif asked as they sat down.

'Is that pistol your own?'

'Sure,' Arif said seriously.

'I assume you have a licence for it?'

In answer, Arif took out the licence from his pocket, and placed it on the table.

'In my opinion, this should never have been issued to you,' said Fiazi, returning it.

'Jinab, come to the point. I did not come here to waste my time,' Arif said smoothly. 'You make a plan for me to meet Riffat for at least an hour. You have saved your son's life, now fulfil your promise.'

'He is not my son. I saved him because he was a human being.'

'Please just tell me, how will you arrange a meeting between Riffat and me?'

'What if I refuse to arrange the meeting?'

'You promised. Will you deliberately break your promise?'

'Yes, I did promise. But if I don't do it, what then?'

'Fiazi Sahib, I have not come here to argue for the sake of arguing.' Arif struck the table-top with his hand. 'Just tell me when the meeting will be and where.'

'What guarantee have I that you will not misbehave?'

'Misbehave? What do you mean?' Arif said uneasily. 'I have already told you that I love her. I only want to talk certain things over with her.'

'The fact is, Arif, I don't trust you. A man who tells someone to jump from a three-storey building is capable of anything. You are a dangerous man. You are only in control of your consciousness for a few hours or in some particular situation; the rest of the time you are quite impulsive. You need to discipline yourself. This means that you should develop a capacity to examine your own actions and their consequences.'

'Fiazi Sahib, I respect you. I do not want to have to talk to you in crude words which might offend your sensibilities. I know well enough what I am and how my consciousness works. Tell me your plan for me to meet Riffat.'

'I cannot arrange for you to meet her. I am prepared to fulfil any other practicable desire of yours, but the further that girl stays away from you the better for her.'

'I have no other desire. I wish to meet her, that's all.'

'All right, in that case I shall put forward some conditions. If you agree to these, I will arrange for you to meet Riffat for an hour.'

'Name the conditions,' Arif said impatiently.

'There are four: the first is that during your meeting with her you will carry no weapon of any kind. Second, a third person will be present, and if your meeting is in an open place, then that person must be able to see you. Part of this condition I will tell you later. The third is, you will not try to touch her. Fourth and last, after this meeting you will never again try to meet her. It is another matter if she comes to your house or meets you somewhere else.'

'I have a serious objection to the second condition, in fact I am unable to understand it,' Arif said excitedly. 'Why should you impose conditions? If I had laid down conditions before sparing the life of your son, what would have happened?'

'Arif, never again refer to him as my son. Thinking him to be a human being, I saved his life. As far as the conditions are concerned, you will have to accept them all.'

'The only one I object to is the second. Can you not withdraw it, then we can settle for the other three.'

'Arif, do you love her or are you going to purchase her that you are bargaining in this manner? You should know . . .'

'Fiazi Sahib, you are a ridiculous man,' Arif interrupted Fiazi rudely. 'If you and the artist did not have some good qualities, I would have scorned even to look upon your faces. He is a good artist, but he has a disgusting mind, and you with your fertile brain are a most mean person.'

'And what kind of brain have you that you say these things? You talk about love, you should have gone to see the words painted on his door.'

'My curses on both of you. I only ask you to keep your promise. Otherwise I don't want to hear your sermons or anything about that old animal.'

'You must accept the conditions. There is no alternative.'

'Fiazi Sahib, what are you talking about! You are annoying me unnecessarily. Anyway, what makes you think that you can arrange a meeting between us? How long have you known her? Are you in love with her too, or . . . ?'

'Arif, have you taken leave of your senses? Hearing you talk reminds me of site excavations where heaps of useless, broken things are dug up. Don't worry about my arranging a meeting.'

'All right, all right. You make the arrangements then.'

'I have already told you the conditions, and I will not withdraw the second.'

'In that case, I cannot guarantee that the person you appoint to watch us will remain alive.'

'Perhaps you are forgetting the first condition: you must not have any kind of weapon on you, whereas the other person will be armed. If during the meeting you break the third condition or do anything unseemly, Riffat will leave at once.'

'What nonsense. It must have taken you a couple of years to think up these conditions. I am not going to accept any one of them'.

'Even if you accept the second, I have yet to tell you another part of it.'

'What is that?' asked Arif in disgust.

'You will not be informed of the meeting place beforehand. When the time comes I will take you myself to where Riffat will be waiting.'

'And who will be watching us?'

'There is no need for you to know that now.'

'He must not be either of the men we left on the roof.'

'No, he will not be. You don't know the man,' Fiazi said, watching the waiter remove the tea things.

'All right. Fiazi Sahib, tell me one thing,' Arif said, speaking rapidly. 'That day in my house, Aziz said as he was leaving, that there were still many days before the year ended. I did not understand what he meant. Do you know anything about this?'

'No, I couldn't understand what he meant either. The artist asked him on the way back, but Aziz just repeated the same words.'

'Tell me, did anyone else say this?'

'No, no one. What is the problem? There are many days before the year ends, everybody knows that.'

'All right, let it be. Fiazi Sahib, arrange the meeting with Riffat in such a way that it looks like a chance meeting. It would be better if you bring her to my place. Tell her that you have to go somewhere and then come to my house, and you could leave after a while, making some excuse. That is all you have to do, and then you can come back after an hour.'

Fiazi laughed in reply.

'Why are you laughing? What is there to laugh about?'

'Nothing, nothing at all,' said Fiazi, still laughing, wiping his eyes with his handkerchief.

'You are a strange man,' said Arif. 'Let me tell you, you laugh sometimes without any reason.'

Fiazi laughed again and then suddenly stopped, and he said in a serious tone, 'Arif, you are spending your life obstinately pursuing desires. You are not aware of the fact that when these peculiar desires appear in the shape of one single demand, they try to come to terms with the time spent in the fulfilment of stronger desires. The unfulfilled desires do not remain quiet, nor do they depart to other lands, but lie in wait for suitable moments. When the suitable moments come to help them kill the stronger desires they show up as united desires. You are the helpless ground upon which these desires move and trample you down and all you can do is to watch them ride rough-shod over you. Arif, what evil fortune is dogging you, why are you destined to be trampled under filthy feet?'

Although Arif listened to this attentively the expression on his face showed that he had not fully understood. He wanted Fiazi to repeat what he had said so that he could listen to it in parts, but he rejected this idea and said confidently, 'Fiazi Sahib, stick to the purpose we came here for.'

'Arif, you will wear yourself out from the exhaustion of trying to attract attention to yourself. You will burn continuously in the fire of unfulfilled desires. You will keep seeing a herd of these peculiar desires treading over you and they will leave such ugly marks of their trampling feet on your feelings and imagination that death will become difficult for you and you will experience great pain in passing through the door of reincarnation.'

'Fiazi Sahib, stop preaching and come to the point,' Arif said, putting his hands in his pockets and then taking them out again.

'Arif, why are you willing to become the abode of pain? You know that desires are passing over you and you make the mistake of thinking that they are in sympathy with you. Desires can never be sympathetic to anyone. They are so greedy that the extent of their greed and the pain hidden within them cannot even be imagined. We build cities, we develop life, we cultivate fields and gardens, but the herds of these beastly desires which we have failed to curb, destroy everything. The real task for mankind is to control desire and to choose proper outlets for it.'

'Fiazi Sahib, you . . .'

'What I want to tell you is that between desires and needs, we should always choose needs. Desires bring us nothing but sorrow and pain. They bring us discomfort. They disgrace and demean us. It is better to give them up. If you nurse them they multiply like germs. It's strange that when some painful or horrifying apprehension takes possession of us, we seek an escape in the world of desires. We try to change the situation by running from one desire to another and so are tossed about in all directions. And when the task of choosing has exhausted us, we regress to a state of lethargy, and the apathy and carelessness which we had buried deep down rise up again in our bodies and desires start up their mechanisms to disturb our stability and to make us valueless and meaningless. They laugh at us, and when we hear their laughter we are driven to seek shelter in holes and corners of loneliness where we hide till the bleeding wounds of our disappointment heal. Once we regain our peace of mind, we again start choosing the same desires which caused us sorrow and pain. This is the worst choice of direction for a man to make.'

'Fiazi Sahib, I tell you plainly, I feel great love for this girl. I fully accept your condition about not touching her. I could meet her on my own, but I don't consider that proper.'

'What actually do you want from her?'

'I . . . what I want? Fiazi Sahib, I do not want anything from her.'

'Do you remember my once telling you that if you loved her, you would stop meeting her? Forget her for ever. Only this would prove that you love her.'

'This is nonsense,' Arif said, grinding his teeth. 'There is a conspiracy against me.'

'Arif, there is no conspiracy. If you really love her, this is what you should do, and if this is not so, then drop this matter, put an end to the affair. Look for women who sell themselves and if they agree to satisfy your wants, fine.'

'Don't you believe that I love her?' Arif said desperately.

'Stop this kind of talk. I don't know where you got the concept of love that you hold so cheap. Arif, our souls are fragile, our bodies weak and our intentions shaky and we groan under the burden of many desires and that is why we either fall in love or begin to hate someone very quickly. The longings of our selves and the hollowness of our personalities demand such hasty actions that to find the immediate results of our efforts we are lost in the ruins of expectations.'

'Fiazi Sahib, some day you will be convinced that I really love her,' Arif said softly.

'Perhaps you may pass through a good door and we may meet one another under new conditions. Only then might I change my opinion.'

'What do you mean by "pass through a good door"?' asked Arif. 'Fiazi Sahib, my love is pure. I am sure of that. All I ask is that you keep your promise. I did not know that I would see Bashir today. I had come in the hope of meeting Riffat.'

'And why did you go there with a pistol?'

'Fiazi Sahib, the bullet was destined for someone else.'

'What do you mean?' Fiazi asked quickly.

'Fiazi Sahib, when I was about to leave the artist, I met two people unexpectedly and after parting from them, I felt I should go home at once and prepare myself for some eventuality. No one was there. Then I felt that Riffat was in danger and that some kind of violence was being done to her in Aziz's house. I took my pistol and, with the intention of saving her, went to that drug-addicted boy. Thank God that my hunch proved false. Fiazi Sahib, tell me why I had this idea?'

'We dream our own dreams and no one shares them.'

'What do you mean?' said Arif, feeling a little ashamed. 'I have told you everything honestly. I would not be capable of thinking about her in that way.'

'Arif, I am beginning to suspect that even your thoughts are not yours. Come. Let's go,' said Fiazi, getting up. 'I have promised that I will arrange a meeting. The day after tomorrow I will come to tell you in the afternoon when she can meet you.'

'Will you bring her to my house?' Arif asked. Fiazi did not answer. They came out of the restaurant after paying the bill and walked on together. It was dark and the shops were lit up. It was Fiazi's day off. He wanted to go and sleep till late the next morning.

'Then you will bring her to my house?' Arif repeated.

'She will not be coming to your house. You will meet her in some public place out of doors. I have already told you this condition.'

'Rubbish. You will have to bring her to my house. Make an excuse that you have to ask Arif's servant something. Tell me the exact time and I will talk to her.'

'Arif, you are forgetting that she is not a society girl, or a hired girl that I can walk around with as I please.'

'Tell me one thing,' said Arif. 'Do you know that the artist also loves a girl? He has his own philosophy of love which he was talking about.'

'What should I say about that?'

'Well, I want to know what kind of love he has for the girl.'

'I know nothing about this, so how can I say?'

'Come, let's go and see the artist.'

'See the artist?' Fiazi asked surprised. 'Now? What for?'

'To talk to him. What would be the harm? We would not stay long. You may have dinner with me afterwards.'

'Thank you very much.'

'Please, come. We will talk to him for a while and then return here,' said Arif. 'Come on.'

'You can go by yourself if you want to see him,' Fiazi said, stopping to cross a road. 'I am going somewhere else.'

'Where?'

'There is no need for you to come with me. I will come to your house in two days' time to tell you when you can meet Riffat.'

'Where are you going?' Arif crossed the road with him. 'I will come with you.'

'With me? Where will you go with me?' Fiazi stopped. 'I am going somewhere on business now.'

'What of it? We'll go together.'

'Arif, go back,' said Fiazi in an angry tone. 'You are not so stupid that you cannot understand. Whether you have a pistol or not, I can call any passer-by and say that you are pestering me and then you will have to go to the police station to clear yourself.'

Arif was startled and looked at Fiazi and at the people walking around them. 'Where do you live?' he asked in a harsh tone.

'That is none of your business. Wait for me at your place at five on Tuesday afternoon.'

'What guarantee have I that you will really come to see me on Tuesday?'

'I do not tell lies.'

'Your veracity is not written on your face. If you don't want to tell me where you live, then don't. I only want a surety that you will come to see me.'

'Keep on walking with me and you will see where I am going. You must know, it is wrong to try to solve all your problems with the help of a pistol.'

'All right, just tell me where you are going. Afterwards I may be able to suggest something which you will agree to.'

'I am going to eat. Then I want to be alone.'

'In that case I will accompany you and afterwards you may go wherever you want.'

'I am going to eat at a cheap eating place. What will you do there?' said Fiazi a little surprised.

'Sit with you.'

'Arif, this is not right, it is not proper. Please go your own way. I will see you on Tuesday.'

'But what is the harm in my coming with you?' asked Arif.

'Arif, I say again, you want to do everything with the help of your pistol and this is not right.'

'I will take out all the bullets and give them to you,' said Arif. 'Then you will believe that the pistol is no more than a toy.' He did so, and included the three extra bullets he had in his pocket. Fiazi looked strangely at the bullets in his hand. 'Now you should be satisfied that the pistol is nothing to me. Put the bullets in your pocket.'

Fiazi started walking again, holding the bullets. Arif was now very quiet. His presence made Fiazi uncomfortable. Fiazi looked at the bullets in his hand and put them in his pocket. They were walking down a quiet road with timber shops on either side, closed for the night. There were beams and old doors lying outside and in the yards were saws with the blades removed. The place was deserted, the labourers who worked here in the day were nowhere to be seen. After some distance they saw an old man coming out from a side alley carrying his hookah with burning coals in the earthenware bowl containing the tobacco. He sat down and blew out the extra water in the hookah and then fixed the earthenware bowl to the pipe and started to smoke, inhaling deeply. Nearby was a brightly lit barber's. Through the glass doors customers could be seen sitting on cushioned iron chairs. A man was standing near the door looking in the mirror, combing his hair. As they passed, someone opened the door and spat noisily into the street. Further up were tea shops and sweet shops. Here Arif found a cigarette vendor from whom he bought a packet of cigarettes, and lit one. On the left was a short cut to a government hospital, made by the removal of a railing from the fence marking its boundaries. The gap was so narrow that only one person could pass through at a time. It was deserted. As Fiazi entered, he saw someone coming towards him. He recognized him at once. Meanwhile Arif had also reached the other side of the fence. As soon as he saw the man, he took out the pistol from his pocket and said, 'Your destined death has brought you here.'

It was Bashir, standing in the dim darkness some eight yards away. Nearby was a gardenia hedge about half the height of a man and a few large sheesham trees which made the place look even more deserted. Bashir looked helplessly at Arif.

'I let you go before, but I will not spare you now.' Arif's voice was fierce as he aimed the pistol.

Fiazi fingered the bullets in his pocket. He was smiling inside, intrigued to see what would happen.

Once he was sure that Fiazi was not going to tell Bashir that there were no bullets in the pistol, Arif advanced a few steps towards him and shouted, 'Come here, come over here.' He led him some distance away from the gap along the fence to the left. Fiazi followed them.

'Bashir, your death has dragged you here. At the request of a respectable man I spared you. I thought that you must have left town, but when your own fate is against you, then what can I do?'

'Arif Sahib, I am not scared. You must know that after my death that woman will curse you all her life.'

Arif gave a loud hearty laugh and without taking his eyes off Bashir addressed Fiazi, 'Fiazi Sahib, this man is standing in front of me, staring death in the face, but he is worried about the lives of other people. Fiazi Sahib, judge for yourself what kind of man this is. How frightened he is.'

Arif and Bashir were about four yards apart, staring at each other. The only light was from the dim streetlamp. The gardenia hedge was very thick and in the semi-darkness its leaves looked black rather than green.

'Where have you come from?' Arif asked.

Bashir did not answer. This made Arif angry. 'Tell me where you have come from! I will kill you like a rat!'

'I will tell you. But it is most unfair to point a pistol at me and force me to speak.'

'I can wound you seriously, too. My intention in making you jump from the roof was either to kill you or cause you serious physical injury so that you would remember it all your life. I let you go on a particular condition which will be fulfilled, but I did not promise to let you off every time. Believe me, I would have followed you and would have killed you when I could. That moment has now come.'

'You said that you would tell me of one way I had to escape.'

'That's enough. Tell me your last wish.'

'Take Kulsoom to a good place. Do not hand her over to her parents, because she does not want to go back to them. Don't keep her to yourself. Take her to a safe place and do not let her know that you are the person who has made these arrangements. Assure me of this, and then you may kill me if you want.'

'Why are you so concerned about her? Why worry about that deaf-and-dumb woman?'

'I want to marry her. That was what I came to tell you. I tried to find you at your home.'

'You were not born to marry. There was no father in your destiny, so how can there be a marriage? Fiazi Sahib, now I am sure that this person really has no father. Bashir, what a shame for you that you do not know your father. Who was he? Where was he from? At least answer these questions.'

Bashir did not say a word.

'How can you know? If you had met him you would have known. The first brick of your body was prepared from dirty, unknown mortar at that time when the circulation of the blood was hot in the veins and you were put into a pleasure-giving oven to be baked. You were nine months in this oven and when you were brought out, the mason had gone elsewhere. Bashir, you search for that mason. That is your task. When you find him, ask which sorrow he got rid of when he was making you.'

'Arif!' said Bashir with great intensity. He could have been heard a long way off.

'Keep quiet, if you raise your voice again, I will shoot you in the leg. You are a dirty blood stain. You point out misleading paths. Your being manifests sin. Those who were the sinners, the masons, who were the makers, helpless and disturbed by their hot blood, reached a destination, but did not consider it their destination. You are their living curse.'

'Arif, I promised myself that I would keep quiet. At the same time I must ask you not to say such things,' Fiazi said to him.

'Fiazi Sahib, I know that he has been slandering you,' said Arif, his eyes still fixed on Bashir. 'He does not know who his father is, and he is searching for his father's mistake in people's faces.'

'Whatever it is, do not mention it. I want to see what you do.'

'Very well, very well,' Arif agreed politely. 'Fiazi Sahib, one day he said that my name reminded him of stretched rope. Today I will tell him how strong the rope is and how necessary it is for binding someone. Bashir, you told me that you had been dreaming. Today I will put an end to this dream, or I will disfigure it in such a way that it will be finished.'

'I don't care about anything except that the girl should live a secure and protected life. Arif, why did you keep her with you in that condition?'

'You are asking me!' said Arif laughing. 'Ask me all the questions that are weighing on you.'

Bashir did not speak.

'Do something quickly,' Fiazi urged Arif.

'Bashir, I can forgive you on one condition: that you tell me where Kulsoom is at the moment and then never again show me your face.'

The darkness seemed to be deepening. The three of them looked fixed, as if in a photograph.

'Speak up. I am talking to you,' Arif snarled again.

'Arif, I ask you to put the pistol in your pocket. You know that she was not your wife, and I am prepared to marry her. Let us forget all that has happened and . . .'

'Stay there,' said Arif, taking a step back. 'If you try to come close again, you will be a dead man. Tell me where Kulsoom is.'

Bashir was certain that, if he told Arif where Kulsoom was, he would shoot him and go away, or at least would wound him so badly that he would not be able to walk. He called out Fiazi's name and looked at him and as Arif also turned to look, he leapt on Arif and brought him down to the ground.

Bashir had risked his life. Arif knew that the pistol was empty, but still he pulled the trigger. There was only a clicking sound. When Bashir realized that Arif had been merely scaring him, it made him wild and he started fighting in a frenzy. Fiazi was standing near them, but he felt no need to intervene. Bashir hit Arif hard on the face with his right fist. Arif was dazed for a moment then he recovered himself and gave Bashir a powerful push and before he could control himself picked him up by the waist and threw him into the bushes, raining blows on him. His hands got caught in the undergrowth. Bashir managed to emerge to catch Arif by the shoulders and shove him in turn into the bushes, falling on top of him. For a long time the two of them grappled. When they finally re-appeared, Fiazi saw that their clothes were torn and Arif's jacket was ripped in front. Arif punched Bashir in the stomach and as he doubled up in pain, struck him another fierce blow on the face. Bashir fell to the ground. Arif leapt on him, but Bashir turned aside and Arif fell on his elbow. Bashir stood up and, catching Arif's hands from behind, sat on him. He paused for breath and then started banging Arif's head on the ground. Arif no longer had strength to free himself and began to feel the pain of the blows he had received earlier. He lay limp. Bashir left him and looked for a heavy stone or brick to disfigure him with. Arif raised himself by the palms of his hands and Bashir had to give up his search to attend to him. Again he shoved Arif to the ground and struck his face. Then he tied Arif's hands firmly with his own belt. Bashir was himself hurt. His mouth was bleeding and he was spitting frequently. He turned Arif over. Arif looked at him with half-closed eyes. He made an effort to sit up and then stayed still. His nose was bloody and there was a wound on his forehead. Fiazi watched him attentively, while Bashir tried to open an iron chain, probably used to tie a cow or buffalo to the fence. He gave up after a while and dragged Arif over to it and tied him up with the chain. Then Bashir looked for the pistol and found it lying a little distance away. After examining it carefully, he came to Arif.

'This is the pistol with which you have been threatening me since this evening. If I had known that there were no bullets in it, I would have beaten you up there on the roof.'

'Release my hands,' Arif said in a broken voice.

'Is this chain not strong enough? Is it not good enough to bind someone?' Bashir sat down beside him. 'Arif, you said that you would tell me how strong a rope was and now you are asking me to untie your hands.'

Arif moved his lips a little as if estimating the amount of pain that he was feeling.

'No punishment is sufficient for someone like you. I came to talk to you in a civilized manner and you wanted to take my life. You told me to jump from a three-storeyed house, so now I will burn you to death. It won't be difficult. I feel justified in treating you like this.' Bashir stopped for a moment and then went on, 'You really are a devil. And what about the way you were keeping that woman? What a despicable person you are.'

'That's enough, I'm tired,' said Arif, quite helpless. 'Stop talking and untie my hands.'

'Listen to him!' Bashir laughed. 'I am thinking of setting fire to him and he dreams about getting free. My dream is not to be shattered. But what are you dreaming? Today a strange thing will happen. In a dream one man will set fire to another who will feel its heat.'

'No, no,' said Arif in panic. 'You will not do this.'

'Why not? Who can stop me? From a distance people will think that the bushes have caught fire. Where were you going with Fiazi? And Riffat, who is she?'

'Riffat is the girl that boy followed,' Arif said in a low voice.

'I don't know what nonsense you are talking about, but I know that if you had not let me go then, you would have shot me after you finished counting.'

'You are mistaken, I was only frightening you.'

'Then I, too, will merely scare you. After lighting the fire I will extinguish it. Where are the bullets for this pistol?' Bashir brandished it. 'You should not carry a useless weapon. Let me search you.' He began looking through Arif's pockets. He found a comb, a lighter, cigarettes, a handkerchief, a bunch of keys, a hundred and five rupees, and the licence for the pistol. He put them back.

'How did you manage to obtain a licence for the pistol? Anyway, tell me where the bullets are.'

'I don't have them,' Arif said listlessly, not looking at Fiazi. Fiazi took them out of his pocket.

'Arif, I have them.'

'Don't give them to him. Fiazi, throw them away,' Arif said excitedly.

'Throw them away? Why should he throw them away?' Bashir said sarcastically. 'A pistol is useless without bullets. Fiazi Sahib, give me the bullets.'

'Fiazi Sahib, throw them away,' Arif said in panic, and groaned with pain.

'Arif, listen to me carefully,' Fiazi said, putting the hand holding the bullets into his pocket. 'I am not your bodyguard that I should throw away the bullets. I don't know what Bashir will do with them. If you want me not to give him the bullets, then you will have to release me from my promise to arrange for you to meet Riffat. He will do as I ask, because I have saved his life. Tell me, what is your wish?'

'Don't give him the bullets, I don't want you to give him the bullets.' Arif tried to speak very fast, but he could not articulate properly.

'Fiazi Sahib, just give me one bullet, please. He is a bad lot and should be got rid of,' Bashir said.

'Don't give them to him. As for Riffat, let's forget about her for the moment.'

'So, you don't love her?' Fiazi asked with a smile which remained hidden in the darkness.

'Fiazi Sahib, don't give him the bullets. I will meet Riffat on my own.'

'Fiazi Sahib, please give me one. I need it very much,' Bashir said, coming close to Fiazi.

'Leave it. It isn't important,' Fiazi said and walked away, laughing.

'Arif, the first time I beat you I took Kulsoom from you,' Bashir said, sitting down beside him. 'This time I am taking your pistol. Put Kulsoom out of your mind and remember that this pistol can shoot you at any time. You have already told me the price of a bullet, and I can buy one at the bazaar.' He put his hand into Arif's pocket again and took out the handkerchief. Then he removed the laces from Arif's shoes. He stuffed Arif's handkerchief into his mouth, placed his own handkerchief over his lips and tied them up with the laces. Now Arif was incapable of speaking, or uttering a sound. All he could do was see, breathe and move his body a little.

'You will spend the night here. If you wish to call anyone you may do so by making gestures and signs. You, too, should know what it means to live without speaking.'

Bashir left him and walked in the direction that Fiazi had gone. He had some questions to ask which only Fiazi could answer. He had hoped that Fiazi would be waiting somewhere, but he did not find him. He came into a street with some shops and, further along, a restaurant serving tea and simple food. He still did not see Fiazi. Disappointed, he went back to his hotel. He picked up his things and went off to catch a bus to the farm where he worked.

Arif remained tied to the fence for about seven hours. He tried to free himself, but every movement caused him pain. The gag was intolerable. He began to think that the handkerchief stuffed in his mouth was the same which Riffat had given to Aziz, but she had not given Aziz any, and the one he had in his mouth had been taken out of his pocket. Bashir had also taken out a handkerchief. Arif began to wonder whose handkerchief was in his mouth, his own or Bashir's. The handkerchief kept him busy for a while. Then he heard footsteps. He tried to shout, but only muffled sounds came out. Rattling the chain did not make much noise either; it sounded more like a cow rubbing her horns against the fence. The footsteps receded. Two other men passed, and they, too, did not notice him. Fatigued by his efforts, he lay still. One reason he did not get any attention was that the gap in the fence was some distance from the place where he was tied up.

Arif felt as if Bashir had wrapped up his head and gone away. Breezes rustled past without making any impression on his senses. Fiazi could have returned the bullets to him. If Arif had given Fiazi the bullets, then Fiazi could just as well have given them back. Given them back to whom? he asked himself, to Arif or to Bashir? Yes, that was worth considering. Bashir had already taken possession of the pistol and if Fiazi wished, he could have given the bullets to him. Then he would not have had any need to say that he should give up the idea of meeting

Riffat, there would have been an end to all the promises and conditions. Did that mean that Fiazi was keeping him alive as some sort of punishment? They, father and son, the bastards, were acting according to a well thought out plan. Fiazi should not have done this, thought Arif. The next moment he forgot what Fiazi should not have done. Fiazi should not have done this, Fiazi should not have done this, he continued thinking obstinately. His mouth, hands and body were bound and his mind was heavy with sleep. He looked around with drowsy eyes at the darkness and went to sleep.

He could not make out how long he slept. The surrounding darkness was the same. Time seemed to have stopped. The silence was so deep that it was like a sharp knife piercing his veins and nerves. His body ached. Pain shot through him in waves. He did not have the strength to move his arms even a little. It was torture. He was afraid that a snake might come out of the thick gardenia hedge and bite him, bringing him to a worthless end. He wondered what lay on the other side of the hedge. Suppose someone was walking there barefoot and he could not hear him? Arif kept looking helplessly at the bushes around and the hospital building in front of him. If he had taken Fiazi's advice and had not obstinately walked with him then he would not have spent this miserable night. Tears came to his eyes and he closed his eyelids to squeeze them out. He felt as if hot iron filings were entering his brain and it was pouring out in agony. Insects seemed to be crawling along his jaw towards his ears and although both his hands were firmly bound, he thought he was brushing insects from his face. The moment they fell to the ground they rose again and crawled back over his face. He brushed away the insects for some time. Then he realized that he was not removing the insects with his hands; it was the blinking of his eyelids that he attributed to the action of his hands. Then he felt as if innumerable fingers were growing inside his brain, soaked in black ink. He wanted to fling off the ink, to chew up these fingers, but one bullet seemed to be missing. If he had the total ten bullets that would be enough, one for each finger. Then he remembered that Fiazi had taken away the bullets and he had nothing left. Fiazi would return soon. Nine bullets would be sufficient. Let the nine fingers break. Nine fingers should be broken, nine fingers should be broken, nine fingers should be broken. A distant train became the rhythm of his thoughts. Now the fingers of pain were dripping poison in his whole body. Filthy insects of black darkness clung tightly to the fingers of his imagination. He tried to straighten these fingers, but found that he had lost the power to bring any movement to them. Now these hateful fingers became hateful eyes and on their eyelids darkness was gathering. It was difficult for him to open his eyes. He felt something floating on his consciousness. He saw a man sitting beside him opening his hands. It was almost dawn. He tried to lick his lips, but could not. He relapsed into unconsciousness.

At four in the morning a man was passing on the other side of the fence when he noticed someone sitting against the railing. He approached Arif and stopped. At first he thought that he was dead, until he noticed that Arif's hands were chained to the railing. He started to untie him. It was difficult. At last he got the leather belt from Arif's hands and removed the gag from his mouth. Arif began to revive and his face flushed with some colour. For a while he did not move. When the man tried to raise him up, Arif forbade him with a shake of his head. The man ran off and soon returned with water in his tiffin carrier. After drinking, Arif still remained on the ground. Bashir had tied the leather belt so tightly that there were deep marks in the flesh. Arif nursed his arms, moved his head about and looked thankfully at his rescuer. Finally he caught hold of the fence and stood up.

'Come, let me take you to the hospital.'

'No, I will go by myself,' Arif answered weakly and started walking slowly. He reached the other side of the fence and saw that the man was still with him. He turned to him and said, 'I am very grateful to you,' and stopped. It was clear that he wanted to be alone. The man went away without saying anything further.

For four days Arif did not go out of his house. The first morning he sent for a doctor who told him to get his nose and jaw X-rayed. Arif ignored him, saying it would heal by itself. He sent word to his office that he would not be able to go there for a week. He did not wish to see anyone. He instructed the old servant that except for Fiazi or Riffat no one was to enter the house and he should tell any visitor that he was not at home. On the third evening, the servant told Arif that the woman with the armless girl had come to see him again and had asked whether he was back from Peshawar.

'Fiazi has not been?' Arif asked.

'No Jinab, if he had come, I would have asked him in.'

'If that girl comes, ask her in too,' said Arif, lifting his eyes briefly from the newspaper.

Arif was confused. He did not know what to do. He wanted to meet Riffat, but how? Her letters were in a cupboard. He took them out and started reading them. This helped to dispel his boredom. He kept thinking about her and wore himself out wondering if she would come and visit him.

Now his wounds were almost healed. The swelling on his nose had subsided, and the continuous pain in his jaw had also disappeared. Only the wound on his head required constant attention and medication. On the fourth day he decided to meet Riffat on her way to school. Just to see her, he would not try to talk. Then, he thought, this would be even worse since she would be scared and wonder why he had come merely to see her. No, he would speak to her, and for this he should wait for another week. It was about two in the afternoon and he was reading a magazine in his bedroom when the servant came and told him that Riffat was standing at the gate, and there was a boy with her.

'Boy, who could he be? It must be that sick boy.' The thought of Aziz upset him. He told the servant to show them into the drawing room.

'Jinab, I have already asked her to come in, but she is standing outside the gate and says she has only one thing to say.'

Arif quickly took off his pyjamas and put on his trousers. Buttoning up his shirt, he came out on the verandah and went to the gate. Riffat was standing there with a seven-year-old boy.

'Is this your brother?' Arif started the conversation, speaking most respectfully.

'Yes,' said Riffat and stood silent.

'Come in, please come in,' said Arif, pointing to the door.

'No thank you. I'm all right here. I don't have much to say. I have come to tell you only this . . . that I will not be able to come here again.'

'Why not?' All of Arif's pain was expressed in the tone of his voice.

'Arif Sahib, the fact is,' she said, catching hold of her brother's hand and looking away, 'I am getting married. I will request you not to trouble me in future. I am not that kind of girl.'

Arif was dumbstruck. Riffat looked frightened.

'Riffat, Riffat, my dearest,' said Arif and stopped, he could not say anything further.

'These things are not permitted in our family. Last night my future husband's people came to our house and I became very worried when I thought of you. Please promise me that you will never tell anyone that we ever had even the lightest kind of affair. You have my letters, for God's sake, say what you like to me, but after today never think of me.'

'Riffat, Riffat . . .' Again the words stuck in his throat.

'I will leave now, it was very hard for me to manage to come here. Please tear up my letters.'

'Riffat, you are afraid of this place, but please meet me once. I realize that you are in a hurry. I want to have one meeting with you and I will accept everything you say.'

'What is the use of meeting? Whatever I did, I am sorry.'

'Riffat,' said Arif, growing perturbed, 'please meet me once. If you don't want to come here, then anywhere you suggest. Only once, and I will tell you everything. Meet me once.'

'What is the . . .'

'I beg you. Just say the time and place and I will be there.'

'No, no, it is not possible,' she said in a fearful voice. 'Please forgive me if I have done you any wrong.'

Riffat's brother drew closer to his sister and looked at Arif. Arif said again to Riffat, 'Give me just one opportunity to meet you and I will do exactly as you say.'

Riffat named a place, added nine in the morning, and left.

There were nineteen hours between then and nine the next day, and Arif spent them in a mood of indescribable impatience and restlessness. To pass the time and shorten the long period of uneasiness he went out for dinner which he had in a quiet corner of a restaurant all by himself. After dinner he walked about aimlessly and then went home to bed. He could not sleep for a long time, thinking about Riffat.

Arif reached the appointed place at half past eight. It was a park and he stood where Riffat had asked him. He was thinking only of her. There was a flower-bed on one side. The white roses were particularly attractive in the light of the morning sun. Arif plucked a flower and looked at it. Time and again he went to the place where he could see Riffat coming. At last she appeared, walking fast. She was alone. He hurried towards her and touched her cheek with the hand holding the loose rose petals. They gently brushed her cheek and neck and fell to the ground. She shrank back, while Arif was too engrossed in feasting his eyes on her.

'I was sure you would come,' Arif said in a low voice.

Riffat did not answer, as if she was waiting to hear something more.

'Riffat, I love you, I love only you.'

'And your wife also,' she said, looking him straight in the eyes. 'Why do you pretend to be in love with every girl?'

'No . . .'

'No? I have heard that you have got into the habit of saying this to every girl. I have told you before, I am not that sort of girl. Whatever you may be does not concern me. I want to stay far away from you.'

'If I wish to marry you, what then?'

'No, Jinab, excuse me. How can I marry you when you already have a wife?'

'She is not my wife, she is not my wife,' Arif screamed, emphasizing every word. 'How can she be my wife?'

'Why not, is she not a woman? Do you think she is made of stone? Arif Sahib, I have not been able to find out what you really are. You don't consider her to be your wife, then in what capacity is she living in your house? Please listen, I tell you with my tears to forget me. For God's sake, do not poison my life. I saw you a couple of times. That was my mistake, for which I am prepared to ask your forgiveness a thousand times.'

'Riffat, I can give you fifteen hundred rupees a month.'

'What for?' Riffat asked in anger and in a troubled voice. 'I don't need money. The money that man gave me he gave to my father.'

'What money?' Arif asked without hearing her out.

'We had refused to take money, but he insisted and thrust it on us. I will take no money from you. What need have I to take money from you?'

'Who gave you money? Whom are you talking about?'

'The artist who lives in the hotel.'

'That old mule?' Arif said, his eyes narrowing. 'Tell me, how much money did he give you?'

'Not me, he came to our house and told us to keep the money for my marriage. He said he had no one else in the world, and he wanted to give the money as a gift.'

'A gift?' Arif gritted his teeth. 'Riffat, he does not want to give this as a gift, he is in love with you. He is a strange kind of fool, who says he loves you.'

'Loves me? How can he be in love with me? He told my parents that I had come to see the paintings and that he had no relatives in the world, therefore he was giving the money as a gift, and apart from this he had no wish or desire. If he loves me, then I love him too.'

'Riffat,' said Arif emotionally. 'Tell me what I should do? This is all being arranged to destroy me. I will marry you and we will not accept any money from this despicable artist. How much money did he give you?'

'Arif, let me tell you again, he did not give me the money, but gave it to my father in the presence of my mother. My father told him that there was a boy in the family who is all right for me. The artist said nothing when he heard this. He had asked for my address when I was looking at the paintings with Aziz in his room, but I had no idea that he would visit us two days later and give us such a large sum of money.'

'Riffat, I love you truly and I want to marry you. I cannot live a day without you. I told you that I would tell you everything and this is that I have been a very bad man, but now I am not the same, this is another Arif Nawaz.'

'Arif, the artist also told me that he would give you another Arif Nawaz. What did he mean?'

'Don't bother about him; he is a bastard of an artist. We will not accept a paisa from him and there is no need for you to go to that ugly hotel.'

'Arif, I want to tell you that you are a bad man. The artist is not a bit like you. We told him to leave the hotel and come and live with us. He refused with a laugh, saying that he did not want to trouble anybody. Arif, you do not know how good at heart that old man is. Even if he had not given us the money and talked like that to us, it would have been enough.'

'How much money did he give you, I mean your parents?'

'He gave us a cheque for thirty thousand rupees.'

'Thirty thousand rupees?' Arif was startled.

'I am now leaving. I came because you insisted. If you are really good, you will say nothing more.'

'Riffat, don't take money from him. Riffat, what are you people doing? Riffat . . . Riffat, forget him. I am prepared to make that house and forty thousand rupees over to you immediately. I want to marry you.'

'But I don't want to marry you. In fact when I think of you I feel uneasy.'

'But why? Why?'

'I don't know, all I know is that I don't like you.'

'Am I not good?'

'Not at all good,' Riffat retorted. 'And today I will go to the artist and tell him everything and I will do exactly what he advises. Then he will in some way tell my father everything about this affair.'

'Riffat, that old man is a devil. No doubt he is a good artist, but his ideas are all wrong. Actually after your marriage he will have your husband murdered and then marry you.'

'Then why do you want to marry me? If you know that he intends to do that, why do you want to be killed?'

'He can do nothing to me. I will frustrate his diabolical plans. Just as he has given your parents money, he can also ask them to return it, and when your parents have none, he will propose marriage to you. Yes, I know that he is old, nevertheless your parents will send you to him for money.'

'Yes, I will marry him, but I don't want to see your face,' said Riffat as she walked away from him. 'I'm leaving and I will not be able to meet you in the future.'

'Riffat, listen.' Arif darted after her. 'Wait, listen, wait just one minute. Why don't you want to marry me?'

'You are not a good man, that is the main reason.'

Arif said nothing. He stood before her like a guilty man.

'Riffat, tell me, do you think that I love you or not?'

'What can I say? All I know is that you are evil. No woman in the world should marry you.'

'Who told you to say this?'

'Who would tell me? It is my own opinion.'

'Your opinion. Why did you reach such an opinion, Riffat? My dearest, I love you and I can prove to you how much.'

'I don't need any proof and I do not wish to stay any longer,' she said, turning to walk away. 'I am going, I only came because you said that you wanted to meet me once more.'

'Riffat, you . . .'

'Arif, why don't you go to some other city?' said Riffat, not letting Arif finish his sentence. Arif heard her and looked away. He was silent, as if all his justifications, truths and desires had come to an end.

'Now may I leave?' Riffat asked.

'Don't go.' Arif's answer was brief and he spoke strangely. After a pause he said, 'Riffat, my dear, I am a very bad man. Believe me, for your sake I can reform and become good. You are the only girl for whose sake I can mend my ways. I love you very much, so much that I cannot fully express it to you in words. That woman was my wife. My mistake was not keeping her as a wife. Today I realize what a heavy punishment I have received because of this. Please forget that and if Fiazi or the artist have spoken against me, pay no attention, and only think that if I was like that, I am no longer the same. I swear by all that is sacred that I cannot lie to you. How can I make you believe me? All right, don't trust my words. Now I tell you to consider everything I say as lies. This is all a lie. I wish that you could at least believe it. A man is fallible, I can make mistakes. Forget everything and give me an opportunity to prove that I am worthy to be your husband and can show infinite love for you.'

'I feel afraid of you.'

'But why, why, my dearest?'

'No, no, don't come near, don't touch me,' said Riffat. 'You are evil.'

'Can I never reform and become good?'

'I can't say,' Riffat retorted. 'Now you must let me go. I am going.'

'Only two minutes, stay two minutes more,' said Arif, seeing her walk away. 'Who is the boy you are marrying?'

'Someone in the family,' Riffat replied innocently.

'He lives here?'

'Yes.'

'What does he do?'

'I don't know,' said Riffat, tired of his questions.

'Will you meet the artist again?' Arif asked.

'What's the harm in that? He can come to our house.'

'May I too?'

'Have you gone off your head? How can you come to our house?'

'I was just asking.'

'This answer also shows that you are not in your right mind. Now I am going.'

'Does this mean I will never be able to see you again?'

'It is not possible,' she said, trying to make him understand. 'If I have nothing to do with you, what is the point of our meeting?'

'Riffat, let's go to some other city. A little while ago you said, "We'll go to another city".'

'I told you to go.'

'Riffat, I will never forget you. I need you. Without you I may never be able to reform myself.'

'Arif, stop this talk. I hope that you will never in the future create any trouble for me. You will find some other girl. There is no shortage of girls in this town.' Saying this, Riffat walked away.

'Riffat, why do you talk like this? Riffat please listen, Riffat, Riffat!' Arif called after her. 'I will get you, I will certainly get you.'

Two days later Fiazi went to see the men he had met when he was with Aziz and the artist. In the past two days he had not gone anywhere. He had wanted to go to Aziz's place, but could not manage it and stayed at home. It was obvious that Aziz had not taken the drug for the first time. Why was he in this world? Why was he just a dirty rag only good for cleaning other people's shoes, with no identity of his own? He was a minor rusty part of a machine which did not fit anywhere; the sound of a racking cough which someone got in his mother's womb; the imprecation which exiles call down upon themselves; a bit of society's spittle and the last throb of a fading pulse soon to stop altogether. The thought of Aziz caused him pain.

On the visiting card he read, 'Albert Whiter, Jan Building'. That was some two miles away. It did not take Fiazi long to get there. He knocked on the door and stood back. Whiter opened the door and invited him in. The younger man with glasses was also there.

'Did you have any trouble finding us?' Whiter asked.

'Not at all, I know this area and someone below directed me to your apartment. What is your name?' Fiazi asked the man with the glasses.

'His name is Paul Jefferson. He is employed in a pharmaceutical firm and lives near here.'

'Do only Christians live here, or are there other religions too?'

'No, we all live together. The first three portions when you come upstairs are occupied by Muslims, and there are Muslims downstairs, too. What are you?' Whiter asked Fiazi. 'Are you a Muslim?'

'I am surprised that you ask me this question again. Did you not get the idea that day that I do not believe in the conventional God?'

'So you do not believe in God?'

'Which God?' Fiazi asked. 'You just say that I don't believe in God. First tell me what do you mean by "God"? If you are talking about the Christian God or Islamic God or the God of some such religion, then my answer is "no".'

'In your opinion religions serve no useful purpose, the principles they present are worthless, and nothing good can be expected of them?'

'The principles that each religion has given currency to and the origin of things that it has preached have not done much good to humanity. If instead of this, theology had been based on purely metaphysical concepts and people had acted upon it, the condition of mankind today would be much brighter. How is it that hundreds of Muslims and Christians are not good men or specimens of humanity of which one can be proud?'

'This is not the fault of religion,' said Whiter. 'The man who invented the fountain pen did not think that someone would draw lines on the earth with the nib. If anyone does, it is his own fault.'

'It was also the fault of the pen that it could be used for a wrong purpose. If we suppose that the pen is religion, then the idea of drawing lines on the earth with it should not have occurred to anyone. Religions do not warn their devotees that they are being misused. Even if someone swears falsely in God's name they remain utterly helpless. Religions are based on fear and hatred. Men are taught to fear God and to hate followers of other religions. There are other aspects of religions that are quite disgusting. One of these is, that the way of life they wish to present should be the only one and that all other ways are wrong and false. This makes men blind and they then justify all kinds of hatred, doubt and suspicion. These are the components of hateful religions which confirm a hateful God. The greatest weakness of religions is that they do not present any acceptable concept of God. They oppose environments free from coercion, and do not allow freedom of discussion and natural relations to grow between people, and the principles they uphold are so pregnant with negative consequences and innumerable evils, that they have to create a hell where they consign all the harmful effects of these principles.'

'No, you have misunderstood the concept of hell.'

'All right, you tell me the correct concept of hell,' Fiazi said. 'What I want to say is that hell does not exist. Religions understand their own inner hidden contradictions. They were aware of the evils that these contradictions would give birth to, and therefore they concocted the concept of hell where these evils would be consigned. If it is supposed that God created hell, then why should an evil thing be created? Can one who is perfect goodness make something which is evil? After all, why should the creator want to send his own creatures down to hell? The way I understand the universe, there is no such God in it. How can I believe in a cruel and wrong kind of God?'

'Wrongdoers and evil persons go to hell to receive punishment for their evil deeds. Look at it from this point of view and you will see how necessary hell is,' the man with the glasses said.

'If wrongdoers and evil people are to be sent to hell, where should you send Him who made them? The kind of God that religions present is no friend of man. To accept such a God is not wisdom.'

'What you are saying is all wrong,' said Paul. 'It is impossible to conceive of life without God. God exists and His existence is proved by every particle that exists.'

'You may think that He exists, but I cannot see it that way.'

'If you are suffering from jaundice, then all things will appear yellow to you, when in fact they are not,' said Paul. 'This is your own disease, not the fault of others.'

'There are three basic defects in religions which will not appear yellow to anyone. First, they cannot manifest their God, and it is easy to disprove God. The argument is that God does not exist; how can one prove the existence of something which is not there? Second, they promote a slavish mentality which has a direct bearing upon man's action, and hence man deviates far from the path which can lead him to true happiness. Third, they impose upon man a never-ending system of worship and useless religious ceremonies which are nothing but a waste of human labour and time. Religions state that God is the creator of this universe, that He is all-powerful, He can do everything. I ask, what has He done? What has He given us? Hunger, theft, murder, loot, plunder, hatred, destruction, misery, and a thousand other such cursed things, the very thought of which makes one sick. If man had the power to do everything, he would have created a much better world. How sad it is that despite having power and control over everything, God has not been able to do anything. It is wrong to say that God has made this world. This world and the whole universe came into being through continuous changes and the power that controls these changes is another power.

'Whether religious principles are good or bad can be decided later, first we should examine if they are perfect or not. When a man commits a murder it seems to him right that he be sent to jail rather than worry about what punishment God will give him, and although no religious book states that God will give a double punishment, he is actually punished twice for the same offence, once by men according to the laws of society, and then again by God Himself who after the man's death supposedly sends him to hell.'

'Your ideas are dangerous,' Whiter said, looking uneasily at Fiazi. 'Whatever may be the case, a terrible punishment awaits you.'

'If that punishment awaits me, then I would like to see for myself what kind of punishment it will be. All that matters is the defence and support of humanity. Religions have played a prominent role in the destruction of human lives, and have been behind all the great wars and the usurpation of human rights. If instead of destroying others, religious people had worked in the larger interests of humanity, the world would have been much happier. The promise religions make that every man will be rewarded for his good deeds in the next world, turns people selfish, and each one works for his own salvation unmindful of others. Not only does he cease to care for his neighbours, friends, and people around him, but he even becomes formal with his relatives and children. Wrapped up in his own religious preoccupation he loses his capacity to see what he can do for others. Instead of striving for a place in paradise for ourselves, all mankind should make an effort to create a paradise for the living. So much human thinking is being wasted, so much human labour is proving fruitless. Look at the large space taken up by churches and mosques, when thousands of people are homeless. We should arouse within ourselves the capacity to love. The lamp, the light of which has been eclipsed by the dust raised by religions, should be allowed to turn bright with the help of our intellectual power. Gods want to be worshipped, they do not care to understand that a man might feel hell crawling within his veins. They remain unconcerned, they do not answer his prayers. They themselves are floating in space, what can they do for others? We should understand the universe in the light of the principle of action and reaction, and keep man's basic needs in mind. The concept of private property should be wiped out as soon as possible. It creates ill will between men and does not permit the growth of mutual confidence. Religions support the concept of private property and propitiatory offerings and alms are thought proper for the poor. This is hateful and should be condemned. Besides, religious people do not accept God in the proper spirit. They openly disobey the commandments and injunctions of their God. They do not accept, or understand God, rather use the word 'God' mostly to swear oaths, make promises, and compel others to believe them. They drag the name of God into all their individual petty affairs and business matters. They don't do this deliberately, but the fact is that their God commands them to do things which are impracticable. In trying to carry out these impossible commands man is reduced to a state of utter helplessness and hence he is made sorrowful. It is necessary to rehabilitate man's dignity and status, and this can only be done when he sets aside all religions and starts thinking in a rational and objective manner. Does man need religion in order to help him establish proper relationships with his fellow men? The New Testament states that without faith all work is lifeless; here Christianity gives its view of human relations and it is most regrettable. Other religions also state that to those who do not believe in their God, their deeds will not be acceptable. Does this mean that if a man does good deeds, but has no faith, the goodness of his deeds will be annulled? Speak the truth. It's a good practice, religions preach that too. Now the question arises, if a non-believer speaks the truth, does that mean that his truth will not remain as truth? You must admit that doing good things without faith is better than doing bad things with faith. The Gods of religion were once powerful. Now they are dwindling day by day. They are slowly dying out since there is no reality in them.

'If we compare the state of religions down the ages, we will find that they have weakened, so why should we wait for the end of something which is slowly being wiped out, why not discard it right now? Those needs for which we in the past prayed to God we should now seek through scientific means. Nothing comes from the heavens not even the rain: it comes from the vapours rising from the oceans. If we hope for the solution of our earthbound problems to descend upon us from the heavens, it would be sheer folly. Religions can give man nothing; instead they devour him and squeeze him dry. They trap man in a net of doubts and take him away from his own reality. They know how to pour poison into a man's mind. Religions say that soul is within man. What an absurd concept, what is the dimension of this soul, what is its volume, what is its weight, what is its character? Once a man comes to believe that he has a soul within him, it mesmerizes him and drains him, and makes him for ever dependent upon a non-existent god. It kills man's beautiful plans, and the variety of his ideas, flowing like a sunny stream carrying its gentle waves towards the aspirations inspired by nature. When man abandons religion he does not find himself in a vacuum. There is a real god towards whom no one has paid any attention.

'This god is a true friend of man and he enters into a partnership with him in the wide field of experience. This god has been alive and will always be alive. He is everywhere. He does not want to be worshipped, nor does he wait for our prayers. He does not coerce those who do not accept him, nor does he get angry and talk of a hell. He only hints and seems to say, 'You don't believe in me, then don't, but consider this: your bodies and ideas have cracked in the splashing rains of your desires'. When someone accepts him after having understood his reality, he assists them in all that they want to do and life becomes easy. To know him is to get to know a great secret, and the acceptance of this god is the only way to a peaceful and satisfied life. The complete and perfect god is Time.'

'What?' they said simultaneously.

'Time is the most powerful god, and the acceptance of this fact is amazingly beneficial for us.'

'What do you believe happens after death?' Whiter asked.

'I will die in the confidence that I will be reborn, having forgotten everything pertaining to my former life. I will keep on being reborn, and therefore I have no fear of death.'

'You do not like religion. Do you think that the whole of the Bible is unacceptable?' Paul asked Fiazi.

'No, I do not say that the whole of the Bible or any other so called revealed book is altogether unacceptable. The Bible has many things which have been proved correct by Time.'

'Give some instances, the Bible is before you,' said Paul and gave him a copy of an English Bible. It was the Authorized King James version.

Fiazi opened it at the Gospel according to St Matthew. He placed his finger on this passage:

> Ye have heard that it hath been said, Thou shalt love thy neighbour, and hate thine enemy.
>
> But I say unto you, Love your enemies, bless them that curse you, do good to them that hate you, and pray for them which despitefully use you, and persecute you.

'And here,' said Fiazi, turning over a page and pointing to the passage:

> Give not that which is holy unto the dogs, neither cast ye your pearls before swine, lest they trample them under their feet, and turn again and rend you.

'And look at this,' said Fiazi, pointing to another passage:

> Therefore all things whatsoever ye would that men should do to you, do ye even so to them.

'And see here.'

> For they bind heavy burdens and grievous to be borne, and lay *them* on men's shoulders; but they *themselves* will not move them with one of their fingers.
>
> But all their works they do for to be seen of men: they make broad their phylacteries, and enlarge the borders of their garments,
>
> And love the upper-most rooms at feasts, and the chief seats in the synagogues,
>
> And greetings in the markets, and to be called of men, Rabbi, Rabbi.

'And look here.' Fiazi turned to another page and read:

> When thou makest a dinner or a supper, call not thy friends, nor thy brethren, neither thy kinsmen, nor *thy* rich neighbours; lest they also bid thee again, and a recompense be made thee.
>
> But when thou makest a feast, call the poor, the maimed, the lame, the blind:
>
> And thou shalt be blessed; for they cannot recompense thee.

'And here.'

> Wherefore putting away lying, speak every man truth with his neighbour: for we are members one of another.

'And see here a little further.'

> Let no corrupt communication proceed out of your mouth, but that which is good to the use of edifying, that it may minister grace unto the hearers.

'And what is written here. Excellent, very good,' said Fiazi:

> Finally, brethren, whatsoever things are true, whatsoever things *are* honest, whatsoever things *are* just, whatsoever things *are* pure, whatsoever things *are* lovely, whatsoever things *are* of good report; if *there be* any virtue, and if *there be* any praise, think on these things.

'You see how many good things there are, how many excellent lessons there are,' said Fiazi, placing his finger between the pages and closing the Bible. 'I am convinced of all these principles and, more than many Christians, am prepared to act on them.'

'But what are the things in the New Testament that you reject, which in your opinion are not correct?'

'Many, many things,' said Fiazi, returning the Bible to Paul. 'In every religious book one finds them. Their worst defect is their insistence on the monopoly of the truth.'

'For example?' Paul handed Fiazi the Bible.

'What do you mean by "for example"? You open the book at any page you wish.'

Paul opened it at the eleventh chapter of the Gospel of St Matthew. Fiazi spent some minutes studying it. He read some verses which were at the end of chapter ten:

> Think not that I am come to send peace on earth: I came not to send peace, but a sword.
>
> For I am come to set a man at variance against his father, and the daughter against her mother, and the daughter-in-law against her mother-in-law.
>
> And a man's foes *shall be* they of his own household.

He that loveth father or mother more than me is not worthy of me: and he that loveth son or daughter more than me is not worthy of me.

'See how greedy He is to obtain honour. All He wants is to have people to bow before Him. If anything is really good, we will be compelled to respect and honour it, but if it claims to be good and asks that you should do this and do that, its goodness becomes suspect. Flowers blooming on branches do not want us to stand before them with folded hands. No good principle or good thing ever demands that once we have accepted it, we should pay a price for it. This is a sick ideology which should be discarded. And then not only are we asked to bow before Him, but only for His sake to abandon brothers, sisters, sons and daughters. What a disgusting thought: what greater sorrow and pain can a man experience than break his biological and blood relationships?'

'If we accept these teachings, then on the Day of Judgment Jesus Christ will be the means of our salvation,' said Paul. 'The Lord Jesus Christ made great sacrifices for us.'

'What sacrifices and what salvation? Look at the facts in their reality. Religions have given us a beautiful concept of paradise and nothing else. Here,' said Fiazi, turning over a few pages. 'Listen to this.'

Then Jesus went thence, and departed into the coasts of Tyre and Sidon.

And, behold, a woman of Canaan came out of the same coasts, and cried unto him, saying, Have mercy on me, O Lord, *thou* son of David; my daughter is grievously vexed with a devil.

But he answered her not a word. And his disciples came and besought him, saying, Send her away; for she crieth after us.

But he answered and said, I am not sent but unto the lost sheep of the house of Israel.

Then came she and worshipped him, saying, Lord, help me.

But he answered and said, It is not meet to take the children's bread, and to cast *it* to dogs.

And she said, Truth, Lord: yet the dogs eat of the crumbs which fall from their masters' table.

Then Jesus answered and said unto her. O woman, great *is* thy faith: be it unto thee even as thou wilt. And her daughter was made whole from that very hour.

'What great cruelty is shown in these lines. He who had come to the earth for the good of mankind and for their welfare, he who was called the Lord Jesus Christ, gave no answer. This example of hard-heartedness and hatred of mankind is before you. This attitude is much worse than that of a doctor who, although he demands a fee for his service, does have mercy on a patient groaning and crying in pain. Jesus Christ, who in one place teaches men to love their enemies and to do good to those who hate them, tells this woman that he has come only for the lost sheep of the house of Israel. Look at this contradiction. How can we believe that such a person can justifiably claim to be a supporter of the idea that one must love even one's enemy? One can suspect that his whole philosophy of love, fraternity and equality is artificial. The Gospels are full of such instances. And look here.' Fiazi pointed out another passage to Paul.

Then Jesus called his disciples *unto him*, and said, I have compassion on the multitude, because they continue with me now three days, and have nothing to eat: and I will not send them away fasting, lest they faint in the way.

'You have noticed that He doesn't have a sympathetic and affectionate attitude towards people but feels compassion for them. He hadn't cared about their hunger for three days; it was only afterwards that He announced that He didn't want to send them away without food in case they fainted on the way. Most of Jesus's behaviour is cheap show. This and other weaknesses have coated a thick layer of dust on His good teachings. Here He is proclaiming: "I will not send them away fasting" and in another place He says: "But when thou doest alms, let not thy left hand know what thy right hand doeth". In fact in the lessons He preached to others, He was not only unconcerned with them but sometimes acted contradictorily.

'Please listen to this too.'

And another of his disciples said unto him, Lord, suffer me first to go and bury my father.

But Jesus said unto him, Follow me; and let the dead bury their dead.

'Don't you think that this selfishness and lack of care need explanation?

And listen to how He addressed the people: 'Ye fools and blind' and this one: 'Ye serpents, ye generation of vipers, how can ye escape the damnation of hell?'

'This is wrong,' said Paul, getting up in excitement and replacing the Bible on the book rack.

'Then you do realize that it is wrong,' Fiazi said.

'There are many corners in hell, and the deepest and darkest one is reserved for you,' said Paul, looking at Fiazi through his thick glasses.

'Paul, we do not have to agree with everything this man says.'

Fiazi laughed in reply and that was an answer in itself. 'One must recognize the truth. This is the real problem. Religions do not help to solve it, but make it more complicated. Religions are themselves hungry, so what can they give to others? They are hungry for worship, hungry for prayers and suffer from various other kinds of hunger. And when their hunger is not appeased, they become enraged and start talking about hell and damnation. They want to snatch everything from us and are outrageously proud and conceited. The attitude of religions towards their followers is neither lively nor acceptable. Their gods are greedy and avaricious, lost in their own solitude and imprisoned in the terrible mirage of remoteness. They are a bundle of crazy demands. All religions will end. They began only so that they may come to an end. Compared to Time they are nothing. Time created them and Time will destroy them. Time wants to set an example before us. They will be buried for ever in history and will leave behind memories of their dire results. If we accept Time as god then it provides us with facilities in abundance. If a fish which is surrounded by water accepts water as its god, then the water will become sympathetic to it. It will help it and tell it not to go where there are many germs in the water. If the fish acknowledges the water as its god, then it will have benefits. Water is certainly the basis of the life of the fish, but for fish, too, the real god is Time. If we accept Time as god, it will protect us from accidents. It will help us in all situations.'

'Let's suppose we accept Time as a god,' Whiter said. 'And even after we die an accidental death, what then in our eyes will be the reality of this god to whom you give the name of Time? Why did it fail to help us, when we have sincerely accepted it as our god?'

'Time is a god, and it thinks about us, keeping all our times in view. It knows that if we had lived longer we would have had to face such a situation in which we would ourselves have longed for death, and to save us from this situation Time brought this kind of death upon us. Death is only a brief interval in life. It is the name for an exit from a door.'

'You should speak to Father McGehan,' Whiter said, shifting restlessly in his chair. 'He is a priest at St Francis's Church. It would be better if you answered his questions.'

'What's the point?' Fiazi replied, getting up.

'Please sit down,' Whiter said, indicating the sofa. 'St Francis's Church is not far. Come here tomorrow morning at nine. I will inform the priest beforehand and he will be waiting for us.'

Whiter looked worried. The meeting with Fiazi and the things that Fiazi had said had disturbed him very much. He was not a regular at St Francis's but he knew Father McGehan was an intellectual and Whiter had great confidence in his depth of study. He was sure that the priest had the answers to Fiazi's questions and he was also sure that Fiazi would soon realize that it was not easy to prove all that he had been saying. In his heart he nursed a secret hatred for Fiazi and he wanted very much to see him worsted.

'I will come at nine tomorrow morning,' Fiazi told Whiter.

'Thank you. I will be waiting impatiently,' Whiter said pleasantly.

Father William McGehan was born in Cardiff. He got his primary education there. Then his family moved to London where he went to high school. During his academic years he developed a special interest in religion and a desire to command religious knowledge. Realizing this he sought admission to Heythrop College, London and was finally ordained as a priest. After that he got the opportunity of working in a local church. He performed his duties well. Noticing his devotion and inclination the bishop gave him his own parish. After some time he took a course at the Missionary Institute and was sent to India, Malaya, Pakistan and Afghanistan on a tourist visa. He had to stay for about two to three months in each country and observe the people; their penchant towards religion and their general view about life. Father McGehan lived in these countries for about one year and during this period he met strange people. Some just came to visit him without any purpose and talked nonsense with him. Others gave him presents and were completely happy that they had a foreign friend. A year later he was sent to a diocese in India where he worked under an Archbishop. After that he was sent to Mozambique with a missionary group. He stayed there for a little under a year. He wanted to go to Asia as a priest, and was sent to Pakistan where he had lived now for eighteen years. He baptized many natives and arranged other facilities for them. Once he fell seriously ill and was forced to go to London. He stayed there for eighteen months, partly undergoing treatment and partly resting. When the time came for him to return, he was asked if he would prefer to be appointed as a teacher at a theological college in England. He declined the offer and came back to Pakistan to his old church. He was an expert in English and French and apart from these he could speak Italian, Dutch and Urdu. He frequently participated in religious debates. He was a learned man and had a strong intellectual personality.

Father McGehan was reading his breviary when his servant knocked to say that someone wanted to meet him.

'Who is it?' he asked, looking down the corridor.

'Albert Whiter.'

'Whiter?'

'Yes, sir, that is the name he gave me. I told him you were busy and could not see him, but he insisted.'

Father McGehan went with the servant. When he saw Whiter, he greeted him pleasantly and offered his hand. Whiter warmly shook his hand and said, 'It was urgent to see you. I would have come last night, but it was too late and I did not think it proper to disturb you. I want to talk about some important matters with you . . .'

'But I am busy with someone else.'

'Sir, I just want to ask you to see me at quarter past nine. There is a strange man I want you to meet. Believe me that I have never met such a man in all my life.'

'Come in,' Father McGehan invited him. They walked down the corridor to the priest's study. It was a medium-sized room. A fine curtain hung over the window, admitting soft light. It seemed to sift the sunlight. Near the window was a desk and a chair. To the right was a tallboy about four feet high, and on it was a candlestick with a candle, some peacock feathers tied with a beautiful ribbon and a metal crucifix. In the middle of the room was a pembroke table with four chairs. Whiter sat down with Father McGehan at the table.

'Sir, I cannot tell you what a strange man he is. I think that you are the only one who can give him correct answers.'

Father McGehan listened attentively, Whiter continued, 'I would like you to meet him and silence him with your arguments. He has a store of cunning and dangerous words. Apart from this he is altogether empty.'

'Who is he?' the priest asked when Whiter stopped speaking.

'He believes himself a prophet of some other world. I think that is what he is. He is against Christianity. He is hateful.'

'But who is he? Where and how did you meet him?'

'Sir, I do not know him; I only met him accidentally. I pray to God Almighty that He keeps you firm in the faith, and that you will be able to contradict his words.' Whiter said this in one breath and blinked rapidly. 'Please sir, let me see the Bible for a minute.'

The priest went away with dignified steps and brought the Bible. Whiter started impatiently turning over the pages. He stopped at one page.

'Father, tell me where family relationships are mentioned.'

'Family relationships?' said the priest and looked hard at Whiter. 'I don't understand.'

'The place where Jesus says: "Don't love anyone more than me" and where it is written: "a man's enemies are in his household".'

The priest took the Bible from Whiter and at once showed him the reference in the Gospel of St Matthew.

'Yes, yes, this is the one I meant.' Whiter briefly told the priest what Fiazi had said about the passage. 'I tell you, Father, he is most hateful. The way he wants to make life beautiful is not possible.'

The priest took two books from the shelf and was going to his library when he saw a booklet lying on the table. He picked it up and said, 'Have a look at this. I will be back in a moment.'

It was a short pamphlet called 'How to recognize the Messiah'. Whiter started reading with interest. It had selections from the Bible, arranged under sub-titles. After some time he put it down and began looking at other books on the shelf and picked up two to look at. While he was looking at them, there came a knock at the outer door just as the library door opened. The priest appeared and opened the door. His servant handed him a piece of paper. 'Sir, this gentleman is standing outside and wishes to meet you.'

It was a page torn from a pocket diary and on it was written in neat handwriting: 'Sir, I request five minutes of your time. Thank you. Fiazi.'

'Fiazi?' the priest said out aloud. When he heard, Whiter jumped from his seat and said excitedly, 'This is the man, this is the man I wanted you to meet. But why has he come here at this hour? I don't know how he means to influence you by coming before the appointed time.'

'Wait, I will be back in a minute,' said the priest and with the motion of his hand for Whiter to sit down, he went out of the room. Whiter waited impatiently for Father McGehan to return with Fiazi. He thought he would hide somewhere and eavesdrop on their conversation, but did not dare lest he be taken to task by the priest. He sat there under the control of a strange mood, as if suspended in the limited atmosphere of the room. The door opened quietly and Fiazi entered, followed by the priest. Fiazi greeted Whiter politely.

'Why are you here? I asked you to meet me at Jan Building,' said Whiter.

'Is it nine o'clock yet?' replied Fiazi with a smile.

'It is not nine o'clock that matters, you should not have come here.'

'Please be seated. We did not decide in our previous meeting that I should not come here.'

'I just wondered, that's all.' Whiter sat down. When they were all seated, Father McGehan addressed Fiazi. 'You wished to see me?'

'Yes, I apologize if I have intruded. I came here earlier than Whiter had suggested, to tell you that I am not particularly interested in such meetings unless I am sure that the other person is also keen and has the time. I will come to meet you, but not carrying a weight of ideas and theories, nor would I want to transfer this weight to the shoulders of someone else lest he drown in the deep waters of apathy and helplessness. Academic or cultural discussions do not mean that one must try to prove the other person is in the wrong.'

'I am afraid that we cannot meet at nine, because I am rather busy this morning. Whiter has told me about you and has given me some account of your ideas. I should like to meet you, but I am busy now.'

'Father, these materialists and atheists are very superficial,' Whiter said to the priest, looking at Fiazi for a moment. 'Unless they see a miracle or experience some revelation, they do not believe, and that is why God has shown them miracles through his prophets. They want immediate action, they want things to appear before them in the twinkling of an eye.'

'You do not understand God,' Father McGehan said to Fiazi. 'To understand religion one must first have an inclination and a willingness for it and once you succeed in this, you will find how true and generous a companion religion proves itself to be.'

'But I don't need religion. I feel that I am self-sufficient.'

'How can you be self-sufficient in yourself? You must have the shadow of a great power.'

'The sun does not need any shadow, if any shadow falls upon it, it is burnt up. The sun is self-sufficient.'

'What makes you suppose that the sun is self-sufficient? There are innumerable other rotations and ways whereby the sun maintains its heat. You consider a lighted electric bulb in a dark room as the whole power, whereas if you cut the thin wire which connects it with the power supply, the bulb will be lost in the darkness.'

'I was talking about the sun, the unity and power of the sun forces other rotations, means, ways and systems to recognize it. The sun has bound these to itself and even if they wish to drift away from it, they cannot.'

'You don't understand religion. At the moment I am busy or I should have tried to make you understand religion and the reality of God with the help of the quantum theory of the solar system. By rejecting religion man becomes unnatural and complicated, his estimates about different things increase and decrease rapidly and this hurts his own temperament and perceptions. How can you deny the beneficial effects of religion on civilization? Religion has given many nations the shape of their national character, and played a vital role in helping them to build up their culture, and assisted them in their progress. Just imagine for a moment what the condition of mankind would have been without religion, what the nature of man's social relations and mutual cooperation. Without religion man's condition would have been disgusting and hateful. It is not possible to abandon religion. It is a need, a part of our senses. Whiter has briefly informed me about your objections to certain parts of the New Testament. All I can say at the moment is that you have not been able to understand these parts properly. Instead of jumping to superficial and quick conclusions, you should try to get to the real meaning of the text. Very well, let us accept for a moment that you wish to discard religion altogether. Then, have you a viable alternative system? Have you principles that are universally good and acceptable? Imagine if a group of students reject their teachers and their books and decide to make their own arrangements for their education, what will be the nature of their organization, their performance and their discipline? Can you in . . .'

Before Father McGehan could bring a new turn to his talk, or Fiazi could say anything, the right-hand inner door suddenly opened and they saw a man with the most remarkable features. On first impression, he seemed preoccupied, but his face cleared as he walked towards them with measured steps. The moment Father McGehan saw him, he stood up and introduced him to Fiazi. 'I must introduce this man to you. He is one of the greatest geniuses of the present era.'

The priest spoke slowly and emphatically as if making a statement on oath. Fiazi got up, looking at the man with interest. The man's head had never known a comb yet his hair was not dishevelled, its form made a comb unnecessary as it was only an inch long all over. He had an extraordinarily broad forehead. His eyebrows were thin and black and below them his eyes were like two separate oceans without any coast or horizon. These brilliantly shining surfaces were unimaginably clear and unfathomable. Below the chin his face matched his broad forehead. Father McGehan asked him to be seated, and brought another chair for himself.

'Father, please give me permission to leave. I will let you know about my next visit in a few days.'

'Please be seated, what is the hurry?' the priest said to the man, and then turned to Fiazi and said a few more appreciative words about him.

'I wish to leave,' the man said. 'I am most grateful for the time I have been able to spend in your excellent library looking at your books.' He shook hands with the priest, Whiter and Fiazi and with the same measured steps walked from the room. His inherent dignity showed itself in his firm tread.

Fiazi told Whiter that there was no longer any need for the nine o'clock meeting. He wished both of them goodbye and left. He was anxious to talk to that man whom the priest had described as one of the greatest geniuses and who, according to the priest, was trying to throw light on certain undiscovered reasons for the origin of man's ideas, and their interlinked problems. The man had not said much, but even his short stay in the room had left a very deep impression on the other people present.